FATHER DONOVAN'S TREE

FRANCIS KYNASTON
KEMBLE

DISCLAIMER

This is a work of fiction. All characters and events portrayed in this novel are either fictitious or used fictitiously.

Copyright 2011 By Francis Kynaston Kemble.

ISBN 978-0-9879062-1-2

First published by: Basiliske Publications, Westloon Gallery, 1300 Hillcrest, Bowen Island, BC, V0N 1GO.
Printed by Lulu Press.

Book jacket design taken from a painting by the late Flight Lieutenant David John Kemble and adapted by Rupert Kemble at 'Pictures and Words.'

DEDICATION AND ACKNOWLEDGEMENT

To all of those whose influence and views created such a firmament of impression and who have consequently contributed unwittingly but invaluably to this literary venture. To Elise Hedges for reciting and bringing to my attention, 'Wind on The Hill' by A.A Milne. To my brother Rupert who so wisely and appropriately selected a painting by my father for the book jacket. To my late father, David Kemble for his painting, for his delightfully corruptible influence throughout my formative years and who once described me as an interesting failure. To my late mother Mary Grace, who instilled in me a great love of literature and of music. To all those many souls so recently and tragically departed from my life. Finally but most importantly, a big thank you to my wife Carol for her endless support, love and the amazing job of tirelessly editing the manuscript. I also have Carol to thank for her beautiful poem 'Reality' that was written 12 years ago which is inexplicably relevant and therefore reproduced in Chapter 33. Without her invaluable input and suggestions, this tome would never have made it onto the shelves.

Invado Pacis. F K Kemble June 2012

THE WIND ON THE HILL

By A.A Milne

No one can tell me,
Nobody knows,
Where the wind comes from,
Where the wind goes.

It's flying from somewhere
As fast as it can,
I couldn't keep up with it,
Not if I ran.

But if I stopped holding
The string of my kite,
It would blow with the wind
For a day and a night.

And then when I found it,
Wherever it blew,
I should know that the wind
Had been going there too.

So then I could tell them
Where the wind goes...
But where the wind comes from
Nobody knows....?

FATHER DONOVAN'S TREE

CHAPTER 1 (PROLOGUE)

Nearly one thousand years ago, there lived an old druid, a venerable man, an aged man though his long life was worn with dignity and pride. He was a man sworn to secrecy in the interests of self preservation, in order that he might do his work. The mystical land of Albion, that was renamed Britannia following Roman occupation, was becoming fervently Christianised by a well meaning but obsessive King of Danish origin who answered to the name of Canute. The druid, clinging to the old ways, was aware that he would invite danger were he not cautious. This enigmatic mystic, enchanter and philosopher planted a tree during the rite of Spring. It was not just any tree but an oak, an example even in infancy that was so celebrated and revered in the days long past by the druids, his compatriots. At that time he knew the tree only by its Latin name, so named by the Romans, 'quercus robur'.

Early that year at the dawn of a very late spring, he stood spell bound, enjoying the sublime solitude and eerie quiet. The howling wind had at last abated although the snow still lay heavy on the ground in an oak grove where the birds had not yet found voice. As he surveyed a scene of post winter carnage where the gods of spring had managed finally to establish a bridgehead, he observed a spindly sapling, a minute and fragile shoot that had just survived berthing pangs having rent asunder the fibrous casing of a barely covered acorn stranded high up on a bank. Those initial tenuous moments were of survival, were entirely magical and a gift from the heavens. Typically each Spring, thousands of such filaments started the life journey but that number was reduced finally to just one or two lucky examples. Miraculously, these few were spared the indignity of being eaten by a foraging pig or stomped back into the earth, mashed and broken by hoof, antler or foot. But this one little tree had survived, the incalculable effort and miracle of nature had prevailed.

It was to be helped however, the fates had decreed that it should endure. The druid observing the lofty and over sheltered position, recognising that this was actually to the tree's advantage initially, saw however, that it could not flourish without adequate space, light and good soil. He studied the fragile plant, his heart going out to it. With the empathy of his druid craft, he could tell from its nearby parent that this tiny offspring was destined, one day, to be a mighty and magnificent specimen. He saw that it would become a sacred tree and that an especial fate awaited the little oak. In order to fulfill that task, the sapling would have to be nurtured and cared for while in infancy. Scanning further, the druid's senses attuned and empathic, he surmised that it might well grow to be over one hundred and forty feet in height and fill the sky with a glorious spatial symmetry. Not only that but he foresaw a trunk that was so broad that it would take six or seven people or more, arms outstretched and holding each others hands to encircle the tree. He saw a canopy so immense that it would accommodate numerous birds and shelter many animals from the wind, rain or sun. He knew also, as he carefully and temporarily transplanted this chosen plant with its promisingly true stem into the protective environment of a small clay pot full of rich damp earth and rotting leaves, that he was never going to live to see the tree in the slightest semblance of maturity. If he lived another twenty years he might see it become strong enough and big enough to survive the ravages of nature, maybe the size of a young cherry tree, too flimsy to climb but too tall to reach the top of.

As one of the guardians of old Albion and a keeper, a trustee of the land, he sensed and acknowledged that the sacredness of this tree was beyond question, it was indeed a worthy offspring. He had seen its future later that night while scrying in the millpond calm of a small lake under the magical silvery light of a full moon. The tree was to play a part in events set far into the mists of what was to come many hundreds of years hence. The land was being torn asunder by a temporal war that had started, coincidentally, when the Romans arrived almost one thousand years earlier. It was too late at that stage to stop the course of events as the damage was like a dry rot in the fabric of a mighty building. It was spreading and undermining the very essence of Britain and tearing the land, by slow degrees, from its etheric counterpart, a magical place that was retreating into the mists, a realm where both original inhabitants and latecomers alike would be denied access were they not to embrace a new way of being. The Druid saw that the land was losings its soul, a gradual but relentless evisceration that would render the enchanted isle a domain of the material and another quite separate place of the immaterial, forever dis-united and lost. At that moment he decided upon a course of action to change events.

A far off 'race' of people, no longer present, the Mayans and worshipers of Venus, had predicted a great spiritual transformation at the end of the 13th Baktun that intimated material catastrophe to the world at that time. Although the druid had no knowledge of the Mayans or indeed, of their prophesies, he did however resonate with their intelligence on some morphic level. He had insight that registered little in the corporeal world but which was so powerful an awareness that ironically, this alone was enough to become an ingredient in that schism and one of which the druid was only too well aware.

Months later and accompanied by his hound, a very large shaggy creature, part wolf, ears erect and ever alert, his eerie pale blue eyes softened by overtures of friendship, his tail wagging and breath steaming, the druid re-planted the sapling in fresh and vibrant earth; soil that had been replenished and then revealed by the retreating winter snows and warmed by the augmenting spring sunshine. The birds had awoken from a long sleep, stretched their wings and pirouetted in the misty sunlight, filling the air with sweet song and happy utterances while they searched for mates and built nests. The winter had been long and hard, the exposed ground was sepia coloured and drab but the druid could see the life in the earth, was entertained by the dance of nature and of all existence and he sensed that the earth was ready.

He chose the site carefully so that the surrounding bulrushes near the lake shore would, to some extent, hide the young tree and act as a safeguard. It was the very lake that he had used for looking into the future on powerful and portentous moonlit nights. The dog snuffled around in the undergrowth then barked at a nearby squirrel then gave a brief but halfhearted chase. Dropping to the ground with a sigh of resignation, he lay in a hollow that looked as if it were made for him. They were in a glade by the lake situated curiously, high up on an elevated plain. The area was perfect, absent from interlopers seeking sustenance and a home in the winter purified virgin ground. The druid put big stones around the sapling and then just inside the tiny fortress, he staked the ground in a ring of protection against the wild pigs and the deer starving after a long winter of harsh frosts and deep snow. Every few days he would check to make certain that all was well, he cleared fast growing weeds and brush that was proliferating and hogging the increasingly balming rays of a radiant summer sun. The tree grew straight and true, radiating vitality and great promise and a willingness and even an eagerness to please the old druid and life preserver; yet another morphic message so subliminal that only the spirits and keepers of the land had access to this exquisite information. When finally the druid's life came to a natural end, he died happy in the knowledge of his life's achievement, this one great achievement. He was satisfied that the oak would live to see out its prophetic life, a weighty burden to be sure but one that the tree was willing and happy to bear.

Just before the druid's death, he became a Christian. This was partly to avoid the increasing persecution of religious zealots who, misguided and misinterpreting Canute's religious aspirations, wandered the land of Britannia taking up where the Christianised Romans had left off. They self righteously sought for sinners and practitioners of the old ways. Once caught, the victims were tortured by the zealots and fire was used to illicit confession. Then the sinners were hung from any nearby tree This was in sacrifice to the new

Christian god whose benevolence and tender ministration could only be enhanced by the paradox of sacrificial purging, or so the persecutors were convinced. The old druid, aware of the blood hunger creeping into the new world of God, embraced Christianity, saw he had great work to complete and saw a higher purpose. Partly also, he saw a glimmer of magic in the religious teachings and felt that good could be achieved under any denominational guise even if many of his brethren were crazed.

On the day of his ordination by a choleric and stout bishop who had chosen to stay awhile with a monastic order living not far from the lake, the druid took the name Father Donovan. Whether he was Irish or not was never known, he most probably wasn't but the Irish were known at that time for the fervour with which they embraced conversion to Christianity; somehow it seemed appropriate to take the name. Henceforth and for the rest of its life, the mighty oak that was to become, would be known as Father Donovan's Tree. Indeed Father Donovan at his end was buried at the foot of tree. This was another concession to Christianity, a direct contradiction of the remnants of druid culture to be burnt alive in the last shaky moments of natural mortality. He was not a coward however, he was Father Donovan and in his druidic alter ego he wanted to be forever a guardian and desired that his body should be given in sacrifice to nourish and nurture his tree.

He had understood all those many years earlier that the 'time' in his lifetime and for those of many future lifetimes progressed slowly and that events would unfold gradually but inevitably. He had foreseen at a young age and been made aware by a last faint but echoing cry from the temporal realm that a change from the future would mend the past and thence to the future. 'Time' would greatly accelerate and continue accelerating exponentially, a phase when events would change ever more rapidly. This was when the changes could be made that would, once more, re-unite physical and temporal to bring synchronisation back to the world. One day, he knew, the faeries, the spirits and the elementals would again become a big part of and integrated with the lives of mortals. There would ultimately be a time when mortals would cease to be so, their gradual evolution from physical to energetic would be assured once the wounds of the world had been healed.

CHAPTER 2

Jessica Stearne lapsed for a moment, enveloped in a sense of physical weariness and feeling the need for a good strong cup of tea. Tea had become an imperative, a thoroughly British rationale borne of generations of 'proving'. At times such as these, tea was was the answer to flagging energy levels and was a panacea for all problems. Jessica considered the dangerous possibility of an indecent lapse into minor decadence, a rich tea biscuit or two, maybe even three? She sat in an armchair, mug in hand and contemplated the first biscuit that had been dunked for just a little too long; part of the over-saturated morsel tilted precipitately and lowering her head, Jessica quickly ate that portion. There was ever the danger in such situations that a piece could subside annoyingly into the hot drink, sinking to the bottom to be rendered irreversibly into a faintly revolting mush.

Jessica had just moved into 'Flat' number 7 in a trendy and upmarket apartment and was unpacking and attempting, without much success, to place her furniture in what seemed initially, to be the perfect places. Likely looking nooks and crannies refused to conform. They were nearly always an inch too narrow or power outlets or radiators were in the way. Her new 'flat' was located, along with a dozen others, at the old prison on Tower Hill, the infamous 'Mort lac', a facility famed during the Victorian era as being the prison for gentleman miscreants if, heaven forfend, such a panoply of misdeed could ever have existed. It was built at the latter end of the eighteenth century during the time of the Hanover's and the reigning monarch, George the IV, by a wealthy merchant family. It was a large and typically imposing house of the time, whimsically named Mort-lac Villa in deference to a lake that had once, it was alleged, existed there. It was also rumoured that there had been many human sacrifices during the time of the druids. The house was situated on what was once a forested plain, in fact a shallow basin, a barely discernible punchbowl at the top of a hill and in a prime location. There were many lives 'taken' over the centuries in the dubious pursuit of 'justice'. Indeed, during the time when the house later became a prison, there had been many public hangings. Both inmates and others unfortunate enough to fall foul of a compromised liver or intemperance by the presiding judges, fell victim.

Such careless dis-regard for life had inevitably left an atmosphere, implications of energy of a tortured spirit world only just beyond the reach of most mortals. Jessica was a pragmatist and not given to imaginative flights or psychic episodes; she just loved the location and the old world appeal of Mort-Lac Villa. Like many sacred places in the British isles, the 'occult' sense was part of the fascination for the hill though few were consciously aware of it. The house, as was typical of that era, boasted many large rectangular sash windows adorned with charming shutters on the inside; the frames were accommodated by sandstone mullions. The windows were mostly arranged on the front of the house, arrayed in a delightful symmetry so typical of the era, south facing and overlooking the gravel drive. The entrance was a hall, a vestibule that stood proud of the front of the house and boasted tall elegant double doors made of mahogany. They were reached after climbing some steps that both ascended and descended on two sides and which were bordered by an ornate sandstone balustrade. The facade was impressive by design but really the house was a not so exquisite though handsome Georgian structure. In essence, it was a pseudo ancestral home, a London town house commissioned by an upwardly mobile family of the time. It was therefore considered a dwelling of the 'nouveau riche', a family who through ignorance, had no real grasp of the subtle intricacies of true artistic design. As a result the concept had not endured success and was a product of concession, an uncharacteristic act of favour to the family. Designed by none other than Thomas Hopper at the start of his career, a man who in time achieved great fame for his architectural ability but maybe, at a young age and with a hunger to succeed, he had augmented compromise. The materials used were sandstone and red terracotta bricks, a material cleverly invented by the Romans that, very regrettably and more latterly, metastasized throughout Britain in the form of countless housing estates of questionable aesthetic value.

Unfortunately for the property, there was little land left owing to Londons increasing density and clamour for housing, there being just two acres in all. The property did however, possess one very redeeming feature. In amongst the apple, pear, cherry, alder and the odd young chestnut tree was an enormous and exceptionally beautiful oak tree situated in the garden but set back some distance from the drive. It showered the neighborhood with acorns, a carpet of russet coloured leaves in the autumn, provided shelter from the rain in the winter, shade in the summer but most of all, it lent an incomparable beauty and dignity to Mortlac Villa.

Over the intervening centuries there had been vague attempts to chop the tree down and one particular time when there had been a much more determined effort. The saga was constantly retold in folklore as being the most mysterious of occasions during the tree's history. At a period in time when the house had stood forlorn and abandoned, a band of brigands trying to survive a harsh winter on the road and needing firewood, had arrived from the ale houses sodden with gin. Holding between them a large two man tree saw, they decided that the stoutest and least inebriated pair should start the proceedings and each holding an end put the blade to the base of the trunk; then they started to cut. Within seconds, so legend has it, there was a terrifying shriek and a powerful chill wind that blew up from nowhere. Despite being quite drunk, the band of men were spooked and paused for just a moment, but then they started again. Witnesses at the time swore to the fact that an apparition of an enormous man appeared, striding toward them with a hand held high and holding what looked to be a large wooden staff. Though startled at first, the brigands were prepared to knock him on the head to prevent his interference. As one of the crew reached up from behind and dealt the giant a cowardly blow with a cudgel, the victim seemed to split into two for a moment as if cloven and hundreds of leaves flew from the point of impact. The shrill wind continued vortex like in the locality and then the leaves regrouped once again into the complete upper torso and head of the giant.

The brigands terrified and fearing that witchcraft was afoot, ran with all their might, instantly sobered. They made haste for an ale house in search of a stiff drink and retold their tale to an incredulous audience who were not as skeptical as one might have supposed. A policeman, in the blinding clarity of sobriety, had witnessed the scene unfolding from across the road and had divined early on, of what constituents the giant was made. Terrified at the events unfolding before him and rendered powerless on that occasion to act in his official capacity, he too made for the ale house beating the brigands by just moments. He quickly demanded a drink as if he had just met with Satan and in between gulps, gave a panic stricken account of what had happened. Just as he finished his story the brigands ran in, obviously terrified and also very much in need of drink. The pub was named 'The Royal Oak', which seemed a fitting tribute; while the tavern existed the story was retold at every anniversary of the event finally to be written on the walls at the entrance until the day the tavern was closed and pulled down.

When the original owner of the house died leaving a trail of debt, Mort-lac Villa was purchased by the Port of London authority for just such a purpose as a prison. High walls were erected at the perimeter of the property to encompass the building and to contain the inmates and to keep out the inquisitive. Strangely, in that increasingly austere environment, the tree was tolerated rather than loved but it prevailed. After the first world war the house was converted into an asylum for the insane. Latterly it was downgraded, after the second great war, into an institution for people with war related mental illness and including brain damaged war veterans. In the early sixties the building caught fire from a freak lightning strike, not enough to do serious damage but sufficient to close forever the doors of the institution. The remaining inmates were either released or relocated to more well equipped facilities. The mighty oak, strangely enough, was spared any damage from lightning despite it's more enticing proximity and height. Some years passed, windows were smashed and architectural features removed by vandals and thieves. Finally the premises was marketed and then spotted by developers who saw great real estate potential in the house in a rapidly burgeoning post-war city. Misguidedly, they carried out a systematic destruction of most that was left of the originally beautiful features in their attempt to convert the old house into apartments, removing the stunning and well established Virginia Creeper, beautiful solid wooden doors, wrought iron stair rods topped with banisters of finest oak, marble fireplaces and a great deal of the exquisite plasterwork moulding. On a more positive note, they had left intact the lofty mahogany doors at the entrance, repaired the crumbling balustrade, lowered the surrounding perimeter wall and amazingly, left the oak tree more or less intact though they were careless of its existence. They almost set fire to the oak tree when lighting an enormous bonfire to burn the waste material removed from the house. A torrential downpour of rain summoned, it was said, from an outraged guardian of the distant past had saved the tree but there were ever more scars and heavily burned limbs, the hallmarks of time. The bluebells that proliferated perennially and enchantingly within the shade of the tree were continuously damaged and abused. Sometimes trampled underfoot, often buried in building debris and even dug over at one point, but they refused to disappear entirely and grew with more abundance and gusto every Spring. The house, when the conversion was complete, bore the indignity of steel fire escapes, asbestos lined doors and flimsy partition walls but the exterior was still quite grand. The future of the property was safeguarded in the awakened sensibilities of later generations who coveted Britain's dwindling and repeatedly raped heritage and one of those was Jessica Stearne.

Jessica was in her early thirties and was already a respected forensic scientist employed by London's metropolitan police force. Forensics was her profession, her passion, the philosophy of the true pragmatist. As a scientist, she maintained stoically if unimaginatively, that all mysteries of life could be explained by algorithm and formula. There was sadly little poetry or romance in her soul, no room for flights of fancy but she did have one 'vice', one hobby that she celebrated within the sanctity of her free time. She was possessed of an almost obsessional love of history which was her principal reason for buying the apartment at Mort-Lac Villa. At that moment, in the midst of unpacking and organising in the attire and circumstance of the newly removed, she sat and contemplated while holding in her cupped hands a mug of strong tea. Jessica was of just above average height, boasted the most amazing long black and very lustrous hair but viewed the world through myopic and bespectacled eyes. They were the unseeing eyes of an over diligent student, eyes that few in the world had ever really looked into and who would never realise just how beautiful they were. So dark, they were almost black and so limpid, one could easily become immersed in them. Her mouth was broad and sensual with a full bottom lip and a delicately and finely delineated top lip. Her cheek bones were high and refined, her nose slightly aquiline but full of character. She habitually plaited and tied her beautiful waist length hair back with clinical severity. The only positive outcome about this being that the world might get a glimpse of her beautiful long and graceful neck. She habitually under-dressed, wore drab and functional clothing that sought to conceal a bosom that was large, firm and prominent. She was quite blind and unaware of the fact that nature favoured her in all respects.

Her waist was trim and her stomach flat and her hips and posterior enticingly rounded without being obvious. Her legs were long and shapely but yet again she sought to cover them up in functional if unattractive slacks fearing that they might actually be looked at. She was possessed of a beautiful speaking voice, rich and with an unusual timbre and she spoke with an accent that was impetuously upper classed, a little theatrical maybe but nonetheless beguiling.

Jessica's father was a true Englishman of the earnest middle classes and established order, a tall, pale, thin man with narrow shoulders and ginger hair and a sensitive, almost beautiful face. Her mother, on the other hand, was a beguiling enchantress from the Punjab. Jessica had taken the best from them both and was genuinely an astonishingly attractive young woman but who conspired with all her might not to be; she saw no value in vanity and failed abominably to appreciate or love herself. Her had mother died giving birth to her and so Jessica had never known her. As a consequence she was deprived of a mother to guide her or to instruct her in that wonderfully intimate maternal way, of the joy and of the divine power of the female. Her father, a self critical and severe man, a civil servant and minor diplomat, had brought Jessica up to the best of his ability in his strange disconnected and entirely distant fashion.

Jessica grew to adulthood thinking herself a constant inconvenience and never realised just how deeply her father loved her. It was true that her father had married again in the curious hope that this would somehow invoke a background of family stability. He really hoped that he might somehow find a way to become a little closer to his daughter. Jessica had unreasonably loathed her stepmother from the outset for no greater reason, typically, than that she had perceived her stepmother as an interloper and this led to great friction. A difficult and combative child and a husband so distant and pre-occupied had finally caused her stepmother to walk out one day. She was a sad casualty of a loveless marriage, an ungrateful step daughter and she had an exceptional fondness for sherry. Jessica was sent away to school by a father, anxious to adhere to his parental responsibility and to avoid any painful connection or discourse with his child. Quite apart from other considerations, his daughter was too obvious a reminder of his only grand and unseemly passion. His choice of bride in a bigoted country of the time, not accepting of racial differences, had cost him a thriving career in the diplomatic service. He died relatively young, just as Jessica graduated from university and only weeks into his retirement. A fatal heart attack while in the midst of compiling a vitriolic and curiously impassioned letter to the local council regarding their planning consent for a block of flats to be built near his cottage in Hurstpierpoint, Sussex. Jessica was fortunate however with her guardian angels, an uncle and aunt who adored her. During as many of the school holidays as she could manage, she had stayed with them and they had virtually raised Jessica as their own child.

Sitting thoughtfully among boxes in the kitchen, she dunked a fourth biscuit into the Lady Grey tea and gazed out of her top floor window at that huge and venerable oak tree with an unprecedented awe and wonder. Sited as it was in the communal grounds of the building but directly in front of her living room window, she was enthralled by its spectacle. Huge and proud, great branches that extended for twenty feet or more, that shaded anyone sitting in deep contentment in a lawn chair. The protective awning so delightfully attenuated the fire of the mid-summer sun. The bluebells had prevailed and once more multiplied happily under the boughs, flourishing in a perfect haven of shaded summer paradise. The tree bore the scars of a long and turbulent history, names were carved into the lower trunk along with the deep scars from an axe. There was evidence of root rot, of a fire and some of the branches having died, had been cut off to preserve the integrity of the rest of the tree. It was near the end of a thousand year long life and the onset of its decline was relatively sudden, hastened no doubt by twentieth century city pollution, greenhouse gases and diminishing ozone layers. It was believed that the origins of the tree dated back to the time of King Canute, the ill fated and well meaning King of Britannia, a Dane by birth, who perished while attempting to prevent tidal ingress by Royal decree.

Though old and dying, the tree was still beautiful, majestic and exhibited the veneration of an old, once invincible but still greatly loved warrior and leader. Jessica considered it abstractedly at first but then more intently as she became mesmerised, drawn in. She studied the tree intently, then looked upon it some more and was besieged by such feelings and reminiscences, as though she had tapped into the trees soul. Fanciful maybe and not like her at all but she had the feeling that the tree was trying to communicate knowledge of some sort? Of course there was no dialogue, no conveyance of feeling or rationale but simply a growing sense of resonance by which knowledge could be imparted and shared. It was an elusive feeling, especially to Jessica who, being a scientist, applauded her continued resistance to the trends of twentieth century 'new age' awareness and fantasy. She never had reason or cause to claim any psychic consideration or susceptibility and in fact would never have accepted such hypotheses. During those fleeting moments of 'connection' however, her scalp tingled deliciously and insistently and held her captive as if she were tuning in to something.

Suddenly, she was rudely interrupted, startled out of her reverie by a very feline chirrup and a ticklish nudge on the back of her neck from a bewhiskered furry head. A fully grown but handsome young ginger cat had come in to the living room for attention and maybe some treats.
" William you rotter, I know exactly what it is that you are after!"
Jessica felt her imperceptible annoyance at being interrupted, ebb a little. She grabbed the cat, picked him and held him up in her arms like a baby, his eyes partially closed, a deep breathy purr and big paws that kneaded the air with happiness, his absolute best cupboard love.
"I wouldn't imagine for a moment that you have come to help me unpack?"
She was beheld by loving but inscrutable feline eyes and a deep rumbling purr that conferred his wish and subsequently, her acquiescence. William held a fascination for rich tea biscuits, he was charmingly addicted to them. He was far from little, in fact a very large marmalade cat with vividly contrasting stripes. He was so wonderfully fluffy and cuddly and his flattened face and large paws belied dominant purebred Persian genes somewhere in amongst his homogeneous mongrel origins. His obsession for rich tea biscuits was such that he would sense when Jessica was about to open a packet whereupon he would appear from nowhere. Sometimes this was heralded by the loud mechanical slap of the cat door when he was outside. On this occasion he had stealthily emerged from the bedroom, his

place of imprisonment until such time as permitted his liberty in a week or so. He smothered Jessica with feline love, rubbing himself against her face, tail erect, purring and meowing while looking up at her imploringly with a hint of dribble on his chin. There had been an occasion once when she had dropped a piece of biscuit down the front of her slightly gaping blouse while sitting in front of the television, cup of tea in hand. William, to her astonishment, had simply inserted his fore paw into her cleavage and retrieved the fragment that had come to rest in her bra.

"Oh come on then Mr Turkey legs, just this one little piece." William purred his delight before leaping to the floor silently and getting down to the nitty gritty of eating his fragment of biscuit. The sound of his munching and crunching once more re-awakened the tingling in Jessica's scalp and set her onto the path of reverie.

The canopy of billions of almost perfect leaves that adorned the branches in unremitting bounty bewitched her. Despite her self professed pragmatism and her unwillingness to embrace the obvious, it was in truth the main reason why she had bought the flat. She loved the lofty ceilings, the large open rooms, the faded glory and grandeur but the oak was the icing on the cake!' She recalled some cruel words when she had viewed the apartment for a second time, trying to decide whether to buy it but knowing deep down that she had already made up her mind.

" You don't need this place Jessica sweet'eart, it's far too big for you, think of the heating bills. If I didn't know you better my sweet, I'd say you bought this place because of that big fuckin' tree, some misplaced and unrealistic romantic notion no doubt, of sitting in the country park of a great house."

This abrasive comment had come from Steven Savage, cockney, long term acquaintance, once boyfriend, sometimes enemy, a charming but crooked snake of a man who operated under the dubious guise of financial services advisor. His only one and great redeeming feature was his love of animals and of course William whom he adored, the admiration being fully reciprocated, provided Steven was armed with rich tea biscuits.

Steven was small, shorter than Jessica by a couple of inches, dapper and an unscrupulous con-man. By various devious means he managed to solicit the patronage of aged and infirm spinsters and widows. He mission was to worm his way into their favours and confidences and then by degrees, take greater and greater liberties with their assets which he 'managed' by gaining ill considered signatures on legal documents. He took care to target people who had few if any surviving relatives and preferably distant. As Jessica often pointed out, it would only be a matter of time before he was tracked down and stoned to death by outraged beneficiaries waving crumpled bequests that no longer held substance because of his skillful doctoring. Steven's uncanny sixth sense was his second major feature which could be considered redeeming in the right person but he abused his gift horribly. He had of course seen right through Jessica's ploy when she bought the apartment. She winced a little at the memory for in truth, she had indeed nurtured dreams such as the one described.

Because of her love of all things ancient, she was an avid reader of good period novels by the Bronte's, George Elliot, Charles Dickens, Anthony Trollope; she adored the dialogue of Jane Austen. She loved to watch good period drama on television, the only thing she ever viewed. Her one great romantic inclination in life was to somehow be removed to a period some two centuries previously and be the grand lady of an extensive family seat. She adored the Victorian era, the clothes, the architecture, the furniture, the rationale by which Victorians lived their lives. It was a great time for Britain, for engineers, artists, musicians and writers alike and while there were indeed awful problems and social injustices, there were some wonderful aspects to Victorian England, a great period of awakening, a time of true plenty for the governors of the empire. Recalling his comment, Jessica felt a huge surge of unreasonable annoyance at Steven Savage, despising his coarseness, hating him.

'What the hell does he know any way, bloody know all? What in god's name did I ever see in him? Was he ever really any fun; strange dysfunctional little man?'

Of course, he was quite right about Jessica and had as usual, enjoyed taunting her. Later that week Jessica heard that another trusting widow had been swindled and that he had flown to Palm Springs with his young female assistant in order to celebrate.

Jessica looking at the tree once again could only utter, "My goodness, that tree is so utterly beautiful, so magical!"

' Mort lac....? Lake of death??? Doesn't London have such oddly evocative names, often there seems no reason for them. But why 'lake' at all? T*here is no lake for miles and probably never was,* it's all fantasy, supposition. I*t's far too high up here?* Maybe I *should look into it?* I do remember hearing *something about a great and bloody battle fought here between the invading Normans and the residing Saxons and of the dead floating in the lake? Didn't Boadiccea fight the Romans here too, she burnt down their settlement? It seems*

so improbable now that there ever was any kind of a battle here in the centre of the city at the site of one of London's most infamous Victorian Gaols. To consider that this beautiful old tree has been witness to most of this, gosh, what stories this tree must hold! I do so wish it could tell me?'
The irony of that brief thought was, that at that moment, Jessica had no idea that this reflection of hers was to become one of the greatest truisms of her life.

CHAPTER 3

Lucius Grey gazed through the prison bars upon the gently undulating boughs of a giant oak tree. He was a man still in the prime of his life, in his early forties, tall, broad and strong. Many would concede that he was a particularly handsome man, sandy haired, supernaturally pale blue eyes, a fine sculpted nose, a broad strong mouth revealing a sound set of white teeth when he smiled, which was not often enough. Beneath his mouth was the robust square chin of a man with principles and kindness. His concession to the fashion of the day was an astonishing set of sideburns, mutton chops, that reached almost to the bottom of his cheeks. Despite his internment at Mort-Lac prison he attempted to maintain his dignity and though his clothes had become worn and were in need of much repair and a really thorough clean, he did his best. He wore a long black woollen frock coat with a satin lined collar and embellished with a top hat when circumstance permitted. His linen shirt with a fashionable winged collar was quite threadbare in places but the wide ascot tie and high waisted double breasted waistcoat with attached gold watch chain helped to decoy any intrusive gaze. On cooler days he wore his 'garrick', a heavy coachman's overcoat that performed admirably at keeping out the cold and the wet. His wide square toed shoes, that had once gleamed like an autumn chestnut freshly revealed from a spiky enclosure, were severely in need of both polishing and repair and they let the water in through soles worn beyond adequacy. Lucius was an educated man and of good

31

family and who had suffered the misfortune of having fallen on harder times. His unfashionable and persistent sun tan, a legacy from years in the tropics and on board ship, was a testament to his status as a frequent overseas traveller. He was not, strictly speaking, a gentleman for his family were compelled to become involved 'in trade'. He was, however, well known in Victorian society and his lineage, up until his incarceration, could withstand petty criticism.

The tree upon which his gaze fell so meditatively was ancient, there was evidence of an attempt to cut it down but the tree was still very much in its prime and resplendent with vitality. Under the canopy formed by the many mighty boughs, bluebells proliferated and thrived in a perfect shaded early summer paradise. The countless leaves of the tree, with those so characteristically lobed margins, sang in the breeze, a sound like modulated white noise that was so quiescently alive and vital. Sometimes when a storm blew hard, Lucius would be partially awakened in the night and he listened to the wind howling through the branches of the tree. In his slumber drugged state, he imagined himself comfortably ensconced in his cabin back on board his ship. The shrieking wind played a phenomenal accord upon the masts and rigging created by the spirits of the tempests. Almost instantly, he would be clutched back into the delicious embrace of Morphius, his cares banished for the remainder of the night. As he surfaced painfully into consciousness in the mornings, the ugly truth would inevitably bubble up through the miasma of his dream state and bring him back to earth with a jolt. Then Lucius would contemplate his true situation while lying on his board in the prison cell, tormented by the same emerging scenarios that plunged him daily into a new abyss of despair.

His bed was a wooden board, a parody, a crude euphemism for a bed upon which he was forced to spend his sleeping or even waking hours. This allied to his angst conspired to make his nights very uncomfortable unless lulled by the sound of the wind in the tree. In the mornings he awoke stiff, bruised and ill rested. The only alternative to the board was a filthy wooden floor that would yield even less in terms of comfortable repose. Yet, whenever the wind blew, he was always comforted by the sound of the elements. The only things that made his life bearable were the tree and the 'music' that was played, a different sound depending upon the time of year. On the long summer days and in the relative stillness of the nights, there was a different sound in the boughs, soothing, mournful but majestic and supremely restful; a voice that transported him to other worlds and helped him to rest. If meditation had been a concept in a Victorian English prison then the meaning would have been well suited to the experiences that Lucius undertook each night. By day he was in perpetual torment, his outrage at the deep sense of injustice, his anguish and his misery was unparalleled in the block. The only thing that truly calmed the volcanic perturbations of his mind were those occasions when the beautiful song of the zephyrs and spirits of the wood got up to their enchanting mischief among the branches and leaves of the Olympian oak; then the music soothed and becalmed his mind and set his scalp all of a tingle.

There were times, while he slept, when he dreamed of other worlds, places where he could celebrate those human sensibilities, awareness of cold, of heat, of hunger, of replenishment, of weariness and of dynamism but simultaneously, he was unhampered in any way by discomfort. It was as if he were weightless, insubstantial, incorporeal. Trekking to a distant mountain range with implausible fairy tale peaks and an impossibly beautiful castle teetering precariously from a spar was no chore at all. He could take as long or as little time as he wanted, there was no difference. He could fly when he put his mind to the task and yet doubt and consternation hampered his ability.

'If I put out my arms and jump, could I become airborne, would I be able to swoop and soar like and eagle.......No? It is not possible..... or is it?'

Then that special sense of exhilaration as he found himself aloft, looking down upon the vibrant canopy of the oak tree way down below. He dared not be too jubilant, dared not contemplate his position too much in case this should bring about his literal downfall, a spiraling plummet earthwards.

The supreme irony in all of this was that these were experiences that he had undergone only since his incarceration in the prison, so far as he knew. These dreamlike episodes, lucid yet forbidden to full consciousness and a life of liberty, were a huge compensation for his dismal situation and he sought them whenever he could. Indeed there were times when he became the mighty tree, anchored to the ground, rooted to the same spot, seemingly for an eternity. This should have been purgatory and even in his dream state he wondered if perhaps he should be anxious, possibly even panic stricken and yet, here too was an uncanny and paradoxical freedom. As he linked into every living form on the planet, he created a network of bewildering connections that fed back to him and thereby, he to it. Every possible signal and stimulus was an all encompassing sensual experience. Sometimes he gained 'knowledge' of people quite unknown to him and sometimes repeatedly. One such ally was an old man living at the beginning and at the end of time, a white bearded pagan and a heathen savage and yet someone with whom he was curiously compatible. The other person he was frequently connected to was a superficially plain, dark skinned young woman wearing glasses and unsuitable, not to say thoroughly unattractive clothing. Yet there was a strange attraction, as if he had known her all his life and he coveted her as he had coveted the recently departed maiden of whose death he was accused.

A rat scurried across the floor. Lucius had hated them at first, was revolted, fearful and retaliatory. He did all that he could to keep them out or exacted a cruel vengeance if he was lucky enough to hit one with his bucket. Over the course of time he gave up chasing them, it was a pointless waste of valuable energy. For every one he dispatched, there were ten to replace the victim. Lucius became used to them over time as the enmity was attenuated. Finally, ennui mitigated his pointless acrimony and the rats became his allies. There was too much death and misery in the world and especially in the prison, what was the point of adding to it? Then he began to talk to them; they said little but listened to him attentively, or so it appeared. Lucius even became curious about his cell mates and studied them at odd times, black, sleek, bewhiskered and scurrilous with dark little scheming thoughts and ugly motives but then of course, that wasn't really true was it? They were both caricature and entertaining and in an odd kind of way they even seemed to adopt Lucius, to take pity on him. Their muroidean sensibilities ever alert, they sensed his softening and warming attitude. While playing and foraging in his cell at night they sought to lessen discomfort and kept away from his bed aware that this was what disturbed him most. Then finally sensing that his animosity had ebbed, the rats became emboldened and would often sit on the ledge in full view between him and the tree and Lucius allowed himself to develop a small affection for his similarly unfortunate cell mates. After consideration he decided that rats have much in common with cats, both creatures aligned with the supernatural but from differing parts of the spectrum. Both were equipped with uncanny skills of survival and each regularly crossed the threshold between this world and others and yet strangely, they were mortal enemies. There was one little creature that took Lucius' fancy and who was a regular companion, who had lost a part of his tail. No doubt this plucky fellow was a casualty of a violent assault from a less sympathetic in-mate? Lucius' heart went out to him but he also admired the rat's spirit and his barefaced cheek and so he became almost a constant companion.

Lucius had named the rat Septimus, a name taken from Lucius's pleasant but completely impotent defense lawyer. He was an unfortunate little man of timid manner who had chosen quite the wrong profession; his name was Septimus Zacharias. He had been set up by his wealthy uncle and had courted friendship within the bar but failed manifestly to be appropriately predatory or unscrupulous in his dealings at law. Septimus, Lucius discovered, was in fact a duplicitous individual, betrayed by his wont of acceptance, a Victorian people pleaser. It was an unfortunate characteristic for a defense lawyer especially one chosen to represent a man accused of a cruel and brutal murder.
" Here Septimus, old fellow if indeed old fellow you be, do me the honour of breaking my fast with me."

Septimus was sceptical at first, cautious, maybe timid, his silky whiskers twitching with anticipation at the proffered crust. Finally he dashed forward in a twinkling of an eye, grabbed the small fragment offered and then scampered across the cell and escaped through his bolt hole.
"My pleasure my little friend- bon appetit!"

Sometimes when the rats became too abundant and a nuisance for the staff, a rat catcher was sent for and traps were laid. The squeals of the injured, trapped and dying rodents became torture for Lucias. The subsequent smell of some of the dead and putrefying little bodies forever trapped in wall cavities was rank; Septimus however, was never caught. Lucius knew then that Septimus's largely missing tail might well have something to do with a former attempt at capture and that he had become wiser for it. During the long days and while the hours of tedium stretched far into the cognitive horizon, Lucius would turn his mind to the tree and he studied it, hypnotised by its beauty, by what it represented. Sometimes he was able to talk with others and in addition to the rat, Lucius had gained another friend during his incarceration. He was an old man named Leonard Champion, bent and twisted, quite crippled and in constant pain from dreadful rheumatoid arthritis. He had been imprisoned as a result of mounting debts. His only real crime had been a lack of circumspection when he had been unwise enough to stand guarantor for a nephew who had devised a seemingly plausible business plan; he was also the sole beneficiary in the event of Leonard Champion's death. This poor sad crippled old man at the twilight of his harmless life was therefore implicated and imprisoned as a result of the huge gambling debts run up by his nephew. Despite his great charm and, it has to be admitted, his genuine appreciation for old Uncle Leonard, the nephew was actually no good, rotten to the core. He was a philanderer and a compulsive gambler and inevitably he, as well as Leonard, became imprisoned, a sad and undignified end for the old gentleman. To the credit of the prison authorities and most of the guards they did recognise the gross injustice despite their jaded and blunted sensibilities and Champion became universally liked though he was often in terrible pain became irritable as a result. He took laudanum to get him through the really bad days and then was rendered incapable of sensible conversation. On his diminishing good days, Lucius would sit with him, chat and play cards.

Leonard, it transpired, was a scholar and had specialised in history and it was through Leonard therefore that Lucius had learned more about the tree.
"There is a legend," Leonard revealed, "that the tree was planted by an old druid."
" Surely the tree cannot be that old?" Lucius remarked sceptically. Leonard chuckled then smiled knowingly and continued;
"Oh but there are druids around today but whether or not they can be compared to the druids of old is open to debate. In fact the man who planted the tree was a lingering follower of the old faith and, it is said, had inherited the vocation from his father as was the accepted practice of the time."
Lucius studied Leonard, his credibility threshold wilting under the onslaught of the man's obvious intelligence and his learned disposition.
"The tree, it is estimated, was planted in the time of Canute and the reason the druid planted the tree, so legend has it, was because he had seen into the future. He wanted to create a spell that would make amends for the terrible damage

inflicted upon the planet by a burgeoning and misguided population over the course of ensuing centuries."

Lucius smiled, the knoll of truth and resonance sounding in his mind.

"Druids, as you may know, held themselves up as the mainstays of justice, temporal and otherwise, where the injustices of man have been widespread and indiscriminate. Did you know that 'Mort-Lac' was so named as, once upon a time, there was a lake here in the middle of an oak grove? This lone tree is the sole survivor of many hundreds that once stood in this region."

"What happened to the lake?"

"Oh it was drained by the Romans, they built a huge dyke along the eastern edge of the hill which, in more recent times became the main road."

Lucius recalled the ascent to Tower Hill and the wide natural looking cleft that brought him to the prison but there was still doubt in his mind despite the 'ring' of intuition.

'How did such legends form, how will I be granted the key to unlock your great secrets oh beautiful tree? How I wish I could look into your heart mighty oak and observe those timeless treasures? That would be a gift indeed and one for which I would willingly expend my life in this enforced tedium?'

A prophetic thought indeed for Lucius, if he did but know it.

CHAPTER 4

Jessica Stearne gazed upon the boughs of the giant oak tree through the old iron prison bars that still barricaded her bathroom window. They were delightful in their original state of rough hewn antiquity, even if trends of the sixties and seventies had left them with a thick patina of creamy white gloss paint. The boughs of the tree undulated gently in the soft breeze, the leaves singing their sibilant music. Every time she studied the tree, she felt odd, disorientated, reality seeming to fall away as though she were hypnotised, rooted forever to the spot. Waves of empathy flowed through her, something to which she was not remotely accustomed, in fact something to which she strenuously rebelled. Yet as each day passed, she felt more and more drawn to the tree and whenever she looked upon it, everything else seemed to lose tangibility. It was almost as if the only thing present and wholly permanent in her field of vision was that towering oak. Her senses normally so ordered and under control, a result of her pragmatism, became strangely alive. There was in her, an increasing sense of abject misery, of hopelessness with each intimately empathic wave of thought.

These feelings were alien to her, she had sensations that she had never experienced before and they were both alarming and enjoyable, an existential episode. She enjoyed the moments of connection, wanted to nurture them, cherish them but was also threatened by them.

' Maybe Julia is right, I am shut down in some way. I think I am happy and content but am I really? Sometimes I just feel so numb. I like my work, I like my life. I could possibly do with a decent man in it, but then again maybe not? More money would be nice but I don't really need it, I think I have my world under control, I'm OK! Am I though, really? I feel like an alien in this world of too much waste and so much stupidity. These thoughts, these feelings that I have now, where do they come from? They don't seem to belong to me, it's almost as if they are not mine. Yet in the oddest way, they are like a beacon, like thought forms that are calling me to WAKE UP!?'

Once again William jolted Jessica out of her reverie by jumping up onto the kitchen counter top and brushing past her in a series of passes, his tail curling sideways and caressing her as he walked to and fro.

" Oh you monkey! You only ever want attention when you want food you shameless fleabag."

When Jessica offered him his afternoon treat, he declined. Not such a strange event really but Jessica had rarely known him to turn down food when he was making a fuss of her, it was simply his way, the habitual exchange between human and feline. She grabbed him around his middle, picked him up and cradled him like a baby, stroking the sides of his face with the backs of her fingers. William purred, partially closing his eyes in a show of feline happiness, kneading thin air with large velvet paws. She loved William more than anything or anyone but there was an inconsistency in his behaviour that, for some reason, rang alarm bells deep in her subconscious. Knowing that she had to go to the shop, Jessica deposited him on the floor; he stalked off, rejected, clumps of hair raised with static, tail twitching with indignation. Jessica grabbed her jacket and car keys and headed out to the garage, which was a tasteless but tolerably useful addition constructed of cinder block. It was a typically thoughtless carbuncle of sixties vintage that was erected on the northern edge of the property, without the slightest consideration for the architectural virtues of the house and was in full view from the approaching drive. The garage had replaced what was left of a small 12th century chapel that had been further damaged by a bomb in the war. The ivy festooned chapel had stood, so Jessica was told, in an oasis of lilac, apple and cherry trees that attracted countless bees and butterflies. Jessica could not even begin to imagine the twisted state of the individual who decided that the charmingly evocative and enticing chapel remains should be removed to make way for a garage block. Then again developers rarely showed insight or architectural appreciation, seeking only to achieve remunerative goals.

Gritting her teeth against the expected onslaught, Jessica wrestled the overhead door open which produced a nerve lancing screech of unlubricated sheet steel. Once open the air was rich, for a moment, with the aroma of vintage car and slightly stale petrol. Her pride and joy glittered, jewel like, from within like a large black insect. Certainly it was the most impractical of vehicles but Jessica loved her car, a 1956 Bentley S1 painted in black and silver, long and low with its distinctive flowing coach-line. She had been given the car by her Uncle Alistair when his wife and Jessica's Aunt Maria, had died. Maria Gray was given the car as a bridal gift and Jessica had always associated the vehicle with her late aunt. One of her greatest treats as a child was to ride in the car and to have her senses deliciously assailed by the seductive scent of old car leather and wood. Jessica had never really been particularly close to her father but had adored her childless uncle Alistair and aunt Maria, who in their turn reciprocated her love in spades. In fact Alistair was a half brother to her father and ten years his senior. Their mother, Jessica's grandmother had remarried and so they had taken their names from their respective fathers. At the much anticipated end of school term, it had nearly always been her uncle and aunt who had turned up in the immaculate Bentley to collect her, along with her large leather trunk. Even at a young age, Jessica was attuned to the magnificence of the Bentley which, compared to her father's utilitarian Hilman Minx, had seemed so huge and effortlessly powerful as it sped along, accompanied by the smooth but subdued purr of the big six cylinder engine.

Alistair was an accomplished but quite unconventional law professor and one of his more 'bohemian' traits was that he loved to tinker with old cars and was in fact a surprisingly able mechanic. Jessica was mesmerised as a child and had tried to learn all that he had to teach. At Maria's funeral, Jessica's recently bereft and deeply mournful uncle had hugged her and handed over the keys with his blessing.
" There you are my dear, Maria always said she wanted you to have the thing; Lord knows we two have spent enough precious years tinkering with the old relic, that exsequiae. You know that I bought the car brand new in 1956 as a wedding present for Maria, my new bride? I teased her on our wedding night that I wasn't sure who was prettier, her or the car."
Jessica had heard the story a million times but still loved to listen to him speak of that time. Despite his sadness there was the ghost of a twinkle in his eyes and a doleful but sweet smile as he handed her the keys. Jessica was miserable at

losing her beloved aunt and then initially aghast that she should be given such a responsibility; she was speechless at first and held fast to her uncle, giving him a long and emotionally charged hug.

"Don't be sad for aunt Maria, uncle Alistair," Jessica finally managed to say while wiping away her own tears.

"She's really still here you know!"

"Oh good gracious lovey, its not Maria I'm sad for, its handing over the bloody car."

Jessica smiled then laughed a little despite herself, dear old Alistair, that prevailing sense of ironic British humour; he didn't like embarrassing scenes, long farewells or displays of gratitude.

Having been used to her Vauxhall Astra which was boringly efficient, driving the Bentley was something of a shock and fraught with anxiety. The steering was excruciatingly heavy, the brakes were effective after a fashion but only after a brief but frightening lag which made parking a nightmare. The robust but out-dated 'allegedly' automatic transmission needed a psychic connection in order to operate successfully. The car was profligate in the extreme and was also a constant target of vandalism in the city. Jessica refused to give up on it though and was always enchanted anew as she slid across the soft red leather, placing her hands on the large steering wheel and gazing at the wonderful old Smiths speedometer with its curiously distinctive dial and needle that pointed at two o'clock at rest. Out on the open road the car was a dream, soaking up the miles in true old Bentley style, accompanied by that typical subdued purr. It seemed almost sacrilegious to use the car as an everyday work and shopping vehicle but to Jessica, it was her haven, the place where she sorted things out in her head.

She had been inconsolable when her aunt had died but the only slight compensation for Maria's death was to have been given the car. The Bentley immortalised her aunt, preserved her animus, kept her 'alive'. In this way the car was haunted, a manifestation that added to the other influences that the car had collected in its curiously rich fifty year history. This anchored Jessica to the distant past with which she resonated and so adored. She always felt at her safest when in the Bentley, almost as if her beloved aunt Maria were there beside her, talking to her, gently criticizing or praising, making her feel safe and secure.

Alistair was an exceptionally robust man with an iron constitution; Maria, on the other hand, had always been fragile, a victim her whole life of anaemia and recurrent and spiteful migraines that often left her in a stupor for days. She died of complications following a serious stroke that had started off as a migraine. Among the Gray's lovably eccentric traits was that, as they had failed to have children of their own, they had taken a deep proprietorial interest in Jessica. As a matter of course, she had stayed with them during school holidays, was taken on outings, picnics at a beautiful and much favoured spot at a nearby river, to the cinema and also the theatre. They taught her to ride a horse and while Jessica never really warmed to the saddle she did have very happy memories of riding high and looking out over the world and down upon the crowns of people walking nearby. She had long suspected that Alistair and Maria had approached her father with a view to having an even more active role in her upbringing. The subject was so tangible on one occasion that despite her fathers worse than usual state of abstraction, Jessica was convinced that her father had just turned down an offer from the Gray's to foster her but it didn't matter at the time, not really. Jessica was so much a frequent visitor and resident at their beautiful rambling house, so much their child in any case. Some of her happiest memories were of when she had played for hours on her own in and around the house and grounds, a skinny, tragic and solitary little figure that always seemed so content with her own company. The doting pair were enchanted by Jessica when, as a little girl, she had asked precocious questions and spent hours playing out on the lawn at the edge of the woods, often swinging to and fro on an old rope swing hanging from a mighty chestnut, while reading countless classical novels. On those wet days which nostalgia had rendered mercifully few, she instead went into the attic and explored the universe and the boundaries of time itself in a space ship which she had constructed and when tired of that, read more Austen, Forster, Bronte, Elliot, Walter-Scott and so on. In fact the space craft was a very large and comfortable wooden trunk into which Jessica had installed an inoperative and dusty wireless that had lost its Bakelite cover. In later life she could still recall the smell, that evocative, musty, aged electrical apparatus odour. The wireless of course with its innards mysteriously full of intriguing silver filigree, glass encased thermionic valves, was the guts of the machine and the engine of time travel.

Jessica was not pretty at that age, not remotely doll-like with her long skinny legs and scabby knees, her black unruly hair, dark skin, angular features and bespectacled eyes. Nevertheless, Alistair had always maintained that one day she would grow into her looks;
"She'll be an absolute stunner m'dear, you mark my words."
Ironically, Jessica had never appreciated her own beauty, was never really in the least bit aware of it as she wriggled out of

the awkward caterpillar cocoon of childhood, to become a promisingly beautiful young independent woman who started to widen her horizons. She went for long late night walks across the fields and by the river hoping to meet a kindred spirit, a kindly and handsome Knight who would lift her gently up on to his mighty destrier and take her away forever to his castle sitting atop the clouds. On occasion she went on pilgrimages, to Avebury or to Silbury hill or some of the neolithic burial chambers, the long barrows, that exerted a fascination upon her. Whenever Jessica thought about it, all of her happiest childhood memories were undoubtedly of her time with the quaint childless couple in their impractical, large and outrageously beautiful home. Alistair had inherited the house which really was beyond his means to run and in which they lived, rattling around like dried peas in a big tin.

The Bentley had not been used for two weeks or more and so Jessica was compelled to adopt a ritual, the priming of the carburettors. This was achieved by opening the carburettor side of the longitudinally split bonnet and depressing the float buttons with the ignition on and the fuel pumps ticking away encouragingly. A brisk opening of the throttle to activate the choke and then the Bentley started with no fuss at all and settled to a steady idle with the oily rustle of the valve gear amplified by the garage enclosure. Jessica maneuvered the Bentley through the snug aperture of the garage door. She popped a compact disc into the player that was sympathetically situated behind the facade of the original but long defunct valve radio in deference to the car's vintage. The music was played through four weighty speakers hidden beneath the rear parcel shelf and inhabiting what was previously the storage openings low down on the inside of the front doors. Jessica navigated the heavy traffic while basking in the stirring and massive dynamism of 'A German Requiem' by Brahms. After locating a parking spot and achieving a surprisingly well executed and successful berthing in limited space, she listened for a while to the music while gradually turning the volume down. Maria had always maintained that it was so irreverent to simply shut the power off. To have turned the music off suddenly would have been like being harshly awoken from the deepest refuge of a dream woven sleep.

The supermarket visit was typically uneventful. Jessica deliberated over and finally selected some packaged fast food meals, organic fruit by ironic contrast and then she picked up a durian. She had always held a fascination for these exotic 'ugly' fruits, they looked unappetising and they smelt terrible and there was no obvious way of preparation or consumption. There was, however, something so appealing about them that she was always so tempted though inevitably, she would falter at the last hurdle for lack of courage. So far she had not tasted the fruit and simply lacked the spirit to ask how it was prepared. As an alternative she took a Spanish seedless watermelon as she loved watermelons but suspected, as she hefted the specimen into the shopping cart, that this factory farmed eunuch would not live up to expectations. She added potatoes, carrots and of course, cat food otherwise she would have William to answer to; finally there were the essentials of her toilette. While deliberating over the wine, seasonally appropriate refreshing whites and full bodied reds, she espied and impulsively bought a swinging garden chair; a big sign indicating that it was on 'special offer'. Jessica needed no encouragement to nurture romantic notions of reclining on the chair, glass of wine in hand, under the shelter of the oak

tree, reading classic novels during the remaining days of summer. After paying for the chair she realised then that she could not fit it into the car. Finally the Bentley was submitted to the indignity of having the box tied onto it's roof.
' What would Alistair think- sorry uncle!' Jessica smiled at the probable result of his amicable disapproval though Maria would have been thoroughly in agreement. The Bentley bore the burden well apart from seeming to idle a little roughly in the heavy traffic in the soaring summer heat. Upon her arrival back at Mort-lac and with the car still laden, Jessica flipped open one of the aluminium bonnet halves again. Guided by intuition, she fiddled, for a moment, with the air screw adjustment on the rear S.U carburettor and noted with satisfaction as the slight roughness changed to a smooth idle.

A new neighbour espied Jessica grappling with the box containing the swinging chair and much to Jessica's irritation, came sauntering over to see her.
" It is so gratifying to see a woman who knows her way around a car, and what a beautiful back end, I often admire it."
Realising immediately that she was the focus of this deliberate 'double entendre', Jessica became flustered, her hackles raised with annoyance. The man's name was Rob Dryden, a good looking young fellow with a full head of blonde hair, pale blue eyes and a look of self assurance bordering on conceit. He had approached Jessica with offers of help when she moved in. On the face of it, this was a good, kind hearted offer but Jessica quickly divined that he had evidently added her to his list of potential conquests. It was apparent that she was seen as another candidate from whom he might add a further notch to his bedpost. He had become very persistent of late and had repeatedly attempted to

intercept her whenever she ventured outside almost since the day she moved in, she really started to feel quite hunted and was becoming extremely resentful. He carried out a frankly nauseating but practiced and appreciative study of Jessica's form as he spoke to her. He surveyed the long slim legs, the beautifully modeled hips, narrow waist and the abundant bosom but all so carelessly hidden under rather functional and shapeless clothing. Her hair was tied back severely as an aid to function and she was wearing her most practical and least attractive work spectacles. Jessica had sought a mate for many years, a partner with whom to converse, to share her joys and her sorrows, her views, opinions and life's experiences. The last thing she needed was just another fickle man looking for an uncomplicated sexual escapade. She had been very unlucky in love and did not know why.

'Maybe all men are just fuckwits by nature! No surely not, there must be some good ones out there?'

Jessica's natural naivete was in point of fact her biggest problem and she was shy and awkward around people and most particularly her admirers. She could be very gauche, saying stupid things and laughing inappropriately. None of this was helped by her dubious choice of wardrobe. Her astonishing natural beauty was shrouded and further attenuated by a total lack of self esteem. On the other hand she wasn't stupid nor was she blind and recognised a predator when she saw one. Rob helped her unload the box from the roof of the car, attempting to ingratiate himself but once the task was achieved Jessica wanted to be rid of him as quickly as possible.

"I can handle this on my own from now on but thank you very much, erm Rob isn't it?"

He smiled beguilingly, a little boy's expression of charming contrition.

"Oh but I like to help, I can never resist a damsel in distress, I could even help you assemble it, run my hands over the intricacies so to speak".

Jessica was becoming increasingly annoyed and despite his charm and good looks she felt the mild stirrings of revulsion. There was something surprisingly deep in her dislike of Rob which surprised her. Also her brittle ego bristled indignantly at the inference that as a mere woman, she would not be able to assemble the chair. It never would have occurred to Jessica in her myopic and defensive way that to have casually batted her eyes at him would have had him eating out of her hand. She would have found herself a willing and helpful slave and all in trade for the mere possibility of uncomplicated sex. Having solicited his help she could then have charmingly sent him on his way. Jessica did not have these skills and was just not equipped in the subtleties of dealing with predatory men, instead she became resentful and distrustful.

Rob was immune to rejection, thinking that some women put up token resistance as part of the interplay; how could they resist him? Normally they didn't but Jessica really wasn't interested. Extraordinarily and quite out of character, she embarked upon a tactic once used by an attractive friend, admittedly with great success.

"Well okay then, thanks for the offer, if we could just pop it on the ground for now, my 'girlfriend' has promised to come over and help me assemble it."

She emphasized the word 'girlfriend' as in partner and was gratified to see that this had the desired effect. Rob cooled off noticeably, finished helping Jessica drag the box over to the tree and then beat a tactical retreat.

'Thank god for that, don't suppose he will be quite so persistent now.'

Then an uncomfortable thought occurred to her. Within hours the news would be all round the block that she was, 'one of those', a 'dyke' as Rob would no doubt refer to her! Then Jessica laughed despite herself and picked up William as he passed by.

'Oh well, if it gives me some peace! Ah William, you are the only chap for me my only love.'

William gazing up at her through golden eyes, chirruped briefly, half meow and then purred, he sensed food was about to be offered and possibly even some morsels of broken rich tea biscuits.

That evening Jessica assembled the chair by the bluebells under a great mossy bough and then, satisfied with her work, lay on it with a glass of wine in one hand and a book in the other. After a while she stopped reading in order that she might absorb more of the soporific calm of a magical summer evening. The only sounds were that of distant traffic, the buzz of insects and an occasional creak from her new acquisition. Jessica, while relishing the moment, the delicious tranquility, was also hoping that no one would come to her with the intention of starting a conversation. She put up a kind of psychic forcefield around herself and then satisfied that no one would dare encroach upon her, snatched these precious moments of serenity. She took another long sip from the wine glass and then, with a sigh, returned to the book immeasurably satisfied that all was well in her world.

As the sun went down, a capricious chill stole into the air and Jessica was finally compelled to stir, she was sleepy, just a little tipsy and wanted to go to bed. Once there, feeling happy and at peace with the world, she fell almost immediately into a deep sleep. That night, Jessica dreamed an odd meandering dream, atmospheric, powerful and quite uncannily real.

CHAPTER 5

It was a magnificent summer evening, warm and dry, the drone of the insects and chatter of the swallows being the only sounds to break the tranquility of those precious moments before dusk. Lucius Grey gazed spellbound upon the gently undulating boughs of the giant oak tree through the prison bars which were slightly crooked and rusty with age. Lucius wiped away some of the cobwebs, the innumerable empty husks of a thousand dead insects and all sorts of detritus that obscured his view. Another day was almost spent with nothing achieved as he whiled away the time sitting upon his bed in a state of mindless dejection. It was just the same as countless other days that had passed in his life of ennui and predictability, a life of degradation and demoralization. The only high points in his days were events such as the observance of the setting of the sun when the weather permitted. The tree demanded his attention regularly, a ritual that he allowed himself was to observe the magnificence of nature, a constant reminder that there was indeed true beauty in the world. Apart from that, the only contrasting emotion was the anxiety and anticipation concerning whether one would actually eat that day. Lucius was wholly at the mercy of benefactors on the outside whose consistency of character represented the only frail hope of a diet that would be both edible and nutritious. The only alternative was a hideous gruel in the morning and weevil infested stale bread and brackish water in the evening courtesy, if that was the appropriate word, of the prison authorities. To be permitted to obtain food by other means was a gift indeed; to actually receive it was nothing less than miraculous. This was a perilous position to be in and in great part, owed its success to the ironic dis-honesty but possible morality of the gaolers. To a great extent, success depended upon regular donations, bribery in other words, to ensure the safe delivery of the food and that cost him dear. The gaolers in general liked Lucius, he had earned a degree of respect and this rendered the service a little more reliable. With prisoners less liked, the food was often appropriated en-route or maliciously tampered with. Leonard Champion was the only person in the complex who was offered, unconditionally, quite deferential treatment and received his victuals unmolested and unimpeded.

Lucius often reflected upon the reason for his predicament, he really had little else to do. His family, once prominent and successful, had withered over generations and had fallen progressively upon harder times. His were an old and established family dating back into a distant and a quite remarkable past. Their wealth had been founded upon the ownership of considerable lands on the east coast of England and in the county of Kent. Over generations, an estate of several thousand acres and situated on fertile low lying coastal land was farmed very successfully and initially, had grown and thrived. A great house was built upon the foundations of a once lavish monastery which had been looted at the time of the reformation under the direction of Cromwell and was subsequently destroyed. The land and monastery were then given to Lucius's ancestors; the estate flourished and the reins of responsibility were passed from father to eldest son.

Unfortunately, as so often happens with families in such situations, there inevitably arises a time when a young man taking on the burden of his fathers wealth has no head for business. A life of profligacy and leisure becomes more enticing and with seemingly inexhaustible reserves, there is little incentive to carry the harness of responsibility. Gambling, lavish parties, philandering and a general excess of self indulgent behaviour eventually reversed the tide of the family fortunes and eventually serious debt ensued. To make matters worse, this also coincided latterly with the claims of nature as rising water levels, caused by Britain's gradual but relentless tilt, claimed a portion of the farmland that lay already perilously close to sea level. The four thousand acre estate was reduced to mere hundreds as land, year by year, was inundated and crops and livestock were lost to the elements. Along with their loss of fortune was a gradual erosion of family status as enmity with other families leached at their good name. By the time Lucius came into the world during the heady days of Victorian advancement and accumulation, the Grey family were declining. Lucius was a good man and well liked, as indeed his father had been, but it was his grandfather who had been the great rogue and philanderer. He had also, through the affairs of the heart, fallen greatly out of favour with an up and coming neighbour named Adam Brogan who owned and was adding to, great tracts of land adjacent to but inland from the Grey's property.

Sebastian Grey, Lucius' roguish but charming grandfather had solicited friendship with and patronised the neighbour who was a man with no status. He had risen remarkably from the grip of poverty like an air bubble released from the watery depths, some twenty years previously. He was a shrewd business man who worked hard and deployed immense sagacity. He was of course flattered by the attentions of a gentleman of the Grey family and it has to be said that Sebastian was an easy man to like for he drew people to him like moths to a flame. For all his faults he was a most charismatic and attractive individual and initially, he was very helpful to his new neighbour. Only his wife, Elisabeth, suspected Sebastian's motives as she had known him long enough to realise that he was incapable of selfless behaviour and she despised him for it. In the event, Sebastian's prime reason for befriending Adam Brogan was not a noble one and had more to do with the fact that Adam's eldest daughter, Diana was reputedly the most beautiful young woman in the south east of England.

Sebastian's wife was a very accomplished and still youthful young lady with whom he had produced three children, the eldest of whom was Lucius's father. Elisabeth had long since fallen out of love with this charming rogue but was powerless to prevent his exploits and simply shut her eyes to his dealings. Sebastian was not to be deterred from any chance of personal gratification and secretly, he pursued Diana artfully and relentlessly and like many rogues, was a clever psychologist. Diana's tendency toward vanity, willful self indulgence and romanticism was the ingredient that the callow naivety of youth was not able to suppress. Sebastian had no respect for the Brogan family, thinking them 'yokels' with ideas above their station and he lost no time in divining Diana's passions, scoundrel that he was. Finally after winning her love and ultimate submission through his own particular brand of charm and witchcraft, he left her with child.

In point of fact Diana was so easily led, susceptible and inclined to follow such a course that remarks were made by many after the fact. With the right catalyst and genetic inclinations, she was her mothers daughter right enough. Her mother, Adam's wife, a buxom and attractive lady even in latter years, was once a milkmaid with a lusty disposition and with a tarnished reputation when Adam had first fallen for her charms. Subsequently, Adam had spent many an exhausting night in the marital bed at the behest of his insatiable bride. Diana, unbeknown to her father, was endowed with a similar appetite. Furthermore, it was to be admitted that Diana was denied nothing, was consequently wealthy and at liberty to indulge her whims. She was neither well educated nor had she the benefit of several generations of sound breeding and deep rooted moral sensibilities that might have deterred her from such a precarious course. She was neither discreet nor even considerate of her parents feelings and fell headlong into a tragic adventure with Sebastian Grey.

Adam so worshipped and adored his eldest daughter that, at the beginning of the affair, he was completely blind to her shortcomings and refused to listen to gossip. As events unfolded he still refused to acknowledge her folly and her part in the liaison. As soon as he was finally aware of his daughters predicament, he sent her away to live with a family in France during her confinement. Diana died while giving birth and Adam, tortured with grief and twisted with a sense of self righteous vengeance, swore an awful curse upon the Grey family and embarked upon a path of unremitting revenge from that day forth.

Adam started by strategically buying up every bit of land surrounding the Grey's property. It could have been financially ruinous for him but the gods of fortune smiled upon him, the climate at that time being very much in his favour. In effect the Greys became increasingly land locked, their rights of access being reduced almost daily, a river running to their property and a main water source, was deliberately diverted away by Adam Brogan. Their dwindling assets and Adam's burgeoning fortune made this a legal battle to which Sebastian Grey was clearly unequal. In disgrace, thoroughly hated by his wife and exceedingly in debt, he finally took his own life in a rather macabre fashion. He ordered a local blacksmith who was bemused and too terrified to refuse, to make up iron cuffs and a collar linked by chains, attached to an iron ball and then fitted to Sebastian's person. Sebastian had then thrown himself into the sea where he sank like a stone and was speedily drowned. Sebastian's son was forced into the 'harness' prematurely and did his best to revive the flagging family fortunes. Under normal circumstances, he would have done well, much to his mother's amazement, but what could do was not sufficient. Between the stranglehold of Adam Brogan and the relentless ingress of the north sea, there was little room for manoeuver.

Under pressure as a result of enormous debt, the family homestead was abandoned to creditors and it was Adam Brogan in the main, who had purchased every available note. Lucius' father, unable to cash in on his remaining status was offered a position with the ageing, bitter and dyspeptic Adam as his estate manager but the position was onerous by design. Adam, now that he had a Grey within his grasp, lost no opportunity to make his life miserable and Lucius' father, his namesake, a young man with a young family died prematurely, a broken man. The young Lucius, his mother and two sisters were saved from homelessness by a relative, who was not so much compassionate but feared for his own sense of imminent disgrace if the family honour were to fall further at this critical juncture. Lucius' mother became a part time governess to a family nearby while the sisters awaited suitors. Lucius, a sensitive, intelligent but very angry young man was sent away to school for education and guidance. He worked hard and well and was encouraged to study medicine at university. Lucius however, deciding that he needed to reverse his families mis-fortune, ran off to the Far East and was gone for some eight years. His expenditures, physical and cerebral paid off handsomely whereupon he returned home a wealthy man. While trying to decide what to do and where to spend his life he met Georgina Brogan.

He had enough sense to know that the feud with her very elderly and embittered grandfather, was pointless; he even felt a certain compassion toward the tortured and ill tempered old man. Adam's mind had become a putrefying cesspool of bitterness and hate and his body, as if in parody, became bent and deformed through the influence of gout and rheumatoid arthritis. Lucius for his part was only too aware of the sordid tale of his grandfather's waywardness, though few actually now referred to the episode. By that time, Sebastian's behaviour had become a legend of infamy that was never mentioned in Lucius' family or Adam Brogan's for that matter. Lucius felt that there had to be a reversal of such bitter acrimony. The best way forward was to somehow overcome the fermenting crucible of hate which had latterly become the almost exclusive ingredients for a self fulfilling prophecy. He craved resolution and wanted so badly to heal the rift between them all through kindness, strength and goodwill. Adam, despite himself, could not help but tolerate the boy. He had begun to divert his attention and his considerable love to his grand daughter, Georgina, the legitimate offspring of his third child who rather tragically, had also died in child bed. After spending her formative years ignored by her grandfather, Georgina was suddenly lavished with attention and gifts and might well have been in danger of being spoilt. She was a much more intelligent and sensible girl however, than her ill-fated aunt and she deserved more respect but this latter felicitation was never offered. She was not quite the beauty that Diana had been but she was clever and alluringly feminine and despite his nature, she truly loved her grandfather. Adam however, in his typically masculine way was quite blind to the distinctions between Georgina and Diana.

Lucius had decided to return from his travels specifically to spend some time with his mother with whom, over the years, he had become quite estranged. His intention was to stay for a few weeks, maybe some months? But as decreed by the powers of destiny it was but a matter of a short time before he chanced upon Georgina. He simply fell in love with her as she did with him, so simply, so beautifully and somehow, so rightly. Georgina was wise enough however, not to let a romance ensue in the open, for fear of incurring her Grandfather's wrath. She and Lucius made a pact, swearing allegiance and undying love for one another but for the sake of harmony would refrain from open contact wherever possible. The time would come when they would be able to be together but they both recognised that this would be hard won. They wrote to one another but only occasionally in order that they did not draw too much attention. The letters were typical of those written by unrequited lovers, passionate, emotional, tempestuous, beautiful. They were conveyed by a sympathetic servant girl whom Georgina had much befriended as a child.

There seemed to be no way out of the predicament of enforced non-association but Lucius in his slightly idealistic but essentially august way, sensed a shift, a change of heart in Adam. If only he could somehow impress upon Adam the honourable nature of his intentions, there might actually be great advantages to a union between him and Georgina. There was even the possibility of a soothing balm to Adams tormented soul, an absolution, an exorcism; then he might smile happily upon his grandchildren and die a happy man. What Lucius did not understand however, was that although Adam did indeed have a reluctant admiration for Lucius and did accept him, to an extent, there was a little too much of his grandfather in Lucius for Adam's complete comfort. He was handsome like his grandfather and supremely likeable, charismatic and a social lamplight to the moths of Victorian society. What Adam sensed but would never consciously acknowledge, was that Lucius, though like his grandfather in so many ways, was also kind, trustworthy and thoroughly reputable. However, there was a fateful misunderstanding between Adam and Lucius that re-enforced the barriers that would keep the young couple apart.

Adam's personality may have become ugly and distorted, his faculties aged and impaired but he was no fool. Through his keen and paranoid observations, the attraction between Lucius and Georgina could not remain unnoticed. Moreover his animosity was fuelled by the apparent deceit conveyed by the young couple who strove only to protect his feelings. Lucius' success in the Far Eastern colonies was seen, paradoxically, as not only a testament to the young man's undoubted abilities but also as an additional threat. He had brought about a dramatic reversal of the relentless decline of his families fortunes and Adam observed this development purely in the light of his inability to keep the Greys within his power. Initially his conflicting mix of admiration and dislike for Lucius was an inconvenience that temporarily halted his plans for the family downfall. Gradually however, his sense of injustice, outrage, jealousy, hate, misery and a fundamental imbalance in his state of mind won the day. Judgment fuelled the fires of his belief that there was indeed a relationship between Georgina and Lucius and from that time, he lived in self righteous torment.

Lucius, whose instincts were razor sharp and finely honed, sensed Adam's suspicions. He decided to do the brave and honourable thing and he wrote to Adam as a first step towards building a bridge. A physical representation, he felt, might be misconstrued by the hot headed and bucolic Adam who would give Lucius no time to speak his piece. Lucius was sensitive and aware enough to know that an open attempt at paying court to Georgina might be an assault to Adam's fragile ego and delicate sensibilities. Deciding that discretion was the better part of valour, Lucius decided to tread softly and warily in his attempts to break down Adams defenses. Just as the painter creates his masterpiece in pre-meditated stages, utilising patience as one of the many vital ingredients in his armoury of portraiture skills, so Lucius would skillfully weave his spell. He was well aware that it might take time and self discipline and that he would suffer moments of disappointment but in that he was well versed, having successfully practiced similar methods in his acquisition of great wealth in Hong Kong. He wrote a letter, a plea to Adam to put any remaining animosity behind him.

My Dear Sir,

I consider you to be a patron and a friend if I may be so bold as to address you thus. I hesitate to broach a subject that is painful to you and I respect you and your wishes more than you will ever realise. It is my great desire that you will read all that I have to say and hopefully, observe some earnestness and sincerity in my communication. I implore you to afford me a little merit in your estimation of my character as, simply put, my intentions are quite without guile. In that regard and without wishing to reopen old wounds, I realise that, in the name of my forebear, I have an account to settle and considerable reparation to make to you. In my opinion, there comes a time when wounds must be healed, there must be an unguent poured upon those wounds in order to address the injuries sustained.

I am aware that a member of my family now long deceased, perpetrated the grossest of improprieties against your kin. He is presently and will forevermore be harmless to all that now live on God's earth. I have no doubt that the sins of the past may, to some extent, be alleviated by the heartfelt contrition and the greatest goodwill by those now living. Those holding the reins of family honour and grace, are prepared to account for all the great wrongdoings of the past. I wish sir, with all my heart to convey my sincerest apologies. My greatest desire is to heal the rift that so saddens our families and still so offends you. I pray you will accept my olive branch in truce as it is honestly offered and is indeed a devout affirmation of my desires to repay the debt and obtain your forgiveness.

I am your most obedient servant,

Yours Sincerely,

Lucius Montgomery Grey.

Many years later, he could still recall the letter word for word and furthermore, he recalled, equally vividly, the malevolent response that his letter solicited. Adam, not surprisingly given his extreme state of paranoia, smelled a rat where really there was none to be detected. Lucius' only error was his youthful eagerness and naiveté. This was not a business initiative when all was said and done.

'Sir,

Your communication is abhorrent to me, your hollow sentiments are repugnant. I have been made aware of the discovery of an alliance that has developed between yourself and my Grand daughter and am making arrangements that will ensure that no more counsel takes place between you. If you truly feel that you have a debt to repay then consider henceforth that the debts will be considered settled when you have forever removed yourself and your accursed family from my proximity. I will not tolerate any further intercourse between ourselves. I urge you sir to take the greatest heed of these words for they will not be repeated.

Yours Sincerely,

Adam Brogan

Lucius was bloodied but decided to swallow his pride and wrote a truly beautiful letter of plea to Adam by return of post. He hoped, like the artist adding the final brush strokes, that he might refine the approach and greatly soften the harsh outlines of the portrait, to similarly soften Adam Brogan's wall of impenetrability. He received a further angry and uncivil note of warning, positively sizzling with hysteria and imbalance. Then Lucius compounded an already bad situation by committing a great error. In a desperate attempt to secure a little time to talk with Georgina and knowing of her imminent departure, he climbed the wall to her bedroom window and knocked upon it. The timing was unfortunate however; having scaled the wall, he found himself gazing upon the comely form of a partially clad feminine figure, the object of his abject love. The maid who was assisting Georgina with her dressing let out a loud and dramatic scream.

Gazing, once again, through the bars and into space, Lucius pondered and considered these memories as if he had not already done so a million times. He looked upon the tree as it became progressively silhouetted by the shadowy beauty of dusk rendering the great venerable oak with a cloak of deep mystery and timeless magic. Tomorrow he would be let out for a while to take the air, a privilege that cost a deal of money but to Lucius, it was an interlude that was vital to his sanity. He felt tired, he wanted to go to sleep, to escape to those other worlds. As he prepared to lie down, a marmalade cat walked past him, an unnaturally large and extravagantly well fed fellow with huge feet and a flat face. In the long months that Lucius had been incarcerated in the gaol, the cat had appeared from time to time out of the blue but no person knew anything of the creature. Lucius loved cats and wanted to befriend the fellow but the cat had remained aloof, distant; a fleeting apparition that shied away if Lucius came too close. He went to bed that night and lay awake for a time listening to the rats and to the wailing of mad old Tom Watkins, a solicitor defrocked for defrauding a family whom he represented. Finally, falling into a fitful sleep, Lucius experienced the strangest of dreams.

CHAPTER 6

Jessica was awoken early by a cool breeze blowing though her bedroom window. There was a beautiful blazing red dawn that cast a deep glow upon the world and into the interior of Jessica's bedroom. Despite this she felt oddly out of sorts, cold and uncomfortable but there was consolation in the vibrant dawn chorus even though there had been a heavy dew in the night; by morning, everything was covered in a light coating of glistening water droplets. The plants and trees were bejeweled and the world that day was greeted with a singular glittering assurance. The early morning sun was still low in the sky and reflected off the high cirrus, this created a new world of imagery above that was so different from that below; the bewitching deep crimson light that illuminated a world of phantasm. It was a morning to die for and yet one that failed to rouse Jessica from her unusual despondency.

William, as usual, had elected to share the bed with her as was his wont and his 'right' and in consequence occupied most of her side. Jessica had been forced to shift over progressively during the night as William intruded upon her space while he scratched, washed and groomed, making all manner of intriguing but frankly slightly irritating noises as he perfected his toilette. His frequent scratching shook the bed annoyingly and then when finally, he sprawled out on his back, he made himself very much at home. Jessica was left quite uncovered, wearing little but her blouse and underwear from the day before and she felt decidedly frosty upon awakening in more ways than one. She unceremoniously hefted a protesting William out of the way, dumped him on the floor, pulled some covers over herself and then, lying sleepily in a soporific warmth, recalled her dream as best she could. As William tried to jump back on the bed she threw him out and shut the door.

" Time I had some space fluffums, some bed partner you are you beast, it's like sleeping with someone with St Vitus Dance. I really should put you out at night so that you can join your chums yowling and fighting into the early hours." She remembered with a shudder, that Steven Savage had been an exceptionally restless bed partner. Even when he was actually still, he lay on his back with his mouth open and snored like an elephant.

'How was it even possible that such a little man could have such a loud reverberating snore.'

She felt herself shrink and shrivel just a little as the unwelcome memory invaded her mind unbidden, her already low spirits dragged down further by the recollection.

She had been dreaming in the night, very intensely and the memories were still fresh in her mind. They were lucid dreams, where there is a thin veil between reality and apparition; she was in her own home, exploring the hall and rooms of not only her flat but of the whole building. Unobstructed by partition walls that were present only in some shadowy and etheric form, she was entirely at liberty to roam freely. Her most prevailing sensation was that of profound greyness and of demoralisation. It was as if she were exploring the old prison during a power outage at dusk. There was a little light but all that was visible was apparent in silhouette only with occasional flashes of reflected light off odd shiny surfaces such as the metal bars set in the thick wooden doors.

Jessica had to an overriding conviction that she had somehow been communicated with, not in a language as such, more sensation, an implication. There was a tortured presence, an abstraction so desperate and so dismal and where greyness prevailed, uninviting and miserable. Yet there was also a strangely reassuring rightness to it, a confluence, as if she truly belonged in that realm. In the cold light of day there was little sense to be made at first as Jessica struggled to remember the finer details of the dream. Frustratingly and, as is often so typical, her memory of the adventure was draining away like sand in an egg timer as the burgeoning consciousness of a rudely awakened mind, rapidly refilled with twentieth century clutter.

A connection had occurred which, though tenuous, fragile and ethereal, gradually formed a picture in Jessica's mind. The link was with someone, no one she knew and yet there was a curious familiar masculine presence. She had even spoken with him briefly but could not remember what was said or even, what he looked like. She felt that he was kind, a gentle man, a 'gentleman' but one who was in extraordinary pain. Her biggest recollection was of the amazing empathy between them, a meeting of the mind and of the soul. The man was disenchanted and much in anguish. Jessica experienced the vaguest recollection of him devouring a feast, a meal that was to be his last, without knowing how or why she felt that. There was also the unsettling sense that she was imprisoned, as though her body were rigid, completely immobile and where her perception of the world was divined through the feelings of many others. No it was more than that, it was some kind of matrix, a connection and an intuitive knowing. Jessica really did feel very odd, not at all herself and for a moment she speculated that she might be coming down with flu. Her ears were ringing, an affliction that was usually a sure sign that she was in the grip of some encroaching malady.

She climbed out of bed, her long, still plaited hair awry and resembling a bristle brush. Then she put on a flannelette dressing gown, plugged in the kettle and absentmindedly heated up some porridge, her mind still on quite another plane. She also put a pan of water on the stove for some poached eggs and experienced a completely alien and highly inexplicable urge to eat kidneys. This was a sensation so foreign to her that she speculated for just the briefest of intervals whether she might be pregnant but then ruled that out with some measure of relief, as a biological impossibility. This was enforced by a sense of the coming onset of cramps in her lower stomach, her breasts were painfully sensitive, that 'time' was looming. Maybe that was why she felt so off-colour, tired, listless but simultaneously restless and really not quite sure what to do with herself.

Large mug of tea in hand, Jessica reached for the 'remote', aimed it at the television and acknowledged the response in the form of that characteristic click and 'whoompfh' of highly charged static. This was something she would normally never have considered doing in the morning unless she was sick but she badly needed a distraction and in any case she really did feel unwell. The clatter of the cat flap heralded William's return and recovering from his rejection, decided to give his mistress another chance. Hopping on to her lap, he dug his claws into her knees as he purred and kneaded her legs,

" Hello sweetcakes, God you are so predictable, I know exactly what you want!"

She popped a piece of rich tea biscuit onto the floor and as he jumped off, ever the slave to his desires, he concentrated on his treat both purring and crunching happily. Jessica re-arranged herself, putting her feet up sideways onto the couch and covered herself with a blanket. It was a Sunday and she took a little pleasure in the knowledge that the day was hers to do with as she pleased; she merely wanted to hunker down and hide from the world. There was nothing much on the telly but fascile chat between early morning presenters, American Idol which held no appeal for Jessica but then on another channel was Steve Martin as Inspector Clouseau. Jessica virtually frothed at the mouth with indignation, *'How could they! Peter Sellers was a genius; this is a ghastly abomination!'*

She clicked off the television in disgust, sat back and closed her eyes for a moment. William, having finished his treat and realising that no more were forthcoming for the moment, had decided that he wanted to go outside again and was flicking the cat flap annoyingly and insistently. Jessica got up and opened the door for him even though he was quite capable of letting himself in and out. It was a little game he played with her and thereby, showing her who really was boss.

The phone rang. Jessica shrank visibly, recoiling in horror, sensing invasion but fearing an urgent work call, she picked up the receiver and answered defensively. It was Julia, her lifelong friend who sounded a little deflated at Jessica's response.

"Jess, was it something I said?"

72

Julia lived in Glastonbury with her husband and four unruly children where they ran a small organic farm. They perpetually teetered on the brink of financial ruin but always made it through somehow. What always amazed Jessica, who had been born under the star sign of Aries and who could only survive in the world with a well ordered bank account and taxes paid, was that Julia and her husband cared little for their precarious financial position and had scant regard for banks or for the government. Jessica, in the past, had remonstrated with Julia, suggesting that affairs in order meant peace of mind. Julia snorted at this suggestion and remarked haughtily,

" I have no intention of entering that soulless grey world somewhere in the Phantom zone where people are assessed purely in monetary terms. You know Jessica that these power hungry, money laundering cretins at the head of financial institutions are just vampires. They are incapable of feeling the slightest joy other than when they are sucking the lifeblood out of innocents."

Then Julia had giggled, Jessica could just imagine the beguiling flash of mischief crossing her features for a fleeting moment. She changed the subject and became suddenly serious, instead devoting all of her frustration, anger and attention upon the plight of organic farmers and of the dismal state of affairs in the livestock related food production industry. That was the last time Jessica and Julia had seen each other but now Jessica badly needed to chat.

" Hello Jules, my gosh, its seems so long since I last spoke to you, I'm so sorry my love, I always seem to be busy and time just passes me by! How are you all?"

" Oh you know, same old same old; trying to figure out which way is up, you know how it is here in this crazy country of yours, idiots in government introducing pointless bureaucratic crap. You know don't you that beef cattle have, for so long, been bombarded with medication of all types, which most people ingest constantly, that a strain of antibiotic resistant E.coli is spreading like wildfire. No surprises there and the EEC bureaucrats are running around like headless chickens and of course, all we get is the fall-out from the political crap. Any way, I didn't phone you to bore you about farming; I dreamed about you last night."

Jessica was always slightly amused by Julia and her earnestness regarding matters to do with organic farming and the rights of the common man. Jessica in more recent years made intermittent attempts to eat organically, mostly because of Julia's influence and to be supportive of organic farmers. Unfortunately, she was also a fast food junkie and enjoyed things like burgers and chips, doner kebabs and hot dogs.
" Anything made from mass produced lips and ass, "
as Julia had once remarked in her typically transatlantic fashion. Jessica was bound to admit, even though she knew little of such things, that Julia's cattle appeared radiant with vitality and good health. Despite owning a farm riddled with badgers sets where it was almost impossible not to fall over a badger at least once a day, they had never suffered an outbreak of bovine tuberculosis in fifteen years nor ever would according to Julia and her husband John.
" Jules, I so miss you all, how are those delightful children and John and the cats and the dog?"
"Oh you, know, snotty, hairy and muddy, especially John but we are happy despite it all, we muddle along. Hey Jess, as I was saying, I dreamed about you and then had to walk over to Honeymoon Lake this morning to consult the water; you never guess what?"

Jessica loved Julia's eccentric predilection for old world mysticism and her interest in something she referred to as 'scrying' though Jessica did not understand it at all. Jessica really avoided the subject whenever possible and instead opted to pour fun loving scorn on Julia's pronouncements and predictions.

" Let me guess, Jesus second coming or we are all about to be visited by a reincarnation of Genghis Khan on the 23rd December 2012....? Bloody good idea if you ask me Jules, maybe he would get rid of your despised politicians......"

"Jess be serious for a moment, this is important, I need to talk to you. Don't suppose you fancy coming to stay for a day or two, I'd so love to see you?"

There was actually a note of urgency in Julia's voice which both surprised and slightly disturbed Jessica.

"I'd love to see you too Jules but, you know, farms and me are like oil and water and in any case, I can't at the moment, I've got a suspicious incident to look into."

"Oh, what sort of incident?"

"Julia, I wish I could tell you but I can't, all the usual classified crap but I would love to see you, I miss you all so so much."

"Listen to me Jess, this is important. In my dream I saw you talking with a man. I can't remember any details but it was as if you were communicating with a powerful consciousness. It disturbed me so much that I had to run to the lake in my nightdress and gumboots."

Jessica called to mind the amusing spectacle of Julia leaping and skittering among the windy hills in her night attire and wellington boots.

As was so typical of her, Julia had somehow tuned in again and Jessica could not help but be amazed by the

75

uncanny parallels between her own dream and Julia's but they had been inseparable friends at school and had always been very 'linked'. They had shared ideas, beliefs, interest in music, clothes, books and even occasionally, boyfriends. In many ways Julia was the complete antithesis of Jessica, Pisces, little and dynamic, ash blonde with pale green eyes, a wide transatlantic mouth and an expansive array of perfect white teeth; she was exceptionally pretty. Unlike Jessica, Julia was a dreamer, a poet and a wonderful fiddle player. Despite her private school education in Britain, Julia had retained a pronounced west coast Canadian accent in contrast to Jessica's terribly clipped English way of speaking. Julia had come over as a boarder at school and had never really gone back to live in her native country though she spoke of it often and with evident fondness. She was good for Jessica, partly because she was less inhibited than a typical Briton and wasn't afraid to say things that a British person would only think. As Julia often said herself, one of the advantages of being a North American was that she was not in least restrained by British customs and protocols. Their relationship worked and they were indivisible in spirit.

Jessica was taken aback but attempted levity, the typical egocentricity of an 'Aries'.
"I hope he was good looking and wealthy, just my cup of tea actually come to think of it, someone rich but undemanding, who doesn't snore and who can't help but be tidy- hey.........?"
"Look Jess I know you think I'm just some nut bar hippy with eccentric interest in witchcraft but I know what I feel and more to the point I know what you feel, you can't fool me, you know that."
Jessica had to admit, there had been a couple of times when she had reluctantly involved Julia in some very tricky

76

forensics cases and despite herself, knew that Julia could achieve things that were quite beyond her explanation. Typically, Jessica's pragmatic mind would become obsessed with riddle solving utilising accepted scientific methodology. She tackled cases as one would create a flow chart, a flawless but unimaginative approach that precluded genuine inspiration; she concentrated exclusively on the facts. Then the thought occurred to her that really, it had been quite some time since she had seen Julia and the family. In truth she ached to see them all even if she would have to negotiate glutinous muddy fields and help milk the cows.

" Look Julia, I really am absolutely desperate to see you all, what are you doing the weekend after next? I would love to come now but really am tied up for the next week at least, on a case."

" Oh honey, you will have the greatest time I promise. I'll get rid of Johns motorcycle bits from the spare bedroom, fix the window, make up the bed -ooh Jess I can't wait. I've still got gallons of homemade scrumpy and might even find a bottle of my folks prairie moonshine somewhere."

" Sounds delightful." Replied Jessica resolving in that moment to fill the boot of the car with wine and beer and pack a hot water bottle, an electric blanket and some draught excluder for the doors and windows. Julia did not respond but changed the subject again and Jessica knew that this was because she was 'receiving information' or in Jessica's opinion, suffering another wild outbreak of unrestrained imagination. Julia spoke almost as though she were in a trance.

"By the way, it's just come to me if this helps, the dead victim will have a puncture wound, a hypodermic one I think, just inside her right nostril."

Jessica was mildly astonished and forgot in that moment that the information was classified, quite apart from the fact that she had mentioned no details whatsoever.

" Are you saying that she was killed with a lethal injection?"

" Of course she was Jess; see you soon, can't wait!"

'How is it that she can see all that even though I said nothing but still fail to grasp the simple truth that I loath cider, always have and always will!'

Jessica suddenly felt happier after speaking to Julia, more upbeat. It was Sunday after all, tomorrow she would be busy, back at work. Determined to enjoy the day, Jessica showered, dried her hair but for once, left it loose. Vibrant blue-black in colour, long and lustrous; the kind of hair that a woman could be accused of harlotry and stoned to death for. On a rare whim, as the day was shaping up to be beautifully warm, she quite uncharacteristically put on a very feminine white knee length, swirly summer skirt with a floral print design. She suddenly felt very daring and then smiling to herself, put on a tea shirt with a plunging neck line and a legend on the front that read, 'Save a Horse, Ride a Cowboy'. This gift was, of course, more of a deliberate act of provocation from Steven Savage. He had handed over the package to her with a slightly lascivious and irritating smirk upon his return from the western United States.

" Time to show off those gorgeous hooters of yours to the world my love rather than hiding them as if you were leprous."

Jessica, incensed, blazed a salvo of the purest white hot anger.

" Fuck You Steven Savage and the horse you rode in on."

He had laughed heartily at her response, a phrase which she had obviously used without really understanding its meaning.

This expression was a hand me down from Julia who had utilised the expression years earlier. A physics teacher was pouring scorn on Julia's lamentable, ineffectual grasp of the subject in a practical class experiment, while taking any opportunity to lean over her and peer down her cleavage. Jessica, at the time, could not help but memorise the deliciously transatlantic phrase. Like a piece of music or a song, an ear-worm, the expression played over and over in her mind ad-nauseum. She anticipated a time when she could use the phrase to greatest effect, like an incantation or witches curse and then suddenly, years later, the opportunity arose and the invocation was cast. Steven, while laughing uncontrollably, expressed his opinion that the comment could never be uttered by a 'posh bird' who spoke with such an archetypal British accent. Then seeing his blunder and her evident anger, attempted to make a conciliatory remark.
"It really will suit you Jess, honestly!
  Jessica was surprised to notice however, that he was actually quite shocked. In truth it was probably the first time he had ever heard her swear.

  This event basically punctuated the end of their relationship as occasional and not very satisfactory lovers, preferring instead to be friends and occasional confidantes. Jessica had never really considered herself very sexual, didn't particularly like sex and just endured the process as seldom as possible. She held so little self esteem and having no regard for her innate beauty, she smothered her femininity. Like many ambitious young women, she considered her sex to be at a disadvantage, a terrible weakness that could only hamper her career in a predominantly mans world. Steven's ill-considered remark just fueled the fires of her lamentable lack of self worth. Why she decided to wear this provocative outfit was a mystery. To top it all she rejected her glasses in preference for her rarely used contact lenses. The previous nights dream had not only disturbed her but had left her with an inexplicable sense, for the first time in her life, of flirtatiousness.

CHAPTER 7

Lying in her newly acquired swinging chair under the canopy of the oak tree, Jessica luxuriated in the tranquil hazy heat of summer and felt herself 'blossom'. The tree was a haven for the local birds who sang for a mate and also for the joy of life. A blackbird sitting in a branch immediately above her made such beautiful sounds that Jessica became spellbound, her heart lost to his enchanting music. There was however, a thorn among the blooms. Deep in the dark and murky depths of her subconscious, something predatory and malevolent had stirred and she fought to suppress a memory, a thing so uncomfortable that she dared not go there. The problem was that the enjoyment of the bird song was painfully linked to something far more sinister and in order to shut out the memory she was forced, finally, to close her ears to the beguiling Blackbird and his rapturous song. A distraction came to hand as a large shiny beetle came into view. It was arduously climbing through the grass nearby and Jessica gazed at the plucky creature that glinted like a chestnut in the sunlight. The solemn effects of the joyful birdsong were to some extent attenuated as Jessica studied the busy beetle who was on some vital mission, unknown to Jessica but obviously very important to the large insect.

By the swinging chair were lemon barley water in a long glass frosted with dew and a book, ' The Moonstone' by Wilkie Collins. Jessica rarely had time to enjoy the luxury of becoming completely absorbed in a book but this day she was going to release the ghost of bad memories and indulge herself, become immersed in 'her' time. She intended to enter that world of beautiful architecture, no government buildings or apartment blocks made from concrete or a world buried under billions of tons of vehicles. Jessica toyed with a delightful memory of being invited into an alms house for a cup of tea some years previously. The alms house was one of a row which were situated near a stunning abbey in Tewkesbury, Gloucestershire and she was instantly captivated by the simple utilitarian beauty of the humble abode, radiant with the ethereal light of timelessness. By a process of thought progression, her mind drifted to rose and wisteria covered peasant cottages that were so pretty that they were almost edible; so much like the witch's house in Hansel and Gretal. Then there were the elegant wide elm lined avenues in London paved with cobblestones and illuminated by gas lamps that were whimsically 'haloed' by the fog. There were no cars, just horses and carts or carriages of myriad types and pedestrians of all shapes and colour, in clothes that spanned an enormous spectrum from excessively sumptuous and frivolous to the threadbare and scrimy.

Then Jessica in her typically pragmatic fashion could not but consider the negative aspects; a city of blanket fogs and primitive plumbing, no showers, personal hygiene was as yet an unrefined science and people emitted body odours to greater or lesser degrees as a matter of course just as animals do and few retained a good set of teeth much beyond the age of 30 or so, if they were lucky. Average life expectancy nationwide was just 40 years. People died of simple infections, many of pneumonia, of tuberculosis, or consumption as it was referred to in those days. Many fell victim to untreated tooth abscesses, small pox, measles, the list was endless. Young children forced into service crept up into the chimney flues of large houses in order to clean them and as a consequence many small boys succumbed to testicular cancer. In many ways it was a desperate age, the dawning of the Industrial Revolution, the world then was a cleaner place by far and as yet still relatively untainted by the impact of humanity.

The population of Britain though dense by international standards was just 21 million in the mid- nineteenth century. Apart from the atrocious fogs in London caused by the burning of coal in just about every fireplace in every home in the city and the great industrial blast furnaces burning oak trees by the ton, the country air by contrast, was clean and unsullied by automobiles yet to arrive and scar the face of the planet. This was the time of Dante Gabriel Rossetti, Elizabeth Barret Browning, the Bronte's, Rudyard Kipling, Dickens, Coleridge, Wordsworth, Turner and so on. Jessica's favourite painter, Thomas Gainsborough had been dead for a while at that time but his memory was still fresh in peoples minds. This was an age on the brink of a great discovery, rich in ideas and language. The language was what Jessica most loved as it was considered an art and a science that was taken to poetic form and concise expression. People loved the spoken word, the nuances of speech creating a vivid caricature of the speaker. People contrived to express themselves to the utmost through the felicitous application of well constructed and well enunciated sentences. This was an era rich indeed in prolific writers where typical Victorian reserve and propriety could be abandoned for the sake of art. Indeed it was a great outlet for women who wrote under male pseudonyms in a patriarchal society and who were subsequently able to express freely, often well beyond the bounds of acceptable conduct and to be taken seriously.

Jessica popped back into her flat, opened the windows wider and switched on her exquisite antique radio-gramme. She put on a record, an LP of Chopin nocturnes. This quite successfully drove the sound of birdsong from her mind and the demons from deep within her subconscious had been quieted. With the windows wide open and the volume turned up, she could hear it perfectly by the oak tree and so could most of the residents at Mortlac and throughout Tower Hill no doubt. She felt quite self righteously, and somewhat pompously, that while one could object to hip hop or heavy rock or even jazz at full volume, no one could possibly object to Chopin especially when played so wonderfully and emphatically by a pianist named Ivan Moravec. Jessica had even fallen a little in love with him, an abstract emotion that invigorated her, she experienced a sense of quickening, her bosom heaving for a paramour without the unnecessary complication of ever having to meet him. Life was suddenly blissful, lying on her new swinging chair under the canopy of the huge oak in the balmy summer sun with a good book and latterly, with a glass of white wine cooled to perfection and within easy reach. It was 'Just a perfect day' as Lou Reed had once sung but then Jessica had not factored William into the algorithm.

She was roused out of her reverie by William, evidently high up in the tree and wailing in desperation. Her sense of peace shattered, Jessica stood and called up to him but he merely teetered on a branch, all four feet spread across in a neat row and his back arched.

" Oh William you idiot! How could you? Come on down you stupid cat, oh please do come down!"

William attempted a little manoeuver, tentatively, impotently he put his front paw out to reach a lower branch but it was beyond his reach. William was not known for his ability to suffer in silence and so he wailed anew, a plaintive sound that pierced Jessica to the core. Becoming quite frantic with worry bordering panic, she circled the base of the oak and called up to William, angry and deeply upset.

"William, how could you do this and on my day off too? You must have climbed trees like that a hundred times before and you must surely, know how to get down."

William emitted another beseeching 'wail'.

"Oh FUCK!"

 Expletives were not generally Jessica's style but she was desperate, anxious, furious, compassionate and a hundred other emotions all rolled into one. Then William tried another tack but failed again and cried anew. No one had ever told Jessica that cats always manage to climb down eventually and that really, there was no need for huge concern. The only alternative as she saw it, was to climb the tree and rescue him. At first she was not at all sure how she would do this despite being a very accomplished tree climber as a child, the lower branches were too high to reach. She made a beeline for Ray, the groundsman. She flashed a big but not very convincing or heartfelt, though hopefully winning smile and explained her plight and her need for a step ladder. Jessica at first, nurtured a vain hope that he might offer to help but as he was in his sixties and not terribly spry she had to concede that this was not likely to happen. He simply said sagely;

" In my long experience, cats always come dahn' eventual love so don't you worry your pretty little 'ead about it, he'll be dahn' when he's good 'n' ready, you mark my words."

Unconvinced and a little annoyed at him for his lack of cooperation Jessica walked away and placed the borrowed steps in a suitably level spot between two massive roots, though they still rocked precipitously when she attempted to climb them. She briefly contemplated going in to change into something more suitable but panic overruled her sense and so she decided not to bother, she would just have to manage.

She climbed to the very top step of the ladder including the one that had a legend embossed upon it, 'Do not use to stand on.' Tottering on to the tips of her toes she managed to reach the first branch with her slim but strong arms. Having done so she swung her legs up and hooked onto an adjacent branch so that she was able to pull herself up and stand on the lower branches. Thoughts passed rapidly through her mind but she was powerless to stop herself.

' Not sure if this is wise Jess, have you considered how you are going to get back down? Maybe someone will call the fire brigade- oh William you are a totally exasperating idiot; I can't bear the embarrassment....!'

Without looking down Jessica quickly reached the point where William sat in a demoralised hunch and she even permitted herself some joy at the thrill of being up so high in the tree. Jessica, at first apprehensive, was beginning to enjoy the challenge and also the view which, though not exceptional, was however very different to the one that she was used to. She noted distractedly that she could even see into her living room. She quickly reached William and tried to grab the scruff of his neck without any idea really, how she was going to carry him down. He growled, then tried to back up hissing ferociously, as she caught him loosely by the neck. He struggled and broke free in an instant and jumped nimbly onto the next branch lower down. Seeing a path open up

before him, William jumped from branch to branch and then sauntered to the ground as if he hadn't a care in the world.
" WILLIAM! You utter utter beast, I've just risked life and limb to save you, just you wait mister!"
Jessica was beside herself with anger but in equal parts with, relief.

As she reached out to a huge semi-vertical branch in order to steady herself, she quite by chance noticed words carved onto the inside of the limb. The inscription would almost certainly have been invisible from below but the angle of the sun had progressed to an unusual point where the side of the branch became highly illuminated and overhead glare was minimal. She climbed just a little higher to where William had been supposedly 'stuck' in order to gain a better view. The inscription looked ancient as the knotted, scarred and gnarled bark of the tree had almost obliterated the text. Instead of being recessed as had been the case originally, with the letters cut into the bark, the text now stood out like the proud-flesh of a bad scar. She studied it for a while, forming the barely legible words in her mind, making sense of them. Then she read them aloud in increasing wonder.
" As God is my witness, I humbly protest my innocence and my anguish at this great injustice. I will do so beyond the very grave. Lucius Gray. Anno-domini 14th July 1820."
It was quite an extensive message for something cut into the bark of a tough old tree and must have taken skill and determination. She was amazed, fascinated and elated and it was providence indeed that she of all people should have made the discovery; Lucius Grey had indeed reached beyond the grave. She quickly forgot all about William and memorized the phrase, repeating over and over again the

exact idiom. Jessica really didn't want to have to climb the tree again to refresh her memory.

As she made her way down branch by branch, too absorbed to be concerned and not nearly as speedily as she had ascended, a voice rose up from beneath.

" Ah! We're wearing blue today are we, to match this spectacular sky no doubt ?"

" Erm, no white obviously.....!?"

An odd statement and Jessica was entirely nonplussed for a moment, quite unable to know really how to respond and then realisation dawned upon her........?

'Oh my god!'

She was wearing her full skirt and the awful truth seeped into her mind unbidden."

" Nope, trust me, you're wearing blue ones. I must say, it makes a nice change to see so much of you."

Jessica was justifiably furious,

' Why the hell does he have to be down there, him of all people. Oh shit! I could have stomached anyone but him? What is it about men and their ridiculous obsession with looking up womens skirts any way, dammit?'

Much to her further annoyance, she was compelled to let Rob steady the ladder and help her down. His jaunty chatter and winning smile had obviously worked on many a young woman, he really was an accomplished flirt but he wasn't as good as he thought. Jessica was immune to his charms, more than ever in fact, she couldn't stand the sight of him at that moment. He was admittedly very helpful if rather over tactile. Jessica decided not to be cool, disdainful and angry, he would expect that, she forced herself to joke, to play the incident down.

" Ah well, If I had known it was you Rob I'd have worn my grannies bloomers, I know how you men get all excited over big nickers."

Rob then changed the subject, he was curious and asked, "What were you doing climbing the tree any way?"

"Trying to rescue my cat of course, I don't always cavort in trees wearing skirts."

" You mean the fellow over there by the shed that has been grooming himself in the sun for the last ten minutes and without a care in the world."

' William you complete bloody traitor! No more rich tea biscuits for you sunshine.'

"He came down when I tried to grab him." Jessica added lamely.

" All cats do that you know, they never get completely stuck unless trapped in a hole or caught in some way. He'd just fall down if he got hungry enough any way, law of gravity and all that darling!"

Jessica thanked him civilly and was about to make haste back to the apartment to recover what was left of her dignity.

"Would you, by any chance, like to go out for a curry? Hey, bring your girlfriend too?"

'Not another bloke who thinks that just because I am half Indian that I love curry. Oh God! Here we go again and he has apparently seen through my ploy.'

Jessica made her excuses resolutely and finally extricated herself from his persuasive but cloying web of charm.

The trauma of the preceding half hour was speedily buried under the influence of and the fascination for her discovery. Her first course of action was to establish who Lucius Grey was and then she gasped in amazement as she noticed the date on her laptop as she flipped the lid open-

14th August 2009.

'Good God, this is an anniversary of his writing that message, how strange, I suppose that it is not so strange but still a 1 in 365 chance that the date should be the same.'
But then another fact occurred to Jessica, coincidental, maybe, but in a numerological sense, the year 1820 was the same as 2009,
' Both amount to eleven, Gosh! Must talk to Julia about that, it's the kind of stuff that she knows all about. Not quite the Victorian era though was it? That was seventeen years away if I'm right. This date marks the end of the Regency era? Mortlac prison had only been here for 19 years-imagine? I wonder what it was like then?'

Jessica's, natural curiousity had been well and truly aroused and, allied to her uncanny forensics abilities, started an avalanche of thought, of analytical process. She searched and located the relevant department on her lap top and then typed in a password, then 'Prison records, 1819 to 1821.' Of course, not surprisingly, there were few details of that period and an insignificant mention of Lucius Grey which was confined to name and a brief description of the nature of his crime; pre-meditated and brutal murder! There were a smattering of entries for the more infamous criminals of the day but Lucius, for some reason, was considered a lesser felon and was denied any distinction. Jessica might have lost interest at this point were it not for a nagging gut feeling that encouraged her to search more deeply. Ironically the difficulties affirmed a resolution in Jessica to get to the bottom of this, her curiosity was now well and truly aroused. She resolved then to track down the relevant notes in the prison records office and would have to go to the archives in person when she had some time. Well, as to that, she was just going to have to make time. Lucius Grey had dropped in on her life in more ways than one and Jessica resolved to get to know the man a lot better before the week was out, even though he had been dead for over 190 years!

CHAPTER 8

Lucius had been obliged to pay heavily for the privilege of being permitted to go outside to take the air. It was late summer, not that one could tell in those dank and gloomy rooms with their grime covered and barred windows. He squinted his eyes, so unaccustomed in recent times to the summer brightness and took a deep breath of balmy air, warm and scented with the lingering esthesis of fresh hay. It was an odour that he could not quite find a name for and yet a word lurked on the edge of his conscience, eagerly awaiting disclosure. The scent was warm and evocative and so typical in the countryside, a result of the agricultural endeavours of the inhabitants. The air was alive with a heady a mix of wonderful olfactory impressions. The world seemed to be alive with the vibrant sound of birdsong and he stood for a moment, quite captivated by the mosaic of the joy of life.

On this occasion, Lucius was escorted by the governor and by a prison lackey, both of whom were oddly respectful of Lucius. They also shared a quiet skepticism about Lucius' alleged guilt, though both were also happy to profit by his incarceration, which was the reality of prison imperatives. The lackey was a simple and uneducated soul named John Bentham who had no axe to grind and who, provided he was treated with a little 'deference' as was his right to demand in such circumstances, could be very amenable. He liked and respected Lucius and in his turn Lucius held a genuine affection for John and it really was no effort to be civil and companionable with him and was typical of men sharing convivial sentiments. The governor on the other hand, was a diminutive Scotsman with sallow skin, an imbibers nose and a tendency to dyspepsia and irritability. His name was James McKay, a reputedly duplicitous and ambitious individual with a modicum of education but who, like so many of that era, aspired to be both learned and gentlemanly. Many an incarcerated man had attempted to put James in his rightful place but to their inevitable detriment if not their downright peril. James McKay had a long and incisive memory, low self esteem and a supremely vengeful inclination. If he saw an opportunity to gain an advantage, material or otherwise, then he was quite unscrupulous in his machinations. Lucius held no real regard for him, did not trust him but was wise enough to know that if he were to achieve some semblance of status quo, then he would have to be circumspect in his dealings. In fact Lucius was naturally adept at extracting the best from people simply by being 'himself', uncomplicated, fair and guileless. It was very difficult not to appreciate him and he was immensely likeable.

It was to James McKay whom Lucius had turned finally, requesting a couple of hours liberty, a chance to enjoy the sunshine before his sentence was fully carried out. It was also to the governor that a hefty bribe, a 'testimonial' was subtly dedicated and discretely accepted with that venture in mind. Lucius did concede that James McKay was an intelligent man even if his brand of intelligence was misdirected toward low cunning. He in his turn worshipped the ground that Lucius walked upon, partly because Lucius treated him as he treated all people, with great respect, as an equal and who he sought never to diminish in any way.

Lucius was escorted out of the prison and into the grounds where his cell overlooked the magnificent oak tree, he gloried at that moment in the healing summer sun.

" I hesitate to press you Lucius Grey but I have granted you two hours of liberty and I do not expect that my goodwill shall be abused. Forgive me therefore, if I ask again that give me your word as a gentleman, that you will remain within the grounds?"

James Mackay's accent retained soft underpinnings of his Glaswegian origins but his voice and his diction was pleasant, competent.

"Of course sir, please banish any misgivings from your mind, you need have no concerns on my account."

" Sir....!" added John Bentham shaking his head sadly and forgetting that he had not asked permission to speak.

"It saddens me dreadful' that a man such as yourself should be put to the gallows. I have been here a good many year and it is not often that I have reason to doubt the verdict of a body of twelve good men and true."

"I think that we might manage without your opinion Bentham," James McKay uttered witheringly! It suited him in so many ways to have Lucius in gaol, as he derived great and varied benefit from the situation.

"Very good sir, I am sorry to have spoken as I did sir."

James McKay was still uneasy about Lucius however and glancing sideway at him added,

"I fear that you might be so self persuaded of your innocence, that you might absolve yourself from breaking your word, on the grounds that you are righting a wrong, do I have reason to be disquieted?"

Lucius looked up at the brilliant and eternal firmament, quite beguiled and enchanted. He considered the big world beyond the wall that beckoned to him awaiting his autonomy;

'It would be so easy to walk away, I could easily gain passage on a ship, go back to Asia and be free. Oh what more enticement does a man need? Ironic though isn't it? If I were to run then they would have good reason to think me guilty but if I stay to confront my destiny then they might conclude that really, I am truly innocent. What a predicament!'

" None whatsoever sir, my word is my bond, you need have no fear."

The governor looked sufficiently relieved that he prepared to let Lucius walk in the grounds unshackled; John Bentham however, was to be within a very short distance of him at all times. John could contain himself no longer.

" Georgina Brogan gov, who was it done her in then if it wasn't you?"

Lucius said nothing, grimly and bitterly aware of both the unfair prosecution and of the loss of his one great love. His family seemed to be cursed. Was his grandfather really so scurrilous that his family deserved to suffer eternal damnation?

Lucius was haunted by the events which followed the discovery of Georgina's body. Adam Brogan, hysterical and with tears of rage running down his face, had become quite maddened with grief. The murder weapon, a sword of Eastern origins and admittedly one that had belonged to Lucius, was found near what was left of Georgina's precious but unrecognizable body. What remained of her fine clothes was the only clue as to her identity. Adam's ferocity and his passionate plea for justice had won the sympathy of local law enforcement officers and of the judge; Lucius had never stood a chance of acquittal. The death of a beautiful young woman is always certain to arouse outrage in even the most jaded of people. His family name was historically besmirched. The locals, swayed by the opinions of their lord and Master, shunned the Grey family as scoundrels and people of shallow morality. Few were really familiar with Lucius Grey, he had spent so much time away that, in truth, he was a stranger to many. Lucius' ill advised nocturnal visitation, that had so outraged Georgina's maid, was all too damning as evidence and stacked up the odds against him from the start. He was arrested and tried and was required to suffer the indignity of a long winded and bellicose speech of reprimand and denouncement for perpetrating such an inhuman, nay bestial act. Lucius was entirely aware of his predicament and grasped the sad and quintessential fact that he was doomed. He was unable to account for and never did understand how his sword happened to be found at the scene of the murder, a weapon that he had kept at his home purely as a keepsake from his overseas travels. Someone who knew him and also of the existence of his sword must have planted the evidence. Indeed there were moments when he feared that perhaps, just possibly, he was guilty. Unhinged by desire, maddened by love, he had brutally hacked Georgina to pieces? Deep down he knew that he was not capable of such an act.

The authorities were outraged and the 'press' celebrated Lucius' long incarceration and eventual sentencing for death by hanging in a frenzy of righteous indignation. His mother was utterly inconsolable and uncharacteristically emotional when she heard the verdict. Quite apart from the pitiable loss of her first born, it really was the end for the family, they would never survive such controversy and scandal. Lucius Grey's fortune was confiscated upon his execution and held in trust by the authorities at the insistence of the Judge,

Constantine Butler no less. Avariciousness, greed and spite had propelled some petitioners forward to claim that the family money had been gained by highly illegal and immoral means. In order to subdue the claim of 'hypocrisy' against the authorities by the Grey's defense, there was an underplayed reference to the fact that, at some point, the money would be returned to the family. In the event, the Grey family had not the resources for legal representation to formerly request that the trustees return the fortune. This was the outcome that Butler had banked upon at the outset. Over the ensuing decades, the Grey family withered and dwindled to the very last of the family line who came to an ignominious end. Nearly a century later, this descendant, with quite another name who was a railway engineer and a conscript during the second world war, died in a bloody battle in war torn Europe. He left a desolate new bride and subsequently a childless widow of just 28 years of age and even she was not to be spared. She was driven quite mad by her bereavement, lost her mind and was incarcerated.

Lucius looked up at the tree's reassuring vastness and at the leaves rustling lightly in the breeze. A great wave of peace stole over him as he closed his eyes and felt himself buoyed upon a rushing zephyr, as a gust of wind swept over the hill and buffeted the great tree. Like a giant enchanted woodwind instrument, natures beautiful music played and transported him to the limitless serenity of happy childhood. "Do you know what I'm going to do master John but with your permission of course?"
John Bentham looked suspicious, even a little concerned for just the briefest of seconds, the hardened aspect of a prison guard setting his features into their habitual role. Lucius

wanted to set him at his ease by taking him into his confidence.

"I've dreamed of climbing that tree for months, therefore, I shall climb it and take a first and last look at the world from that lofty aspect."

"Really sir? I'm not sure what the governor will think on it?" Lucius dug into his pocket and handed John something, obviously quite potent with value and consequently persuasive.

"You wouldn't begrudge a condemned man one last harmless wish would you John? Where would I go from a tree? I can't fly."

John became wrapped in thought for a moment, ruminating almost visibly but then a look of acquiescence flashed across his features.

"Well you will have to come down just as soon as I say guv." Lucius smiled, "But of course!"

Lucius had little trouble gaining purchase with Johns reluctant help. He managed to hoop his legs onto a lower branch and pull himself into a sitting position. He rested for a moment and then continued to climb. He experienced a curious little flash of inexplicable remembrance, of deja-vu. The sensation was far more powerful than that especially once the vision gained momentum. A tall white haired druid with a beard plaited to his chest was planting a newly germinated sapling into virgin ground, freshly revealed by the retreating snow. Lucius did not recognize the place. It was a lofty situation almost resembling arctic tundra and was beside a lake, a shallow but broad punch bowl on the top of a hill. There was a breathtaking view over a forest which stretched away below into infinity but which was partially obscured by a blanket of low lying mist. The fragile spring sunshine smiled upon the misty vale below, adding a further touch of magic to the scene. Lucius was moved to silent tears.

'How has this happened? How do I know this place?'
He felt a great lift in his spirits, a moment of profound elation as if he had been picked up and transported to a magical land. This feeling transfused his sense of deepest despair. He recognized, in the moment, that from desperation may come great waves of comprehension, understanding and indeed, hope!

After a little consideration he called down below with an impossible request?
"John, do you have a penknife that I might borrow for a moment?"
" Oh no sir, sorry sir, the governor would have my guts."
" Oh for god's sake man, this is important to me, I mean no harm, I give you my word, I beseech you. Grant a dying man this one last wish. I won't forget this good deed."
Unaccountably John did throw his tatty but wickedly sharp folded pen knife up to Lucius. Never in his many years as a prison guard had he committed an act of such untypical altruism or benevolent 'stupidity'. For many years after, he would ponder upon the impulse that drove him to acquiesce, though he was happy that he had done so. Lucius grabbed the knife, expertly thrown and skillfully caught.
'Forgive me sacred tree but I need to do this for reasons that I am not able to fully comprehend.'
He cut into the bark and wrote an inscription. Just as he had finished, a raven sitting on a branch not far above him clucked and cawed, a sound of approbation and of consent. Lucius had always been an animal lover and had a particular fondness for birds having considered them to be emissaries

of some sort. As a child, he remembered being told by his nanny that Ravens were old druids reborn and that they must be afforded respect.

" If ever you have a burning wish master Lucius, then tell it to a Raven who will be there to listen because you will have already summoned him."

Lucius' mother had an appreciation for the nanny but would often remark in a somewhat derogatory manner and in hushed tones betraying a hint of fear, that she was probably from gypsy stock and possibly even a witch. Lucius in his childhood innocence passed this information onto his nanny as she was getting him ready for bed one night. She said nothing but her expression was forever burned into his subconscious, a wry and knowing smile. In his reverie, Lucius had almost forgotten John Bentham standing patiently down below but who had suddenly become insistent that Lucius should descend instantly and return his knife. The spell was broken but not completely for he had indeed made a heartfelt wish to the raven.

That night, Lucius lay awake for some while contemplating his lot. Septimus scurried into the nocturnal quiet of Lucius' cell and helped himself to the small crust that had been left for him. Sitting on his haunches, he held the morsel in hands that were almost indecently human and then he started to eat. Later, he preened himself in a moonlit area of the floor, his little black eyes glinting like jewels in the moonlight. All the while Lucius watched him, observing and wondering at the tenacity with which this little creature clung to life in an utterly hostile environment and who received no justice. Lucius knew that his outrage and reasoning were tools that would be of no use to him in securing his freedom as his days of mortal existence were fast running out. There would be no miracle in this life and yet he held an inexplicable conviction that there would be a redemption of a kind, although he had no idea of the form that this would take. It had been so good to be outside, the first time for a long time. To have climbed the tree and warmed his face in the sunshine, listening to the birdsong. A day, paradoxically almost idyllic in the light of how his days had formerly passed and with the prospect of a brutally curtailed future. His only hope lay in his supreme wish that had been cast onto the winds via the raven who had cawed and croaked at Lucius and to be fair, most probably in the hope of receiving some modest comestible. Even 'druids' were entitled to their 'testimonial'. Lucius' wish was nevertheless a hope borne on the razor thin but strangely robust ice of credibility and it was all he had. A sense of peace overcame him, of acceptance. As he dissolved gradually through the barrier of consciousness into the delicious realm of the subconscious, he started to dream. He dreamed of the old druid planting the tree and of another, a curious stranger who wove a path into the lucidity of his deepest repose. The stranger was a beautiful dark skinned woman with ebony hair which was plaited and trailed down her back like a silken rope. There was also a feeling, a prevailing sense of being absorbed by and of becoming one with the tree and with the possibility of becoming immortal.

CHAPTER 9

Jessica discovered the prison records in the form of a number of weighty and surprisingly comprehensive tomes, bound in leather though dried out and fissured with antiquity. She easily located the volume that coincided with the dates of Lucius Grey's incarceration and quickly discovered the relevant entry. Jessica lapsed into a state of agitated excitement as she looked through his file which was surprisingly detailed, though somewhat illegible in places. What was unusual was that a strong and obviously well educated hand had added circumstantial notes. It appeared that the additions had been made some time later as the script was far less faded. To Jessica's inflamed imagination, it was as if Lucius had an unknown accomplice or ally who had dedicated him or herself to clearing Lucius' name.

The prosecution had been carried out by a renowned but quite venomous barrister named Karl Hawkins-Lane; the defense being handled by an idealistic 'innocent' in legal circles, a young barrister named Septimus Zacharias. The concepts of true impartiality, though adhered to in fervent exclamation, actually held no place in the courts at that time. A typically Victorian circumstance of appalling double standards still prevailed and judgment was given, dependent upon the whims and digestive condition of the presiding judge and upon the status and reputation of the accused.

In fact the judge at Lucius' hearing was his Nemesis and there could not have been a worse appointment as far as he was concerned; Lucius was doomed from the outset. By some strange 'coincidence', the judge was a farming acquaintance of Adam Brogan and also an unrequited admirer of Georgina. By implication therefore, he was sympathetic to Adam Brogan at the outset. The judge, Constantine Butler, a once rakish, popular and handsome young lawyer with a sharp legal mind, had risen speedily through the ranks. His notoriety as a philanderer and a seducer of other men's wives was almost as legendary as his legal prowess. In more recent years the good life had caught up with him; he had gained an enormous midriff and flaccid jowls to match. His once beautiful ringlets of golden hair and fine white teeth were lost forever; he was also very dyspeptic and given to prolonged periods of gout.

Without knowing the facts at that moment, Jessica detected, with some degree of irony, that there was some self interest implied by Butler's appointment to the case. As it transpired, he had conveniently anticipated the Crown's deepest sympathies for Adam Brogan's tragic loss, spurred on no doubt by his obsession with Georgina. His bitter awareness of Georgina's 'tragic' susceptibility for his rival, Lucius Grey, was fuel for his vindictive fires and he lost no time in bending the attributes of the law to his own ends. Georgina, according to friends, had not taken kindly to Constantine Butlers repeated advances and had soundly and repeatedly rejected him. The ego of such a monster being what it was, he attributed his own failure to win Georgina's hand to Lucius' cunning manipulations. Adam had spitefully recounted the story of Sebastian Grey, the elder, and the subsequent disgrace of his daughter and Butler needed no further encouragement to dislike the young Lucius. Butler was highly susceptible to all of the worst vices and he continued to become soured and poisoned by his own malevolent machinations. Like the portrait of Dorian Grey, he rotted from within but also mouldered from without. Reading between the lines, Jessica divined with some extra-sensory amusement, that like all vain and egocentric men, Butler could not accept the inevitabilities of his own advanced years, ugly mind, unattractive demeanour and terrible halitosis. In short, he was obsessively jealous of Lucius Grey.

Jessica noted that sometime after the pronouncement and 'sentence' was passed, there had been some serious question raised about the inconsistencies of the case. Some of the jurors had spoken out with regard to the integrity of the hearing. This created a backlash and support for Lucius Grey actually began to build but sadly, not soon enough to prevent his death. When sentence was passed, he was pronounced guilty of the charge of slaying Georgina Brogan with a sword belonging to himself, which was then abandoned at the scene. It was considered a most heinous and brutal crime of unrequited passion though no one was permitted to act on strong feelings in those stifling days of emotional containment. On the day of his execution, Lucius, with the greatest dignity, stridently professed his innocence. The priest who took his confession was bound by the obligations of his devotional faith not to yield the content of the confession. He did, however, come away from this final ritual, pale, agitated and angry. It was reported that he made a short speech about the constancy of justice and of the dangers of injustice. By implication he was professing his belief in Lucius Grey's innocence. Constantine Butler however, was not a man to be crossed, having power and support in high places and of course, Adam Brogan, who was relentless in his intention that justice should be done.

The hanging was carried out on the 15th August 1820. Lucius apparently bore his sentence with great stoicism and dignity and even the most ardent protagonists of justice were observed to have been shaken when the sentence was carried out, with the exception of Adam Brogan and the judge. Jessica noticed that there were subsequent details about Adam Brogan and she discovered that he had committed suicide some twelve months later. His estate, left to his remaining family, quickly became worthless as the money was squandered and business matters were left to founder. One rather intriguing but highly incongruous note that Jessica discovered regarding Lucius Grey, was that throughout the process of his execution, a raven had perched atop the gallows and not flown off until Lucius was quite dead. She was puzzled by the incongruity of the addition, this was supposed to be a legal journal and not a diary, feelings had obviously run very high in this emotive case. Jessica noted that this observation must have made a deep impression upon the reporter.

Karl Hawkins-Lane had enjoyed the privileges afforded him from what was a widely publicised case, though not as much as one would have supposed. Septimus Zacharias sank into oblivion, struggling for his daily bread from that moment on. Ironically, it was he and not Lane who became the 'bogeyman'. He was hated by supporters of Butler and Brogan for having the gall to support such a vicious killer and was despised by supporters of Lucius Grey for being so utterly useless.

Jessica studied the evidence that was provided at Lucius' prosecution with mounting astonishment and skepticism. *' DNA testing would have sorted this lot out, not that they should have needed it. Lucius Grey's probable innocence would have been proven beyond all possible doubt, this really was such a simple case! I wonder who did kill Georgina Brogan? I bet Butler was involved? Isn't it ironic that people of that era, so rigid in their adherence with respect to propriety to the letter of the law, were so amazingly blind. Things were only obvious when it suited them. Just goes to show really 'too much law, not enough justice' and far too much hypocrisy.*

At the time of his death, Justice Constantine Butler was acclaimed in a wordy soliloquy of the usual timbre of that time, 'Upright pillar of society, personal friend to the Bishop of Durham and Sir Darcy Capewood, an unblemished and an unsurpassed record, great services to mankind and the nation.' When the eulogy was given there was a continuance of meaningless platitudes in a similar vein punctuated at the end by the obligatory, 'Requiescat in Pace.'
'If the man had any conscience at all he would never rest again but I suppose that he was just another sociopath for whom there is no right and wrong.'
Jessica read between the lines and discerned that he was far from universally liked, especially at the end of his life. She was pleased to discover that there was an intriguing addendum when the judge finally gave up his soul to the good lord. The addition intimated that in his last years, Butler had succumbed to dementia and had raved about demons visiting him by night. One of the principle demons, named repeatedly, being that of a tortured soul of a young

man, Lucius Grey. Coincidentally an additional brief note had been added to the notes on Lucius Grey's records to the effect that in his last days, the judge had been heard to have shouted for mercy and for clemency. It was also noted that the Bishop of Durham had heard his last confession and was apparently, 'very upset' by the experience though he never said why or volunteered any explanation; that of course, was entirely consistent with his office.

Jessica glanced up at the window noticing that the sun had gone down and had been replaced by the disappearing vestiges of a brilliant red sunset. The great tree was quite still in the windless dusk and was silhouetted, a magnificent black cardboard cut-out set against a deep crimson sky. In that light, she could no longer discern just how ancient the tree was though its venerability was beyond question. In the daytime, the tree was undeniably beautiful but what became evident were the great broken branches, quite dead, huge chancres upon parts of the main trunk and a slight loss of symmetry. The thousands of acorns deposited upon the ground in the late autumn were a testament to the fact that the tree was near the end of its life. Like any other living thing it resonated to the cycles of nature, a desire to perpetuate its own species by shedding an ever proliferating number of seeds in its death throes. It was possible that the tree would survive another fifty or possibly even a hundred years but as each year passed, it would lose just a little more of its bloom. Great carbuncles would continue to encroach upon it's surface; its shape and balance continually compromised by a pronounced stoop and deformation of its once aristocratic profile, as more and more branches died. In all likelihood, it would probably be uprooted in a huge storm one day as the roots continued to withdraw and loose their grip.

Jessica adored the oak, she wanted to run out and hug and sooth it and weep onto its calloused flanks as if her tears were an elixir that would sooth its aches and pains. Stranger still was the most extraordinary and illogical compulsion to lie naked in front of the tree and then she realised, with some degree of trepidation and consternation, that she was mildly aroused by its proximity.

'Am I losing my mind, this is all too strange! Is this some sex kink, I'll be downloading images of oak trees from porn sites next!'

Jessica went outside and took some deep gulps of fresh air as she walked toward the tree, gazing up at it reverently. Someone had recently added yet another comment which was deeply and cruelly carved into the trunk with what looked to be a small axe, so horribly administered were the scars;

'All Pakis are wankers' both a monstrous desecration and a vile sentiment.

" I'm so sorry beautiful tree, have we really come to this?"

'Actually no, not all humanity is so ugly.' For no reason that she could think of other than blind compassion, she leaned her head onto the trunk and closed her eyes, listening for who knows what, a primordial heartbeat, natures grandfather clock, a reassurance that life was still within. She sent the tree all her love and respect and begged to be admitted to the tree's secrets, to share it's pains and joys and to be forgiven. At that moment she experienced a curious picture in her minds eye. The vision in itself was unusual enough but what was even more singular was the fact that it was almost as though she were viewing through the eyes of another. For some reason the experience brought to mind a NATO exercise and of a photograph shown to her by an ex-RAF

108

colleague, of a hunted and fleeing British bomber. The shots had been taken by an apparently gloating and self indulgently felicitous crew aboard a US spy plane. Little did they know but the US crew at that moment were being photographed also from above by another British plane. The observer, through which Jessica was attuned, had experienced the vision but then Jessica's lofty and greater picture seemed somehow, to have been ill won, illicit, almost an invasion of the most private recesses of another's mind. The scene that she became aware of however was powerful and captured her and she could not disengage from it.

There was a white haired old man, powerful and feral and still excruciatingly handsome, with a long white beard plaited to his chest. He was planting a newly germinated oak tree sapling of tender age into virgin ground, freshly revealed by the retreating snow. Paradoxically, Jessica did not recognize the place, a lofty situation almost resembling arctic tundra situated by a lake, a shallow but sweeping punch bowl upon top of a hill. There was a breathtaking view over a forest that stretched away into infinity but which was partially but enchantingly obscured by a blanket of low lying mist. The fragile spring sunshine smiled upon the misty vale below adding a further touch of magic to the scene. Despite her sense of her own deliberate invasion, Jessica became enthralled. She had never seen anything quite so beautiful in her entire life and was moved in a way that she had never expected nor had experienced thus far. Tears of joy, of enchantment, of fear, of the awareness of mankind's impending doom rolled down her cheeks.

Out of the blue, the vision was replaced with another, unbidden. It was Spring and the air was rent with the sound of Swifts playing and pirouetting high in the sky, celebrating the poetry of the rites of Spring. She was fighting desperately for her life, for her virtue, her right to retain her maidenhood, though that was forfeit on behalf of the Mother Goddess of the planet. The handsome and kindly old man became over-shadowed by a virile and magnificent stag in his prime and despite her terror and her desperate rejection of him at first, she had finally been subdued and had finally submitted to him. The sexual ecstasy and period of delicious languor and longing that followed became deeply imprinted upon Jessica's mind. Not only that but she found herself suddenly to be hopelessly in love. As the observer, Jessica was almost numb with pain and anguish at the start but the vision brought to her immense comfort and consolation. It was apparent to Jessica that she had been given the vision both as an insight and as solace. Certainly, in her unaccustomed and extremely emotional and highly excited state, Jessica was about ready to locate and seduce the old caretaker if he was the only man around.

'GOD! What is wrong with me? This really is not normal.'

As Jessica wept by the tree in a rare but joyous celebration of a cocktail of human emotions, she was interrupted by her neighbour, old Mrs Wainwright. Upon passing by and noticing that Jessica seemed upset, she had come over to ask if she could be of help.. Jessica was devastated by the sudden break in this divine communication and a fearful panic arose in her as she felt the vestiges of the vision slip away into the ether. For the briefest of moments she was extremely angry.

" Are you alright my dear, is there anything I can do, perhaps a reviving drink...?"

" No, no, it's okay Mrs Wainwright, I'm alright, truly, just something I hadn't expected."

Certainly this was no kind of explanation but it was all that Jessica could think of at that moment in her state of mental disarray. Mrs Wainwright was very elderly, in her nineties or so Jessica had been told, but she was also very spry and independent if somewhat eccentric; it was alleged that she could be inclined to be domineering. Her faculties were un-impaired, her mind was as sharp as a razor and she was undeniably shrewd. She looked at Jessica, piercing grey eyes boring into her soul, sensing something. Then she spoke in a gentle voice, calm, interesting conversation and inflections that soothed Jessica so that she didn't want her to stop talking.

" I remember when this tree was still in its prime when I was but a slip of a young woman like yourself and I remember even then when the travelling folk, the gypsies would come here and talk to the tree. This place was a 'loony bin' by then and it was always assumed that the gypsies were just as mad as the inmates but they claimed to experience visions here, utilising what they used to call 'the sight'. Sounds a bit of a fantasy I know my dear but the funny thing is that I always believed them without question and with good reason too."

Jessica must have looked both astonished and fascinated because Mrs Wainwright, after a brief pause carried on, the kind of loquacity spurred on in elderly people by decades of loneliness and a lot to say.

" My great great grandfather of all people, it was said, claimed that he saw things here and in fact he went quite mad with it, claimed he saw demons and used to come to the tree to beg for forgiveness, quite a rum 'do' by all accounts."

Jessica's analytical mind quickly succumbed to deduction, a welcome substitute for the earlier sense of interruption. Quite apart from other considerations, she found Mrs Wainwright to be thoroughly fascinating and a potential source of information.

" Would you like to come in for a drink Mrs Wainwright, I have whiskey?"

" You must think that I am the most dreadful old sot but do you know, that does sound rather appealing oh, but only if you will join me in a glass."

Jessica would have killed for a drink at that moment.

Once back in the apartment, Jessica found a dusty old 24 oz bottle of single malt that had been in the boot of the Bentley when she took ownership. She had always intended to return the bottle to her uncle but had simply never got around to it. Mrs Wainwright peered about her curiously.

" Certainly this old place has been through some changes since I first came here." Jessica poured two liberal glasses and clinked hers with Mrs Wainwrights.

" You mentioned your great great grandfather, who was he?"

Mrs Wainwright smiled, evidently happy to answer questions and talk of the past.

" Oh he was a judge, Constantine Butler was his name. It was rumoured that he was not a very pleasant fellow by all accounts."

Jessica's mind raced as she tried to recall the facts gleaned from her hours of study regarding the tragic case of Lucius Grey.

" Pardon my curiosity Mrs Wainwright, but in my work, in forensics, I am sometimes drawn to study historical cases and I do recall a case presided over by Justice Butler who was reputed to have gone mad. You are Wainwright by name and as I understand it, Constantine Butler had no issue, he died childless?"

Mrs Wainwright, as sharp as a pin, saw what Jessica was driving at immediately.

" Ah well, my dear, I am a Wainwright but only by marriage. My great great grandfather was indeed Constantine Butler and no, he did not have a child in wedlock that is true. He did however have an association with a woman many years younger than him, who provided him with an heir, though not legitimately I regret to say. I believe that she perished in childbirth if I recollect the details correctly."

Jessica was intrigued, her forensic's sensibilities on fire.

" What was the name of his, 'associate'?"

" Do you know my dear I don't know or I can't rightly remember. She apparently lived like a hermit during her confinement, somewhere in Cornwall. After she 'fell' with child she never communicated with my great great grandfather again, never wanted anything to do with him, hated him by all accounts; screamed like a demon whenever he tried to talk to her. I believe that he saw her for the last time just after she had died giving birth. I gathered that this was when his madness started "

"It wasn't Brogan was it, her maiden name I mean?" Jessica could barely contain herself.

" No dear, no it wasn't, or at least I don't believe so, well not as far as I can remember anyway. It's come to me now, it was Grey I believe. Strange that you should mention the name Brogan and now you come to mention it, there is a very odd thing that has puzzled me for years. I have an ancient book in my library, a first edition as it happens by Sir Walter Scott entitled 'The Monastery' and inside the cover is written, Ex Libris, Georgina Brogan, 25th December 1820. I have always wondered about that name, where it came from. Do you think that this was the same woman?"

Jessica was about to answer but was distracted; she found herself strangely drawn to this fascinating woman and she wanted to know more, lots more.
" How long have you been here Mrs Wainwright."
" Oh a long time, far longer than I care to remember. I am, I suppose, quite stuck here. I feel as though the fates have kept me here, as a guardian of sorts."
" You must have come here in the early seventies then." replied Jessica probing perhaps a little more than she should but driven beyond caution. Mrs Wainwright paused for a moment as if wondering what to say, uncomfortable for the briefest of moments, she paused.
" I came here when I was just 28 years old, in the summer of 1942 ."
Knowing the history of Mortlac, Jessica asked innocently enough;
" Ah, you were a nurse then?"
Again another long pause and evidence of an internal struggle, a terrible cauldron of emotion from within. She then spoke in a quiet voice, almost a whisper.
" No my dear I was a new widow, a casualty of war, deranged by events and I was incarcerated here as a patient for 20 years until the day it closed in 1962."

Jessica was mute with embarrassment and did not know what to say. An elusive memory flashed through her mind before it disappeared as Mrs Wainwright spoke again thereby banishing the shadowy thought. Jessica asked delicately,
" Were you married long?"

" No, not long, just one month. We met in Brighton while Jack was on leave, a whirlwind romance. I hardly knew him but fell completely in love with him, he was 'the one', you know, that one person for me. There aren't many people in the world who find that perfect match. When he died, all I had was a trunk full of his possessions. Many years later I received a letter out of the blue from a lawyer telling me I was the sole beneficiary of Jack's estate. That's how I managed to buy this flat, ironically I felt close to him here. My goodness, I've just remembered an extraordinary thing, another coincidence. Jack's name, as you know, was Wainwright but his mothers name was Grey."

"Gosh that does sound intriguing!" Jessica experienced that same fleeting but unformed and elusive thought again.

" I'll tell you more about it sometime my dear and I know you will think me quite mad. Suffice it to say for now, my great great grandfather wasn't the only one visited by demons or even, what the gypsies refer to, as the 'sight'."

CHAPTER 10

Jessica was anticipating, with conflicting feelings, her visit to the West Country the following weekend. When she had last spoken to Julia, her insights into the sudden death of a young woman was very timely. Admittedly, these insights were to cause some complications for Jessica. She knew from the medical records that the deceased young woman was diabetic and was the wife of a partner in a successful legal practice. He was well liked, reputable and 'well to do', a pleasant fellow but full of sadness and remorse. Even to Jessica's hardened professional eyes, he did appear to be genuine. His grief was silent but all the more devastating, his grim determination to retain decorum at all costs, for the sake of his child, his colleagues and his position of responsibility. Four decades of British conditioning by strict parents and a harsh regime at private school had conspired to create a massive barrier of impenetrability; a wall that contained a seething core of emotion within. Outwardly composed, in credence, yet his torment was palpable and the air thick with his anguish. It radiated outwardly from him like the static before a severe thunderstorm.

The detectives, while questioning him, were not able to hold him for longer than 24 hours and really felt they had no reason to. Despite a typically thick patina of jaded cynicism, deep in their hearts they truly did not suspect him. As far as the detectives were concerned, there was nothing with which they could reproach the solicitor and had fallen into the trap of believing the enquiry to be a formality. The young solicitor had an empty house to return to and a sad and inconsolable child to take care of and they had no desire to prolong his agony. The Chief Inspector, Stringer, was as it transpired, a casual friend of his and while he was basically a good person, an efficient policeman, he was also wearied, a bitter and twisted man with two divorces under his belt. He was abrasive, misogynistic, acerbic and generally temperamental but ultimately, and this is what counted, he was scrupulously fair. It became apparent that he felt that there was no need to detain the devastated young man and was actually relieved when could send him home.

The following Monday, Jessica accompanied the pathologist at the morgue as he performed the autopsy on the young woman. They checked all those obvious places, between the toes, underneath where the the watch strap would have been, the base of the neck above the hairline and of course discovered multiple routine injection sites quite consistent with the corpses previous medical condition as a diabetic. Remembering Julia's words, Jessica examined the area just inside the nostrils and there she discovered, with a bewildering sinking of her heart, a tiny puncture wound consistent with that of a hypodermic syringe in the soft delicately convoluted tissue. The skin around the site did seem an odd colour in contrast to the other injection sites though it was hard to tell. To have administered any kind of injection in that area would have taken knowledge of anatomy and nerves of steel, not to mention a very cooperative recipient. Previous routine tests had shown a higher than average level of a medication (Zoplicone) which had been prescribed just ten days earlier as a sleep aid but

certainly not high enough to cause complications, a red herring in fact, or was it?.
' You cunning bugger!' Jessica thought to herself.

She made her observations known to the pathologist who desired only to submit a routine and wholly acceptable assessment on cause of death. It was only the age of the solicitor's wife that had prompted the autopsy but that was normal under these circumstances. Had she been elderly when she died, then almost certainly a death certificate issued by her General Practitioner on its own would have been quite acceptable. The experienced but somewhat jaded pathologist, although always aware that forensics might show some inconsistencies, was nonetheless surprised by Jessica's observation indicating death by insulin overdose. He therefore peered searchingly at Jessica over the top of his bi-focals as though she were not quite right in the head.
" She was a diabetic you know, you expect all sorts of hypodermic sites in these cases!"
" In her nostrils, are you kidding, how is that normal?"
The pathologist 'hurrumped' self importantly and at a loss to say anything sensible for the moment, he added;
"Credit where credit's due, you did well to find that but I have to ask, what made you look there?"
Jessica didn't want to get into a conversation about clairvoyant messages regarding the mark and merely mentioned somewhat caustically that she thought that the site looked a little angry and also thought it odd that a diabetic, no matter how desperate for a non-ravaged spot, would choose such an difficult place to inject.

The pathologist considered Jessica no less dubiously. With a full work load ahead of him and his daughter about to return from university for the weekend he had no time to be chasing a red herring.

"Well the boys in blue will never admit to this being conclusive evidence because they know a clever defense lawyer will try and make a joke of it but that's not our problem. Leave it with me." he said with a sigh and did she imagine, a little dismissively. Jessica was convinced that he would not bother and was very surprised at the end of the day when she had a brief note along with the report. The note said quite simply,

" It would seem your intuition was spot on, well done!"
The attached report read as follows. ' Death by poisoning intentional or unintentional. Site, soft tissue proximity to right nasal cavity. Bi-refringent crystalline material, probably zinc phosphate, immunohistochemistry revealed granular insulin deposits as well as an insulin staining along the lipocyte membranes. A cellular reaction of granulocytic character was present with an excess uptake of insulin by inflammatory cells. The amount of insulin required to impact upon the tissue in this manner must have been very substantial and in fact excessive. Please see attached toxicological report.'

Chief inspector John Stringer hit the roof, both acerbic and exasperated in the extreme,
" Look love, are you seriously telling me after all this that she was killed, done in by her hubby who is only a fuck'n' lawyer! Where the hell is Wallace, I can trust him even if he is an upper class pouff!"
"I'm not saying anything at all, simply read the report!"
Stringer cast his eyes to heaven and reached for the phone to contact Jessica's boss. Benjamin Wallace was the head of the forensics department. He was a bumptious little man, an ex-

Etonian and the son of a bankrupt minor aristocrat. He marched to a different drumbeat, was eccentric in nearly every way though this was contrived to some degree. He habitually wore a duffel coat and carried a golf club, a five iron that he used as a walking stick, a pointer and at times a tool to forge a path through throngs of people when on a case, or to poke people with when making a point. He was brilliant but had an almost intolerable ego and, like John Stringer, was impossible to get along with most of the time though in a different way. He adored Jessica as a maiden aunt loves a niece, an entirely asexual appreciation. On the other hand, he and John Stringer openly despised and hated each other. Strangely, there was also a grudging mutual respect for one another, though neither would have admitted this. John Stringer was wont to play games and would often mention Wallace's name when trying to put Jessica in her place. Wallace, on the other hand, supported Jessica when she needed him to and sometimes he did this just to annoy Stringer.

Unfortunately for Jessica, Wallace was away on leave as well John Stringer knew. Jessica became annoyed and dug her heels in, steadfastly remaining aloof and objective.
"Ben is still on holiday Chief Inspector but I am sure that he would concur with my my professional findings based on the scientific evidence; to wit, she was administered a gross overdose of insulin by some undisclosed means; simple really!"
Inspector John Stringer held his head in his hands for a moment; his voice heavy with sarcasm.
" Are you saying her husband killed her?"

" No I have never said that. I am however saying, based on the evidence, that someone must have; it's for to find out and draw conclusions as to who committed the offense isn't it?"
" Don't you try and tell me how to do my bloody job. Look love, for Pete's sake, this is a good man, a friend of mine that I would vouch for with my life. There's no need to be so fucking stiff about this! What is it? Boyfriend ditched you, an unexpected visit from Aunty Flo...?"
Jessica should have stood her ground but she was incensed and flounced out of the office like a young girl sent to bed for misbehaving during a party. It was hardly the impression that she would have liked to have given and it made her rage all the more impotent.
'Stringer can be a total bastard sometimes, actually most of the time!'

Later that day she heard that the solicitor had been arrested and charged. He had apparently broken down when interviewed and had unburdened his soul. It was, it transpired, a crime of passion. He had found evidence that his wife, whom he adored, had been having an affair with a colleague, it was a mess to be sure. John Stringer came to tell Jessica in person looking very tired, pale and contrite though he didn't apologise. He had attacked Jessica before and would most likely repeat the performance. In truth he should have been hauled over the coals but Jessica saw his pain and found herself forgiving him, a perennial re-enactment sadly.
" I don't suppose that this would be a good time to tell you that a clairvoyant friend of mine told me what to look for?"
Stringer looked pained.
" I really don't want to know, it's all bloody nonsense to me love, I'm a copper not a mystic but I want you to know that however you did it, you did the right thing, you stuck to your

guns and you were professional and I'm sorry about my temper getting the better of me. That pouff Wallace can't hold a candle to you if you ask me, love."
Jessica gave him another in a long line of forgiving but reserved smiles.

On Friday morning, William was deposited, along with a packet of cat food and a half packet of rich tea biscuits, with Steven Savage. Jessica really wasn't sure about Steven and Julia despised him but still, he was helpful when the mood suited him. Besides, William really liked him and he was probably the only other person in the world with whom William was totally comfortable.
" That cat will have rotten teeth and fucked kidneys by the time he is five if you keep on like this."
Jessica gave him a knowing and tolerant smile.
"Far be it from me to force you to deprive him of his favourite treats Jessica sweet'eart."
"You wouldn't have a prayer Savage!"

She parked the Bentley at the supermarket, went straight to the wine counter in the hope of countering Julia with her offers of cheap cider or even worse, 'snakebite'. With two bottles of Cabernet Sauvignon and two of Chardonnay safely in her bag, Jessica went in search of other gifts. She bought Julia a pair of black satin nickers with a motif in red on the rear proclaiming, 'I'm single if you're rich', which made her giggle, the assistant wrapped them extravagantly in layers of coloured tissue paper. She bought John, Julia's husband, two classic motorcycle magazines knowing what to look for as she shared some of John's passion for British motorcycles. John owned a Norton Commando which spent more time in pieces than being ridden but she empathised with his passion and occasionally delighted him with her budding knowledge of Norton folklore. Jessica's natural appreciation of vintage machines and her innate science based sensibilities had married to create a background sufficient to impress most tinkerers and fettlers toiling in their garden shed or garage while breathing life into their ancient machines.

Jessica had been absolutely forbidden to ride a motorcycle by her over protective father. It was the first time they had ever truly fallen out, a furious row ensued and it was evident that her father was very upset at the prospect of her riding or owning a motorcycle. She promised, in the end, not to. When at university however, an opportunity arose when a friend in desperate straits had borrowed money from Jessica and had given her a motorcycle as security, effectively a trade. Jessica returned home exultant, with a BSA C15 single cylinder. As she had explained at the time to smirking and disbelieving friends, it was a measure of expediency.
She had loved every beautiful moment of motorcycling that summer until she was eventually 'found out' by her father. With a troubled conscience, Jessica put up feeble resistance and then shed real tears as she observed the original owner riding away on the BSA leaving a familiar pungent blue haze in its wake. Jessica was outraged at this injustice and the event drove an even deeper wedge between her and her father until the day he died. When offered the chance, she would ride Johns Commando and usually too fast. She was thrilled with it's lusty bellow, the adrenalin rush, the seemingly unlimited power and the sublime sense of freedom and joy that she felt. But on each occasion her conscience was pricked by the ingrained sense of duty towards her late father who had, in effect, laid a curse upon her which persisted even

after his demise. Jessica just had to accept the sad fact that she would never be able to own a machine of her own.

For the children, Loretta, Hamish and Oliver, Jessica chose a croquet set and a giant 'pick and mix' bag of assorted chocolate treats of varying degrees of delicious sticky perniciousness, which were normally outlawed by their mother.

"Julia will hate me for this but if I was one of her children I would be desperate for a lifeline in the form of chocolate after being offered bran muffins, raisins and nuts for an eternity!"

She left the supermarket feeling strangely jubilant but was quickly deflated by a badly written note stuck under the windshield wiper of the Bentley. This was accompanied by a bold, deliberately administered key scratch along the side. The note read;

"Keep smiling as your driving your enviromental dinosor around Dikhead."

Jessica wasn't sure whether to be more annoyed about the bad spelling or the sentiment but was upset by the deliberate act of vandalism.

'What an absolute beast! Uneducated and bitter people who adopt the moral high ground rarely have a correct grasp of the facts. Basically its just raw envy and hypocrisy.'

Despite her attempt to shake off the 'attack', she was bothered more than she wanted to admit. The energy of the message lingered like a bad smell and the necrosis beneath the intent permeated deep into her subconscious.

' Well it is a dinosaur and to be honest, not conducive to environmental well being but that was horrible!'

Sitting inside the car once again, the smell of old leather and the shine of the walnut burr, highlighted by gleam of the beautiful aircraft style instruments and switches was beyond the material. She felt that driving the Bentley was akin to a spiritual experience, allied to a lifetime membership of one of those stuffy but delightful gentleman's clubs. The sort that had weathered the storm of the inevitable withering of a once great empire, by keeping up a whimsical pretense. The Bentley was more an antique than a mode of transport. *'And in any case, this is my only real link with Aunt Maria. Am I to be judged and chastised for that?'* Driving out of London was a nightmare. Experience lived up to expectation despite the fact that Jessica was ahead of the the normal rush hour traffic. The Bentley was a difficult beast to manage in such conditions and an intermittently fouled spark plug caused a misfire and soaring water temperature did not help Jessica's state of anguish. As soon as the traffic started to thin out however and the car was at last able to breath and stretch it's legs, then calm prevailed. The Bentley was old, built in the days when cars were much more rarefied and the one environment in which the Bentley excelled was on the open road at cruising speed. At 80 mph the temperature dropped to normal, the oil pressure gauge sat reassuringly just a little higher than normal and the big in-line six cylinder engine murmured a subdued and comfortable hum. Meanwhile 'Faure's Requiem' bathed the interior of the car and Jessica with the light of sublime and infectious inspiration.

Aunt Maria loved music, especially choral and had reasoned that the car was the best place to play music really loud since you could not upset the neighbours. Indeed the music spirited one away from the humdrum disrupted road surfaces and slab sided buildings of mind numbing concrete drabness of the south circular, to other, far distant and infinitely more enticing realms. When Jessica first took ownership of the Bentley, it was fitted with a radio/tape cassette player cunningly concealed behind the original valve radio fascia. Two loudspeaker boxes were mounted on the rear parcel shelf as was the norm of the era. As a result latterly, of a virtual absence of cassettes, Jessica decided that a CD player was the answer. A company that fitted stereo equipment to cars was selected at random from the phone book. An eccentric elderly duo wearing coveralls spoke conspiratorially about their plans for the Bentleys in car entertainment system. As it transpired, they were technically competent but also the artists of their trade. The original fascia of the long defunct valve radio was re-installed as a cover tastefully hiding the modern and incongruous newly fitted CD player and it was wired to light up when the lights were turned on. At the touch of a button the fascia folded down revealing the new apparatus and reminding Jessica, who giggled when she first used it, of the subtle but functional intricacies of James Bond's Aston Martin DB5. The original speakers were removed and instead, a pair of much more powerful variants were incorporated into the parcel shelf, beneath baffles and quite hidden from view. Two more loudspeakers were then beautifully installed into the front doors into the spaces that were previously storage pockets. Normally these were little used other than as receptacles for pieces of paper, receipts and empty chocolate bar wrappers where over time the detritus inevitably congealed into a sort of sodden mush. There was still the glove locker for storage and of course, the cubby hole in which to store glasses, gloves and so on next to the huge tiller-like steering wheel. The venerable Bentley remained therefore, completely true to form visually but the innovations produced a marvelous sound. Aunt Maria must have intended to fit a CD player as, curiously enough, a new CD of 'Faure's Requiem' was discovered in the glove locker. Jessica listened entranced, to 'In Paradisum', transported in more ways than one. Her thoughts strayed to the tree, of the amazing vision that had tantalized and enthralled her for a single exquisite moment. It was a glimpse of the Garden of Eden, a place in which she yearned to be, *'But only if I can take you Aunt Maria',* she said as she patted the armrest of the Bentley.

Driving to the West Country became fun especially on the section of the A303 that skirted Stonehenge. Jessica's initial anxiety at the prospect of negotiating deeply glutinous muddy fields and cow pats was replaced with a curious longing as the influence of the city abated. Jessica then realised with wry amusement that there was a part of her which yearned to be transported to a sylvan wilderness without access to showers, washing machines or even Bentleys with impressive sound systems! No matter the number of times she had been to visit Julia and John however, she always seemed to lose her way way. Some labyrinthine conundrum had been installed in her mind and was doomed never to be exorcised. She parked in Glastonbury's main street and reached for her phone which rang the instant she touched it.
" Hi Jess, I know you are lost again! John is on his way, he was itching to be out on his motorcycle, just hang tight for a few minutes!"
Jessica though embarrassed, breathed a sigh of relief.

" I'm in the high street, outside that lovely cafe we went to last time I was here. I can't wait to see you Jools, you and those gorgeous children of yours.... "

Within seconds the booming crisp snarl of an enthusiastically ridden Norton could be heard zinging along the ring road. Moments later, John rode up the street wearing his farmers tweeds and aviators goggles, on a motorcycle which glistened and glinted from every aspect. Jessica stood out in the road and waved to catch his attention. She flung her arms around him just as he stopped and was frantically reaching for the kickstand. John was the only man she had ever truly trusted, apart from her uncle and Jessica loved him like a brother.

" Hey! Steady on girl, you'll have me lying in the gutter!" John lifted Jessica off her feet and gave her a mighty hug in return, his West Country Farmer Giles dialect weighty with warmth and welcome.

" It's really good to see you Jessica." Then he added mischievously, " And I can see an awful lot of you, did you know that the sun at this angle is shining right through your dress?"

" Oh God! Cheap thrills for you then John. Does Julia know that you leer at strange women when you are riding your motorbike?"

"Yeah, of course she does, like I always say to her; just because you admire a car doesn't mean you have to drive it." Jessica smiled,

"You are incorrigible!"

"Yeah that's me alright! You okay to follow me home now?" Noticing the scrape on the side of the Bentley, John looked briefly pained, as if the gouge were in his own flank.

"How did that happen?"

" Oh I don't know, just another self righteous moralistic bore at the supermarket." Jessica showed him the note.

" No Leo Tolstoy though was he my lover?"

John whistled through his teeth in exclamation.

" The Norton's looking good and sounds gorgeous, can I have a ride later?"

" Yeah of course you can my darlin', she still needs few odds and ends though, it never seems to end with these."

" Ah but you love it really, all this fiddling and fettling."

In many ways John and Jessica were quite similar, pragmatic, mathematical, precise. Julia was entirely different, fanciful, imaginative in the extreme, highly emotional, psychic and overtly affectionate; she just loved everyone. There were times when John and Jessica would side with one another, pouring light hearted scorn on Julia's colourful lamentations. They both admired and loved her however and respected her incredible insights.

" Well come on then Farmer Giles, are you going to show me the way or are we going to spend the evening here on the street with me exposing myself to all and sundry."

John sped off into the distance, no doubt showing off, then carried out a swiftly executed and flamboyant 'U' turn just in time to see the old Bentley cresting the hill. Jessica suffered some discomfort at the thought of all the mud she was going to have to wash off the Bentley later, as she navigated a very long, muddy and potholed drive. There were the usual discarded vehicles, dented and mud encrusted that had been left exactly where they had died. In some cases they had been utilised as storage sheds or in one case a chicken coop. Jessica stopped briefly to let two hens and a large fluffy cat with matted fur, amble across the lane.

The house was not an attractive building externally, built in the sterile post war era when adversity had crushed the imagination and where functionality ruled supreme over any other consideration. Basically, it was a cement block rendered in a grey pebble dashed stucco but it was in a sublime location with far reaching views of open countryside and of the Tor. Beautiful Julia stood waiting in the doorway, long straw coloured hair, blue eyes, tanned complexion, broad mouth and transatlantically impeccable teeth. Wearing a long skirt and top of amazing hues, purples, yellows and russets that stood out in a blaze of colour and character. She waved energetically at Jessica, happiness betrayed in every aspect of her being. Then she rushed towards the car, shrieking with excitement and opened the door barely before the vehicle had drawn to a stop.

"Oh my God Jess, is it really you, you are so welcome honey, you are so welcome!"

CHAPTER 11

While the outside of the house was hardly attractive the interior was bewitching and cozy and Jessica, despite her weariness, felt becalmed and quite at home. Her own childhood home environment had always seemed singularly bland and lacklustre; a place to eat, sleep and to do school homework assignments but it was never comfortable or in the least bit welcoming. The management of the household was the domain of her disinterested and widowed father who lived in a world of his own. His hobbies excluded anything of a practical nature but included his passionate obsession with philately; the only books in the house being on the subject of stamps. Jessica remembered, with something akin to fondness mixed with sadness, a time when her father had uncharacteristically shown some enthusiasm for putting up Christmas decorations and eagerly sought Jessica's help. Aged just ten years old, she had indeed pitched in and spent many hours cutting out strips of coloured paper which she had taped together to form chain links, which were to be hung from the ceiling. Her father's rare bout of enthusiasm had lasted the afternoon but by the following day he was absorbed elsewhere and Jessica's enthusiastically made coloured paper chains were left on a chair for weeks and despite constant prompting were finally swept into the garbage. The one family cat that she had been permitted to own, a sickly but endearingly affectionate white cat with one blue eye and one green, had died at the age of two from an untreated abscess. Jessica had forgiven her father most things but the Christmas decorations and the demise of Florence were memories that pained her still, even many years later. She never really knew her father, did not know the person he was other than as the 'distant' and pre-occupied parent who had died long before his time. She always assumed that deep down he had loved her but, maybe that was simply never the case.

Julia's house not only looked good but Jessica was almost overwhelmed by the earthy odour of woodsmoke, a hint of incense and delicious culinary smells. She was utterly seduced in an instant and became deeply immersed in a sensory nirvana, soaking up the comfort of a home, the like of which she had never really known. Julia, combining her North American west coast talents with those acquired in Britain, allied with a vivid imagination had created an interior of exceptional charm. Jessica regarded the wall hangings, antiquities and ornaments that included a life sized carving of a bald eagle with wings outstretched. There were fantastical paintings of other-worldly and surreal landscapes, old stuffed armchairs draped with rustic looking 'throws' of russets, forest greens and deep reds. A life size statue of St. Francis of Assisi, carved from a piece of Mexican saguaro cactus, stood guard by the fireplace. An enormous and very baroque mirror unmistakably originating from the Far East threw back a flattering reflection of herself, though Jessica did a double take and underwent a brief moment of embarrassment. She could swear that, even in the reflection, she could see through her dress in places as the sunlight picked out the myriad of tiny flaws in the reflective silvering of the mirror but also the translucency of Jessica's attire.

Julia hugged her repeatedly, her scent and the softness of her bosom lending Jessica a sudden impression of a maternal warmth that she had never experienced as a child. Then, squealing in delight and laughing, Julia put her arm around Jessica's neck and took her into the kitchen.

" I must admit you've got some nerve girl, wearing blue striped underwear with a white dress and with your colouring too."

" Yes, it would seem that the whole world has seen right through me while I have been blissfully ignorant, I had no idea until John mentioned it."

" Well he would too eh, typical! But that's partly why we love you honey, your amazing naiveté, it's so charming. Here try some of my chai, it's a real pick me up after a road trip. I see you've still got that funky old car of Aunt Maria's; it's haunted y'know?"

" So you tell me every time I see you. That reminds me, I've been meaning to ask..........?"

Just at that moment all three children entered noisily with Jessica's baggage, freshly liberated from the boot of the car. The children were excitable, mud streaked, unruly, noisy but interesting and beautiful in a resplendently pre-raphaelite fashion. Along with their wild hair, blonde like their mothers, they were refreshingly uninhibited and unspeakably healthy; 'Almost feral,' thought Jessica, 'just as children should be.' They were all over Jessica within seconds, talking, demanding, hugging, utterly un-repressed; Jessica suddenly felt inadequate and not up to receiving the unconditional love given so freely to her. Her own up-bringing had been so ordered, so secular, but that was normal to her; this on the other hand was almost too much, a heresy. How could children be so wild, warm and uninhibited? A torrent of mixed emotions scorched through her as she struggled to break down the barriers that would allow her to be warm and loving in return. It was then that she realised that this was the main reason why she feared the West-Country visits. Her world of ordered and grounded emotional calm became suddenly strapped to a Saturn 5 rocket and launched into the cosmos.

Handing out the presents and enduring a brief but consenting frown from Julia, Jessica watched beguiled as the children excitedly distributed the chocolates and aportioned carefully measured shares. Julia laughed with delight upon opening her present, the children giggled. John sidled up to Julia and put an arm around her waist, possessively, intimately, his hand resting suggestively on her behind. Julia pulled his hand away, smiling but then asked him,
" I was wondering if you would put the children to bed tonight my darling, please?"
" All sorted my love but it'll cost you."
" Not again!" Julia rolled her eyes at Jessica in mock horror and them smiled sweetly back at John. Jessica felt just a little embarrassed, her stringent repression and sense of decorum dented by what she considered to be a slightly distasteful and sordid display of carnal humour. By way of a distraction she proffered the bottles of wine in a slightly brittle fashion and then informed Julia of her desire to order a take away curry from a local and 'approved of' organic curry house. John was already 'away with the fairies, a motorcycle magazine in hand with a featured article on a Vincent twin engine powered Norton.
" Well I guess that's done the trick Jess, we'll not have much of a peep out of him for the rest of the evening after he's put the kids to bed. He'll linger tonight of course, as he's fond of

you and wants to join in but tomorrow he will probably go to the pub to get some peace; you can maybe help me then?

The evening was lighthearted and fun and Jessica basked in warmth and contentment, the wine melting her barriers. It was difficult for her to get a word in edge ways with all the happy chatter but she watched them all with a sense of longing for a childhood that had never existed for her. When they had eaten, Jessica felt very replete but suddenly tired from the long drive; also the country air conspired to induce in her an abnormal drowsiness. Excusing herself, Jessica retired to her bed early but took the precaution og filling a hot water bottle. Tomorrow was Saturday and she and Julia would have a night to themselves, a night to catch up on gossip, scandal and to share thoughts. Just before Jessica went upstairs, Julia looked at her intently,
" Tomorrow, I want all the news, I particularly want to know more about this mysterious man that you have evidently fallen in love with."
Jessica was genuinely baffled.

The following morning, Jessica, Julia and the children visited nearby Honeymoon Lake. Jessica had offered to drive and the children, excited at the prospect of being taken in the Bentley as opposed to the muddy and dented family Volvo wagon, shouted their enthusiasm.
"I guess that means you are driving honey." Julia had stated cheekily. The children, particularly Hamish who loved cars, asked a machine-gun-fire stream of questions;
" What's that lever by the steering wheel Aunty Jess," he had asked?
" This one?"
" No the one on the other side!"

" Oh that's for changing gear manually."

"Manually?"

" Yes this car has an automatic gearbox so you don't really need to change gear as it does that all by itself or at least it is supposed to."

Then Jessica smiled to herself, aware of the transmission's eccentric vagaries.

" Then why does it have the lever then Aunty Jess....?"

" Oh Hamish! All these questions?" Julia interrupted,

" Do you think I might be allowed to slip a bit of conversation with my old friend somewhere in there?"

" Hey! Not so much of the old if you don't mind Julia darling."

" What's that button for," Loretta asked pointing to a small bakelite protrusion below the ignition key switch?"

" That's for the ejection seat isn't it Aunty Jess?" chimed in Oliver

" Its an ejector seat not 'ejection' you dumb-ass...."

" That's quite enough of that language Hamish Foxwell, if you don't mind, your brother is not a 'dumb-ass' and you are not to use that vile expression!"

" Well you say it to Dad..."

" I certainly do not. Well okay maybe sometimes I do but only when he deserves it!" then Julia giggled, her eyes dancing with mischief. And so the cheery chatter continued without pause for breath until they reached the picnic area, a large clearing by the lake shore.

Julia and Jessica spent a very happy if exhausting day wiping noses, laughing, playing tag, eating a huge picnic, wiping noses again and finally, later in the day, soothing over-excited and exhausted children.

" Mum, Mum, MUM, Hamish keeps putting his finger up his nose and wiping it on me!"

" Hamish you'll be doing time out in the car if you don't cut that out mister.........and Loretta, don't be such a princess, Jessica and I want to talk, can't you please keep an eye on the boys, c'mon guys give me a break!"

It had been Julia's suggestion that they go on an outing with the children to the lake; the idea being that the children would play to their hearts content while she and Jessica could had a good heart to heart chat but things didn't really go according to plan. Each time they started to talk about Jessica's discovery of the message in the tree and the ill fated prisoner at what was once the 'Mortlac Prison,' they would be interrupted or disturbed by one of the children. Oliver, the youngest, had fallen in the water almost as soon as they arrived and had to be dried and changed. Then of course there were repeated visits from them all for biscuits, sandwiches, drinks and mostly attention. They just wanted to share some of their mother's and Jessica's company. Though Jessica so wanted to talk she could not help but be charmed by the raggle-taggle bunch of wild haired little gypsies. Eventually she and Julia managed to intermittently reminisce over past boyfriends, parties and the various mischievous misdoings of a couple of adventurous girls in their childhood and teen years. It was a conversation that could stand constant interruption without losing the thread. In truth, it was fun to go over those old times.

That night the younger children were put to bed and Loretta, was permitted to stay up for another hour, on her best behaviour, to watch 'Little Dorrit' on the hidden and usually covered television in the corner of the large farmhouse kitchen. Then at last, Jessica and Julia were alone;

they sat either side of the large, sturdy, kitchen table. Over not one but two bottles of wine, Jessica related the story of the tree, the splendid and beautiful oak. She told the tale of Lucius Grey and of her experiences and discoveries including her visions.

" For some reason I feel strangely but wonderfully haunted," Jessica remarked. Julia said little as was her way, devoting all of her attention to Jessica, savouring and emphathising, with an intense gaze. Jessica of course gave away far more than she had intended as Julia's deliberate lack of verbal response prompted Jessica to keep talking, filling in the possible void where a slightly awkward silence might have prevailed, a good listeners art.

" The other funny thing is that in my dreams he arouses me in a way that I have never experienced before. I have to say that I do slightly envy and admire yours and John's close physical relationship but up until now, I have never really understood what it was that I envied. Would you believe......no sorry, I can't even tell you of all people......."
Julia looked at her intently but said nothing.

" I simply can't Julia my love, it's just too embarrassing."
Julia continued to look searchingly and Jessica squirmed.
"How is it that I always tell you everything in the end?
Oh bugger, okay I'll tell! Look, I even get sort of aroused when I'm close to the tree but I'm not kinky about the tree; I sense that this happens as a result of some kind of association."
Looking serious for a moment, Julia was about to give an opinion and then despite herself, the beginnings of a broad smile spread across her face, her eyes twinkling and then she spoke.

" Do you mean that you do understand now? My darling, my only real friend, my lovely naive soul sister, when was the last time you had sex?"

" Oh charming, bloody typical, there is infinitely more to this saga than sexual intrigue! I know that North Americans are obsessed with having healthy sex lives but there has to be a line drawn somewhere, it's just for producing offspring after all! It's all so undignified, the arousal part is only a bit of the story........."

"WHEN?"

" Oh I don't know, months ago I think, some beastly little man at a forensics conference; he kept asking me on a date, I felt so abnormal that I let him talk me into it but......"

"My dear girl we're going to have to get a vacuum cleaner up there to clear out the cobwebs. You've got a figure that women, especially me, envy and that men including John, bless him, go gaga over, you shouldn't waste it! You have a body that should be cause for a bacchanalian celebration"

Jessica was at first shocked, a puritanical reaction rigidly enforced by her stringent upbringing. Then seeing the look of devilry deep in the eyes of her friend she collapsed into a state of mirth mixed with embarrassment.

" Tell me more of the tree and of the man, Lucius Grey; that was his name wasn't it?"

Jessica became silent, contemplative then she blurted out;
" I know that this sounds strange but I've actually been there Jools, I have seen it. I would never normally admit this to a soul but I knew that you would understand. I've 'seen' the prison as it was and I have looked upon that tree when it was younger, healthier. Even then it was as if the tree was trying to tell me something. I have also seen the same place as it was long before there were any buildings there, at least I

think it was the same place though there were no familiar landmarks. There was a vast forest as far as the eye could see, then there was the lake which is the conundrum, as there is no lake there now, though I read that there was one once hence the name, Mortlac. Anyway, a beautiful but obviously elderly man dressed in white with plaited hair and a beard was planting a sapling, which I know, or at least I felt on some deep instinctive level to be the same tree as my oak. The funny thing was, and I can't really explain this, that the old man had a similar essence to the prisoner, as though they were one and the same person. I can't believe I'm saying all this Julia, even to you, my best of friends with whom I have shared all my greatest secrets. I'm a scientist, a pragmatist, I am not supposed to be fanciful. Perhaps I'm going mad....?"

Julia paused for a moment and was evidently giving the matter some considerable thought.

"There's something else isn't there Jess, that you are not telling me?"

" No, not really..."

" C'mon Jessica, it'll be better for you to speak of it now rather than allow the issue to gain too much significance."

" Oh I don't know, this is all starting to seem so sordid."

"I'm waiting."

" I met the druid in my vision, if that is what it was. I was terrified of him, didn't want him, was petrified of being violated and yet I was utterly and paradoxically 'turned on' by him. It was so odd as he was this beautiful old man one moment but then he somehow became a stag, an incredible creature in its prime. I was quite powerless to resist him you know, it was a kind of sublimation, I was utterly consumed and I wanted it, I yearned for him. I had no choice and yet it was the most exquisite experience of my life. I never knew

140

that I had such a vivid imagination but I suppose one might actually thrive in a world of pure fantasy."
"You know what Jess, describing actual events is not fantasy. We form deep soul connections on all sorts of levels and time lines. In fact time ceases to exist when you see the bigger picture, 'time' really is quite meaningless."
" You don't actually believe all this Jools, well, stupid question really because I suspect that you do; but what of time travel, of the paradoxes, time travel is an impossibility, surely?"

Standing abruptly and then making for the sideboard, Julia opened a lid and withdrew papers, lighter and tobacco and proceeded to roll a 'large cigarette', a 'joint',
"Best BC bud," she boasted, "A present from back home."
Jessica did not even want to contemplate how Julia had managed to get her hands on it, *Probably buried in her face cream in the bowels of her suitcase again knowing Julia.'*
Julia then put on some music, the kind of music that Jessica had heard in alternative and funky holistic book shop on her last visit, that smelt exotically of far eastern incense and had large statues of Buddha sitting omnipresently and mirthfully on shelves in portly munificence. There were beautiful, almost alien crystals of stunning colours and intensity sitting under glass counter-tops and, most memorably, books on the shelves with titles like; 'You are a galactic being' or the more ubiquitous, 'Discover your Inner Child.' Jessica loved these places but was inclined to pour scorn on most of the publications that, from her perspective, were appallingly written and also fodder for the new-age gullible.
' God ! It's so lovely to be back here, why did I stay away for so long?'

Jessica smiled at Julia, a big happy smile and Julia smiled back, reading her, seeing her. For the first time in a long time, Jessica truly relaxed.

CHAPTER 12

Father Donovan's original name was Derryth, a Celtic name meaning quite literally 'oak'; a sacred name bestowed upon him by his Druid brethren. Strangely there were few who knew this secret. He preferred to live a hermit's life, an existence of solitude and reflection, rarely communing with people in neighbouring settlements. The only time he did, was when he was summoned in his capacity as local priest, a veiled and reputable front to his druidic alter ego. On those occasions he preached short sermons, baptised infants, married young couples, gave holy communion, performed the last rites and took confession though, contrary to accepted practice, he doled out moderate, if token, penances. He lived in a simple cottage with an earthen floor in a forest glade, rich with the plangent resonance of enchanting bird song and the rushing of the wind elementals on stormy winter nights. He farmed his land in a clearing that he had created many years earlier and this provided him with nearly all that he needed, though he bartered to fulfill any lack. He kept hens and let them roam as they would but at night they sought shelter and he shut them up to safeguard them against marauding predators.

Derryth practiced his pre-Christian faith in the privacy of his domain, surrounded as he was in his forest of beloved oaks, bristling with lush globes of mistletoe. He interacted with the outside world as little as possible for reasons, among others, of personal safety. He was not only a zealous and valued guardian of his pagan secrets but also naturally reclusive. His greatest passion was to tend to the needs of sick and wounded animals and to befriend those that weren't. His ability to soften fear and timidity in animals was legendary among those that had witnessed his great compassion first hand. Squirrels would take nuts from his upheld palm, birds landed on outstretched fingers and aggressive she bears protecting their young were coaxed to relax, becoming almost tame and trusting under his influence; the animals were indeed his true friends. When occasion demanded, he gathered herbs and mushrooms from the forest and concocted plant medicines. These were formulated either to enhance his 'sight' or, at other times, transform him into an animal archetype of his choice. With the aid of these potions, he was able to put himself into the mind of his chosen creature, badger, wolf, bear or raven, whatever was appropriate to gain an insight and a wondrous perspective peculiar to only those creatures. As a hawk, he would survey his realm while soaring in the heavens. The sickness, purging and several days of deep lethargy that inevitably followed the rituals were the price that he paid willingly and without question. Rufus, his dog, took all this in his stride and simply kept a companionable proximity to his adored master.

There were still followers of the old ways, pagans who would seek him out, in a country oozing with established Christian fervour. Derryth was summoned from time to time in his capacity as druid, to give advice or oversee peculiarly supernatural events and closely guarded religious ritual ceremonies, some of which he participated in, though less as he grew older. While cautious by nature, he learned by instinct to know the strangers whom he could trust and was adept at recognising those who were trying to lay a trap for him. The land was full of religious zealots who tirelessly sought to locate and eradicate centres of pagan activity. Often they burnt or hung the 'sinners', dependent upon whether they would recant. Derryth also put great faith in his 'familiar', a beautiful black Raven, a constant companion whom he named Crevan because he was as sly as a fox and bristled with intelligence. Crevan was the immortal ally and willing accomplice in Derryth's vision quest. His enormous and intimidating dog, Rufus who was an incongruous mix, part wolf and part wolf-hound that Derryth had rescued from a trap when still a pup, was ever at Derryth's side and kept a wary eye out for interlopers. Rufus was so named because of his shaggy coat which was of an unusual deep russet hue. His eyes were disturbingly hetero-chromic, one blue and one brown and his ears pointed skywards, ever on the move like radar antenna listening and sensing everything. When Derryth thought of poor little Rufus' heartless entrapment as a puppy and of his tail which was stunted as a result of losing the tip, Derryth still became angry. On these occasions Rufus, sensing something amiss, would lay his big shaggy head on Derryth's knees, a little whimper of concern escaping from him. Derryth would have laid down his life for both Crevan and Rufus.

It came to pass that shortly after planting the tree, Derryth was approached tentatively by a small committee of initiates headed by the high priestess, locally known as the abbess. Like him, they effected an ecclesiastical front in order to deter unwanted attention and passed scrutiny as members of a small and deeply devout convent. In fact, they were ardent followers of the old ways, were priestesses and one of many small bands of protectors of their beloved and immortal Albion. Although details of the foundation of their Sanctuary were lost in the mists of the distant past, it was known that very few of the order were actually born there, their parents being existing members of the Sanctuary, the identities of the fathers were unknown or kept strictly secret. It was at the latterly, more subdued and secretive Beltane festivities that women of the order were impregnated and were then confined to quarters where their clandestine condition would not be discovered. If the child born was female then she was raised in the Sanctuary. If a male was conceived, the child was raised by the women until they were sent away at ten years of age to learn the arts of warrior or priest, depending upon their calling. The Sanctuary presented a front as an orphanage and on the odd occasion when it was considered expedient, they would take in a child from outside the order who needed a home.

The matings occurred by intuition, driven by the desires of the flesh and the energy of the occasion at Beltane, gifts both to and from the Earth Goddess. Sometimes the partners were selected prior to the event by the elders when there were factors of significant portent to be considered. The participating men and women were denied knowledge of their partners and indeed, the sires were compelled to wear disguises so that their identity would never become known. Father Donovan, as a druid, had been required to perform this service and like any warm blooded young male was more than willing to carry out this 'offering' at the fires and the feasting. As he grew much older and his animal urges receded, as ordained by the cycles of nature, he entered the festivities less frequently, almost to the extent that he absolved himself from partaking unless specifically requested to do so. The reason for this recent visitation by the initiates, was to formerly invite him to attend a ceremony at the express wish of the High Priestess. There was hope, they indicated, that he would father a child, a spirit of great presage was awaiting re-incarnation and Derryth had been chosen. He was well aware that to refuse would not only be churlish but would also be a great dishonour to his very being and all that he represented.

The woman chosen as his mate, whose name was Laurna, was a dedicated and long respected resident of the Sanctuary, a maiden who had long since flowered into womanhood but who had remained a virgin by design, a decision taken by the elders. The fires of her youthful passion having been starved of fuel, had been suppressed. She was special; she had been more or less mute since birth although she could hear perfectly well. There were times when she would speak but only when she was encouraged to enter a trance-like state which was induced during the ceremonial administration of plant medicines. She was considered to be a 'seer' of considerable ability. During one ceremony, the High Priestess received information that the woman would speak just once more and that her words would have great significance but that in order to fulfill this prophecy, she must have recently conceived a child. The father, it was said, would have to be a venerated druid with the great knowledge that came with his position and experience. On the night of Beltane, Father Donovan or Derryth as he was to be in his capacity as druid, was to wear a disguise, that of an animal archetype. His favoured and most applicable one was that of the King Stag. He was then to find the girl at the appointed hour, who would be waiting for him in a bower prepared for the occasion.

'Be gentle and sensitive with her' were the last words spoken to him before the event. It was a remark that he found a incomprehensible and slightly distasteful, as if he were just a lustful and insensitive opportunistic old man with only carnal gratification on his mind. The 'Abbess' had good reason, as she recalled a little too fondly, when she herself had fallen under his spell. The memories still vivid, though decades had passed, of the sublime moments of ecstasy she had experienced at his hands. She recalled his incredible strength, virility and energy and his potent and intimidating manhood. She was taken to the brink of ecstasy and finally drunk with love and satiated beyond comprehension.

' Ah such beautiful memories.'

She recalled that she had been a more than willing partner, mesmerised by the raging fires of her passions and of the flickering of sparks that flew up from the bonfires and into the moonlight. She had been bewitched and stirred by the drumming and her belly pleasantly warmed by the honey spirit she had imbibed. She had been erotically fascinated by the sight of couples disappearing into dark corners hidden from the moonlight, then she became aroused by the sound of their lovemaking and was spurred on by her own vital youthful instincts and her desires honed during the intensity of her ovulation. This was a memorable and intoxicating experience and she had been well prepared for Derryth. The maiden Laurna, on the other hand simply wasn't. She was dried up like old parchment, the heartbeat of nature's cycles had ceased to beat within her breast if ever they had which was debatable. Even as a very young woman she had displayed little interest in the opposite sex.

As the festival approached, no amount of preparation or dialogue seemed to change Laurna's demeanor of ill-

148

disguised loathing and fear. True to her strict training as an initiate, Laurna was outwardly obedient and consigned to her fate but the Abbess feared that all would not go well. Her only hope lay in Derryth's advanced years and accumulated wisdom. The time came and festivities commenced; Derryth was directed to the bower in a state of resolution tinged with nervous irritability. He simply felt too old and too tired for what was expected of him. Upon encountering the maiden in her bower, he was even more disquieted to find her mortally afraid, more so than he had ever seen a woman before and she was supposed to be primed and had given her consent. His first thoughts were for her wellbeing as he was a sensitive and compassionate man whose primary concern was ever the safety and welfare of others. He did not know that for Laurna, a quirk of nature, of genetics and of time, sexuality had passed her by. Instead she took solace in her ability, in rare moments, to speak of truths yet to come. Yet she was a good accolyte and showed a complete acceptance of her fate. Derryth for his part observed an unwilling participant, a woman whose desire, like an un-watered sapling, had withered and died. Despite himself, he could not help feeling like an old lecher about to defile an innocent young creature and were it not for the fact that he was bound by his faith and by his word, he would most definitely have succumbed to the impulse to turn tail and run. He burned with a cocktail of conflicting emotions and for the first time in his life, doubted his vocation and his duty.

Derryth deciding that kindness was the only way went to Laurna with the intention of wooing her and putting her at her ease as he did the animals of the forest. He genuinely wanted to console her, to reassure her and encourage her confidence in him. He very gently touched her brow, a gesture, he hoped, of friendship and of compassion. It was an action to which she reacted with thinly disguised horror as she winced and sprang from his touch. Derryth had two choices; accomplish the deed as quickly as possible and get it over and done with or preferably, try and win the woman over but he knew, with a sinking heart, that this was going to be a battle hard won.

Before entering the bower, he had enshrouded himself in a 'glamour', a druids device to make himself appear more youthful and alluring, less masculine and less threatening but this device was strangely unsuccessful in this case. Derryth was still a very handsome man despite his more advanced years, tall, well proportioned, powerful and leonine. His full white beard conspired but failed to mask a very good looking, open, deeply tanned and pleasantly lined face. When people joked about him in a friendly guileless way they would say that his supernaturally pale blue eyes would melt the heart of even the most resistant of maidens; many a grateful young woman had welcomed him to their arms in the past. He tried to talk with Laurna, to calm her, to quiet her apprehension just as he did with the frightened animals that required his medical attention. The smell of the woodsmoke, the drinking of the honey spirit, the smell of incense and the urging of the drumbeat had the absolute opposite effect upon her than it did upon the mating hordes elsewhere in the encampment. The abbess, for her part, would have sold her soul at that moment to trade places with Laurna. Her life of devotion having deprived her of a lifetime with the only man she had ever truly yearned for and loved.

Sitting next to Laurna, Derryth then tentatively put an arm around her shoulder to comfort and to sooth her in his priestly guise. Her body solidified, became rigid with terror and discomfort, her eyes wild and staring, her demeanour verging on the catatonic. He spoke to her gently, reminding her that they were both honoured by the sacred roles they were fulfilling in this ceremony. She looked at him, loathing him, hating the moment, dumbstruck with horror. Finally she nodded a very reluctant acquiescence, numb with obedience. Derryth for his part was not even sure if he was up to the task as any small interest he had held for the occasion had long since waned. He gently laid her on the leafy floor of the bower and kissed her forehead, then went to kiss her neck. Suddenly she leaped to her feet spitting and snarling like a feral cat and despite his gentle but powerful grip, she sprang away from him again, hissing at him. Derryth realised then that anything like divine union would not be possible; he knew he would have to act fast.

He remembered later that despite his advanced years and his inescapable fatigue, he became suddenly possessed. He behaved, to his regret, in a manner that he never had before and never would again. No longer was it a mating ritual but a fight to the death between the hunted and the hunter. He grabbed her, tearing off her robe and pinning her to the floor, attempting to subdue her. Laurna bit and scratched and kicked with all her might and then wriggled free once again. Whenever he did pin her down she screamed and fought all the more and despite her small stature she was amazingly strong as he found to his cost. He circled her as she turned, following his gaze with blazing eyes of fire and he was suddenly at his wits end, consumed with a blood lust and a passion, his manhood suddenly galvanised and straining, he was frantic with desire. Now it was no longer simple expediency to bed this woman at the behest of a religious order, he wanted this woman like he had never wanted a woman before in his life. There were no longer two people in that bower, there were instead two wild animals fueled by their instincts, fighting to the death. Derryth circled her again baring his teeth and she in turn glared at him, standing rebelliously, her hands on her hips, her small but beautiful maidenly breasts quivering slightly in accompaniment to her cold rage. Then he leaped upon her and grabbed her. This time he knew he was going to win, he was going to succeed, the blood pounded in his head and desire rang in his ears as he pinned her to the floor, spread her legs and penetrated her.

To his utter amazement, he realised that he had entered a woman who was quite thoroughly and inexplicably aroused. As the initial barriers of maidenhood were breached she cried out briefly as he pushed deeply into her, making good his claim upon her. She in turn wrapped her legs around him and began to moan with unrestrained pleasure. Suddenly he was eighteen years old again, energetic and virile and she repaid him in kind as she wreaked havoc upon the skin of his back with her razor sharp nails. Finally, after they had cried out at the peak of sexual frenzy as he honoured his commitment to sire a child, he collapsed beside her, consumed and spent by the entire process. He quickly fell into a deep and exhausted sleep but was awoken many times more that night by the young initiate. Her previously dormant and withered instincts had evidently been activated, the dam breached and this yielded an inconceivable torrent of desire and she acted with basic animal wantonness. That drive and undiluted instinct was truly alive after all, and she used all and every means to make certain that a conception was cemented and consecrated. Derryth and Laurna consumed each other repeatedly, on fire with an otherworldly need and lust, a sublime luminescence of fused souls. The plan, finally, could not have gone better though the start, admittedly, would send conflicting and unsettling messages into the multi-dimensional void .

Derryth departed early the following morning, a beautiful dawn enchanted by the chorus of birdsong and for the first time in his life and far too late, realised he was totally love struck. Laurna, pretending to be asleep, had regarded him unhappily as he got up to leave her, as he was bound by his office and his pledge to do so. She studied him with newly softened wise brown eyes full of tears while an amazing new being had already started to form in her belly. Derryth was forbidden by the faith ever to set eyes on Laurna again and he would live the rest of his life a saddened man and a rather tormented soul, his heart broken, lost to a woman still living and who later bore him a fine son. Laurna was also denied even the merest glimpse of her beloved from that fateful night, a cruel but apparently necessary twist of fate.

In the depths of his desolation and while tending the forest one day accompanied by Rufus, Derryth experienced a vision, the only one of its kind that had occurred for him in the cold light of day. As he sat by the lake shore to take a breath, a truly exceptional and beautiful young woman with dark skin, black hair and curious clothing walked by. Though Derryth could at times see right through her in places and to the forest on her far side, he knew that he had been visited by a kindred spirit, one that was linked to both him and Laurna. So too did Rufus, who had somehow crossed that threshold of time to accompany her in person. He acted as if he were guiding her in some way and he trusted her entirely. It was the most powerful vision Derryth had ever experienced.

Twenty eight nights after Laurna conceived, her breasts heavier and more sensitive and bearing a fine filigree of new veins characteristic of her condition, his scent still vaguely upon her, the delicious soreness between her legs a not so distant memory, she spoke at a ceremony but for the last time ever. Laurna's long awaited speech was disappointing and incomprehensible. In a part of the country where early English or Anglo-Saxon, Brythonic and a smattering of Latin were spoken, she spoke in an unknown tongue which was to become modern English but it was barely recognisable then and difficult to comprehend. Under the direction of Derryth and endorsed by the Abbess, the speech was then written down by three sympathetic Brothers, accomplished and trustworthy scribes from a monastic order, in the far sighted and almost prophetic hope that one day someone would be able to transcribe the text into something intelligible. The words meant little but were written phonetically, the scribes interpreted as well as they were able and then collated their interpretations into just one exquisitely handwritten document. Little had it occured to anyone but Derryth, that the speech had never been intended for this time but was destined for another. Laurna it transpired, would never speak again until the day she died when in her last gasp she uttered the word 'Derryth'. Quite evidently she had known all along who her partner had been. It was shortly before meeting Laurna that 'Father Donovan' had planted the young oak sapling in homage to his beautiful bride to be and to his son whom he would never meet. The son whose name was to be Dewin, was destined to become a great druid in his own right and was to play a key role in a country shortly to be invaded by the Normans.

When Derryth had been gone for many decades and Dewin was by then much older, the monastery and Sanctuary were sacked by Norman soldiers. The sacred box that contained Laurna's speech was in danger of being discovered and taken or destroyed. In his nightly visions and his dreams, Dewin had long ago seen the import of the parchment upon which his mothers speech was written and in which the lineage of his parents was described and he felt bound with all his heart to protect it. One sacred day on the eve of a full moon he planted the parchment, enclosed in a bronze chest, deep in the ground at the foot of a beautiful young oak, the very one planted by his father. He took great pains to wrap the document in waxed cloth and many layers of preserved animal hide and finally enclosed it in within the sanctity of the heavy bronze chest. As he dug into the ground and heaped the earth into a mound alongside, he sensed a presence. From time to time he would catch a fleeting image in the corner of his eye only to see nothing when he paused and looked about him. Then he sensed that he was being watched and looked up again. This time it was evident that he was accompanied by an ethereal sprite of the woods, a dark and very beautiful, tall, long haired woman stood in front of him. Just as he prepared to lower the chest into a small neat rectangular hole in amongst the bluebells she spoke to him. Upon the prompting of this apparition and as he covered the chest, he disguised the burial site by casting a spell over the ground so that the scarring of the earth was rendered invisible by the speedy growth and regrouping of the bluebells.

Having fulfilled his life's mission, Dewin lived a long and fruitful life, a highly regarded druid and seer in a country ruled harshly by the Normans. He died quite suddenly and painlessly, alone beside the lake shore and close to the sacred oak, near to his father and to his mother, neither of whom he had really known. Finally, when he was found, he was buried there with all the ceremony afforded by his office.

CHAPTER 13

The sun was blazing from a pinnacle in a sky that was unblemished by cloud, relentless and most especially ferocious at midday. Despite being on board a boat that should have benefited from cooling breezes, the humidity was indescribable and runnels of sweat ran into his eyes, seeming to seep from every pore of his skin like spring water welling up through the soil of a freshly dug well. He was in familiar terrain and to some extent used to the stifling heat and yet, he was not entirely certain how he came to be there in the first place; the knowledge eluded him, but inconspicuously, as if recollection was unimportant. The memories just did not exist for him and were rendered therefore, inconsequential and needless by their very lack.

His boat was of unknown origin and must have been a beautiful and sleek craft once. He was familiar with the material from which it was constructed, originally white and boasting a perfect sheen but he could not think of the name. There were large windows on the bridge including a 'French window' to the rear that slid open reluctantly and noisily on badly corroded runners to permit access and exit to and from the salon. The quarters down below decks were cozy and boasted the expected port holes. The hull, that must have gleamed like a new pin once, was weathered by the environment and was sporadically covered in a lush layer of verdigris. The boat was named 'White Heron' (though latterly that could have been changed to Green Heron) and was about 55 feet long, streamlined and exuded a sense of purpose but it was entirely alien when he came to think about it. This was his home and was all he had ever known as far back as he could remember. What were evidently wind turbines were placed at intervals along the deck and had a look of being fabricated, lashed together. They were constructed from bits and pieces and looked home-made and anachronistic; they did not belong on such a streamlined machine. In fact, he realised, as he sat and contemplated them thoughtfully from high up in his vantage point on the bridge, they were entirely incongruous and completely ruined the lines of the boat. Also at intervals along the open deck were rectangular areas of soil, bordered by make-shift driftwood frames, in which grew various vegetable plants, carrots, tomatoes, squash, potatoes, even an apple tree and were hardly a compliment to a craft designed with only aesthetics and self indulgent leisure in mind.

On a flat area of the stern section stood a motorcycle that was fastened to the deck with hooked ratchet straps. The motorcycle was badly weathered and corroded, the paint faded or gone altogether leaving in its wake patches of surface rust. In one place on the petrol tank, the rust had caused a huge hole in the side where the corrosive effects of salt had created a chancre. The alloy engine covers were white with residue and the wheel spokes rusted to the point of being quite useless. The seat cover had long since split and peeled away revealing a rotting foam pad underneath. On the originally black mildewed gas tank were written the words 'Triumph' in upper case and the descending leg of the letter 'R' was extended and looped around to join the crossbar at the end of the letter 'H'. Though the 'logo' seemed vaguely familiar, it meant nothing to him as he knew little of motorcycles and never had shown any interest in them. There had been times when he had almost unsecured it and tipped it into the ocean as it took up useful space, but then something always stopped him but he was unable to identify this curious inhibiting force. He sometimes felt as if he were in a waking dream, as so much of his mental faculty seemed to be drastically impaired. Had he been ill or maybe badly injured, was that what clouded his memory so invasively? No memory of any adverse experience came to mind no matter how hard he searched. Curiousity as to the origins of his few possessions was marginal, as if that too was becoming rapidly and similarly buried into the mists of swirling pools of oblivion, along with everything else about his predicament. It was as if his life had started just moments previously and that there were no reference points to give him any indication as to who he was or where he might be going.

The wind turbines turned slowly in a sluggish and steamy breeze in the primordial swamp-like atmosphere and had been doing so for many hours; his experience told him that this was enough but what experience, what memory? By the evening the batteries would be well charged and he would have enough power for light after sunset and enough also for a little propulsion before then. He might be able to go fishing, as his stocks were running low. He needed to contact the community nearby and trade fish for some other food. He needed rice, fruit and especially diesel if at all possible. More fish would ensure a greater stock of those provisions but they were increasingly hard to find. The most commonly caught fish were mackerel and dogfish, both of which seemed very hardy and had survived the climate change well. Even these did not come in abundance any more but he knew where to find them and also where to trade them. Mackerel and dogfish, once considered undesirable by many, were actually in great demand as the seas were not nearly as bountiful as once they had been. Fish was pretty much the staple source of protein for survivors like him but the outlook for acquiring fish was becoming increasingly bleak.

Domestic or wild animals were also very rare as any land that was not excessively poisoned had become hostile in other ways, usually reverting to jungle where the reptile species had thrived and evolved. It was a lucky man indeed who brought home a deer or even a rabbit, an event that could be measured in months with his own people. He had never liked dogfish, they made him nauseous but the mackerel were glorious if eaten within a day of being caught. There was a time, he remembered, when shellfish were more than unusually abundant and a good haul was a good excuse for feasting but those days had long gone. Dogfish were more easily caught near the shore by the rocks but under normal circumstances, to get a reasonable haul of mackerel, it was necessary to travel far out to sea. This was fraught with danger since the weather was unpredictable; vicious and malevolent ship-sinking storms could blow up from nowhere. Diesel was therefore a vital ingredient to survival in these times of environmental ferocity.

Hurricanes were increasingly common and had become a manifestation to be greatly feared, such was their intensity and potential for destruction. Not only that but the planet was in constant turmoil, shuddering and shaking as if trying to shake off lice; violent earthquakes had become a frequent event. If they occurred out at sea and the epicentre was not deep then the resultant Tsunami could and often did sink the rusting hulks of great ships. Back in the lagoons and in the relative safety up river, fisherman, upon hearing that familiar and persistent rumble as the ground trembled and heaved, would head as far upstream as possible before the water ebbed. Then they would securely anchor their craft before the retreating waters could drag the boat back out to sea. The boats often became beached as water was drained in incomprehensible quantities to feed the burgeoning and towering monster far far away out at sea. When finally the encroaching tsunami was broken by land mass, then it arrived up river in the form of a giant ocean swell. Though still a risky situation, the boats were often lifted high but relatively harmlessly on the swell and swept further upstream by the tide; then they were sucked back as the water once again retreated. It was a dangerous roller coaster ride; the prevailing risk being that once the anchor had lost purchase on the river bottom then the boats could be left hopelessly beached upon high ground among rotting piles of stranded but still highly venomous purple jellyfish. He had managed to avoid that ignominious plight so far, partly through good seamanship and partly through luck and he had a good craft, shallow bottomed but surprisingly stable and well built.

He did have one memory that throbbed continually and insistently like an abscess. After having been swept far upstream, he had found himself, as the water ebbed, in the middle of a lake and near to what was once a great oak tree standing magnificently in a watery stillness. It's mighty branches dipping into the shallow water some considerable distance from the trunk. Most of the branches were devoid of flora, bleached and quite dead. Some of the branches higher up still showed signs of life with many leaves and acorns weighting the limb with astonishing abundance. Certainly the tree was a miracle, standing as it was, trunk deep in brackish water. He was marooned there for some weeks as the retreating Tsunami partially drained the lake and closed off the exit. He was able to survive on fish also similarly entrapped. There were also thousands of purple jellyfish stranded on the muddy shoreline, dying in the desiccating heat, not to mention those struggling in the shallow and super-heated lake water, he was careful to avoid those.

While he was there, he became gradually entranced and captivated by the tree, especially when it was in silhouette at sunset. He felt energy, melded with it's spiritual life force and pondered upon the oak's no doubt incredible past, wishing that he was able to tap into it. He spoke to the tree like an old friend and at times, climbed the low branches and held on to it tightly as if the tree were his only anchor to sanity. The oak was undoubtedly extremely old, venerable and was in the latter stages of decay. The number of huge limbs dead and entirely bereft of foliage were a testament to the incredible fortitude of the tree despite the effects of the encroaching saline water that was destroying the roots and hastening the process of death.

After a few weeks, he contemplated abandoning his boat and heading back to the coast on foot through jungle and across broken and cracked land, rent asunder by the endless geothermal activity. He considered the labyrinth of huge and endlessly deep smoking canyons that were all but impossible to cross. The original roadways had been ripped apart and short stretches effectively relocated by earthquakes, with sections lost entirely into any fathomless abyss that had opened up beneath. Untouched stretches had been reclaimed, as invasive plants took root in the paving and becoming established, forming jungles that entirely absorbed the old highways. Just as his predicament was becoming precarious and fresh water was running short, the tendrils of another swell reached up river, breached the boundaries of the lake and clutched him back into the estuary. In more recent times, as water levels had continued to rise, he heard that the lake had been fully inundated and had become navigable though the narrow entrance was still perilously shallow and could not be accessed at low tide.

On the boat, there were two huge purposeful engines which lurked under a cover deep in the hull of the mid-section and which glittered potently from within. The engines had been unused for as long as he could remember. In the fuel tanks was a small amount of diesel, maybe 30 gallons which he was saving for a time when he would, by necessity, be forced to start the engines but diesel was an luxury almost impossible to obtain. 'White Heron' was obviously capable of great speed, though once again, he didn't know how he knew that. As far as he was able to remember, the engines had never been started. In any event he kept them spotlessly clean and checked fluid levels regularly, engine oil, hydraulic oil and coolant and he kept the many, if aged, deep cycle batteries charged with the wind turbines. The batteries also provided his lighting, power and motivational energy for the electric 'kicker' that hung way down over the deep stern. This was sufficient for gaining momentum in calm waters but useless in a strong current or rough seas. The mighty engines were as mysterious as they were beautiful, glistening alloy and steel, gleaming cast rocker covers, black enameled exhaust manifolds, twin turbochargers, fascinating, mysterious. Where on earth had he obtained the knowledge to understand them and to so expertly work on them? When he reflected upon this for any length of time, he realised that they were, in fact, a complete anathema to him; just like a word that is taken and then repeated out loud time and time again, eventually the word loses all meaning.

The bridge was similarly mysterious, a whole host of levers and controls, the helm was the only place where he felt at home. A flotilla of gauges and flickering lights were his eyes into the workings of the boat along with a semi-operable GPS satellite navigation system and radar, depth sounder and a largely irrelevant but beautiful compass, the inner workings of which were suspended in pure alcohol to remain upright at all times. The galley was extravagantly equipped with all manner of gadgets and cooking utensils. A refrigerator to keep the fish cool, that needed constant power; a stove that needed propane or electricity though there was none. Instead he had built a fire pit on the rear deck from an old forty gallon oil drum with a steel mesh grill which was a wonderful way to cook fish. In the saloon there was a drinks cabinet full of clinking glasses of all types but now quite devoid of any liquor as he had long since drunk what was left of the dregs, with the exception of one unopened bottle of 'Edradour', an aged single malt that he was saving for a special occasion. Oddly, he could not consciously remember ever having drunk the rest but knew that it was he who had exhausted the stock.

In the saloon was a very large flat-screen television that was suspended on a wall above a DVD player. In an adjacent cupboard there were a few DVD's and also CD's to play when the mood took him. He would watch DVD,s and be fascinated by scenes from a world that he felt certain that he had never seen. Great cities, enormous tall buildings, millions of people, roadways covered with vehicles that conveyed people and goods to a myriad of destinations. The people appeared well fed, excessively so in many instances, well groomed, smartly clothed and clean looking. The mariner caught his reflection in the windshield of the bridge. He surveyed his deeply tanned and weathered face with its sunken cheeks, long hair gone wild from lack of attention and the beard of Methuselah. His scanty clothing hung from him in tatters and his feet had been bare for as long as he could recall. He wondered if this strange world that he had seen portrayed on the screen had ever existed and yet, he knew that once upon a time, it had.

Remembering suddenly those images of clean, well shaven men and beautifully attired pretty women, he self consciously sniffed briefly and with distaste, under his arms. Then disrobing his minimal attire and depositing it on the deck, he threw himself from the upper deck into the water with a long, graceful and well practiced dive. Although a little warm, almost tepid, the water was nevertheless refreshing and helped to temper the stifling muggy heat of the day. There was a time, he was certain, when the seawater was a lot more brackish than it was now, water that was so salty that you had to spit it out as soon as you took an unintentional gulp. He remembered also that there had been a higher buoyancy and that he had been able to float easily without having to tread water. Now he had to work harder to stay afloat especially, as his body had become so lean, almost bony. Although he went to nearby rivers to get freshwater supplies the seawater could probably be drunk in dire emergencies without too many ill effects. With that in mind, he paradoxically relieved himself, swimming as he did so, keeping a wary eye open for the giant and highly poisonous jelly fish that inhabited these waters. They could grow to ten feet in diameter and had tentacles that trailed up to sixty feet behind them.

The jellyfish were a recent evolutionary product and were to be avoided at all costs. He had seen men and women who had been stung by these terrifying creatures, scream in agony for hours before finally succumbing to the fatal effects of their corrosive poison. The jellyfish were forbiddingly toxic and contact left the victims skin and whole sections of soft tissue burnt, eaten away and gangrenous, where the lethal tentacles had brushed against them. They would leave an array of dreadful nematocysts that were both exceedingly pathogenic and almost irremovable since they blended with the victims flesh on contact. Swimming in deep water had always been a source of some trepidation for him but now that these decidedly malevolent dwellers of the sea were in such plentiful numbers he took great care. Then, his senses highly attuned to approaching danger, he swam back to 'White Heron' and hauled himself up the ladder at the stern, just in time to see an enormous purple violet dome rising from the depths to where he had been treading water only moments earlier.

The jellyfish had arrived relatively recently and were some diabolical product of evolutionary change as the earth, ruined by mankind, used mother nature to fight back. They had somehow developed as a 'marriage' between their natural predecessors and chemical or natural effluent dumped into the sea by man, They had effectively evolved a differing pattern of DNA which enabled them to absorb some of the ocean borne chemicals and incorporate them into their wholly poisonous structure. This was the main reason why they were so toxic and also very large. Overfishing and the near annihilation of the edible fish who were the natural predators of the jellyfish, meant that they had proliferated and existed now in enormous blooms, sometimes covering hundreds of square miles. Hunters had become the hunted, which was why fish were so hard to come by. The jellyfish sensed animal activity, their subterranean antenna twitching in response and they were attracted to animal life rather like a wasp is attracted to citrus fruit or a tick attracted to body heat. The oceans were certainly no longer a safe place to be.

After an unusual and surpringly successful days fishing, he decided to head for the closest community with whom he could trade. There were indeed others like him, people who had clung tenaciously to life and who had formed small communities, tribes which helped to ensure greater safety. He called them 'his people' though in truth he really did not belong anywhere, spending little time with others and only when he wanted to trade. He raised sails that were also a homemade addition to this sleek anachronistic craft and after a moments thought, engaged the 'kicker' to aid the sails that were struggling to properly fill from the lank sultry breeze. It was high time to do some bartering. As an afterthought, he decided that he wanted also to take an uncharacteristic detour to a place, an area, that held a kind of fatal fascination for him, a special place to which he had not been for some years.

The sun had fallen to the east and was far less intense but the resultant increase in humidity made breathing a typically laborious process and kept the temperature at a far from comfortable level. As the boat motored noiselessly up river, he studied a green tinged roadway shimmering in the watery depths beneath his boat, that emerged finally on land approximately forty feet or so from his starboard side and then disappeared into jungle. Either side of him towered the remains of a couple of structures whose origins started way down below in the invisible murky depths. He manoeuvred through an island of plastic bottles, corroding pop and beer cans and other flotsam carelessly discarded by a former civilization and rounded up by ocean currents. Then he studied the trash abstractedly, accepting that it had always been a part of his life but ignorant as he was of the past, he wondered where it had all come from. He shut off the power to prevent the propeller from becoming fouled by the detritus and was attempting to navigate using a large wooden oar to fend off waterlogged tree stumps and large pieces of floating garbage. He ruminated again for a moment on the water-borne trash, a monument to consumerism, a past age when industry spewed such vast quantities of material whether edible, cosmetic or utilitarian, that even the containers and packing materials not recycled had progressively clumped together. None of this stuff would decompose and was carried therefore by the winds, oceans and river currents and then sucked into innumerable tidal vortexes or dead zones where the waste formed enormous islands.

He had not been to this place for many years, not since being stranded at a time when the water levels were much lower. His memory, atrophied through a pragmatic lack of necessity, became suddenly triggered by the scene and the place. Through the blanket fog of his mind, recollections started to bubble up to the surface like the effervescence of some deep submarine galvanic activity. A mind latterly almost numb and incapable of sensation, of pain, was suddenly suffused with a billion-fold cocktail of conflicting emotions. This flood of reminiscences and thoughts became the emissaries of great hurt, as forgotten sensations and ideas that had been carefully buried, came back to haunt him. Like the heroin addict going cold-turkey and once again being able to suffer and to feel after months or even years of sensory deprivation and the abdication of his soul, so too did he recoil and flinch. He had stayed away from this place for a long time and did not really want to return but something compelled him. An elemental, a being of his super conscious had recently been whispering to him, enticing, pleading and urging him to visit the lake and he really had no idea why. In truth, a beautiful but painful sense of nostalgia beckoned to him.

Even as the sun was setting and the mosquitos had come out in their billions, it was almost 100 degrees and exhaustingly humid. He worked up even more of a sweat as he guided the boat into the stifling millpond calm of the lagoon. As he drew closer to the object of his fascination, his level of fear was forgotten as his excitement increased. His awareness of what it was that he was heading for evoked a further flood of recollections. The landmark was something that he had honestly never expected to find, never dreamed would still exist. Through the island of trash in this murky and dismal lagoon poked some majestic branches of an old oak tree. It was completely dead but still standing like a monument, almost as if it were petrified for eternity, the tree was entirely unbowed, as proud in its mummified form as it had been during its prime.

He sat on the stern section of the boat and attempted to grab a hold of one of the branches, when he noticed what he perceived to be an inscription, crudely carved into the wood, although time and decay had rendered it all but illegible. He had climbed the tree and read it once long ago but the secrets of that occasion were still locked away in the deepest recesses of his mind. He tried to read it again but then for some reason he turned his newly awakened mind to his life partner, someone he had met far too late in life and whom he had buried at the foot of this very tree. This event had taken place many years before the waters had risen and had engulfed her burial site along with a nearby building and most of trunk.

" Ahh Jessica where are you now? Such a tragic end to so beautiful a person." Now he understood why his memories had forsaken him for so long, why he avoided this place.

Suddenly he felt that it was time to get away, to go home, wherever that was and he prepared to set sail, his eyes falling for a moment on his days catch. Then he turned to a large black and exquisitely glossy Raven who had just returned from a flight from who knows where, with a rusty beer tin in his beak. A very muscular and sleek marmalade cat emerged from under a small upturned boat on the fore deck, after a day of being asleep;

" Well! Umm, gentlemen, looks like we will be dining on fish tonight, I do hope that this will be acceptable fare to you both? I only wish that it could be accompanied by a crisp, chilled Chardonnay"

Just then, a lone solitary rat with a stunted tail scurried out from a hidey hole, stopped for a moment to sit on his haunches and sniff the air. He too divined the distinct impression that he would be dining on fish yet again but then made haste as William prepared once more to pounce on the hapless rodent, a game, a routine that was re-enacted umpteen times daily.

The effort of manoeuvreing the boat out of the lagoon was laborious and caused the sweat to run into his eyes. Overheated and exhausted by unsolicited memories in the sultry evening oppressiveness, he craved the beer that was once inside the tin that was in the Ravens beak. Gasping for breath he cried out inadvertently to the only one who really should listen;

" A cold beer would be nice and a little breeze if that could be arranged. C'mon, how about it, just this once eh?"

But God wasn't going to cooperate that day and despite Father Donovan's ordination long ago, God never really had!

CHAPTER 14

Jessica found herself reaching out to take the joint from Julia without really knowing why, it was so oddly out of character and not her scene at all. She had never liked the idea of marijuana but the wine, good company and the excitement of the moment had lowered her resistance and broken down her defenses. All those years of opportunity at school and then at university but the shadow of her conventional father had barred the way. Julia delighted in repeating a Timothy Leary quote;
" Reality is a refuge for people who can't handle drugs."
Jessica giggled and then she belched, looked a little shocked momentarily and then giggled again. However, the music was mesmerizing and with the influence of the marijuana, the perennial clutter of her conscious mind was quieted and she was taken on a joyride to an unknown realm on the fringe of her subconscious. Somehow, ironically, her thoughts became more ordered and effortless; she lost her inhibitions and experienced a heightening of her sensibilities. The vast impregnable wall of her credibility barrier began to dissolve, first at the edges like an old vinyl record tossed onto a bonfire and then came the delicious sense of some higher awareness. Julia was silent for some time, pondering, but also giving Jessica time to relax.

There was a period of absolute stillness and total serenity despite the ambient music; but then a female voice originating from somewhere in the room, powerful and invasive;

" There's a lovely William Blake quote, ' I must create a system or be enslaved by another man's.' Well I for one wholeheartedly agree, we must all follow our intuition and not allow ourselves to be swayed by external forces or doctrines."

Jessica listened, unable to do otherwise and noted that the seemingly distant echoic quality of the voice suddenly became clear.

"What I am talking about Jess, is just my interpretation, my own awareness, which may not fit in with yours, as we all have our own ideas and beliefs that we resonate with."

Jessica nodded, she loved it when Julia got to this stage of eulogising upon a topic of which she was so passionate. In the past Jessica had laughed at Julia's eccentric take on the world but now she listened apparently spellbound;

'she was indeed becoming enslaved herself!'

"Time is a concept of the physical being, it is a convenient and necessary marker of a process of events that have been, are and will be. By marooning ourselves in this earthbound single dimensional plane, we have relinquished the awareness of unfettered thought and movement and have created boundaries which prevent us from being free. Jess darling, are you with me?"

The voice, distant was an echo again, then suddenly close and urgent.

"Oh yes, good heavens, rather! Rapt attention I'd say, it is jolly interesting, do go on?"

Julia laughed.

" Jess, you really are quite stoned aren't you? I can tell by the silly expression on your face, you'll be saying 'jolly hockey sticks' next." There was a moment of mirth, then all of a sudden, she did not want to be labeled as 'stoned'. The mere concept of this thought suddenly brought her down to earth with a painful bump, a place from which she had escaped probably for the first time in her life and she had tasted freedom.

" No no, please Jools, do go on, I'm a bit out of my depth, it's not my realm as you know but I like to listen to you."

"Time has to be measured chronologically but in fact time does vary, even if the atomic standards say that it doesn't.

" I'm sorry Jules you've lost me there, a standard is a standard."

A moment of lucidity, a satellite of thought, an interlude of painful clarity came from god knows what diabolic recess of her mind.

"Okay, say you are waiting at home, unable to go anywhere because you are expecting a repairman to fix the hot tub or the dryer? He will arrive at some undefined point in the day because he couldn't give a precise time for his visit. Or, you are in a class for religious studies, I remember how much you hated religious studies!"

Jessica felt the tendrils of reality snaking into her being and took another hit on the joint and swigged some more wine from the bottle. The pragmatist was being set free for fear that her mortal soul was in peril; freedom finally identified and embraced. She never wanted to let this feeling go.

"Okay, I'm all ears."

" Then compare that to a time when you had a particularly gruesome and curious forensic case and the corpse of a mysteriously mutilated person to study."

Jessica did recall a case that appeared to have been an example of spontaneous human combustion which she truly did not believe could happen. She had told Julia of this at the time as she had become so fascinated by the subject.

" I remember you saying that you had stayed up all night working on that case and that you were amazed to have discovered that whereas, you thought only a couple of hours had passed, in fact you had spent all night, nearly ten hours working without a break. I remember you saying that you did not know where the time had gone, well it literally sped up; the intervals of time measurement actually contracted, became smaller; you time travelled girl. In comparison, the religious studies class seemed to take hours when the lessons were only thirty minutes long; the wait for the washing machine man was interminable except that in fact he came earlier than you expected."

Jessica was tempted to interject, to protest but stifled the impulse and was actually incapable of being present. Julia continued;

"As far as we know, 'time' is variable depending on our state of consciousness. Chronology means nothing. We live in a world of time that is speeding up because there is a thirst for knowledge that is creating an impetus for increasing awareness. Look at us, thirty thousand years or thereabouts and most of the most amazing advances and events have occurred in the last hundred years and this is a phenomenon that is speeding up exponentially."

Jessica could see where this was going but was fidgeting, suddenly uncomfortable.

"Sorry Jools but I have to pee."

That distant sensation which had just nagged for a while was suddenly all too imperative.

"Sorry, I really don't mean to interrupt but nature calls rather desperately and the clock is ticking," she added grinning inanely like a naughty school girl.

Jessica sat on the loo, knickers around her ankles, studying a most beautiful and elaborate spiders web that glinted in the evening sunlight and she was absorbed for a 'timeless' period. Through the fug, the sense of what Julia had been saying gradually breached her credibility barriers and enveloped her. Suddenly she was back in the room with Julia and didn't even remember leaving the bathroom.

'How did I get here?'

She was gripped by a spurious and sudden presence of mind.

"Alright Jools, sorry about that, I hope I didn't break the flow, it does sound jolly fascinating."

"Okay, we take this one stage further and leave the body behind and enter the domain of Spirit." Julia's voice became huge, it dominated the room, a solid mass of sound like an enormous monolith.

" As Spirit, we encompass all of time, are able to experience the past, present and future simultaneously. We don't age, we just 'are'. As a mortal being we see reality in tiny chunks, little pieces of measured 'time' but as spirit we see it all. Here's an example, if you take a holographic image and then take a tiny piece of that image and examine it, what will be revealed will be the whole image intact."

Jessica nodded her head in agreement because she was on a firmer footing with holograms. She smiled at Julia who had become so absorbed in her subject and was so earnest.

Julia's voice was comforting and although Jessica was listening, it was as if she were dreaming, as if she she had entered the domain of her subconscious.

"Humanity has always striven for singularity, they have a need to understand in order to feel more secure. Paracelsus, a Greek alchemist, had an expression which represented what he felt was the start of it all which was 'prima materia.'

Basically, that everything has its origin in a pile of shit. I know what he meant; that we all started from chaos, and thence to chaotic physicality and then a burgeoning grasp of reality!"

Jessica was past caring, she reached for the joint again, a fresh one recently lit. She was dispassionate, lost in a world of semi-reality. Sensations, not thoughts swept in upon her like the waves of the ocean and then suddenly, out of nowhere came an incongruous notion.

" God Julia can be so literal sometimes, North Americans are so wrapped up in analysis! Life is beautiful, hapless poetry. Hold on a moment, who's the dreamer here, me or her, I'm not thinking straight."

Julia paused for a moment as if reading Jessica's thoughts. "Did you ever come across a book by John Wyndham called 'The Midwich Cuckoos?'

" Well, I know of it, I know he wrote 'The Day of the Triffids'?"

Julia continued as if she had not heard Jessica, "Basically, it was about a bunch of kids that appeared in a small town. They were separate people and with separate consciousness but were simultaneously connected and aware of each others thoughts and feelings. Well this is what I feel about us as individuals and as a collective. We think, so we create and in thinking and creating, we create not only our own reality but contribute to the one great consciousness. It is the essence of creation for the particles to join and become one but still remain as particles; the complex bacteriological structure of the human organism being a perfect example."

Jessica, by this stage was becoming too inebriated to care but nodded anyway.

"Having said all this, at the end of the day, we seek to rationalise by converting feelings, thoughts and emotions into words which is an inadequate process to say the least. If you don't mind my saying so at the risk of sounding a tad preachy, you do have a tendency to rationalise a little too much and this might perhaps demean or even undermine your experience. There is so much more to learn and 'receive' if you don't halt the process with your mind."

Jessica noted that Julia said 'process' in the American way when she was stoned as in 'prossess' rather than proessess.

"A deeper understanding will come of this, I am sure. I am only speaking from my own limited experience so don't assume that I know anything. However, think of your life and experiences as the very essence of a beautiful poem and not as individual words. I'm really boring you aren't I?"

Julia stopped at this point with a sudden quizzical look on her face. Jessica became aware that a wall of noise like the sound of many voices in an echoing school room had suddenly gone; there was utter cold silence. She felt compelled to speak to fill the silence but desperately wanted to go to bed, they seemed to have been talking for hours.

"What is it that you truly wish for Jess, tell me as I have a feeling, a sense that you are searching."

" You'll think I'm mad."

" This is me Jess, your absolute best friend so don't be silly." There was a brief pause and then Jessica spoke, suddenly very earnest.

" I know this must sound ridiculous but I feel such a connection with this man, Lucius Grey! I want to get to know him, I've never felt like this before Jools, I have never had experiences like this before, my life has always been so ordered and so bloody boring!"

Then Jessica started to weep, tears welled up in the corners of her eyes and trickled warmly down the sides of her face.

They were interrupted by sound of the door creaking, heralding the tentative appearance of John who entered clutching his motorcycle magazine looking a little bleary eyed.

" You know I've just found the most fascinating article on a wildly fast Norton that has a Horrocks Supercharger fitted; you girls having fun?"

He walked over to his chair and sat down, oblivious. Jessica was jolted back to reality, she wiped her eyes feeling suddenly vulnerable wanting to creep away to bed.

"I'm sorry John, it's nothing you said but I'm so tired after a brutal and draining week and have had far too much to drink and I need to sleep." Jessica rose, a little unsteady on her feet and headed for the stairs.

"Night night Jess, sleep well." He blew her a goodnight kiss and got back to his motorcycle magazine. Julia stood up too and hugged her warmly.

" Sleep well Jess darling, I will bring you some tea in the morning. Are you sure you want to be woken up early, I warn you, it'll be very early?"

Jessica mumbled acquiescence as she had asked to be called when Julia woke up, she didn't want to miss anything.

Jessica hardly remembered getting into bed other than the sense of contact with extremely cold but crisp sheets as she climbed into a single Victorian bed with both head and foot boards and she sank into an exquisitely soft mattress. Once inside the covers, a delightful sense of warmth and comfort rose up from her feet in all enveloping waves and she quickly fell into a deep sleep. As she entered the realm of dream, forces were already at work that were going to take Jessica from her path of convention and safety and that her life was about to change very significantly. Paradoxically, she was about to wake up in fact.

CHAPTER 15

Jessica found herself in a strange but beautiful place. The air was rich and vibrant, a fresh, sumptuous smell of damp earth and verdant greenery assailed her senses. The birdsong was prolific and almost deafening, a myriad of exotic sounds, sad, argumentative and jubilant. Indeed they were the sounds of life, a life of bewilderingly rich variance and quite devoid of the clutter of mechanisation. Her surroundings were fresh and invigorating and the earth voluptuous and positively sizzling with life force.

A horse stood nearby, a bay, curious, friendly; ears pricked forward in greeting and flanks gently steaming. Jessica walked up to the the horse who exuded a scent so typically equine that was both heady and seductive. She stroked his muzzle and he snorted happily, blowing warm air and water droplets onto her as he gently nuzzled her neck. A dog, quite wolf like but with hetero-chromic eyes, one blue, one brown and also with ears erect and alert to all sounds, sat nearby, panting and smiling. He jumped up and made off into the woods, obviously responding to something which demanded his immediate attention. He re-emerged a few moments later accompanied by a man who smiled at Jessica as he approached. She found herself deep in conversation with this man who introduced himself as Dewin. He was a druid but to outward appearances he resembled a priest or cleric of the Christian church. He wore a simple dark brown rough woollen habit with a hood draped around his shoulders and carried a long wooden staff upon which he leaned. As he bent forwards, Jessica glimpsed deep blue tattoos, the colour of woad upon his chest and shoulders. He was handsome and well proportioned though, strangely, Jessica's attraction was something akin to maternal pride as she gazed upon this young man as they spoke.

Jessica spoke no languages other than English, flawed Hindi and halting French and yet she found that she was conversing effortlessly with a man who was speaking a language she hardly recognised at all. Without resorting to sign language or any other medium, she simply spoke and listened and yet somehow there was perfect communication, as though they were at the Tower of Babel. Dewin told Jessica that he had an important task to perform and he suggested that she accompany him and sit under the canopy of the oak. She indeed felt compelled to watch over him as he worked. The young man dug a deep hole in which to bury a large metal chest that was ornate, heavy and impermeable. He buried the chest reverently and at a considerable depth, six feet or more as though it were a corpse. He then covered the burial site with rich soft earth, tragically flattening many bluebells that were unfortunately trodden into the earth.
"No secrets are safe under Norman rule. The chest must be hidden as it contains a great treasure, not of material value but a key pertaining to how the land of Albion or more recently, Britannia, will evolve in the future."
Jessica realised that she was being put in a position of great trust.
" I don't know who you are or where you have come from but I know I am strangely compelled to reveal the truth to you, to tell you that this land is more than just a small island in the middle of the Atlantic ocean."

Then as if spurred on by the revelation, he continued;
"Albion was an isolated and mystical land, a final refuge for
those few who remained of a once great civilization that
existed many thousands of years before on an island
continent that is no more. They had been driven from their
home by a great cataclysmic event. This disaster," he
continued, "changed the face of the world, covered it in ice
and created a wobble in the planet's yearly orbital circuit
around the sun that led to the concept and form of seasons.
Jessica listened intently, drawn in by his revelations.
Dewin looked at her for a moment, as if trying to make his
mind up about something.
" I am going to give you a brief history lesson, as I think it
may help you on your quest."
"Okay, I'd love to know more?"
"Well as the refugees made a new land for themselves, they
sought to protect themselves in a wholly non-confrontational
way by avoiding all contact with man, their distant cousins in
the rest of the world. These people were both physical yet
elemental, powerful in a mystical sense and able to live in
harmony with nature. They travelled between worlds and
traversed universes, unimpeded by boundaries. They were
physically small, dark, elf like and though not strong in a
physical sense, were able to evade capture by disappearing
into the mists.

"Albion was once a part of mainland Europe but was cut-
off at the end of the last ice-age partly by design, these early
inhabitants retained enough of their mystical abilities that
they were indeed able to influence the forces of nature to
enable them to make Albion an island and a natural fortress.
It was they who constructed the great pyramids in other parts
of the world and later, the circles of standing stones in

Albion, using no more than sound to move the massive monoliths. The pyramids were built as amplifiers so that their power increased exponentially. They could create cataclysmic earthquakes and tidal waves a mile high if they chose to do so. The island was made safe for thousands of years but finally invaders came across the seas, greedy for the treasures of this land. At first it was the Celtii, a warlike and fearsome people originating from the east. In some respects they were very different from the island people but they also had great similarities; they had a caste system, females were traditionally afforded the same privileges and positions as males, though they took differing roles to which the abilities of the sexes were more suited. Though the Celtii were deeply steeped in battle especially amongst each other, they were strangely peaceable with the local indigenous people and honoured them as the original inhabitants, as mystics, philosophers and deities. They lived in harmony and even learned from one another; the Celts were such good craftsmen that they were admired and appreciated by the Pretanni, as the locals became known. In time the Celts were welcomed as people with whom the Pretanni co-habited and then many were assimilated from both sides. The Celts benefited from the mystical structure of the Pretanni and indeed, ultimately took over to become guardians of the land as in many ways they were better suited to the task. The whole druid caste, that is so peculiar to the British Isles, was one created by the assimilation of mystical and philosophical customs from the Pretanni by the Celts. Basically the safekeeping of the island was left to the Druids and the Celtic peoples as the Pretanni retreated more and more and traveled into other domains. I myself am from a line of both Druid priests and philosophers and also of the Pretanni line of mystics though I have not their great power. I am here to assist in the protection of this small island."

" Why would you want to protect this land from overseas immigrants?" Jessica asked; " Look at me, surely you've noticed that I'm one of them?"
" No you belong here far more than you realise. We have a system that works, we have a culture that is magical and we have a land that has benefited from thousands of years of occupation by us and has indeed become a blessed place and our true home now that we have no other. Nevertheless, we are losing it, first the Romans came and raped and pillaged and then slaughtered the mystics. Then the Angles and the Saxons and the Vikings did likewise. For a time we had a Champion, a great King of mixed but old blood who was able to draw upon his skills as a warrior and his abilities as a sorcerer. With his powerful Druid ally, he almost succeeded in expunging the Saxons and partially reclaimed the land from the Romans to give back to the people. He had many powerful advisors and a half sister who indeed, was herself one of the line of Pretanni. Sadly for us all, he was finally undone, betrayed and fatally wounded by his son whose name was Mordred. He was a tragic result of the union between Pretanni and Celt gone wrong for he had power and ability which was out of balance with his lust for power and control. And now the worst has happened, the Normans have come and we finally have to accept that we are unable to protect our diminishing habitat any longer, we are effectively doomed to be subdued, dominated and assimilated. My father was a respected druid, Derryth was his name and he was indeed a wise man and a true magician of the old world. It was he who planted this beautiful and mystical oak tree as

part of a great invocation. His intention was to set events in motion that would, one day, bring this land back to us."

"You tell a pretty story," replied Jessica, "But I am merely dreaming aren't I? You don't really exist, I'm tucked up in bed, although I believe I might have been here once before?"

"Yes indeed you are here in this physical space! You have accessed these worlds as we do because that is your destiny. The blood of the Druid and Pretanni sing in your veins and we have reached out to you from the past. You have experienced much that is inexplicable and have just begun to uncover the truth of your destiny as until now, you have been asleep in an eternal dreamless sleep. There is another with whom we have made a connection though he is less open than you and is living in a different time domain, sadly his life is destined to be tragically short."

"I'm just a half caste girl from Sussex who is a scientist and doesn't believe in all of this and why should I? This other person, who is he anyway?"

"You have no choice and now you have seen where I have buried the chest. Besides which, if you were truly a scientist then this would all seem quite in order. The other person that I have spoken of is of no consequence to you at this moment but you will find out sooner or later as fate dictates and the mystery unfold, as it shall at the appropriate time."

Jessica looked over to the base of the tree.

" It doesn't seem like a very good hiding place, look at the heap of fresh soil, the trampled flowers, the scar that has been left?"

" What scar, what disturbed earth?"

She looked again and to her astonishment saw that the ground was as it had been before Dewin had dug the earth, bluebells intact, a radiant blue sheen basking in the sunshine, an undisturbed cluster at the base of the oak tree with bees droning in hazy industry all around.

" Aha!" she said, that is indeed a cunning and glamorous ploy."

The comment was incongruous, ridiculous in fact, this didn't sound like the kind of thing that people normally said but this was a very surreal event.

It was then that the realisation came upon her that this was a dream, a pure fantasy. Reading her thoughts, Dewin remarked;

" Yes of course this must seem like fantasy, how else did you imagine that you were going to bridge the gap of nearly one thousand years. We, you especially, are physical beings separated by the obstacle of time. The only way we can communicate is to eliminate the physical boundaries. You are a pagan you know, a person who worships the elementals of the universe in all their forms who does not adhere to the belief that there is only one God."

" Didn't think I was anything really, I rejected the rank hypocrisy of Christianity, didn't like Hinduism or any religion for that matter; I never could stomach dogma. As I see it, we are borne, we eat, sleep, defecate, urinate and we procreate and then die answering only to the rules of nature, no less and no more. I am not, as I have mentioned, remotely religious."

"Nor am I but we are here aren't we, talking, enjoying the spring sunshine."

As he spoke, he walked to a nearby apple tree and removed an impressive though patently unripe fruit. He cut it up with a knife, giving a chunk to the horse who wrinkled back his lips and took the proffered apple with obvious glee.

" He'll get colic. Unripe apples are not good for horses."

Then she felt stupid because of course, this young man would have a far greater understanding of horses then she could ever have.

" No he won't. The apple is quite ripe, here try this."

She bit into the fruit and was both incredulous and delighted, it was not only ripe but it tasted glorious, the best she had ever eaten.

"You came to me for enlightenment, do you think you have achieved this?"

" Did I? I don't really know to be honest, you were not the person I was looking for as far as I know. I really don't understand the significance of the buried chest or of meeting you for that matter."

" No, but as I have said, you will. It may not seem that this discourse has any relevance to you but it does, as you will soon find out."

"Could you perhaps tell me what is in the chest please?"

"Unfortunately not."

" Oh..., why not?"

" Because you are dreaming of course............!"

Jessica rubbed her eyes as she awoke, in an attempt to gain a clearer view of the world she knew as quickly as possible.

'That was such an amazing dream, what can it all mean?'

She was reluctant to let the atmosphere of the dream fade away but little bits and pieces of information filtered through the morass of her barely awakened consciousness and she realised, after a moment that she was in Julia's spare bedroom. Jessica felt out of sorts; various fragments, recollections of the previous night came into her mind and she squirmed with embarrassment.

'Oh God, that's the last time I behave so stupidly, me smoking pot- Oh my God, how hideous!'

Then the dream took prominence again, overriding her sense of shame. Even though it was still dark and painfully early, she reached for a pen and paper, wanting to write everything down as Julia had suggested but she was rendered inert for a moment as a feeling nausea swept over her. Jessica lay still in bed, the world spinning, as chronic vertigo held her in a billious grip. Then as things settled, she reached again for the pen and paper and scribbled rough notes while lying on her back. Already she was losing the more subtle details and wanted to capture as much as possible before this dream, like so many others, was dispatched to some forgotten corner of her subconscious, only to lie dormant there for the rest of her life.

Julia, keeping to her promise, knocked on her door, breezing in, full of the joys of Spring, leaving in her wake a pleasantly fresh aroma of toothpaste, lipstick and soap. She was holding a tray upon which was a plate of home baked cookies, a large cup and saucer and a teapot of steaming chai tea. Jessica could not help but wrinkle her nose in slight disgust,

" Good morning Honey, did you sleep well?"

" I have to tell you that I had the oddest dream, do you think it was something to do with the marijuana?"

"It is possible, actually very likely in fact but I have to run Sweety, it's my turn to do the milking and I'm late but tell me about it later okay, don't forget any details!"

Jessica held up her notebook, opened onto a page of spidery hieroglyphics. She lay in bed eating the biscuits and drinking the chai tea, marvelling that she actually felt better with each sip. She luxuriated in the warmth of the bed for a while in the semi-darkness, at the dawn of a truly beautiful and very still morning. Looking out through a crack in the bedroom curtains, she could just make out ghostly and ethereal silhouetted shapes high up in the sky which were thinly scattered cumulus humilis cloud formations. They were almost black against a deep blue firmament that progressively lightened and glowed with a stirring carmine on the eastern horizon.

Even with the prospect of another complete day off, Jessica was aware, with a kind of nagging dread, that she was expected back at work the following day. Two days previously, she would have felt quite differently. She would have been looking forward to returning to work as an attractive alternative to a freezing bedroom and fields of mud. Now she felt that the weekend was slipping away and she was so looking forward to talking about her dream with Julia. She feared yet yearned for the truth of possible revelation. There was, however, trepidation on Jessica's part, as though Pandora's box was about to burst open.

It was still early, being one of those beautiful days of crystal clarity where there is a promise of warmth once the morning mist has burnt away. Jessica was torn between staying in bed and going back to sleep or dragging herself up and striding out on a 'purposeful walk'. The former idea was the far more attractive proposition but she knew that she would bitterly regret missing such a magical opportunity. Julia would be busy for a couple of hours and so this would be the perfect time for her to revisit the lake in solitude She had so enjoyed her slightly chaotic outing with Julia and the children the previous day but now she needed time on her own away from the lovely but disorderly household so that she could think. She decided to go back to the lake remembering how beautiful such places could be in the misty early morning light and as she showered and brushed her teeth, she became very animated at the prospect of going there again. Somehow, she felt, the lake would help her to process the empty, unresolved sensations that she had been dealing with since discovering the message carved into the tree branch.

She quickly dressed, putting on a warm jacket in anticipation of a bracing walk on this chill mid-September morning. John was obviously up and about and tending to his chores, judging by the crumb littered bread board, opened jar of organic marmalade, jug of milk left on the counter and a still warm coffee pot on the stove. Wishing suddenly to escape, Un-noticed, Jessica crept through the front door, putting on her boots while sitting on the front step. She strode purposefully across the farmyard and through the apple orchard and then onto the path that she knew would take her to the lake. There wouldn't be an awful lot of time before the household was in its usual state of pandemonium, when the children were up and about and demanding all sorts. Jessica wanted to be back in time for breakfast to spend time with the family, making the most of them as she was only too painfully aware that she was leaving later in the day. Staying with Julia was always noisy, cold, fraught, uncomfortable and muddy but Jessica had to admit that she came alive during these visits and then realised with a sudden wave of deepening discomfort just how dull her life really was.

CHAPTER 16

Lucius Grey awoke feeling very uncomfortable, stifled and gasping for breath; he quickly ripped the lice ridden blanket away. He had pulled it up to cover his head in the night to keep out the ever predatory mosquitos and as a result, his body and clothing were saturated with sweat. What was left of the lake at Mortlac, after which the facility had been named, had become a sort of open sewer for the prison and was therefore the perfect breeding ground for countless air borne parasites. Lucius found himself to be in what he perceived, initially, to be a completely alien environment. He rubbed his eyes then held his head in his hands.

" My goodness, what an extraordinary and singular experience."

Though almost awake, the vivid atmosphere of the dream remained with him and was almost entirely intact in its detail. The normal attenuation that so affects and drains away those nocturnal visions within minutes of waking, seemed not to have had the usual impact. He contemplated the memories and the details, dwelling on the oddities of a reality that had appeared relatively normal at the time but which were impossibly surreal from his waking perspective. Lucius observed Septimus, who was sitting boldly upon the floor without a care, he was thinking of his twin in that spectral place of illusion. He addressed his ally, the dry croaky quality of his own voice startling him for a moment:

"It does seem to me that I have become very prone to these diurnal phantasms. Quite why I should be having these experiences at this rather precarious point in my life is a mystery, what can it all mean Septimus?"

The rat on the floor by Lucius' bed continued to sit on his haunches. In his frighteningly human but very miniature hands, he held a morsel of bread, the remainder of a piece that Lucius had let him have the night before. He looked up with beady inscrutable eyes, his whiskers twitching as he sampled the air, permanently on the look out for danger or for food or both. Suddenly and without preamble, he scurried away to his hiding place among a labyrinth of passageways accessible only to creatures of his size. Lucius, still half asleep, looked around for his feline companion. As he bridged the chasm between sleep and consciousness, there was still the sense of a large cat lying comfortably next to his leg but when he raised himself up on one arm and rubbed sleep from his eyes and looked around there was no evidence of a gritty hollow on the prison blanket, the weighty and vibratory warmth he had experienced so vividly, quickly faded into the obscurity of the twilight dream world; the illusion had seemed so real.

He was not sure of the time but had an awareness that he had slept later than normal, a curious event indeed given that this was the day of his execution. Upon retiring the previous night, nervous and in an understandable state of extreme trepidation, he had tossed and turned restlessly. Scenarios had flitted persistently into being in his hyper-excited and anguished state of mind. Even when he did fall into fitful sleep, the scenarios simply jumped the slender threshold from conscious to subconscious and taunted him anew. In the early hours of the morning, he had started to think of his times on board ship, happy times during his merchant days. In those days, his face was deeply but unfashionably tanned from constant exposure to the sun and his body was honed by the vigorous daily work and with these happy memories he had finally fallen into a deep sleep. It was then that he had experienced the amazing dream. The world he had entered was hostile, alien, impossibly hot and barren. He was aboard some strange craft in the otherworld though his role as skipper was not so very unfamiliar. Lucius could not think for the life of him, an unfortunate choice of words indeed, why he should want sleep at all, what was the point? Why would he need to be so well rested in order to survive the rigors of the day, an execution by public hanging? Sleep wasn't simply rest to Lucius but was instead a recourse, a submission of his being, where he could gain access to all that was denied him in his waking state and his currently miserable conditions. His life, his travels on board his beloved ship, his encounters with natives and his knowledge gained from meetings with shamanic priests had changed him and his previously pragmatic existence. He had come to believe that this reality was a hologram, a perspective of one reality. Lucius was a dreamer, had always been so. He was a man for whom the world held no great allure and this had made him a seeker, open to the influence of other realms. Even his impending execution, unjust though it was, did not present any great fear to him. Ever since the fateful day when he was accused of the murder of his beloved Georgina shortly after hearing the news of her demise, followed by his subsequent conviction, he had lost his love of life. To surrender at this impasse, presented the exciting prospect of being able to start again, to live another life. He had tactically withdrawn from his life in order to gain insight into another and in that presumption he was more correct than he had any right to realise.

Lucius' last long introspective gaze fell upon the tree, he loved the beautiful oak. He admired its mighty flanks, the billions of leaves, the mystery of its thousandfold acorns and the tenacity with which it gripped the soil with its deeply embedded roots and subsequently life. Lucius thought back to his vision that previous night and was aware that, even in death and mostly submerged in water, the tree had refused to give up, had steadfastly held its immortal grasp of terra-firma. For a moment he felt ashamed at giving up on his own life but he wasn't giving up, not at all, he just desired that 'this' life be brought to a satisfactory conclusion. He felt a kinship with the tree, as though he and the oak were bonded in some way, their fates intertwined. Briefly a vision of the sylvan glade by the lake shore came to him; the vibrant and healthy young sapling so recently planted by the druid, with a long and portentious life ahead of it. Then this vision was replaced by another, of the mighty but denuded limbs of a dead oak tree reaching to him from the depths of a flooded plane. It seemed to Lucius in his fanciful state, that the tree was pleading for his help, was communicating with him somehow. There was an intent inherent within the tree, a deep, abiding and desperate urge to remain intact, to remain standing for all time or at least until Lucius saw what it was that he was supposed to see. He recalled for some reason, the North American Innukshuk, structures made by the northern Indian tribes, the 'Inuit'. They stacked the stones until they resembled a symbolic form of a standing man. They were simply points of navigation as observed pragmatically, by scholars of the day but Lucius always felt that there was

more to an Innukshuk than simply being a marker. They were reminders of mans ability to survive in that harsh environment. He felt that these were catalysts for a philosophy necessary in the arctic environment to help the populous transcend the basic needs of daily survival. They helped people to see the bigger picture by opening their minds to the staggering array of possibilities for their reality. Lucius continued to look at the tree, lost in a reverie.
'What can it all mean, I know I am being told something, some vital facet of my fate and I am simply too obtuse to see it. Maybe these visions will continue for a while longer, perhaps beyond the very grave? Maybe only then will I understand!'

The crowd outside was gathering and full of morbid interest; he likened them to opportunist hyenas awaiting the imminent birth of a newborn antelope calf. Lucius observed that they were filled with an eerie and incomprehensible blood lust. The hypocrisy of the degenerate nature of their own harsh and precarious lives in that Victorian era of raw survivalism, could be swept under the carpet for a time in a frenzy of self righteous indignation. Onlookers to the government sanctioned murder of a man accused of taking the life of another, were awaiting that moment when justice would be satisfactorily dispensed. Then they would crow and cheer in the reassuring knowledge that the good Lord's work had been done. Murderers must, after all, be punished in mortal existence and then banished to an afterlife of eternal damnation. Although he slept long, until well after sunrise in fact, his execution was not scheduled until midday. The crowd could see him through the barred windows of the prison and they waved clenched fists at him and shouted insults, knowing nothing about him, they would in most cases have found him to be a very moderate and likeable man, had they not been consumed by zealous judgment. Strangely, in that time, humanity had never grasped the ironic concept that murder could also be sanctioned by the ambassadors of Holy precepts as a good thing! That many of those worthy men who had been accepted into military service were just as guilty of mortal sin and more so, as Lucius truly was innocent of the crime in any event.

Shortly after he had completed his toilette, he had been brought his last meal, a repast that for once, he did not have to pay for; the identity of the thoughtful benefactor being a mystery to him. It was a substantial platter containing a bowl of porridge with a liberal sprinkle of cream and sugar, poached eggs, kidneys, still warm bread fresh from the bakery, a generous pat of butter, coffee in a silver jug and sweet meats. At first he had no appetite for any of the victuals left for him but the dream came to him and gave him a glimpse of privation, himself as skin and bone and half starved. A tentative sample of poached egg and toast on a fork rendered him suddenly hungry for more and then he became voracious, stuffing the food down quite without decorum. The egg and porridge dribbled down the sides of his chin and onto the front of his shirt. It was as if he were grabbing at this one chance to nourish himself at the start of a long journey. The food, the mainstay of physical life, had a power to feed him through the ordeal. This was what his disordered imagination and stimulated palette urged him to believe, for there was nothing else left to believe in.

At 11.30am on a beautiful sunny day on the 15th August 1820 AD, he was taken by the guard and ushered gently through the labyrinthine passages of the prison: the guards at least, had grown to admire and respect Lucius and were really not so overjoyed at carrying out their task. He had paid them well but never in a way that implied or demanded subservience. He simply indicated his great appreciation of their friendship and help. He was guided outside through throngs of angry hecklers, then to the gallows that stood facing the glorious oak tree. He was immune to the mob's angry gestures and foul curses and even tolerated the thrown eggs and rotten cabbages with deep forbearance. He felt all alone, deeply desolate and abandoned. A priest and a friend of Constantine Butler had volunteered, unbeknown to the worthy judge, to come and take Lucius' last confession. So convinced was he of Lucius' great guilt, that he desired with obsequious self interest, to take news of the condemned man's secret back to Butler. The priest, full of false piety, sickly compassion and hypocritical kindliness had made a great plea to Lucius. He had urged clarity and candour in Lucius' last moments as it would bode well for his soul in the afterlife should he unburden himself finally of his sins before entering the heavenly realm. Otherwise he would be condemned to eternal damnation in the everlasting fires. Lucius took the priests hand and looked into his eyes. "Bless me father for I have sinned as God alone knows." Just at that moment the priest experienced an unholy sense of victory; he knew he would get his confession from Lucius Grey admitting to the murder of Georgina Brogan. He would then be able to imply to his friend, the judge, without giving details which his ordinance forbade, that the accused man had given himself up to the Lord. If he was able to return to Butler with the news that Lucius had admitted his guilt and had been hanged fairly, he hoped that Butler, whose conscience would no doubt be eased, might look upon him with favour. Maybe he would become Bishop one day? Unfortunately for the self-interested priest this was not to be. " Father forgive me for I cannot confess to a crime that I did not commit, I would sooner burn in hells eternal fires than purger myself by making a false confession. I have nothing to lose Father but please understand, I did not commit this crime for which I am grossly and unjustly accused."

Lucius, standing erect and with great dignity, turned to the crowd, now almost silent with suspense and expectation and then he re-stated the content of his confession, repeating the exact phrase to them. He was not booed and hissed-at for his impertinence other than by a hardened few, sensing the possibility of escape by their prey. People reluctantly recognised an innocent man when they saw and heard one. Meanwhile the priest, who had turned deathly pale, scurried away a beaten and worried man, his plans foiled and his folly shown to him. Lucius was determined to remain composed to the end until he caught a glimpse of his mother and his sister. Despite his resolve, he shed silent desolate tears, not tears for himself but tears of sadness for the plight of his remaining family and for the vacillating inconstancy of mankind. A raven stood on top of the gallows and looked down upon him and the sight of the bird gave him a moments great comfort. *'Hello beautiful creature, have you come to rescue me?* " Christ! These people do need to be saved," he remarked to the bird conspiratorially as the trapdoor fell away. His brief fall was arrested jarringly by the noose around his neck that savagely jerked him to a halt. He wanted a quick death and that particular blessing was acknowledged. Just at the instant of death he experienced a moments elation, even jubilation and knew that he would, in some way, be re-united with Georgina Brogan for eternity.

CHAPTER 17

One of the perennial mysteries of death is that no mortal has any real idea of what happens at the moment of demise. Certainly Lucius, before his own death, was as vague about these matters as the next person. For millennia, men and women have speculated, pondered, theorized and written great treatise on the subject but have failed to reach any universally accepted explanation.

'Is it possible that a lifetime of thoughts, experiences, the rich vitality of consciousness and super-consciousness can be simply removed without the faintest trace?'

Lucius was never terrified of death although predictably apprehensive in the final hours. Even at that brutal moment just before the trapdoor opened, he felt no real fear but instead, surrendered to his fate.

As he dangled from the rope, his sub-conscious mind racing to find a way to extricate himself from the predicament, he did experience some moments of deep and unbearable discomfort. His hands were tied and his automatic reaction to reach up and grab the noose was fruitless. He was vaguely aware of something giving in his shoulder, a muscle or ligament tearing as he struggled with all his might. The hangman's rope by then, had been pulled as taut as a piano wire around his neck. His body was quite beyond his control and he reacted autonomically, kicking and squirming involuntarily but impotently like a rat caught in a trap.

As is typical in a 'hanging', the odontoid peg on the topmost vertebra, the atlas, was severed, had snapped during his violent convulsive movements and the peg was then driven into his brain stem, the start of what was actually a very quick death. Lucius had felt something give, a sickening sensation, a rupture, a sudden surreal separation from pain. A calming warmth enveloped him and a delicious sense of being drawn into a place of oblivion; at the very last a warm balming light suffused his being and then there was no more.

Just as Lucius withdrew from consciousness, as he almost entered the immortal realm of eternal peace, he felt a tug. It was as if someone had rudely grabbed his coat tails as he was leaving a room and he became aware of the same kind of sensation that one has when in the midst of sleeping off a vast excess of alcohol. That refuge when one has withdrawn, where there is nothing but an unending cozy oblivion, but then an insistent shake and loud voices unkindly draw you back into the painful realm of consciousness. Lucius experienced a moment of searing anger, his frustration intolerable. To be so cruelly treated when at last he thought he had found peace was too much. In a kind of nether world of partial cognition and of dubious reality, he experienced vague impressions. Initially he felt contained, as if in a capsule and he was quite unable to move. His mind was also restrained, powerless in the face of his present circumstance to think rationally. There were no prevailing sensations, no sound, no vision and no light. Lucius was trapped in limbo for what seemed an eternity. As time passed, he became aware of a sensation of heat, of light, a curious sensation of absorbing moisture and of 'swelling'. It was the strangest and most unexpected sense but not really unpleasant. Finally and under the onslaught of mounting internal pressure, he felt something crack, then followed elation as the promise of liberation became an actual possibility, a delightful sense of release and of liberty. He desired so much to burst out and leap and dance on a seashore and to watch the swallows in their curious pirouetting low level flight. He yearned to be free to face the wind and to feel the rain, to run forever along a bewilderingly beautiful woodland trail in the gentle spring sunshine. There was a promise, so full and so enticing, to be amidst a symphony of birdsong, to observe the myriads of small insects and to sample the seductive fragrance of spring flowers, crocuses, daffodils, daisies, buttercups, primroses and bluebells. Then he experienced more relief, a sudden release of pressure as if he was able to escape through a fissure but his greatly anticipated joy was curtailed; the sudden liberation never happened. He became just vaguely conscious of sunlight, of standing in the wind but of being sightless and deaf. He had a sensation of life-giving heat, of drawing energy from the sky and of absorbing sustenance from the earth. Most of all though, he had an overwhelming sense of being literally rooted to the spot.

When viewed in human terms, it is almost impossible to assess the extent of the sensory array of an oak tree. The ability to hear, see, taste or to become excited at the tender touch of a life partner are abstracts denied to a tree, at least in animal terms. In this incarnation he was no different from any other tree, although he enjoyed the privilege of some form of conscious separation and could think, cogitate, meditate and ruminate. There is no way of knowing if there is a natural interface between a human mind and tree physiognomy and any such process must therefore be subjective. Lucius of course, no longer possessed a human mind and although he was quite unaware of the fact at that moment, his mind had actually been tremendously expanded. Lucius explored with his mind in his state of vaguely comfortable solid imprisonment and he started to discover a new aspect of freedom. Though he had no 'vision' in the human sense, he experienced sensations that could be worked upon and interpreted, fresh new sensations and novel methods of perception. As he became aware of his growth from acorn to sapling so too did his awareness increase, a new armory of hitherto unknown senses sprouted. A strangely familiar being tended him and protected him; though he could not see him, he could sense his kindliness, wisdom and radiance. Lucius could even discern a certain impression of this 'being', based on the complex patterns of energy that represented the old druid's vital body. What was strange to him was that while he could envision and even communicate with the 'druid' for this was the particular energetic signature of this being, he was not able to do so with very many other humans. They varied in intensity, some were fairly bright and coherent, others were literally dim and beyond his reach. The druid often spoke to Lucius, hummed prayers, mantras and communed with him daily, their minds at certain times becoming one.

As the years passed, Lucius gathered strength and girth, growing bigger and stronger with each decade. At the passing of the seasons there were great changes. As Fall progressed, the joy of feeling the sun on his branches and the exquisite expedience of drawing life force through a multitude of leaves, became replaced by a sense of creeping tactical withdrawal. Leaves were shed, seeds were dropped and big ethereal globes of mistletoe proliferated on his upper branches. He didn't feel the cold as such but there was an intense sense of deadness and emptiness when the snow and ice hung from his branches. In the spring, his joy of life returned as the leaves grew and flourished and the warm summer wind brought a gaiety to the tree's immortal soul.

Time had far less meaning for Lucius in this incarnation; many human lifetimes flashed before him, his was a life of sensations, of awareness, of a strongly compelling need to reach out and connect with his mother earth. He gradually came to the exquisite realisation that he was not one single and wholly isolated organism but in fact was connected to every part of the entire planet, every microbe and every creature. While on some conscious level, he resented his lack of liberty in the early days, he realised that he was, for the first time ever, entirely free. He could be anywhere and the fascinating electro-dynamic diversity and character of all who dwell on the planet became known to him. Birds nested on his great branches in the spring, he sensed their urgency, their excitement and most of all he worshipped their ability to fly, to dance with a joy of life in the mating game, to pirouette and to soar in the sky beyond the clouds. Birds were his emissaries to and from the heavens. They helped him to endure the pain and anguish, along with his brethren, of being cut and harvested to provide food for others, of being trimmed to keep nature in check. Nothing compared however, with the agony he experienced when mighty oaks, chestnuts, maples, beech and others of their kin were brutally hacked down by machinery, their great root structures reaching to the heavens, unsecured and un-nourished. Their collective souls remained alive but in great torment for weeks, even months, as they attempted to flourish despite their loss of physical grounding and connection to their Mother Earth.

Father Donovan's Tree experienced the tragic loss of his close brethren on the forested plateau and each time, he felt himself die just a little. For some reason his position by the lake shore was unassailable, as though he were guarded and kept safe in some way but there were times when he felt an impending sense of mortality. Father Donovan had planted him there for a purpose, a task for which he had no knowledge. He knew on some level that his own fate was intermingled with that of the druid. At his planting, he had been aware of the conjuration of magic, of divine forces, a swirl of colours, the awesome beauty of a star nebula and the sensational energy of the Aurora Borealis as the druid invoked the powers of the universe. Many decades before and just as he had breached the threshold of adolescence in the tree world, when he had grown from a mere sapling into a promising and beautiful young oak tree, he had become aware of another being. This person was a nature spirit, an elemental, who had buried a chest deep in the earth and into the realm of his burgeoning root structure. To be in such close proximity to so inanimate an object, had at first filled him with disquiet but then he sensed energy within the chest, an impression of enchantment that he recognised from his own beginnings. Within the chest lay a great secret that was but a seed and was to await the prophetic day of its germination. In veneration of the old druid, he vowed to protect his charge which had been entrusted to him by the druid's son. In consequence, he forgave the trampling of the bluebells and encouraged them to regrow, obscuring the site of the burial from the forces of evil.

Fox and deer sought shelter underneath the boughs of the oak when hunted. Stags rubbed the itchy, dead skin from their antlers on his rough flanks. Rabbits and badgers built warrens nearby and mated profligately, making the most of and contributing to the great bounty of Mother Nature. Lovers in human form were enticed by the enchanting shade of the tree on hot summer days, spending intimate and happy interludes under the great protective canopy of the oak's mighty limbs. Once, a rope was thrown over a lower branch by militia-men during the civil wars and a man, with his arms tied and sitting on horseback, had a noose put over his head and around his neck. This brought back painful memories for Lucius. Sensing that the condemned man was an essentially good creature, Lucius suffered this limb to suddenly wither and break away as the horse was slapped on its rear end and the man fell to earth with a bump, along with the mighty limb that felled the ugly men of the militia, who had death and pillage in their battle-rotted hearts.

Lucius was aware, during his long life, of the occasions when he was almost uprooted by powerful and sinister winds but the old druid's spells preserved him while the last of his brethren perished. The commonsense of the age decreed that the environment high up on the plateau was hostile to tree longevity. It was decided that the mighty tree should be cut down which it almost was, twice in fact. In a welter of panic and fear, he shed leaves and acorns, his only chance to perpetuate himself, a being multiplied and re-confined to a million seeds with a chance to be reborn and to, once more, reach for the skies. A being not of this earth, a wraith, the ghost of old Father Donovan had yanked himself from the comfort of his immortal realm, had shown himself and had frightened away the would be tree cutters. On those occasions, a huge raven and Father Donovan's familiar, also sat on his branches squawking loudly, invoking spells. Being aware of this 'curse', any proposed felling was abandoned by the custodial authorities. Once a man with whom he felt the strangest affinity, climbed his branches and cut into his bark with a knife. Though violated, the tree felt an understanding as to why the man was doing so. He felt that it was right that he was being used as a guardian or messenger, that somehow his skin was being branded with intelligence that would be utilised at an, as yet, undecided time. It was then that he pledged that he would hang onto life for as long as he was able to remain standing. To guard over the chest was paramount, as was his intention to protect the message carved into one of his limbs. Even when there was a failed attempt to burn the tree to the ground, he suffered scorched and charred branches, some of which died and dropped to the ageless earthen floor while others took decades to heal in an excruciating process of regeneration. In latter times, he was aware of being cared for and of being loved and then he luxuriated in the grooming process. Among other things, the gardeners cut away long established ivy which was winding an ever constricting path up the trunk of the oak. He sensed that there was care in the hearts of the men who tended him. They melded with him as the druid had done. Not all of mankind was bent on destruction.

CHAPTER 18

Following Julia's instructions, Jessica headed for the lake. The bridleway quickly gave way to a dense wood in which the beautiful early morning light became gloomy and the footpath serpentine and barely discernible beneath a low ground fog. Julia had indicated that the foot path went directly to the lake and so Jessica became puzzled, wondering where she had gone wrong. She encountered an array of little yellow toadstools clustered upon the bark of an enormous but long dead tree and bending down, she touched one tentatively. She could not help but be rather intrigued by them. In the dim and damp confines of a wood and growing on a rotting tree, they looked oddly incongruous but almost 'pretty'. Despite her training and in full knowledge of the possible toxicity of the fungus she reached down again and picked a whole one from the tree. Then she rubbed it experimentally between her fingers, brought it to her nose and inhaled. She wrinkled her nose in a reflex action as there was a very subtle but an oddly invasive and very astringent odour. It was then, for the briefest of moments, that Jessica experienced a sudden flash of uncertainty and apprehension. *'Julia never mentioned the woods, I'm sure that she would have. This is more like a thick forest, maybe I meandered off the track somewhere but where?'*

The trail followed a gradual incline that seemed interminable and wound a sinuous path for many miles with no lake in sight. Jessica would have been charmed had she not started to become panic stricken. She encountered several more clumps of the curious yellow toadstools along the way also growing from felled tree stumps that also boasted well established bracket mushrooms. Suddenly, quite out of the blue, a very large shaggy dog, alarmingly wolf-like trotted up to her, its ears erect and alert, its one pale blue eye and one brown eye softened by overtures of friendship, tail wagging in greeting. *'More weirdness'* Jessica thought. *' Not the kind of dog that one would expect to find in rural England.* Jessica's most fervent but unrequited wish as a child was to have had a dog as she had a special affinity with them. Invariably, most dogs would greet her when she was out walking, with a mixture of trust, respect and friendship and often surprised owners of the more neurotic or ferocious of the species, with an uncharacteristic show of affection toward Jessica. Were it not for the fact that she lived in an apartment in London, she would have kept a dog, though William no doubt, would have been very miffed. Jessica sat down on the trunk of yet another fallen tree in order to catch her breath. The dog too was also panting from exertion and exhaling clouds of steam from his mouth; he nevertheless, made the most of the attention that Jessica gave him while sitting at her feet and giving her a quaint lopsided smile as he looked up at her. As she prepared to walk again the dog was obviously determined to accompany her and trotted alongside happily, tail still wagging.

"Go home beautiful, go back to your master. You will surely be missed"

He completely ignored her suggestion but during the rest of the walk he periodically dashed into the bush then, re-appearing far in front of her, waited for Jessica to catch up.

" I don't know where you come from gorgeous but won't your master or mistress be getting worried about you?"

The dog who was slightly ahead stopped for a moment, turned and looked at her and obeying only his own guileless instincts, evidently tried to convey something, some intelligence to her with his baleful mismatched eyes and then resumed accompanying Jessica once she had caught up. Periodically, he stopped to sniff at the bases of selected trees and cocking a leg, peed, marking his territory. At one point he emitted a deep and loud but strangely muffled "woof" at a squirrel that had appeared overhead on a branch and that was chattering at them both in hostile consternation.

With the aid of a sunlit break in the dense forest, Jessica espied a lake and was fascinated to discover that, just as the footpath had been, it was enshrouded by an unutterably beautiful low lying mist. She lapsed into an uncharacteristic moment of whimsy and fantasy and found herself wondering if she had indeed strayed into the world of the Undines, the spiritless but beautiful elementals of the netherworld. She half expected to see one such creature sitting on a rock in the middle of the lake, combing her hair with a comb made from a shell. Jessica walked slowly around the perimeter of the lake then tiptoed through a thigh-high bank of mist that was rolling onto the lake shore and once again, became quite spellbound. On the western edge, the forest had thinned and was replaced by a large area of bullrushes. As her panic slowly ebbed away and just when she could imagine no other feature that could improve her experience, she encountered countless spiders webs, beautifully erected and hung skillfully between the heads of the bullrushes. Each web was covered in a heavy early morning dew and was illuminated quite supernaturally by the radiant light of a beautiful autumn sun.

In the clearing was a sapling oak tree, though not much taller than her it was quite perfect and held a wonderful poise and symmetry, one of natures great successes. Suddenly, her reverie was broken as she was assailed with a fearful sense of deja-vu, this all appeared to be so eerily familiar; she felt suddenly a desperate need to get back to the safety and familiarity of the farm. Paradoxically, Jessica lacked the motivation, as though under a spell and found that she could not help but linger; simple inertia dogged her every attempt at thought or movement. She sat on a large moss-covered rock becoming weighed down by lethargy, her mind was 'still' but something within her was moved by this poignant and haunting scene. The lake of course, was nothing like the one that she and Julia had visited two days earlier and Jessica assumed that she had become hopelessly lost and had stumbled upon another far more mysterious lake hidden in a vale on much higher ground. The dog, who had settled for a while as Jessica sat and rested, was neatly curled up in a hollow that looked as if it were made for him. Then he stood up, stretched his front legs as if bowing to Jessica, yawned and trotted over to her, sitting close and leaning against her leg. After a short while he gently lay his great head on her knees, looked right into her eyes and emitted a short, plaintive little whine. She stroked his muzzle and scratched him behind his ears, tears streaming down her face and she had absolutely no idea why, though the world had started to seem very surreal.

A scene came into Jessica's mind, not quite a vision but a frighteningly vivid recollection of a conversation that had taken place between her and Julia the previous morning about an old school friend. Why this should come to her at this moment, Jessica had no idea but each intricate facet of the interchange came back to her. The subject had not seemed so important at the time, maybe even a little trivial, but in that moment by the lake, Jessica became suddenly obsessed by these revelations. Julia had abruptly become silent, almost secretive; Jessica had asked her gently what was on her mind?

"Oh nothing really, just life!"

"Julia, this is me?"

"Oh, it's just a guilty little secret that bothers me from time to time."

"Go on....?"

"Oh it's nothing really."

"Jools! Its not like you to keep quiet about a juicy bit of gossip, this must be a guilty secret indeed if you won't even confide in me. Now I have to know!"

"Oh, now there's a rich irony."

"Julia, whatever do you mean?"

She was quiet again, as if making a momentous decision and then having decided......

" Do you remember when we were in the upper sixth and you went out with that catholic boy who later became a priest?"

Jessica looked surprised.

" Good Lord yes, of course I remember him, Andrew Morley; I went out with him if you can call it going out? He was so tall and good looking, always very neat, wore a blazer. I remember that he parted his hair on the side, similar to those cheesy photographs that you see outside barber shops."

Julia nodded.

"That was him, far too nice for his own good, always so civilised. I never told you this because you were dating him but I had quite a crush on him at the time, can't think why

looking back on it now especially with his side parting."
Then Julia grinned impishly, slightly embarrassed.
Jessica looked at her thoughtfully for a moment.
"I know that a lot of girls did, it was part of the attraction for me but I remember that you were always a bit mean to him for some reason, weird behaviour really for someone with a crush, actually perhaps not, now I come to think of it. Why are you bringing this up now?"
" Well, two reasons; firstly, I seduced him!"
Jessica was mildly incredulous in that way that someone is both appalled and amused by a revelation simultaneously. She put her hand over her mouth to cover her amazement, combined with evident amusement but her dancing eyes betrayed her.
" What! Well honestly Julia, I'm appalled! I went out with him quite a few times actually. I really thought that he was the one for me, my gosh, I can't belive it. You absolute tart!"
" I know, I know! It was really mean of me, you're not angry with me are you Jess?"
" Good heavens no, of course I'm not, it was such a long time ago, I'm just rather astonished. What made you do it and why tell me about it now? "
" Well truthfully, I've always been just a little haunted by the episode and for some reason, more so recently. You know he really was very attracted to you, he always seemed to be just there staring at you wherever you were. If I spoke to him, he would just go red, mumble something and then disappear. I used to catch him looking at you. Of course I teased him about that as much as I could just to taunt him. I was so jealous of the fact that he fancied you and not me- Jeez, teenage girls! God help me when Loretta reaches that age. There's a kind of hormonal insanity that prevails in us girls from about fourteen to eighteen. I know what monsters

young women can be, no wonder they used to be chaperoned. Anyway, I teased him, y'know, sidling up to him and brushing against him with my chest thrust out or making innuendos. I even lifted my skirt and gave him a flash of my panties once; actually that was for a dare. "

" Julia, You didn't! Who dared you?"

" Lizzy Atkins, she knew I had the hots for the guy. I'm not proud of myself. My only excuse is that we Canadian gals are much more brazen when it comes to catching our man or someone else's man, y'know, a bit like the Mounties. You Brits are so damned repressed."

Jessica looked thoughtful for a moment, Julia's little joke had passed her by.

" Well it's such a long time ago but I suppose I never gave him much encouragement, I was so painfully shy, so prim and frigid basically. A deeply entrenched family sense of morality stopped me from having any fun. I was rather in love with him though, I wanted him to grab hold of my hand and send me illicit notes or poems. I supposed, or at least hoped that he would catch on but I was far too young and naïve to know how to make the next move. I did go to the cinema with him once and he tried to kiss me but I was eating cheese and onion crisps and I thought that my breath would be a bit off-putting frankly, I was so self conscious. There was something about him though. He was the only boy at school who stirred something in me, made me feel sexy. I suppose I didn't really understand what it was then, I was so inhibited."

Julia uncharacteristically serious, listened to Jessica's confession and much to Jessica's surprise, was obviously in pain. Jessica took her hand and tried to comfort her, confused as to why her friend was behaving so strangely as it was all water under the bridge as far as she was concerned.

They sat in a contemplative silence for a while and Jessica starting to think that the subject was exhausted, reached for a sandwich when Julia continued, on the verge of tears;

"It all happened when I saw him again at a birthday party, do you remember John Cotter, he was actually going out with that slut, Lizzy Atkins, at the time? Come to think of it I think every guy in our class went out with Lizzy. Anyway, it was John's 18th and he had his parents house all to imself for the weekend. I decided then and there to seduce Andrew. He was a challenge I guess, I found his goodness hypocritical and so I played all the tricks, chatted, flirted and finally on the pretext of wanting to talk about you, I dragged him into John Cotters parents bedroom, which of course was out of bounds. Even though he was quite drunk, he was resistant at first but weakened by my feminine assault, well lets face it, what man wouldn't be, we finally did the dirty deed, we made out."

Jessica looked rueful for a moment;

" Don't be too hard on yourself Jools, most teenagers get up to mischief, it is what the teenage years are for after all. All except me of course, Miss Prim, Miss Frigid, I deserved to lose him."

" No that's not true Jessica, I just distracted him but I wounded him and actually you too, it was a nasty trick. It wasn't very good sex, we were both drunk, he was completely inexperienced and it hurt a bit and then he actually called me 'Jessica' at the end, I was furious. The worst of it is that he broke down and cried like a child afterwards, I just didn't know what to do, it was all so embarrassing and so I just left him, sobbing half naked on the bed."

Jessica looked thoughtful for a moment,

" Did you ever see him again?"

" Well here's the thing, I did. He avoided any contact with me for years after that time and then he left town. Much later he became a minister or a priest or something in London and evidently all the middle-aged and elderly lady parishioners were making sheeps eyes at him and trying to do everything in their power to win his favour. I bumped into him quite by accident in the Natural History Museum of all places. He recognised me instantly but was a little awkward, though courteous and polite. Of course I did all those stupid teenage things again, batted my eyelashes at him and made him feel uncomfortable even though I was happily married to John and very pregnant at the time. I really was genuinely pleased to see him and wanted so badly to make amends but of course, I overdid it. He became defensive, I got on my high horse and he got angry and said something to me that has haunted me ever since. He told me that what happened between us ruined any possibility of his having a relationship with you and that he had always loved you Jessica. He told me that he would have given up his vocation for you. He also told me that he could not even be a good priest because his soul had been tarnished, alluding of course to the ah, interlude. Of course I should have known better but felt downright hurt actually, my God, after all those years, it was so childish. I thought he was a freak and told him so. I said that he had always been a hypocrite and that he was just blaming others for his own weakness and that he should get a life. It was stupid Jess, just like we had actually become teenagers all over again and then I flounced away. I'll never forget the look of mortification on his face as I left, it still haunts me."

Jessica looked at Julia with mounting disbelief, she was horrified.

" You know I never knew he cared for me to that extent, how strange. As I mentioned I think, I used to pray that he would sweep me off my feet but we were both so horribly shy. It does sound as if he had a lot of stuff to deal with though, poor chap."

" I should tell you the reason why this has bothered me so much recently. About a week ago he was found dead in his church. He died of a heart attack of all things; he was only thirty four years old. For some reason I sensed that his death was linked with his anguish. He seemed to carry the weight of the world on his shoulders. I experienced his pain; y'know how I feel these things. Here's a newspaper cutting that I kept."

Jessica read the obituary and studied the photograph of a much older Andrew Morley, a man and not a boy, filled out, some heavineess but far more handsome in fact. For some reason she was reminded of the man in her dreams. She concentrated on the picture, trying to conjure more images from her subconscious. She was aware that there was a link, nothing tangible, just some vague elusive sense teetering on the edge of her consciousness.

Jessica came to with a start, the shifting sun opened up a clearing amongst the dense foliage illuminating her surroundings and her mind as her reverie was broken. She was awed by the strangeness of it all and was comforted by the eerie intransigent silence. She suddenly became aware that much time had passed and felt a sense of urgency to find her way back to the farm. The dog, who was asleep in his hollow, sensed her movement and raised his head, suddenly alert. Then he jerked up onto his feet, swiveled round and dashed off at speed as if summoned, yet there had been no sound. Jessica was on her own again.

" Well thanks a bunch Mutley, I thought you might at least have helped me find my way back."

As she rose to her feet, she felt unaccountably woozy, there was still a subtle but insistent chemical smell which reminded her of the mushrooms and which refused to dissipate. She carefully retraced her path. Gradually things started to become a lot more familiar, though she still felt light headed and disorientated. She was more relieved than she could ever remember being before when she finally reached the farmyard gate and ran hastily towards the farmhouse and the comforting prospect of a warm kitchen and breakfast with the family.

CHAPTER 19

Entering hurriedly through the kitchen door, cold, weary and evidently very relieved to have found her way back, though perplexed and quite shaken up Jessica nevertheless experienced a tinge of unreality, as if she were in a twilight world where nothing seemed real. Julia, John and the children were however, sitting around the kitchen table amidst the usual family pandemonium but seeing Jessica looked sddenly relieved and welcomed her reassuringly.
" Gosh I am so glad to be back, that was an incredibly long walk and I got hopelessly lost."
Within no time, the warmth of the kitchen, the deliciously lingering odours of a hearty fried breakfast and coffee set her mind very much more at ease. Julia evidently very relieved to see Jessica, leaped up and hugged her, holding fast just in case she disappear again.
"Jessica, honey, you were gone so long, we were starting to get a little worried about you, John mentioned that he had seen you heading off in the direction of the lake over four hours ago?"
" I know, I'm sorry Jools but I just got a frightfully lost."
Julia looked momentarily confused and somewhat baffled but the cloud passed and then she added brightly,
"Well I fixed us a real Canadian breakfast, what you people call brunch; pancakes, maple syrup, hash browns, bacon, sausage, eggs and good stove top coffee, I hope you're hungry?"

"Famished actually Julia darling, it smells absolutely glorious. Gosh! I'd forgotten just how much a long walk can make one so absolutley ravenous."

" Oh my god Jess, I forget just how incredibly British you can sound at times, I'll never get used to the way you speak but promise me you will never change, please! Tell me this though, how does a distance of just under a mile and a half along a straight path translate into an epic hike, and how on earth did you get lost. You're a scientist for God's sake and with a mind that's far too analytical for your own good, what happened?"

Jessica leaned back against the solid, reassuring warmth of the Aga where she was gradually thawing but then, encouraged by Julia, made her way over to a place set for her. A plate piled indecently high with delicious comfort food was passed to her, a biological time bomb guaranteed to send cholesterol levels soaring but bursting with properties of glorious sensual indulgence. The food really was sublime, warming and satisfying and Jessica ate voraciously, as if she hadn't eaten for a week. She reached over to the stove for the coffee pot and paused for a moment before filling her cup as if this simple ceremony would help her to gather her thoughts. While eating, Jessica gave a detailed account of her protracted walk and of the dog who had appeared from nowhere and who had befriended her.

"Which way did you go Jess?"

" I went down the footpath that you told me about, past the orchard and into the forest, then up the hill which seemed to go on for miles up to the plateau. Finally, I found the lake; I didn't recognise it from that perspective, it seemed so different from yesterday?"

Julia seemed genuinely puzzled.

" Y'know there's no forest there Jess, there are no forests within miles of here and no high ground apart from the 'Tor'. This is the somerset levels don't forget, swampy, flat land, flood plain, that's why it's called, 'the levels'. Y'know, the lake is actually just visible from our bedroom window."
Jessica stopped chewing for a moment, unable to provide an account that would both satisfy her and properly explain to Julia the nature of her extraordinary adventure. Feeling just a little foolish, she replied inadequately;
" But there must be, I was there, look I have this in my pocket which I picked from the big rotting tree."
Julia looked briefly at the astringent smelling fungus.
" I don't know of a big rotten tree near here. In any case, as soon as a tree falls hereabouts, people will rush over to it with chainsaws and cut it up for firewood."

John, reading his motorcycle magazine and only partially taking in the details of the bizarre conversation, chipped in at this point;
"I'm always looking for wood for the stove for the winter Jessica and would love to get my hands on a fallen tree if you can remember where you saw it?"
Jessica divined the impression that both Julia and John were being rather simple and frankly, quite annoying. There remained with her, just the faintest undertone of discord and surreality that Jessica could not quite put her finger on.
" After breakfast Jessica my love, we will walk up to the lake together. You can show me the path you took, okay? John, please could you keep an eye on the kids for a little while?"
John looked momentarily peeved, caught unawares.
"Yes, well I do have to change the alternator belts on the tractor so don't be too long will you?"

Jessica was resolutely disinclined to walk again and wanted no more than to sit in the kitchen by the Aga with a book, enjoying the busy but cozy environment through a drowsy miasma for the rest of the day.

" Must we, really Jools?"

" Yes we must, this is really important Jessica!"

This time, they set out for the lake in an entirely different light, the sun was up, it was warm and everywhere looked bright and cheery. Within twenty minutes they were standing at the shores that Jessica recognised from yesterdays outing with the children. She looked out across to the other side as if that might provide her with an answer to this most baffling riddle.

" This isn't the one, this is not where I came earlier this morning, I followed the same path but must have accidentally taken a different route. I did find the most beautiful lake though, surely Julia, you must know of it?"

" John and I have walked literally hundreds of miles around here and know this area like the back of my hand. I swear to you Jessica, there is no other path along the way and no other lake."

Jessica experienced goosebumps, a tingling that started on top of her head and worked its way down to the occipital region of her skull, an alarming sensation.

" Honestly Julia, I was there! Oh, I know you both think I'm mad but I know what I saw, she said defensively"

Julia thought for a moment before speaking.

" Did you ever consider that you might actually have had some kind of psychic experience Jessica?"

Jessica was momentarily irritated.

" Oh no, that's your domain and I would never presume. I

just don't have time for all that nonsense, sorry and all that but I don't. As you quite rightly pointed out, I'm a scientist and I don't have room in my life for fantasies. I know that you have helped me in the past in ways that I really cannot account for but I am way out of my comfort zone with all this mumbo jumbo. Maybe I fell asleep and it was all a dream, oh I don't know, I really don't? Do you have an ordnance survey map?"

"Yes but it won't do any good Jessica. We have explored every interesting site for a twenty five mile radius from here. There is no other lake or at least not one that fits your description in any way, just seasonally flooded fields basically."

They walked back to the house and in slightly awkward silence until at the back door.

" Jess?"

" Yes"

" I have a suggestion, something that has come to me."

"Oh!"

" Well it's not a suggestion exactly, its an idea, I can't quite get my mind around it just at the moment but I will work on it. I will say that I feel that there is a link between where you were this morning and that guy that you are doing the research on, the one that was executed."

" Lucius Grey?"

" I don't know how to describe this but I am getting all sorts of weird scenarios. It's almost as if he were a multiple consciousness, a person that has been separated, sliced up into different parts and each of those somehow isolated. Oh don't look at me like that Jess. I know this sounds stupid to you but let me think about it some more okay? Don't dismiss my idea."

Jessica was reflexively guarded, skeptical but then attempted to open her mind to Julia's thoughts. They were so different the two of them, how had they become such close friends with such opposing views of the world.

'We really don't operate on the same wavelength, how is it that we have such a close connection? Maybe we compliment each other or maybe we just think that we do!'?

A cup of strong tea and a slab of rich farmhouse fruitcake revived them both and to some extent banished the tarnished portion of the day. Then it was time for Jessica to leave. John had finished the tractor far more quickly than he had expected and was itching to nip into town on the Norton just as soon as the girls were back. Jumping at the opportunity, he offered to escort Jessica as far as the town.

" Hang on a minute guys," Julia shouted as she grabbed a helmet. She extorted a solemn promise from the children that they would behave themselves for ten minutes knowing full well that they wouldn't.

"Loretta, you are in charge, Oliver, listen to your sister, that's an order."

Then she ran out to the yard in her wellington boots and climbed, a little indecorously, onto the pillion seat behind John on the Norton, wrapping her skirts around her legs as best she could. Hamish stuck his fingers in his ears and grinned when the Norton started. Jessica kissed and hugged the children and then climbed into the driver's seat of the Bentley. Just a few minutes later they were in Glastonbury where they stopped for a coffee and then chatted hilariously for the time remaining to them thought there was a perceptible brittle quality to their hilarity. Before departing, Jessica hugged Julia and then John, an emotionally charged connection and had been embraced warmly in return; the true strength of their amazing friendship was communicated to one another unreservedly. For the first time in her life, Jessica felt the impenetrable walls of her personal defenses start to crumble and she welcomed the warmth that this let in. Despite the length of time they had known each other, there was still a whole aspect of Julia to which she had no access and no knowledge but she was indeed her absolute best friend and the closest thing to family that she knew. Curiously enough, similar thoughts were bubbling to the surface in Julia's mind and she threw out a parting shot.

" Find yourself a boy honey and try to have some fun, you are way too serious!"

Jessica realised, just as she was driving away, that she had still not told Julia of her dream of meeting the young druid in the woods, maybe that really would have been too much? It would have to wait until the right time. She was persistently nagged at by an odd feeling, a discord, a dissonance, something that was not quite 'right' but once again, she forced the 'sense' to the back of her mind. Nevertheless, she so wanted to make Julia aware of the similarities between the dream where she met the young druid burying the chest and of the place where she had found herself wandering earlier that day but she could not bring herself to speak of it. *Was that all just a dream too?'* There was of course the overwhelming part of Jessica that was forever the pragmatist, science was her god, her raison d'etre. This was this restraining force that prevented her from falling headlong into an abyss of fantasy; she held back, fearing that she was becoming 'fanciful', maybe it was simple fear, a terror of the unknown but for the moment her sanity had to remain more or less intact, her reason, unimpaired.

She popped a CD into the player, she needed something rousing and solid, grounding, she craved something upbeat that would bring her back to earth. At first it was 'Jamiroquoi' which normally she loved and which, for her, was daring and wild but on this occasion, the music seemed jarring and uncomfortable. On a whim she selected a CD that Julia had given her just as she was leaving but which she had resolved not to play. Julia's music was usually far too 'new agey' for her. Julia in turn, volubly disapproved of Jessica's taste which she described as middle aged chick music.
" Just been sent this by my folks back home, it is truly wonderful," she said as she stuffed the CD into Jessica's pocket. Jessica was tired of her motley collection, mostly foverplayed classical music, light rock, a sprinkling of Andrea Bocelli, Frank Sinatra, Whitney Houston, Celine Dionne and others of a similar ilk. The only musicians that Julia and Jessica had once shared a passion for were Neil Young, Roy Harper and Nick Drake but those days, sadly, were long gone. In desperation Jessica put the new disc in the machine expecting to hear mournful and repetitive synthesized melodies accompanied by the sounds of waves breaking on a sea shore and soulful whale song. In fact Jessica was pleasantly surprised to hear something quite new and rather wonderful. The musician, Julia had explained briefly, was a Mexican/Canadian singer named Lhasa. In some delicately indefinable way, the music started to dissolve some of Jessica's massive preconceptions. She was, she realised shockingly, in every way a material girl, status, success and money were important to her. She had always been a high achiever, was very ambitious but lately life had seemed to Jessica to be increasingly pointless.
' We have a responsibility in this life to succeed, or fail and be consumed. What else is there? Maybe Julia does have a

point. Maybe there is a part of me that's dead. Maybe that's why my relationships fail too, not satisfied in life, really not satisfied in bed, comfortable though not wealthy. BUT WHAT ELSE IS THERE?'

Julia sometimes talked of her old home in Canada and while driving, Jessica pieced together many a school lunchtime conversation to build a picture of Julia's formative years. She had confessed to Jessica of missing her home and family desperately. Before moving to Saltspring Island on the west coast, Julia was born and had been raised in a small arid dust laden town with an odd name, 'Osoyoos' was the name as Jessica recalled. The town stood at the northern end of the Sonora desert just on the Canadian side of the border with the United States. Jessica found herself envying Julia's roots, wide open spaces, clean, healthy, modern and apart from a wide smattering of crazed evangelists, and haggard, starving, drug-raddled hippies, pretty 'normal'. Julia would often talk of wonderful places there, Okanagen Lake, the vineyards, Oliver, Naramata and the sublimely untarnished Kettle valley and Jessica would ask in astonishment what on earth drew her to England.

" Magic!" she had replied and Jessica had laughed.

" There is a spirit in this country which is stronger than anywhere else I have ever been, it's so blatantly elemental, deeply rooted. Maybe this country is overcrowded and polluted and the EEC is comprised of a bunch of scum sucking freaks, but Britain really is so magical despite all the problems."

Knowing of Julia's and John's constantly precarious financial situation, Jessica had stated more recently and somewhat spitefully;

" You can't survive on magic Jools, magic is just a fancy for an over active imagination, you're just hippies trapped in some make believe world."

" You don't understand Jess but you will one day. 'Majick', not 'magic' is a little word that defines everything about us, what makes us tick. None of this is truly real you know, none of what you think you experience is really happening."
Jessica had snorted a little derisively, loving Julia for being the 'nut' that she obviously was and yet there was an attraction for Julia and her family that had kept their friendship alive and that, ironically, had to do with the 'majick' to which Julia referred. Then suddenly the recollection of the 'reality' statement hit her like a sledgehammer; her thoughts struggled to identify what it was that chivvied at her conscious mind.

Jessica's friends were nearly all professional and successful people and Julia was the only aberration in this regard. The curious thing was, now that she came to think about it, that while all of her other friends were successful to wildly varying degrees, they were also snorting cocaine, drinking to excess, spicing up their love lives with illicit affairs and buying ever faster and more gadget ridden cars to bolster their jaded sensibilities. Julia was the only person that she found to be fundamentally and deeply happy. She may have miserable moments while fighting pointless bureaucracy, fending off the bank manager, the tax man or trying to buy shoes for the kids with a depleted credit card but these were just annoying superficialities really. Julia's life was on track and she had an inexhaustible love of life and to Jessica, this was both very attractive but inexplicable. Departing that morning and leaving the family had been both a relief as Jessica's life was so well ordered and neat, but something within her had been awoken as so often it did when she visited Julia. She had been immeasurably sad when she left and silently wept in the car as the music played, twice in one day and something of a rarity for Jessica. The morning adventure was becoming lost in the mists of that hazy dawn of reality and Jessica mourned the loss but she was persistantly haunted by that weird smell that seemed to have stuck with her with a vengeance.

It started to rain as she approached London, darkness was encroaching; she reached for the headlight switch then turned on the quaintly minuscule wipers. The surreal dawn and later the welcome warmth of a dwindling autumn sun had gone, banished in the same way that her sense of wonder of the day had fizzled away; it was oddly prophetic. London loomed like a foreign land as she approached the outskirts on the manically congested motorway. Countless lights, bewildering in their number made shadowy patterns on the interior of the Bentley through the rain streaked windows. Somehow all of those things that she loved about London, or at worst tolerated, became quite unendurable. The apartment that she knew so well seemed odd, strange, like it was someone else's home. Even the faintly discernible odour, that quintessential characteristic that all homes have, seemed discordant to her, almost alien. Jessica felt flat, depressed and exhausted and went to bed early that night accompanied by William who lay in a warm cozy spot in the crook of her sideways turned legs and purred resonantly. Before going to sleep her mind replayed some of the events of this long and eventful day and she recalled Julia's suggestion.
" Maybe if John can spare me, I'll come to London and stay with you for a few days."

Jessica had a brief and amusing vision of shopping sprees with a petite but dynamically pretty women with a trans-atlantically wide mouth, flashing white teeth, long blonde hair and with the glorious golden glow and patina of someone who spends much time out of doors. Then she inwardly giggled when she thought of the figure wearing a tie died T shirt, long skirt and purple wellington boots sitting on the back of Johns Norton. Moments later and all too quickly, she plummeted through the threshold of consciousness and into blissful nirvana, utterly dead to this world but altogether very alive in yet another.

CHAPTER 20

As Jessica went to sleep, breaking through the boundaries of her daytime reality and into the world of subconscious illusion, she dreamed. Her initial escapade was strangely lascivious in nature, a concept not usually encountered by Jessica as she spared little thought for anything other than the stark practicalities of life. Her semi-dormant sexuality bubbled sluggishly into wakefulness as the random bursts of forays into sensual realms gradually coalesced into one powerful dream.

She was a princess whose husband had tricked her into marriage. He usually left her to her own devices in his magical kingdom, to roam at will and to be free to do just as she wished. There were, however, occasions when he would seek her out or rather, hunt her down and impose his obligatory conjugal rights upon her; after all she was a Princess and was required to produce children. Her husband was half man and half beast. On a visceral level she was repulsed by him, an ugly freak of nature that could never conceivably sire offspring that she could love and nurture. Nevertheless, there was something about him that stirred her, despite herself.

She was lying in a beautiful woodland valley adjacent to a some rapids that lavished a vibrant rush of tinkling water into the bright balmy sunshine. There were strange bird-like mammals, beautiful semi-naked people, evidently happy and content and enjoying the paradise in which they lived and blithely toiled. The kingdom was an idyllic but also strangely unlikely world where colours were enhanced and where the true powers of nature had little sway on the events of the paradise in which she found herself.

One day, dark storm clouds interrupted the serenity of a perpetually azure sky. As the clouds swept in, a chill and capricious wind arrived from nowhere, fluttering canvas cloth and blowing sun dried leaves into a frenzy of swirling vortexes. Along with this unwelcome and unwholesome weather front, someone appeared, a man like creature; it was Jessica's husband in fact, ever the spirit of whimsy. He was very tall, over seven feet in height, beautifully proportioned and muscular, a giant with extraordinary black skin that reflected dazzling hints of glittering metallic blues and greens. His wings had a reptilian quality and were webbed like those of a bat. They were also thin and translucent and in between the long bones, the tissue exposed a fine filigree of blood vessels. His disturbingly dead eyes were of the purest ebony and like those of the great white shark, a total void. They seemed to absorb positive energy, sucking the life force from whomever they were brought to bear. Jessica's awareness in the dream was that this creature, her husband, needed her energetically but that he also wanted her sexually.

As he approached her, the darkness of his gaze paralysed her for a moment, she was quite incapable of movement and became increasingly terrified. Like any Lord, he was in a state of obvious expectation and excitement, his impossibly meaty and burgeoning phallus betraying his want. She ran for her life, just as she always did and tried desperately to escape but the creature, powerful, athletic and able to fly, was impossible to shake off. He played with her as a cat plays with a mouse, letting her think that she had got away and then catching her. A thrilling terror and panic overtook her, seeping from her world of dream into her normal domain of semi-consciousness. Jessica became aware that she must wake up. Julia had attempted to teach how to do this in her lucid dreaming exercises. Jessica tried with all her might but to no avail, she was as trapped mentally in that temporal world as she apparently was physically.

In the midst of her terror, she became aware of a hint of sexual tingling and started to become excited by the chase despite herself. When the creature finally grabbed her fully, he did so in such a way that it was firm but actually quite gentle and a tingle of sexual awareness flashed through her like the jolt of an electric shock. She was caught like a moth in a web and there was nothing that she could do about it. Finally, she was brought to ground and turned onto her back, the creature gripped her shoulders and supporting himself on his elbows, lay on top of her. The Princess's awakening excitement quickly became a fire of desire, from her womb, her breasts, waves of desperate arousal spread throughout her whole body. The creature, as if reading her mind, tore off her clothing. He kissed her breasts and then began to lick them with a long wet black pointed tongue that caused her nipples to harden. Her thoughts became enslaved by and centered on exquisite nodes of stimulation and she could not imagine a moment when this would stop. Simultaneously, she greatly feared and was actually petrified by her imminent impregnation, a divine paradox; a struggle of sensibilities often typified in the conflicts of sexual union but in this case, magnified tenfold.

Brought to the brink of inexpressible and uncontrollable wantonness, she clawed at him, desperate to draw him to her. When the moment came she cried out, sublime pleasure rippling through her whole body and echoing further into the realm of fantasy. She raked his back deeply with her long demon nails. Slow and very gentle at first, he increased tempo as the urgency of his need compelled him to utterly consume her. His excruciating enormity was almost too much for her. She felt hopelessly and wholly possessed, wanting him to stop but also completely incapable of bringing the proceedings to a halt. The sense of pleasure boiled up in her exponentially when suddenly a tidal wave of a sensual storm ripped through her being and she cried out, long and loud. His own climax coincided with hers and he gripped her powerfully, massively, a deep feral growl escaping from between his clenched teeth. Incomprehensibly, she found that she did love him afterall and so was happy laying along side him afterwards with his arms wrapped around her protectively, possessively. They basked for a while in a contrasting hiatus of peace and lassitude that quite consumed them both in an entirely different way.

The storm clouds dissolved as suddenly as they had arrived and once more they were bathing in the healing glow of a soft summer sun. He started to change form, his skin lightened, his eyes became a beautiful pale sky blue and he looked upon her with kindness and with love. His body changed in form, became smaller, reduced in size to that of a moderately tall and well proportioned fair haired young man. He opened his mouth to speak, uttering the words;
" I was lost but I knew you would find me. You know that across the boundaries of the past and the future I have always

loved you Laurna, we are destined to be together but you must continue to help me."

" I, help you?" she replied, questioning, confused?

" How so; anyway my names is Jess..........?"

" I have been imprisoned by a power that you cannot imagine. You don't know yet how you will help me but you will, you have already begun the process. You were once a powerful priestess, though you are unaware of this in your present incarnation. You alone are the only person that can help me. The Earth needs the Mother Goddess, beseeches her for help."

Then the voice echoed as if he were suddenly distant from her, his form rapidly losing opacity. Jessica reached for him, grabbed at him and then at thin air.

" Quickly tell me your name? "

There was a dying whisper of a mans voice in the wind.

" Oh I have many names, all of which you know, search within the quiet of your mind."

Jessica felt suddenly alone, bereft, he had gone. As a mistral came from nowhere and whistled across the plain so too did a tide of sudden depression sweep over her.

Jessica awoke, both frightened, wet with perspiration and shaking hypo-glycaemically in a curiously incomprehensible and thoroughly unfamiliar state of post coital exhaustion. The appalling but exciting thought crossed her mind that this was the first time in her life that she had ever experienced and enjoyed the thrill of sex. Throwing on a dressing gown and going into the kitchen, Jessica looked at the clock and was surprised to see that it was just 1.30 am. The night had seemed so long and she felt that she had been asleep for ever. She heated up some of the chai tea that Julia had given her and made toast thickly coated with crunchy peanut butter.

She slumped onto the couch then tucked her legs up beside her and was then joined within seconds by William, who had just popped in, a little damp but bristling with health and smelling fresh and outdoorsy. He demanded and was given love, rubbing noses with Jessica in a frenzy of feline furry abandon and sniffing exploratively at the toast. Finally he settled down and cuddled up to Jessica, purring loudly and contentedly, a tiny drop of dribble on his chin. Jessica reached over to the overladen coffee table for the file on Lucius Grey and as she moved she squeaked as William extended supporting claws into the skin of her leg. Then she opened the tin containing rich tea biscuits to go with the chai tea and gave William a small piece.

The rain had stopped and even without going outside, Jessica could tell that the temperature had dropped. The great dense clouds were breaking up with deep chasms in between, permitting the moon to gaze down upon the earth and to highlight patches of southern England. In London, of course, there was too much background light to notice much enhancement or even to be able to see the stars but the moon, highly visible through the window, drew Jessica's attention for a languid moment. It did seem to her that a great void had opened up directly over the silhouetted oak and that the tree was being smiled upon by a benevolent lunar enchantress. It was a beautiful and moving sight and she wondered, for just a moment, if she was truly witnessing this magical vision or if she was still dreaming. She suddenly felt very moved, overwhelmed and once again shed tears of both sadness and joy. It was in those special moments that Jessica realised that she was actually waking up, was veering off the path of control and emotional stability. Perhaps life was worth celebrating after all. Julia was quite right, there was more to life than money, material possessions and status.

Jessica was filled with a sudden irrational impulse to remove her clothing and to circle the tree under the moonlight, in celebration of life and in delicious ceremony. A light flicking on in another apartment, suddenly and rudely illuminated the lawn and the tree in a sterile, brash light bringing Jessica back to earth, the surreal but special opportunity was lost. There would be no yielding to the temptation for naked abandonment and so she returned her attention to the file on Lucius Grey and also to the note that she had added concerning old Mrs Wainright. It was then in the glorious quiet of very early morning, in a moment of total clarity that she realised that Mrs Wainright's husband must be a descendant of Butler's. Constantine Butler's mistress was obviously Georgina Brogan but she had taken the novel and acrimonious step of naming herself Grey, following the death of the 'worthy' judge. Jessica also realised that the child born of Georgina Brogan was Butler's but was named Grey and had passed into the care of Lucius's family when Georgina had died.

"How ironic is that?" Jessica said out loud and rather transatlantically, "That Mrs Wainright should marry a man descended from the Grey family though genetically of the Butler and Brogan line."

Jessica conveyed this startling information to William who looked impressed but Jessica knew that really, he was just hoping for a rich tea biscuit. Then a glimpse at his big striped furry tummy as he lay on his back in a state of unadulterated bliss was enough to convince her that he deserved one. Later, Jessica went back to the bedroom and put on a movie and then drifted into dreamless sleep ten minutes into the film.

She was awoken by the alarm at 7.30am which startled her. It was so warm and cozy in the bed with William taking up three quarters of it in his favoured spot in the middle. Jessica was loath to get up and she lay for a moment, studying a spider whom she had named Bill, with a rousing sense of sadness. The spider that had moved into her bedroom, was larger than life and twice as ugly and had constructed a beautiful web in the far corner of the ceiling. Jessica liked spiders and always felt that they were a welcome addition to any home. One of their most attractive traits was that they consumed less welcome insects. Bill, although Jessica thought her female, looked to be a successful predator at first and was a very proud, round and a well fed looking specimen who strutted confidently on the ceiling. Over the ensuing weeks and despite the handsome web, she caught nothing. Her self assured rovings and impertinent step were gradually replaced by days of stillness and occasional stilted creeping to the edge of the web. She appeared to Jessica to be becoming malnourished. Jessica tried catching insects and sticking them to the web but Bill did not stir. It was probably that the victims had to be actively moving in order for the spider to respond, a stimulus necessary to the whole process of capture and ingestion. At a loss as to what to do, Jessica periodically observed her and pangs of impotent pity rose up within her.

That morning, Jessica noticed with sadness that Bill had gathered in her eight limbs and turned herself into a ball. She had, Jessica thought, given up and was preparing to die. Enough was enough and full of pity for her plight, Jessica scooped the spider up in her hands and moved her to the outside window ledge in the vain hope that she might build a new web and then hopefully flourish; Jessica knew deep down, that it was too late.

" So like life when you think about it. One stakes ones claim and hopes for the best. One either survives or one goes under, depending where we are geographically and monetarily speaking. Life really is just a lottery."

After showering, getting dressed and breaking her fast too hurriedly, Jessica hurried outside into the bracing wind to get the car. The weather was seasonally fickle and unreliable in the encroaching months of autumn and had changed once again. The previous mornings burst of rejuvenating sunshine had been replaced by a wintry blast of wind and rain. The temperature had plummeted and a bracing chill easterly wind agitated and loosed the leaves of the tree whose colours had changed to russets, yellows and golds. They were falling from the great oak like snow with each gust; captive passengers within the grasp of the blustery wind, blown far and wide, they collected finally in the guttering, in ponds and other depressions, an undignified and anti-climactic end.

It was then that Jessica noticed, several feet from the base of the tree where the bluebells grew in the summer, the slightest hint of a small rectangular delineation of the most subtle kind. Were it not for something akin to 'prior knowledge', the unusual light and the pattern of the falling leaves, Jessica would never have seen it. There was not time to investigate, even though her head tingled with a sense of curiousity, foreknowledge and expectation. She hurriedly picked up some small stones and carefully marked the corners for further investigation at a more appropriate time. For some reason, this reminded Jessica of a time when she had dropped her purse near the house. After a panic-stricken couple of hours while she looked in vain, cancelling credit cards and trying hard not to remember how much money she had left inside, she gave up. Weeks later and when the event had been completely forgotten, she happened to be passing some iron railings near the garage and had seen her purse wedged between two upright poles, completely visible and yet untouched. Much to her surprise the soaking wet purse and the money within were completely and incomprehensibly intact. Jessica, among many other people, must have walked past it a hundred times without seeing it. This was a curious lesson indeed, in the premise of concealment. Certainly the square patch in the ground was, if not highly visible, at least conspicuous to those who knew of its existence. To Jessica, it seemed odd if not astonishing why no one had noticed or explored the site before.

She opened the garage door, mentally shutting her ears to the atrocious squeal of un-lubricated sheet metal that set her teeth on edge. Once opened and seeing the Bentley within, her mind was instantly taken away from the subject of the tree and its imaginary prize buried beneath the bluebells. Jessica gazed with horror at the poor mud spattered and grimy vehicle. Like a great white scar, the key scratch along its right flank contrasted horribly with the otherwise pristine deep blue paintwork. Rob, her annoying neighbour, walked by and stopped, his breezy smile turning to a look of mock concern as he surveyed the old car.
" Oh Dear! If I didn't know you better love, I'd say you've been off- roading again." Then he added with an ingratiatingly cheeky smile,
" What you need love, is for me to polish her up a bit, buff up your bits and pieces so to speak. I'd concentrate on those lovely bumpers of course."

Jessica gave him a withering look as she climbed into the drivers seat and turned the key. She drove out of the garage and stopped briefly. As she reached up to close the garage door, she noticed him studying her outline, flatteringly enhanced in that moment of extension. It had never occurred to her before but Rob actually gave her the 'willies'.

When Jessica arrived at work, John Stringer popped in, greeting her with a surprisingly cheery 'hallo', announcing that there was a 'stiff' to be examined, a man who had apparently been shot through the neck in a shoot and run incident and needed to be looked into right away.
"That pouff Wallace says he hasn't got time and we need to check it out a.s.a.p."
"Poor Stiff! You seem strangely cheery about this John?"
" Ah well you could say that. This man's a 'crim' of the highest order, we've been after him for decades."
Jessica raised her eyebrows questioningly, in expectation of more fulfilling information.
"The file is on your desk but basically he was a coke dealer and a hard porn merchant, Micheal Larkin's the name, did a little time 20 years ago for possession but apart from that we haven't been able to touch him. He's squeaky clean on the surface but he was up to his neck in it; we could never prove anything. He and his wife and kids live, or rather lived, in a huge house in East Grinstead, hob-nobbing with the famous, wealthy and influential, gave millions to charity and was an all round good bloke as far as the world was concerned. He even had elocution lessons would you believe and sounded quite different latterly to the nasty little con that I knew back in the seventies. We knew what he was up to but I have to say he was a clever bugger, always seemed to know when we were onto him, had friends in high places!"

Jessica was intrigued. Having become so absorbed in the case of Lucius Grey and the appalling miscarriage of justice, she speculated that the man might actually be completely innocent, a victim of a questionable past and ultimately, a dreadful murder.

" Any idea who shot him?"

" Well, we have a suspect, just need some proof, some ballistics details in order to prosecute, though he's done us all a big favour if you ask me. We've cordoned off the incident spot and thrown the victim in the morgue."

"Okey dokey, right-ho then!"

On the table in the morgue was a man in his early sixties, of average height, balding but with good strong features, quite handsome. He wore exquisite clothes, expensive Italian designer labels, well chosen and well matched. There was a lingering but not unattractive smell of expensive aftershave. On his wrist was a very understated antique Cartier watch, pure class, nothing vulgar about him at all. He appeared to be a man of culture and class. Jessica had a job to do but there was nothing about him that shouted illegal, immoral or amoral. Upon investigation, his ghastly injuries were consistent with gunshot wounds, the bullets had gone right through his neck, ripping out chunks of soft tissue and lacerating the carotid artery. Later while at the scene of the crime, Jessica found the bullets embedded in a wall which indicated that the shots were taken at close range. Suddenly she remembered her dream about the giant with the scales and the dead eyes and Jessica became unusually susceptible to the concept that impressions can be very misleading. Her forensics training had taught her to beware of the dangers of pre-judgement; impartiality was the watchword under every circumstance. She picked up the phone and dialed Julia's number; it was answered almost instantaneously;

" Hello Jess, how are you? So lovely to hear from you so soon, have you recovered from your weekend yet?"

"Thank you so much for having me, I really did have a gorgeous time, even my long walk, I loved it all. I miss you all so much and especially the mud!"

"Very funny, are you at work now?"

"Yes actually, I am and that's partly the reason I'm calling Jools, hope you don't mind?"

"Oh, 'erm no, not at all."

"I have a case concerning a man who has been murdered and I know that this sounds crazy but I was wondering if you could 'tune into him' or whatever it is that you do and let me know what you feel?" Jessica gave Julia a rough outline of the case

"Jessica, are you asking me for help?"

"Jools?"

"How soon?"

"Yesterday!"

"Oh, as soon as that eh Jess, Just give me ten minutes to finish kneading the bread and a moment to wipe Oliver's nose and I'll get back to you."

" Big kisses to you and all your lovely family."

Back at the morgue, Jessica started to examine the corpse, looking for clues that might be of help to the police but there wasn't much to go on. The injuries were nasty, brutal and despite her conditioning, her heart went out to the man and in that moment, her cellphone rang;

"Jess, It's me, Julia. Listen Jessica, that man, he's been shot hasn't he?"

"Yes, gosh I don't know how you kno.......?"

" What I feel is that he has been very cruel. I feel an intense energy of pure hatred that is focused upon him, by someone who he has harmed very deeply."

"Go on."

" This man is, was a snake, he exudes a veneer of respectability, of culture, intelligence, a philanthropist too but it's all a cover."

"You always amaze me Julia my love, how do you do it? In any event you have confirmed my suspicions......"

" Don't be fooled Jessica, despite his appearance and his reputation this man was an empty vessel, a shell that absorbed evil because it was the only thing that made him 'feel', he was almost inhuman, inanimate, a stray entity. All his money and all his influence meant nothing to him really, he couldn't enjoy anything and had no concept of true joy. He did not understand people, there was no empathy with anything or anyone. Ironically he envied people with advantages, he desired money, wealth, influence, class, but really he was incapable of understanding what it was that made these people he so admired, tick. What he really enjoyed was misery, extortion, brutalising people, killing people. Raping young women a third of his age was his favourite tipple. He was a lowly evolved being of the worst type, a dark and quite lost entity. I feel tainted having tuned in to him"

"My God Jools, I would never have asked you if I had known, I never dreamed that he was such a person...?"

"Jess! One more thing; he was killed by an essentially good man, driven to distraction and to utter despair. You would be doing the world a favour if you didn't find much evidence leading to the arrest of his killer, do as little as possible, hide the evidence."

"You are joking Julia, that would be a huge breach of my professional etiquette. In many ways I would be no better than this corpse, or the man he was."

"Think of the greater good Jess, trust me in this. The law is not always right just because it's the law. His killing was not revenge, just pure justice, something had to be rebalanced. I'm sorry Jess, I have to go now, take care, call me soon."

"Bye Jools, I love you all and thank you, thank you for everything."

Once more Jessica's pragmatic mind was thrown into a turmoil knowing what she had to do but unequal to the task of reconciling this with her well ordered sense of duty.
' Ben Wallace will have a thing to say about this if he ever finds out. I do hope he doesn't study my report too rigorously. Julia has never been wrong though, has she?'
For the first time in her life Jessica did her work, meticulously but she knew that Ben Wallace would sense that something was amiss as he was so familiar with her methodology. John Stringer wouldn't care less and would probably be relieved deep down. Jessica's sense of professional integrity would be compromised but she knew she would be doing the right thing.

CHAPTER 21

The sun blazed unrelentingly from its pinnacle in an essentially unclouded but perpetually brumous sky. The whole planet felt as though it were a steam bath, the humidity so high that it was difficult to draw a really good breath; on top of which the sun was ferocious, especially at midday. From time to time the water saturated sky would loose its incredible burden in a torrential downpour that lasted whole days. Then, though the heat of the sun was less intense, the rain was not cool or refreshing and the temperature drop being negligible, there was very little respite. Today was one of the hottest that Father Donovan could ever remember.

He manoeuvered the boat out of the lagoon and in between the towers of two long vacant buildings that jutted upward into the sky. They appeared monstrous, sightless guardians of the entrance, as the glass panes in each window had long since been smashed. Each window represented a dark pit of despair. Father Donovan so badly wanted to be out at sea that day, way, way out, away from the piles of rotting garbage, the smell, the appalling squalor and the people, mostly sick from malnutrition and disease; sick in mind as well as in body. Survival really was the domain of the fittest, the aristocrats in an impoverished and dying world. Father Donovan survived by his practicality, well honed wits and astonishing intuition. He traded what he caught and gave what he could afford to give but the situation was hopeless and he barely had enough for his own needs.

He felt perpetually guilty, overwhelmed by the pain, misery and suffering of those less able to cope. On some days he felt an urgent need to escape and if he sensed that his catch for the day would be further out to sea then that was an added incentive to leave the land far behind him.

It was well known among the fisherman that it was very unsafe to venture far off shore as the weather could change in an instant, whipping up into a frenzy as if purged from the bowels of hell. Hurricanes, or Typhoons, as people had latterly come to refer to them, an old seafaring term, were frequent and supernaturally violent. Boats far bigger than his were often lost as men, tempted by the prospect of a richer catch, would be lured beyond the safety of the headlands and well beyond the reach of the sheltered harbour. Without engine power, the boats could be driven onto barely submerged but indiscernible buildings or rocks or were sunk by enormous waves that dwarfed even the biggest of ships. Father Donovan, on the other hand, did have fuel for his engines. He had been, collecting diesel over the years, dregs from rusting cans or fuel tanks, priceless fluid ounces won in fights or bets or bought at the cost of many fish. He had even cut it with fish oil and occasionally he added the dregs of gasoline. Some instinct told him that the highly tainted and stale fuel would still work; what he didn't know was if the engines were in any state to run any more. He could not remember when he had last tested the engines, for the fuel was far too valuable. Nevertheless he did have diesel, he had clean and maintained engines, charged batteries and he therefore stood a better chance than most of escaping a storm.

'White Heron' was built in the early sixties, a strictly 'for pleasure' craft but unusually, it was actually very seaworthy.

She was a sturdy, well built boat with a broad beam and a deep heavy keel that had so far endured stormy seas with apparent ease. She was a good craft, obviously named by some previous owner with a sense of humour and a battered bank balance. Underneath the name 'White Heron' was a sub text in italics *'Overdraught'* which slightly irritated Father Donovan for some reason and he considered painting over it. There was, in him however, a prevailing maritime suspicion that changing the name of a boat or even removing part of it was a heinous act that would lead to bad luck or worse. Remembering suddenly how he came by her, he was just grateful that White Heron had broken her moorings in the rising water and had literally drifted into his life at a time when boats were increasingly sought after; his previous boat had been inadequate. Certainly to Father Donovan, steeped as he was in the mysteries of the temporal world, he was sure that White Heron's arrival was an act of Divine providence. Certainly it was a manifestation that helped to assure his survival in such a harsh environment.

He did not feel particularly well and was quite depressed, unusual for him as he was normally such a positive person and enjoyed excellent health which something almost incredible under the circumstances. He so badly wanted to be entirely alone that day; he wanted to imagine, actually he positively craved a world that was not waterlogged, excessively hot and oppressively humid. Most of all, he needed his beloved Jessica, the partner that had made him delirious with happiness and contentment for a cruelly short period of time, to be beside him once more. This woman, Jessica, as if in answer to his prayers, had appeared one day, had seemingly materialised as if conjured into existence by magic. While on an extended fishing trip that had led him as far west as he could go without losing sight of land, he had been forced to turn back east but kept to a more northerly bearing. He had found himself, for the first time ever, in unknown territory on the northern side of the remaining land mass, in an area dotted with small islands, one of which had attracted his attention as it was a steep prominence, rising out of the water with the remains of an old church tower perched at its peak. As he had drawn closer he had become more curious about the island and had decided to weigh anchor and step ashore. It was a fairly brief walk up to the tower but when he arrived, he was astonished to find a beautiful young woman sitting on one of the stone benches inside, reading the remains of a very dog-eared pamphlet. As he entered the tower, he had walked over to her and greeted her albeit slightly awkwardly but was set at ease in a moment as she had looked up at him captivatingly and disarmingly. What was most puzzling was that upon being questioned, she did not seem to know how long she had been there and could not, or would not tell him where she was from. Although he could ill afford to take on another person to feed and to take care of, there was no question in his mind that she should come with him but then what would he do with her?

In those harsh days of austere survivalism and rampant madness, women were outnumbered by men to the ratio of ten to one and were not well treated. If he was to release her into a community, she would starve and become just another sorely used toy as so many surviving women were by men whose sanity and reason had long since deserted them. The more he gazed upon her, the more he had felt a connection. It was more than recognition, he knew her from somewhere but could not think where he had seen her before. When he spoke to her, she appeared to be studying him intently with

249

her deep, dark brown eyes in what he perceived as recognition too. He wanted to keep her for himself, wanted to look after her and the survivor in him realised that she could also be of considerable assistance to him. The paradox of starvation is that the more deprived an animal is of food, the less able they are to gather or hunt and this woman was evidently healthy in every way. When he had taken her on board and was showing her around, she appeared to have an inexplicable fascination for the old motorcycle, the Triumph. A friendship was speedily forged between them as he navigated the coastline back to his familiar fishing grounds. He skippered the boat while she laid nets and put out lines and caught fish quite successfully despite her limited experience; it was good teamwork.

As time passed, the friendship had been superimposed by a more intimate connection and each time they accidentally touched, there was a charge and a sexual tension that increased as they made contact. The 'accidental' touching had become more deliberate and then they would hug each other at every opportunity, such as in celebration of a successful days catch. Finally, Father Donovan, throwing caution to the wind had kissed Jessica for the first time and had been almost overwhelmed by her response, which was warm and urgent. Their kisses led inevitably to the fusing of their souls and of a sublimation of their physical needs. Within no time at all they were dedicated to one another, desperately in love and rarely apart at any time of the day or night. It was as if they had always known each other. An almost cliché concept, he thought but there were so many recollections, numinous, shadowy and elusive and yet there they were and there she was, for a while at any rate. She had loved to swim, often depositing her clothes on to the deck without any hint of self consciousness. He was openly beguiled, charmed by her lack of embarrassment and had studied her form, long shapely legs culminating in a black almost perfect triangle of hair at their apex. Her hips were delightfully rounded and shapely and her lower stomach, betraying just a hint of prominence, narrowed to a slim waist that led finally to her large and lunate breasts. He yearned to hold her in his arms forever.

He had warned her repeatedly about the deadly jelly fish. Despite his dire warnings, she was almost oblivious to the dangers of the ocean, almost as if she was unaware that there was genuine peril. One fateful day, the tragedy that he had most feared came about, she was stung by a monster jellyfish while she was in the water and untangling a fishing line from the rudder. His attempts to save her had been herculean but she had died three days later in his arms in mortal agony, along with his unborn child who lay still in her womb. The experience was so catastrophic to him that he had not wanted to live at first, he had desired with all his heart to end his misery and to join her in eternal paradise.

In tragic Irony, it was a giant purple jellyfish that had postponed his demise. Jessica had adopted a cat and cats were a rarity as no one could afford the luxury of keeping one as a pet when the effort of holding onto ones own life was so perilously tenuous. In fact cats were often eaten when caught. Jessica's cat was a delight and the exception; he was an exceptionally large fellow with a flat face and big feet and an enchanting penchant for lying on his back, eyes closed and kneading the air with his paws, exposing a large but very inviting furry underbelly. He was astonishingly well-fed looking and Father Donovan could not help but wonder where he had been getting his food. In truth, he had never had much time for cats but this almost supernatural creature had become his constant companion, just like a faithful dog. Then a raven had joined them, had appeared one day and was welcomed as a member of the crew but he was an incorrigible thief, although very intelligent and evidently cunning. To complete the menagerie, a rat had found his way onto the boat, a shiny black fellow with a stunted tail and one blue and one brown eye. He skillfully resisted all attempts at removal or capture and therefore also became a part of the team by default. Father Donovan grew to admire his tenacity and even fed him along with the, cat whose name he was told by Jessica, was William. The rat and the raven had so far escaped being given names and were simply called Rat and Bird but somewhere deep in Father Donovan's mind was a word, a name maybe and occasionally the word surfaced unbidden, 'Crevan'- it almost sounded like Raven and sometimes when calling 'Bird' he would instead say 'Crevan' and astonishingly, the raven would respond. William occasionally made half hearted attempts to catch the rat but there was more game in the enterprise than hunter and hunted.

When the disaster had struck, were it not for the animals whom Jessica had loved, he would have taken his own life in despair or would have died from a broken heart. Just moments before she had died, her nervous system neutralised, destroyed by the poison in her system, there was a hiatus, a moment of relief. She had rallied her thoughts for a moment and had spoken to him, breathlessly but coherently and clearly.
" Don't think you have got rid of me just yet priest," she had said and there was the faintest hint of a smile,

"You and I have unfinished business, you know the truth of what I'm saying?" He had nodded, tears streaming down his face, knowing that they would be together again, somewhere, somehow and that helped but only a little.

" Promise me one thing," she had said and he looked straight at her with his blue eyes, there was, in that special moment, a consecration of their spirits.

" William and the Raven are a part of us and also the rat, they are part of a matrix which is more complex than you can imagine just at this time. Guard them all with your life, this is really important. We will be together again in a different time and a different place. None of this is real."

There was a dark pragmatic part of him that felt that she was not quite in control of her faculties, that she was speaking nonsense while in her death throes; however, he had simultaneously felt a resonance and a truth in what she said and besides which, her eyes had told him so. He had promised that he would take care of the animals, that was his sacred duty to her.

Some weeks later, while sitting on the prow of the boat, rocking himself over and over again and gazing into the water in semi-catatonic oblivion, he saw William, who had evidently been chasing the rat, fall into the water. William could swim very well and made for the boat without preamble but Father Donovan noticed, to his horror, the purple domes of two jellyfish rising rapidly from the depths towards William. Like 'ticks', they were attracted to body heat and in their ponderous way they were able to migrate relatively quickly towards their victims. Father Donovan grabbed his shotgun, aimed and blew the nearest jellyfish into pieces. Then he leaped into the water and hauled the hapless cat out by his tail and threw him up onto the deck of the boat, bedraggled and dripping water. William had hissed and snarled in fear, an automatic feline response. In the process of removing William, Father Donovan had been stung by a stray piece of the hapless jelly fish tentacle. Luckily, the contact had been fleeting, a mere millisecond and not enough time for real damage to have been done, especially as life in the detached tentacle was ebbing fast.

After scrabbling out of the water, he had reached for his razor sharp knife, cut out a small portion of flesh from his calf where a lone nematocyst had adhered. He had doused the wound with rubbing alcohol that he had found in the first aid cabinet which helped to staunch the prolific flow of blood and then, with his dwindling strength, he had bandaged his leg. The self inflicted surgery was brutally quick and inexact and he experienced the shooting nerve pain from the poison that was flashing through his nervous system in repeated bursts, pulsing with his heartbeat and it was like nothing he had ever experienced before. As his muscles tightened up due to the effects of the poison, he had lain on the deck and was quite unable to move for hours. During the heat of the day he had sweated profusely, unable to escape the intensity of the sun or even to be able to reach for a drink. He was aware that his sweat gave off a strange odour, almost chemical, astringent, a smell that invaded his sinuses like ammonia. William, sitting nearby and still wet from his ordeal had studied him constantly with an unflinching inscrutable feline stare. Crevan had kept to his perch and did not move. The rat scurried past constantly as if on some mission and for the briefest of hysterical moments, Father Donovan became convinced that the rat was considering eating him, maybe they all were? Occasionally, the rat would sit nearby and preen himself, his beady jewel-like odd eyes and all too human hands were strangely fascinating. His presence, along with that of the raven and of William became infinitely comforting .

As the sun went down and the mosquitoes came out, he had sensed a respite, the mosquito's for once, left him alone. His apocalyptic and anguished state of mind began to rally as he gained a sense that the worst was over. Sometime in the night, he had been able to crawl to the galley where he had drunk deeply from a flagon of water that had been collecting run-off from the the condensation unit. Like the morning drunk desperately seeking to slake his thirst with water upon awaking but then upon drinking, feeling intoxicated again, so too did Father Donovan feel the pain return a little. He had also started to feel nauseous and was on the verge of retching but that awful moment was postponed, then finally avoided; the water would help. He then fell into a sleep which was fitful and interlaced with strange disconnected nightmares but latterly his sleep was healing and deep; he did not awake until noon the following day. The only thing he could really remember upon awaking was having a brief dream about an old man planting a sapling in a wooded grove by a lake shore deep in the middle of an immense forest. It was such an uplifting dream and had seemed so idyllic that it left him with a sense of deep longing. It was a world that he did not know but a world nevertheless, that was undeniably beautiful and paradoxically, strangely familiar.

During the night, there had been of a torrential downpour. In his toxin drugged state of illusion and shadow, it felt like the end of the world had come. Then he thought he felt, or heard, the sound of a particularly prolonged and ominous rumble. In the dim murky depths of his subconscious mind he vaguely registered that this was an earthquake, a huge one by the sound of it which sounded far off and in any case he was quite incapable of responding at that moment. By mid-morning the pain had receded to a vague throbbing, accompanied by a monumental headache and a sore leg where he had so speedily eviscerated part of his calf muscle. He vaguely recalled the sound of rumbling hours earlier but maybe it was just another phantasm of the night? The clouds had cleared and the sun was up, hazy as usual in the water-saturated atmosphere. He studied the ocean which was millpond calm and he was sure he would make it back to shore without undue drama. Though the nausea had abated he did, however, have a terribly upset stomach and was hardly able to stop relieving himself, the waste running from his body and over the side of the boat. Though he was weak and dehydrated, he saw that he was on the mend and that he must cleanse his body to purge the poison from his system and drank all the water that he could. William had ambled over and rubbed up against him, a half purr and half meow. This was both encouraging and soothing, things were looking up. Later that day he had begun quite suddenly, to feel extremely well, light, clear headed, full of energy and with a gnawing hunger in his belly. Most of all, he felt almost happy for the first time since Jessica had died; there was a change in the air, he sensed it.

The memory of the rumbling in the night returned to him and despite his buoyant mood, there was an underlying sense of unease, though maybe the rumbling had been thunder? While looking about him, he realised that he had drifted far out into open sea and he was not able to discern land on the horizon. The atmosphere had become electric, another storm was brewing and within the hour he would be in the thick of it. He had no notion of where he actually was, in relation to his home mooring and the safety of the natural harbour, surrounded by the semi-submerged high-rise buildings. Remembering that the nets had been left down for a long time he dragged them up and was pleasantly surprised to find that there were quite a few fish, an amazing catch in fact. There were of course a couple of small specimens of the usual purple jellyfish along with some squid and he weeded out the jellyfish, throwing them into a bucket. He threw the squid and some of the small fish back into the ocean. He put the jellyfish on top of the bridge in direct sunlight to frazzle in the sun as an outright act of revenge and looked anxiously to the skies again, noticing thickening black clouds on the southern horizon but a fiery red sky to the north. It was then that he decided that the moment that he had been anticipating for years had come; he would have to start the engines and make a run for it.

He figured that the two big diesel engines would use about six gallons an hour between them at cruising speed and so, if he was lucky, he would have three hours of run time maybe more. He checked once again, the filters and the water separators and he bled the diesel lines with the primer; the ritual and ceremony adding to the spell. Then he turned the key to pre-heat the glow plugs on the starboard engine first, adding precious seconds to make sure the motor would fire and he prayed that there was enough juice left in the very old batteries to crank the diesels over. The first engine gave out big clouds of black smoke, almost running but reluctant to run clean. Feeling a little panicked, he had tried the port side engine knowing that the batteries were getting weaker, once again adding precious moments and valuable battery power to the 'pre-heat'. He thumbed the starter button and the engine fired, more dense black smoke and a tantalising few seconds when he was not sure if the motor was going to run but finally the smoke cleared and the engine shouted a mighty bellow of triumph! He warmed it for a few minutes and then engaged the propeller, opened the throttle and then headed north and towards the fire in the sky, in the hope of finding land. With the batteries now charging briskly, he could risk trying to start the second engine. It too blew a mighty cloud of black smoke which then settled to a vague blue as it cleared and he ran the motor for a few minutes at fast idle. Then he opened up both throttles to about three quarters to bring the mighty craft up onto the plane and having achieved that, throttled back a little. Father Donovan became exhilarated as the propellers bit into the ocean and propelled the boat at high speed; he had never known the boat was capable of such spectacular performance.

For the first time since Jessica had died, actually as far back as he could remember, he felt alive. It was such a wonderful feeling to be racing along with his hair blowing in the wind and his eyes squinting against the blasts of sea spray. He had felt a little chilly for the first time ever, that he could remember. The raven flew into the air and hovered above keeping pace, William sat on the dashboard next to Father Donovan on the flying bridge but ducked behind what was left of the windshield. The rat was nowhere to be seen but that was normal during the day. Father Donovan selected, at random, a CD and put it into the player wondering if it still worked. Within moments 'Smoke on the water' by Deep Purple was booming through big heavy speakers while enormous storm clouds accumulated in gathering malevolence behind him to the south. The sea was already becoming choppy and the boat bounced and jostled over whitecaps, the wind developing a capricious bite that made him reach for a rain jacket which was hanging on a hook near the helm; such a glorious revitalising sensation after decades of insufferable sweaty heat. Who knew if they would make it? He no longer cared. Maybe Jessica was right and all of this was just an illusion? It was a matter of fate, if he ran from the storm and found shelter then it was 'meant to be'; on the other hand, if he was engulfed and consumed by the ocean and taken forevermore into 'Davey Jones Locker', then so be it. The opportunity to be mercifully released from this incarceration on a ruined and decaying planet and to be free at last to find another promised land in another realm, another time, rendered him immune to fear.

He had put his hands on the throttles and pushed them to full. The boat leaped forward, shouting its thunder gleefully now that it had been liberated and used as was intended, flying over the troughs and bouncing off the whitecaps of an increasingly angry ocean. The stereo was turned up to almost full, just under distortion level. Remembering suddenly that he had saved some single malt, he opened a rusty tin toolbox on the deck and withdrew a 24 ounce bottle that was half full. Just as he took an extravagant swig from the bottle, excess spirit spilling over the sides of his mouth, it was then that he saw ahead of him, yet some distance away, an encroaching wave of monstrous proportions, an enormous solid black mountain of water. Tidal waves were a frequent phenomenon but this one was truly the monster that they all knew would come one day. He realised then that the 'thunder' that he had thought he heard in the night was indeed an earthquake of titanic proportions. He knew then that his time had come and he knew also that this was to be his nemesis. Terrified at first but in a state of surrender, he gloried in his fate accompanied by the cat, the raven and the rat. He reached for the volume

on the stereo, turning it all the way up to full and took several more deep gulps of the fiery liquid;
'Never mind the bloody distortion, Deep Purple would approve!'

At this most pivotal moment, he had a vision of a half submerged tree in the lagoon, withstanding all that nature could throw at it, it appeared to be beseeching him. In his minds eye, Father Donovan had 'seen' the thousands of acorns deposited upon the ground decades previously, a sign that the tree was near the end of its life, as it resonated with the pulse of life and death. He wanted to be able to run along the once solid ground and to hug the mighty oak, to weep onto its calloused flanks, as if his tears were an elixir that would sooth the tree's pain.
'We all came out to Montreux
On the Lake Geneva shoreline,
To make records with a mobile
We didn't have much time.
Frank Zappa and the Mothers
Were at the best place around
But some stupid with a flare gun,
Burned the place to the ground.
Smoke on the water, a fire in the sky, smoke on the water.........'
Just before he hit the wall of water, almost a mile high, a sight too terrifying to contemplate, he had experienced a powerful vision. A man was burying a large chest at the base of the oak in a deep hole that had been dug in a bed of bluebells. For some reason, the memory of the chest being buried was important. Even more important was what was in the chest, there was a fleeting acknowledgment that contained within that chest, was something that would

change mankind's destiny. He knew that he had to adhere to and somehow carry that memory with him into the next world. As the giant tidal wave approached, with only seconds to go before the boats inevitable destruction and his death, he made a vow to retain this knowledge.

As the craft and its motley crew encountered the steeply ascending edge of the great wave, Father Donovan became certain that they would all be together again as Jessica had predicted. In that moment of utter acceptance of his fate, his mind was purged of all thought, replaced by an insistant and prevailing clarity, he saw into the past and into the future and everything suddenly made sense, the previous conundrum of his limited perspective banished in the light of crystal clear vision. Moments before the boat capsized, bow over stern, the huge engines raging and the propellors scrabbling impotently for bite in the frothing spume, he had seen Jessica standing in front of him, naked, beautiful, hands held out to him, an expression of elation upon her face and he understood.

CHAPTER 22

Jessica knew in her heart that Lucius Grey had been wrongly convicted; the evidence that she had found so far allied with her finely honed instincts supported this. There had undoubtedly been a gross miscarriage of justice and as a result, generations had suffered. The world was full of injustice, always had been and always would be but there was something about this case that really niggled at Jessica. It was as though this 'blip', this outrage had created waves, a ripple effect with far wider and undetected ramifications. After some deliberation, Jessica happened upon the phrase, 'butterfly effect'. She was not even sure what it meant precisely but there was such a resonance with the expression that she looked it up. She read the text and was aghast, it was so appropriate to her feeling, her 'sense'. The butterfly effect, simplistically speaking, is the sensitive dependence on initial conditions, where a small change at one place in a non-linear system can result in large differences to a later state; for example, the flap of a butterfly's wings in Mexico setting of a tornado in Kansas.
'But I could not possibly bring this case up for a review, everyone would think I had gone quite mad to even suggest it! Who knows, they might even be right?'
Jessica however, driven by some unseen force was entirely determined bring light to this iniquity.

The first person she spoke to regarding the case was Detective Inspector John stringer. She subtly mentioned the case in conversation, hoping to elicit some response. In the event he could not have been more disinterested and after a few mutterings of, "Is that so?" he changed the subject. Jessica brought up the case in conversation with colleagues whenever she felt she might receive a positive response but people weren't the slightest bit intrigued. She eventually cornered Stringer and brought up the subject again, citing the premise that this would be a good test case and a public relations exercise for the police force. He evaded the subject, hoping to diffuse Jessica's ardour until finally, ever on a short fuse, he became angry. Still Jessica persisted.

" Oh, for fucks sake, Jessica!" He had shouted in frustration. "What drugs are you smoking love, because I think I bloody well need some? This is nonsense. It's all lost in the past! It's done and dusted love and an investigation is consequently well out of order. Quite apart from the fact that there is no legal precedent to re-examine the case, I personally can't be arsed. In any case you know as well as I do that the force has got a billion unsolved modern crimes to deal with and no time or resources to do so. In any event, we'd never get the thumbs up from the boss."

" Yes but don't you see? If recognised gross miscarriages of justice, even from long ago, are allowed to slip by without so much as a raised eyebrow, then what chance do we have of engendering a respect for the law and a moral understanding of what is right and what is wrong."

Jessica knew she was on dodgy ground.

" No one's got any respect for the law anyway love, what we do is mostly a total waste of time!"

" What's the point of it all then John, why are we doing this. Why are we here?"

John Stringer was a jaded soul who wanted as quiet a life as he could manage. Once he had been a bright and upcoming detective, a veritable trooper representing the powers of good over evil, a firebrand. Sadly and like many of his fellow officers, he gradually lost his zest for life and his work over the years, along with most of his hair and inversely, he had gained a large stomach. He simply wanted to solve crimes as quickly and as unproblematically as possible, collect his monthly salary and dream of his yearly caravan holidays to Provence or to the Algarve. True to his volatile inclinations, he would invariably explode in a fury if pushed, would lash out, hurling invective at his tormentor; Jessica knew what was coming.

"Listen to me girl, just listen okay! This is not your job, it's actually mine, I'm the fucking copper and as I said, I really can't be arsed. You need to let it rest now! Miscarriage of justice or not, it's all too long in the past and I know for a fact that there will not be an investigation because I say so. I couldn't give a tinkers cuss for the old bloke now, it's too late. Bloody pushy feminist lesbians, give me strength!"

This last expression was uttered as he turned away from her and then he masked his eyes and his forehead with his hand as if in pain.

" Right-ho then John, I'll leave you to wallow in your self righteous hypocrisy!" Jessica's response was icy with disdain. There was no more to be said and John Stringer knew that. Once again, he had grossly transgressed the boundaries of social interaction within the workplace. He had also wounded someone he actually respected and the damage was done. In the days that followed, there was an inevitable impasse which would be almost impossible to breach. Jessica was not sure she could forgive Stringer this time, he really had gone too far.

Feeling beaten and deeply angry at first, Jessica was on the brink of giving up on her crusade but after tactically withdrawing and rallying her defenses, she went on the offensive with more determination than ever. She was known to be tenacious in her work but her colleagues were about to discover a whole new side to Jessica's determination. She felt such a sense of responsibility to this man even though he had been dead for well over a century. Ever the pragmatist, she would question her motives time and time again,

'Why is this so important to me? Why do I have this insane desire to help a man who is well past caring and will never have the slightest clue about what it is that I'm trying to achieve.'

When Julia had told her that she and Lucius were inextricably linked across differing time lines, Jessica had snorted with derision and yet how else could this obsession be explained. She just could not let go and despite the rampaging inner conflict and her never ending self doubt, she knew that once she got the ball rolling, events would take care of themselves. Her role was akin to lighting a fire, a momentary input of energy to spark a reaction which once started, could never be stopped while there was still fuel. She so badly needed impetus to gain the initial momentum, her battered sense of enthusiasm was bloody but remained unbowed, especially once she developed a plan.

The idea that Jessica came up with was, like all good ideas, remarkably simple. Later in the week and resorting to a little bit of duplicity, she decided to enlist the help of her beloved uncle, Alistair Gray, who was a retired lawyer and professor who had retained some very useful contacts. Jessica experienced a little twinge of guilt, remembering that she had hardly ever been to visit him since Maria's demise. Wistful and nostalgic thoughts came unbidden, of Alistair, dear Aunt Maria and of their home in rural Wiltshire. She remembered it as a place of permanent but softly embalming sunshine, idyllic atmosphere, fairy tale architecture and rolling fields, covered in a permanently undulating low lying mist. Such a domain of sylvan charm was one which Jessica's mind often returned to during times of stress. She had loved her uncle and indeed her late aunt, more than any other human beings on the planet with the possible exception of Julia. While thinking of them, a spurious thought occurred to her. *'Interesting that Alistair should also bear the name Gray, though admittedly, the spelling is slightly different.'*

Part of the reason that she decided to ask her Uncle Alistair for help was because Maria's brother and also good friend to Jessica's father, Sir William Briggs, was a high court judge. 'Briggsy' was an enormous rotund man who tottered like some vast unstable structure when erect. He was of benign temperament however and was charmingly solicitous if not a little flirtatious with the ladies. Despite his veneer of empty headed, waffling amiability, he was an intelligent man. Part of his talent for legal evisceration was in presenting himself as an absent minded doddering old gent. Many had underestimated him to their great detriment. "Just the man for the job!" thought Jessica while in the midst of quite unashamed scheming. The possibility of a positive outcome was slim but she intended that she would wade into this case, guns blazing and with a good General in charge.

Jessica took the stone path that crossed the rear lawn of Abbotsfield House and stepped up to the entrance of an entirely familiar, exquisitely beautiful and baroque Georgian

266

conservatory designed by an architect of flamboyant renown named Thomas Archer. Jessica was assailed by the strains of music, Cecilia Bartoli singing 'Selve Amiche', cascading like a waterfall through the long sash windows that opened into the conservatory from the library. Her uncle was sitting among a bewildering array of flowers, basking in their exquisite scent. Gerbera, snapdragons, lilies, geraniums and lisianthus surrounded an elderly man wearing spectacles and studying a newspaper. He stood to greet Jessica, smiling broadly, though she was surprised to see that he was stiff and slightly stooped with age, considerably diminished in height from his original lofty 6'4".

" Jessica, my dear, how are you but more to the point, how's that lovely old Bentley?"

There was still that twinkle of mischief in his eyes and really the question was not so odd, after all, the car was a huge link between him and his late wife, Maria. Alistair's own car was a much loved Alvis TD21 soft top that made lovely sports car noises when driven exuberantly, which was most of the time. Unfortunately, like Alistair, the car was past its prime and was tired, fissured, with fading paintwork, seats that were dry and cracked, rough woodwork and an engine that emitted more than a faint blue haze from its exhaust. Jessica had phoned him a few days earlier to warn him of her visit. He had, of course, invited her to join him for tea, sandwiches and a chat. He desired, so he said, to catch up on events and general gossip. He had always been so handsome she remembered, so full of fun, tall and vigorous but as he approached his mid-seventies, he looked old and tired, his legendary vitality starting to desert him. Jessica was immeasurably saddened to see him wilting like a dying flower and wondered whether subconsciously, this was why she had not been to see him, the fear of seeing someone she loved so much becoming so fragile? Then his twinkling mischievous eyes and his famous sense of fun came to the fore and she realised that this, at least, had not left him. She sidled up to him, sliding her arm through his and looked up at him searchingly;

"How are you dearest uncle?" He laughed good naturedly.

"Aha the same old Jessica I see, You always were engagingly precocious but absolutely lovely of course. I simply don't see enough of you my dear but I know that you are fearfully busy and have no time for a decrepit old man."

Then he became serious realising that he had not answered the question,

" Oh but, you know, 'senium quod infirmitas!' Still alive, just. Still game but as old as the sodding hills. Oh do forgive my language my dear.

"Oh, Uncle Alistair, you are the only person that I have left since aunt Maria and father died. It's so good to see you."

Alistair reached out to her and squeezed Jessica's hand.

"I do miss your father so you know. God the stories I could tell you, the shenanigans that we used to get up to my dear. My goodness, we were such scoundrels, you would be shocked! Your father was of course, my greatest friend but he was a sobering influence when things got a little out of hand. Our other great pal, Billy, was a terrible lout, always playing appalling jokes on people and misbehaving horribly, usually as a result of too much too drink, may God forgive us."

Jessica was astonished that Uncle Alistair should mention William Briggs, whom he had referred to as 'Billy', synchronicity indeed. Jessica realised, with a pang of sadness, that he was being more than usually guarrulous, as lonely older people so often are when suddenly presented with company. She felt remorse for not having been to see him more often. He still had his beautiful voice, rich in timbre, baritone and effortlessly modulated. Age had not diminished that at least and once more it made Jessica's scalp tingle in some delicious and oddly sensual way as he spoke. Then summoning up a lively response to familiar stories too often recounted, she looked at him, smiling.

"Gosh, yes, as to that, I can so very well imagine you all up to no good Uncle Alistair. I can even remember bits and pieces; you at a garden party dressed in a suit of armour and on horseback, absconding with a screaming Myrah Briggs! That's one one of my favourites." Alistair gave a hearty stentorion laugh and then became sad, nostalgic memories flooding his mind for a moment; then he chuckled again mischievously.

" God, that woman had the most collosal bosom! Her brasierre gave out when she was laid across the horse y'know. That bugger Briggsy was in stitches!"

Maria had been dead for just three years and even though Alistair had always been a natural flirt and a secretive philanderer, he had loved his wife very deeply. Interestingly he appeared to have aged more in the last three years than in the previous seventy three. In the absence of his late wife, he had become efficient in the ways of the solitary householder and made Jessica a pot of tea, some biscuits, rich tea, ginger snaps and orange osbornes and also a plate of cucumber sandwiches. As Maria had done when preparing for their numerous outings, he had sliced the cucumbers with an aged, tarnished but frighteningly sharp steel kitchen knife honed to a razors edge which had given the cucumber a unique taste, quite unparalleled. Then he drizzled the sliced cucumber with balsamic vinegar and a sprinkle of pepper. The smell and then the taste took Jessica exquisitely, back to her childhood.

Her memories were of endless summer days, of picnics and wickedly daring explorations into the wooded wilderness that once belonged to Abbotsfield. Sadly, the meadow and most of the beautiful big trees had been sacrificed to rapacious development as debts had encroached upon the Grays. All around the perimeter of the three acre property were modern streets of semi-detached or detached houses built in the neo-Georgian style in some vague, uncomprehending and highly insensitive effort to blend in.

Jessica was jolted out of her reverie as Alistair handed her a glass of whiskey, single malt in fact, even though it was only ten in the morning.

" Uncle!" She had remonstrated in mock horror.

" Well what else does an old man do apart from gaze at beautiful women and pine for the time when he was young and carefree, 'adeo tripudium.' You don't mind though do you?"

" Not at all, chin-chin! Aha, well as to that comment about having nothing to do, uncle Alistair, I have a case I want re-opened."

"Heavens! You don't beat around the bush do you. I knew you were up to something of course; Cheers my dear!" Holding the glass to his nose he inhaled with his eyes shut and then took a gulp of the whiskey.

" I'm retired you know my dear and rather out of touch to be brutally honest!"

Ignoring the note of doubt in his voice, Jessica smiled enchantingly at him and carried on undeterred.

"Yes it's the one I told you about on the phone, concerning a a man who has been dead for over a hundred years; Lucius Grey."

His great white furry eyebrows shot up in surprise and his heavy lids opened to reveal eyes that were still as blue as the summer sky and the twinkle flashed brighter for a moment. Jessica gave a few basic details in the hope that his interest might be piqued.

" If he has been dead for such a long time, I'm not sure if it would be possible to re-open the case my dear? There are laws that prohibit such an action after a length of time has elapsed."

"Oh Uncle, this was probably the greatest mis-trial of the millennium, so much misery and ill fortune was inflicted upon the family as a result of this debacle. Surely it is time that Lucius Grey's name was cleared?"

Alistair looked thoughtful for a moment, unusually serious, as if he knew that what he had to say was not going to be well received.

"I'm not really sure that it is Jessica and such is life I'm afraid. My goodness, you do seem to have got rather caught up in all this "

Jessica knew that she had to get his interest, rouse him from his torpor, he needed to be given a lift. Already oiled by the heavy hit of the mid morning whiskey, Jessica topped up both glasses, then, basking in the sunshine and the scent of the flowers in the conservatory she talked animatedly for what seemed like an age, noticing after a time that he was staring at her distractedly.

" You know Jessica, it's the most curious thing and I know it has occurred to me before but I've never mentioned it for some reason?"

Jessica was expectant, thinking that he had pulled some legal rabbit out of the hat. Her hopes started to germinate, delicate filigree roots gaining purchase.

"You don't really look at all like your mother and you certainly don't sound like she did but the most curious thing is that when I close my eyes, it really could be your mother in this room."

Jessica's mother was a mystery to her, someone in a motley selection of faded and creased photographs and one larger framed photograph that had sat on her fathers desk in his study for as long as she could remember. In the photograph, her mother was wearing a very traditional and beautiful wedding dress that, as was explained to her once, had belonged to Jessica's grandmother. There was an incongruity in the photograph, as Jessica's father looked the epitome of a senior British civil servant in his very well cut but rather drab suit and jaunty panama hat. Jessica's mother on the other hand, looked frightened, lost, like a new girl at school, in a uniform to which she felt she did not really belong but she looked strangely jubilant too, proud, an odd combination. Unlike Jessica's skin colour which was a rich dark brown with a tinge of deep red, her mother's skin was dark, her eyes and teeth flashing white in contrast. She was extremely slim, petite in fact, not statuesque like Jessica, but undeniably beautiful and she boasted refined features and held herself proudly like a queen. Probably for the first time in her life, Jessica felt a sudden fervent wish that she could have known her mother and to have been spared the string of lacklustre nannies that had raised her.

It was brought home to Jessica that the concept that Alistair had known her mother, very well in fact, a living mortal whose eyes had rested upon hers and whose hands had no doubt shaken those of hers and whose cheeks he had kissed was altogether very odd, not real.

" What was she like Uncle Alistair, would I have liked her?

"Oh yes, you would have adored her and she you. When she was expecting you she was so happy, never a moments sickness, always so animated, planning, yearning to hold her new born child. It was a cruel trick of fate that took her from us. She made your father very happy but do you know, their association, their marriage ruined his career, but those were the consequences you came to expect in those idiotic days from mixed marriages. He was never the same when she died. No one realised then that she was really quite ill, as she had appeared so vital."

Jessica was both comforted by the conversation about her mother but also discomfited, her not being there had meant a long period of maternal austerity during her childhood and there was a little part of her that was angry with her mother for abandoning her. Much as Jessica's father had loved her, or so she had surmised, he was just not equipped emotionally or practically to deal with her.

Suddenly, Jessica wanted to change the subject, abruptly. "Uncle Alistair, I'm sorry to go back to this but I wondered if there was any chance that you could give this case some thought; look at my notes, the evidence."

"What case?'

" The one concerning Lucius Grey's hanging, or rather, his innocence."

He sat silently, brooding, maybe he was upset by Jessica being so brusque. She became aware that he was evidently contemplating a pure white chem trail in the unblemished blue sky. Jessica started to suspect that he really had forgotten what they were talking about.

" You know that those vapour trails persist for far longer now than they used to do even fifteen years ago, something to do with carbon emissions. I'm starting to think that my time on this beautiful planet is up, I don't want to live to see it ruined any more by man. People really are so stupid!"

Jessica looked at him and reached out to hold his bony and venous old hands, with their arthritic and swollen joints. Momentarily she had a vision of her uncle, handsome, young and raffish, dressed in a dinner jacket, his hands delicate and dexterous, beautiful; hands were important to her. She felt sad for him, wanted to make him young again, wanted him to regain his magnetic attraction to women.

'He may be an old roue now but there was a time when his charm and his good looks caused women to fall completely in love with him, they would yearn for him. The only damage he did was to womens ego's and possibly to the odd marriage but that damage was a part of the beauty and the poetry of life. Without such yearnings and longings and drama where would we all be? Old age is such a terrible thing, a blight that gets us all in the end. There's nothing remotely gracious about it; the inevitable dwindling of life force as natures cycle is completed. Oh, I'm just being maudlin.'

She sensed that he was not interested in her project or even, for that matter, in life. Quite simply, she realised, he was too old and possibly even a little senile.

It was in that final and tumultuous moment of letting go of her obsession, her fully embraced acceptance that re-opening the case was an event that would never happen, that he spoke again, somewhat wistfully.

"Yes I have been listening to you Jessica my dear, and you are quite right. I'm bored you know, bored with life, bored bloody witless and lonely. Old age is a repugnant period in ones life, there is nothing dignified about the process of decay you know, well of course you do. 'Quo vadis,' eh, my dear?"

274

He sat in silence again for a moment, swirling what was left of his liberal second glass of whiskey around in his tumbler. "Do you know my dear, this project of yours does sound rather fun and intriguing actually; I need a purpose in my life. Things have been too easy for me really, I've always had what I wanted, never had to work very hard, apart from during the war; that was rather tedious at times. I had the best woman in the world as my wife, may she be blessed. I had everything and to be absolutely honest I feel a bit of a fraud, always have, I really need to do something worthy before its too late. Now look at me, here I sit judged by a higher authority, incapable of stopping the clock- serves me right, eh-haha! Do you know of that famous quote m'dear? 'Alcohol, hashish, prussic acid, strychnine are but weak dilutions, the greatest poison of all is time.' Emerson, I believe, 'Society and Solitude?' I've always had a taste for the good life, too much booze as you know and I have even been known to try hashish in my youth though who exactly knows of this, I am not willing to find out. Oh how I have loved life but I'm sure you don't want to hear all this nonsense from an old man raving in his dotage."

Jessica was just about to leap up and hug him but he held out his hand.
"I have to say that I'm not entirely sure if we can make this fly but I will make inquiries right away starting with the Lord Chancellor, my old friend Billy Briggs and I'll bloody well give it my best shot; God! That sounds so American. What do you think of that eh?"
"Jessica was stunned, speechless."
" Do you think Sir William be interested?"

She pretended innocence but her uncle had played right into her hands, knowing that if he came to the conclusion himself then he was far more likely to follow it through.

"Yes of course; I caught him in bed with their au pair once, actually I was always catching him and I know his wife would flay him alive if she ever found out. If he is at all awkward about this I'm just going to have to blackmail the bugger!" Alistair's eyes twinkled attractively, the fires of mischief illuminated them once more and made them fully alive. Jessica smiled at him, wanting to hug him.

" Do you have nothing to say my dear; 'Decorus silentium."

"I'm sorry uncle, I really thought you weren't listening, just not really interested but gosh, crikey, that's wonderful! You won't regret this!"

" I'm sure I will my dear but I really couldn't give a stuff any more, this is just what I need in my dotage and just what Billy needs, whether he knows it yet or not. He's become rather too complacent and pompous in his old age.

That night Jessica slept like a baby, in her old room on the eastern side of the house that overlooked the trout pond. Everything was falling into place. In the morning however, she awoke to a heavy mist that shrouded the world and locked her inexplicably into a zone of deep apprehension. What had she started?

CHAPTER 23

Within months of Jessica and Alistair's conversation, the investigation was re-opened. John Stringer became positively radioactive with fury, newspapers were intrigued, local television muscled in, bureaucrats were amazed, tax payers indignant and diocesan authorities outraged. Nevertheless, the remains of Alex Grey, Constantine Butler, Adam Brogan and Georgina Brogan were located and exhumed. After taking countless samples for DNA analysis, forensics tests were carried out on the scant remains; Jessica was itching to see the results knowing that the evidence would be irrefutable.

Once the avalanche had started there was no going back and it assumed monstrous proportions as it increased in speed, gathering mass and intensity. Due to the unrelenting efforts of Alistair Gray, who pulled in an extraordinary number of favours with many people including a grudging and grumbling Sir Billy Briggs, the whole case was not only reopened but was represented on national television. Benjamin Wallace was in his element and hogged the limelight shamelessly. Initially, Jessica was asked to give an account of proceedings. So unused to being in the public eye, her delivery was stilted and desultory, Ben Wallace was encouraged to speak in Jessica's stead. Though his 'performance' was scientifically accurate, his natural ability as a raconteur lent the tale so much flavour that viewer ratings soared. He was narrowly upstaged by Alistair Gray who, predictably enough, won the hearts of the women of the nation with his intelligence, charm, melodic voice and Latin epithets. Newspaper reporters circled like sharks in a fervid feeding frenzy and recorded events on a daily basis. Even Jack the Ripper was surpassed in notoriety by Judge Constantine Butler. Diminutive Benjamin Wallace, brandished his golf club at over inquisitive and pushy reporters; many learned that it was a mistake to be in close quarters when he was working, bumptious and annoying as ever, he was nonetheless invaluable and irrepressible, now that he had the bit between his teeth.

According to Benjamin Wallace's account, forensics had deduced from various DNA samples, that the exhumed body of the allegedly murdered Georgina, was not in fact her at all, could not have been. The maid's clothing, though rotten and falling to pieces, was evidently not hers. Servants were rarely fortunate enough to wear expensive jewellery, fine silk gowns and brocade; the clothes therefore, must have been Georgina's. Furthermore, the remains of a note was tucked into the maid's under skirts where she must have put it before being abducted and then brutally murdered. Presumably her killers, fearing to breach the customs of social etiquette of the time, had not the temerity to search her for evidence which might implicate them but this did not deter them from hacking the poor creature to pieces. This vital piece of evidence finally removed the cast of judgment from Lucius Grey. Following a brief but well televised and dramatic hearing, he was vindicated entirely.

The grave of the latterly tormented Judge Constantine Butler was also exhumed and his mortal remains were analysed by a team of investigative scientists, including the strutting Benjamin Wallace. More self important than ever, he brandished his ever present golf club and lapped up the publicity. Constantine Butler, it was discovered, was found to have had advanced tertiary stage syphilis at the time of his death and was pronounced 'most probably quite insane.' As Jessica had surmised, it was Constantine Butler who had arranged to have the maid 'done in'. There were evident similarities in stature and age between Georgina and the maid; the worthy judge had evidently utilised this convenient and happy element in his plans to remove Lucius Grey from the scene, leaving him free to win Georgina for himself. Somewhat surprisingly, it transpired later that Butler had also murdered Adam Brogan who was alleged, at the time, to have committed suicide. Quite why Butler had done this required further interpretation of the evidence and Benjamin Wallace was up for the challenge in his inimitable style. Utilising his vivid but often useful imagination and his vast store of knowledge, he filled in the blanks to create a scenario. Like a sermonising priest in the pulpit drawing from the commendation of the almighty and with the patronage of an awed and silent congregation in front of him, he pronounced his interpretation in a vigorous, self righteous and censorious bellow. Jessica noted with some degree of amusement and irritation, that although a little over dramatic, he was, as usual, quite accurate.

Butler, out of his mind with disease, desire, jealousy and anger, had chosen a moment when he knew Adam Brogan would be absent and he had abducted Georgina, in the apparent hope that she might weaken, concede and finally agree to be his. He must have been confident of his ultimate success, as abduction, especially by an upright pillar of society, was an extremely serious crime. Some evidence was miraculously found which indicated that while Butler was en-route to Cornwall with his captive, they had stopped off at an Inn. The tattered remnants of an old register were found in which Butler had registered as the Right Honourable Constantine and Mrs Georgina Butler. Wallace produced evidence in the form of notes from Butler requesting an audience with Georgina with the intention of adhering tenaciously to his plan to win her over. Allegedly, having been horribly but justifiably vilified and rejected, Butler had ravished and raped Georgina. Two of Butler's hired ruffians had dragged Georgina's maid into the forest and mutilated her with a knife that they had stolen from Lucius' house. Further evidence supported Butler's intention that she should appear to be the victim of a sexual predator but also to be un-recognisable. When she was found by the side of the road with Lucius' knife beside her, her clothing which was torn and bloodied was obviously the attire of a lady. Lucius Grey was doomed from that moment. Constantine Butler, in his madness and fearing discovery, bullied and chivvied and did all that he could as presiding judge, to make Lucius fully accountable for the heinous crime. Evidently, Butler was so consumed with passion for Georgina that he lost any remaining reason. He locked her away in a Cornish country cottage where months later she gave birth to his child and then died rather tragically in child bed, most probably of a broken heart Wallace surmised. The child did however survive.

Adam Brogan, having giving great thought to the matter, had been increasingly suspicious of events in connection with Lucius. He discovered after the judgment and quite by accident, that Lucius, true to his claim, had indeed been away at the time of Georgina's alleged murder; he was in fact overseeing the unloading of a trade vessel recently returned from overseas. No witnesses came forward as Butler had evidently seen to that. What Butler had not realised was that one crew member was a friend of Lucius' and though initially silenced by the bribes and then threats from the 'worthy' judge, the man had finally been overcome by his conscience. He had come forward to substantiate Lucius' claim that he had indeed been far away when Georgina had been murdered. Adam Brogan's subtle digging finally paid dividends with an unexpected turn of events, Constantine Butler confessed. Evidently a broken man, deranged by Georgina's relentless but vicious rejection of him and then of her death only the previous night while giving birth, Butler broke down and made a tearful confession to Adam Brogan. He repeated over and over again that all he had wanted to do was to marry Georgina and to make her happy. Adam realised that he too was implicated by virtue of the fact that he identified the maids body as Georgina's and had pointed the finger of suspicion at Lucius. He had allowed his hatred of Lucius to cloud his judgment and had let Butler whistle the tune.

As events unfolded, it transpired that very conveniently for Wallace, Adam had kept a journal of unfolding events which included the dreadful confession of the the judge. He had clasped the journal to his bosom, taking it with him to the grave where, of course, it was discovered. Broken hearted over the loss of his daughter, Adam was devastated by the fact that Georgina had actually been alive when he had supposed her dead and then to his dismay, learned that she really had died on the eve of his discoveries. Indeed, as was mentioned in the journal, he was intending to have it out with Butler and planned to shoot him. Following Butler's distraught confession and comprehending his deep psychosis, Adam began to relent. Butler at the last minute, fearing repercussions, had seized his gun and had shot Adam, leaving him for dead. Adam, though badly wounded, lingered for nearly two painful weeks while he wrote feverishly in his journal. Finally, he succumbed to virulent infection and gave up the struggle for life. His journal was buried with him in eternal repose.

Constantine Butler had been truly on the ropes, his life a mess. Diseased, his true love dead and being guilty of the greatest hypocrisy and perjury, he had killed his only real friend. Yet in his madness, some thread of instinct for self preservation had prevailed and so it was that he safeguarded himself by creating the evidence to suggest that Adam Brogan had killed himself. Butler, apparently lived for some years more but then had died a raving lunatic, no doubt haunted by his past sins. According to the legend he was plagued by night demons and tortured by hallucinations from sleep deprivation, exhaustion inevitably overtaking him, he would awaken screaming Lucius' name.

One further piece of information that turned up, was in fact located by an ancestor of the Bishop of Durham at Jessica's request. He had watched the unfolding events on television and learning of the involvement of a forebear, had responded speedily to Jessica's appeal. Miraculously, some diaries in his possession had belonged to his ancester, none other than the good Bishop of Durham. Contacting Jessica in a state of great excitement, he had subsequently arranged for them to be delivered into her hands. The journals were leather bound and filled with entries made in the same fine hand. Though the leather was cracked and peeling, the bindings broken, some pages loose and the handwriting faded, there was no doubting their legitimacy. Jessica examined them tirelessly and eventually found an entry that looked to be chronologically correct. Judging from the entry, the previous Bishop was obviously deeply disturbed and well he should have been in Jessica's opinion.

'He should have spoken out, Butler was of completely unsound mind, he was a raving lunatic!'

The Bishop's bitter prose in his entry questioned the very core of his faith and the episode, no doubt, troubled him deeply until the day he died.

' My faith prohibits me from speaking out, words spoken in the sanctity of a confessional are inviolate, yet what monster may supposedly gain the forgiveness of the Almighty and yet walk as a free man, his conscience purged. What a dilemma, shall I allow this man to escape the justice of mankind and to be forgiven by God having perpetrated such horrifying acts. As the Almighty's emissary, I forgave him as I was bound by my office so to do. Should I have done so, could I refuse? I gave him an exhaustive penance but a man so bereft of guidance by his true conscience or in possession of a lucid mind, will be unable to understand the implication of his penance. What then will be the nature of his forgiveness? Should I break my oath and speak out? It is the right thing to do but I find I cannot. It is a cruel twist of fate indeed that I have invested so much of my life in The Faith only to be confounded by my own hypocrisy. He was my friend but no longer will I countenance the existence of that man. He is a true monster.'

Jessica saw then that it had been the Bishop of Durham who had somehow accessed the prison records for Lucius Grey more latterly and had made the additions that she had noticed when originally studying them; everything fit.

Jessica was not religious and moral issues in connection with religion were easy for her to pronounce a judgment upon but she did feel the Bishops pain and empathised with his stricken conscience. He was evidently a good man and he was obviously in a sorry state of conflict over the whole issue of Constantine Butler. Jessica could afford to be dispassionate however and to put the blame where it was due. The Bishop had a responsibility to mankind and as such it had been incumbent upon him both morally and spiritually, to have spoken out. There was a cynical part of Jessica that speculated on the possibility that the worthy Bishop felt bound, on some immoral level, to forgive the Judge, as he was his friend and was a 'gentleman'. What would have happened had the Judge been instead say, a sailor, a drunkard and a wife beater, a man considered of lower order in those days of established 'class' guidelines? Only the worthy Bishop, searching deep within his heart, would have known the answer to that.

Shortly after the case was over, poor Alistair Gray died very unexpectedly, in his sleep. A smile on his face indicated that he was happy with his release and had passed away a contented man. Jessica had been with him the previous day and had enjoyed hearing of his younger years; he was always so fascinating, amusing and informative to the end. She remembered listening to him that previous night as she had done so often before, in a state of rapt attention, while curled up on a large dusty Knole sofa upholstered in a musty but evocative William Morris print. Later that afternoon they had played croquet. Alistair, who was surprisingly limber for his age when up to mischief, cheated or played dirty, chuckling with schoolboy-ish glee as he did so. In the evening he had taken Jessica to the pub, The Royal Oak; he had joked with locals, showing off his pretty niece Jessica and chatted with the owner; he drank his allotted three pints of good Real ale, his 'quota' as he described it; 'A satis vis.' They both enjoyed a hearty pub meal, beef in guinness pie with peas and chips followed by treacle pudding and custard. Alistair was in an ebullient mood and quite on form when he went to bed that night but in the morning he didn't appear. Jessica, becoming alarmed by about eleven went to see if he was okay but found a man no longer, an unrecognizable and shriveled stranger lay in his bed. He had obviously died peacefully in his sleep. No doubt he was driving his revamped and immortalised Alvis in celestial star bursts from universe to universe, doffing his cap jauntily and waylaying pretty ladies as he went on his way. No doubt he was also endorsing his bewitching sentences with charming if slightly pretentious Latin epithets. Jessica immediately phoned Julia and gave her the sad news and then sobbed into the phone.

Curiously enough, he had finally left Jessica with the secret of his surname. There was an envelope addressed to Jessica with a note enclosed propped up on Alistair's desk as though he knew what was coming. To her amazement, Jessica found that, like Celtic knot-work, the fates of people in her life seemed to be woven in and around her own life. She was the only person to have been curious about his name and it must have been what spurred him on to do some digging. It transpired that he was a great great grandson of none other than Constantine Butler and of course Georgina Grey. The child born of the tragic union between Georgina and Butler, a boy, had inherited Butler's fortune. Little was known of him other than that he was given the name Gray with an 'a', Walter Gray. Walter had married happily, bought a house and fathered two boys. There were more surprises as Jessica found that the younger of the two was Mrs Wainwright's great Grandfather. The elder was Alistair's great grandfather who, by the rules of primogeniture, had inherited the estate. The property eventually ended up in Alistair's hands in an attenuated form and that included the house that Walter had originally bought. The amazing irony in all of this was that not only was Alistair related to Mrs Wainwright as a distant cousin but to Jessica's astonishment, so was she. Even more amazing was the startling news that they were actually descendants of Constantine Butler. It was a chilling concept for Jessica who suddenly felt the disreputable and toxic elements of her ancestry running though her veins. No wonder she had taken the case so much to heart.

Alistair died intestate; a dusty old Will was discovered but evidently had been drawn up many years previously. He had bequeathed the house to Jessica but sadly, the Will had never been signed or witnessed. There was a previous Will naming Jessica's father as executor and Maria as sole beneficiary. Some odds and ends and pieces of furniture were left to Jessica in this one along with a sum of money to be put in trust for her. It was all strangely ironic considering that Alistair had been a professor at law but Jessica had always suspected that he in fact, loathed the legal profession and couldn't cope with any sense of this organising jural influence in his private life, meaning of course, that at the time of his demise, his financial and legal affairs were in chaos. The house, it transpired, was heavily mortgaged. Alistair had always led a life of delightful frivolity and extravagance. He knew how to live the high life and he had style, loving expensive cars, well fitted suits from Saville Row, hand made shoes from Crockett and Jones in Mayfair, expensive aftershave and Cuban cigars. His income and inheritance had never been sufficient and he had lived beyond his means. At the reading of the 'will', sharks of course, appeared on the scene, people vaguely related, supposed friends and helpers and they circled ominously in the hope of scraps. A nurse turned up at the inquest who had apparently helped Alistair when he had spent time in a nursing home following a bout of pneumonia. Without preamble or scruple, she demanded that she had been promised a large sum of money. A birthday card had been discovered in his possession that had been sent to him by the nurse. It was stacked among other correspondence including tons of unopened bills. Jessica was appalled when she read the card and found a message inside; "To dear Alistair with much love from the daughter you did not know you had."

It was a shockingly low and obsequious tactic, transparently motivated by pure acquisitiveness and greed. Jessica was quietly outraged on Alistair's behalf. She decided to walk away and let the law intervene and do what it must to disseminate the estate. Mrs Wainwright was also a likely beneficiary which was ironic as this would not have come to light had Jessica not reopened the case.

Jessica made arrangements to have some family momentos and pieces of furniture delivered to her flat. They were things that she knew, had been important to Alistair and Maria. As she drove through the gateway at the end of the drive, she experienced pangs about the house and a sense of debilitating sadness settled upon her. For Jessica it had been the only security in her life, a mooring from which she had set out to sail the waters of the world but to which she could return when she needed safe harbour and to recharge her batteries. She knew that Alistair and Maria had meant her to have the place. She was compelled to admit however, that in the same way as the Bentley, the beautiful old house was a true dinosaur, a relic from a time when position and affluence meant that you could legitimately demand a bigger slice of the world. It was a work of art, bewitchingly beautiful and full of enchanting nooks and crannies, just the kind of place that many people would dream of inhabiting, of playing lord of the manor while fundamentally missing the point. Such an abode was more than just a home, a work of art or a status symbol, it was a temple too. A spell had been woven when the house was created and subsequently lived in by generations of happy families. It was a bewitching and delightful spell that crossed celestial and temporal boundaries while the physical substance of the building remained anchored to the earthly realm. Jessica saw all this but recognised in those painful moments just as she was leaving, that the cost was just too high in so many ways. No doubt there would be a solution one day but to Jessica, the price of being involved in litigation for years in the hopes of a resolution was just too much; almost obscene and she wanted simply, to let it go. The memories of the fictional characters, 'Jarndyce, versus Jarndyce' in Charles Dicken's 'Bleak House' were a reminder that the wheels of justice do indeed grind exceeding slow.

For her part, case solved and her beloved uncle Alistair buried with his beloved wife in the churchyard in the village nearby and beneath an enormous copper beach tree, Jessica felt herself in a state of permanent anti-climax, of ennui. It was as if her life's work were over, as if her lover, children and her home had been taken from her. After all the months of work and the tide of strangely unbidden esoteric experiences that had swept in, everything had just stopped; suddenly the world seemed so empty and life meaningless and so very sad. Over the ensuing winter she became deeply depressed and even her best friend Julia, was quite unable to rouse her from her lethargy. Jessica lived from day to day, just coping with her work and life. Gradually, she became more lacking in her previously unique vitality, she wore the death crones shadowy cape which spread a greyness about her; an atmosphere of despair surrounded her. Even the intransigent John Stringer became concerned for her welfare. Shortly after the case, she had fallen out with Steven Savage during a very heated and cruel argument about a mere trifle and refused to speak with him any more: Jessica was by degrees, becoming noticably more unreasonable as each day passed. She was no longer visited with strange and exhilarating nocturnal dreams now that the ghost was laid to rest and she mourned their loss almost more than she could bear. The dreams while they had lasted, had quite taken over her life, had absorbed her into some magical temporal world, a life that seemed in many ways, so real. Without this other dimension, her world became empty, a void and increasingly tragic. There was an all pervading sense that some cataclysmic event or catastrophe was just around the corner as well as the impending threat of economic collapse. Even the knowledge that incomprehensible quantities of carbon emissions were poisoning the air, causing wildlife to dwindle. A dying and increasingly acid ocean, indeed the very lungs of the Earth, that was horribly over-fished haunted her, making her feel hopeless. Ironically, she had been blissfully happy in her recurrent dreams of living in a tortured and battered world of the future, but that was different; she had been with the man she truly loved, her true 'soul partner' a cliché and overused expression but which in

Jessica's case was particularly apt. Paradoxically, in that tortured polluted world, there was actually hope of a kind, a potential for improvement, she could feel it just the same as she could sense the hopelessness of her own world in the 21st century. No more though, no more new life in a burned out future, that door, she felt, had been abruptly closed to her and she had not the least idea why.

William was her only friend and ally during all of this and seeming to sense her anguish, he did his best to adore his mistress. He circled around her legs peering up at her lovingly or alternately, he lay on his back with his feet in the air. He repeatedly attempted to open the rich tea biscuit tin and when a morsel was offered he would jump onto her lap and purr, rubbing noses with her. He tirelessly entertained her and while she loved him for it, she seemed to be no longer capable of love. The only thing that aroused her attention was a raven that repeatedly sat in the great tree. Whenever she walked by, often deep in thought, he would singler out, stretch his wings and 'caw' at her. If she sat outside on her swinging chair, he stood nearby under the tree preening his exotically blue/black and lustrous feathers with his intimidatingly sharp and shiny beak.

Then one day Jessica noticed that the raven always stood in the same spot and despite the fact that she was in a state of permanent semi-consciousness, her sensibilities dormant, she became curious about the bird. The raven, she remembered, was a creature of her dreams, always there whenever she had dreamed of Lucius Grey. The prison report on Lucius Grey's execution had mentioned the raven sitting on the gallows. Very much akin to black cats, these were creatures of the twilight world. Indeed she had heard a story from Julia that there was a legend that ravens were actually old druids re-incarnated in bird form.

'So odd that the bird should always sit in the same spot,'
she thought repeatedly

" Oh my Goodness!" she cried out loud, her first animated utterance in weeks in realisation. Her subconscious had uttered these thoughts first and it was only after listening to the echo of the words that the penny dropped. There was a moment when she wondered how someone so scientific and so rigidly adherent to detail could have let something so potentially monumental pass by.

" The ground at the foot of the tree, how could I forget that some treasure might be buried there!"

These thoughts however vanished days later, clouded amidst the dynamic and tempestuous perturbations of her mind. The knowledge, so keenly won, simply deserted her. Oddly enough, the raven too disappeared from her life and so any means of reminder were removed.

CHAPTER 24

There was no more dreaming. Jessica had been deserted by that world or rather that particular reality was now denied her. She was effectively isolated from the only man that she had ever loved and she felt quite abandoned. Was it even possible to find ones true soul partner in a dream, an imaginary character created from within the depths of ones subconscious,
'But he was real, wasn't he?'
Jessica was hollow and empty, the cold-turkey withdrawal was a harsh reality indeed. There was, paradoxically no other life for her now that her elusive and ethereal partner was suddenly and cruelly absent. Jessica became gradually more distraught, broken hearted and her life ever more meaningless. She started to go downhill; her health, her state of mind and her astonishing vitality diminished, being daily attenuated by a loss of the will to live in the world, this world.

While sitting upon her swinging chair one day and rocking to and fro in a state of mindless dejection as she was wont to do, Jessica lapsed into a meditative state where immediate thoughts were banished but where sounds and impressions came to her in crystal clarity. That old sensation of her scalp tingling lulled her and quieted her tormented mind. A blackbird inexplicably voiced his joy at the threshold of what was soon to be a wintry gloom and Jessica's reaction to his song was of joy but of a deep discomfort, as though a memory was being summoned that she was fearful of, this time she let herself be wholly absorbed by the sound. At that moment of clarity, an image came back to her of the subtle evidence of excavation of the soil at the foot of the Oak tree. Misty concepts lying in the dark recesses of formlessness in an ethereal void gained resolution, crystallized and became manifest. It was then at this sudden recollection of the shape in the ground that an altogether more concrete resolve overcame her to shed her melancholy and to investigate the ground at the foot of the tree.

At this timely juncture that Jessica's nocturnal inter-dimensional world returned; her strange alternative life becoming gradually less mysterious. So vivid were the dreams now that Jessica was haunted by graphic recollections of them during her waking hours. She withdrew more and more into her world of shadow and illusion. In a way she was genuinely at peace though the source of her contentment was derived from quite another place. The dreams were always meandering, sometimes erotic, occasionally a little disturbing in a way but always tragically beautiful. These nocturnal experiences left her feeling permanently languorous, having form and sequence and evolving, each nocturnal adventure a natural progression from the previous one. For Jessica, this was becoming her life and reality, albeit in some other dimension. On some level, she knew that she was inextricably linked to Lucius when she strove to clear his name, as though, her life, her very soul depended upon it.

Inevitably, Jessica was relinquishing her grasp on life in her twentieth century world. She tried to work in an effort to escape from other aspects of her life. She ate sparingly and lost weight, her hair lost its lustre and her fingernails cracked. In contrast were her eyes which gained in intensity, becoming bright, jewel like, limpid and they burned consumptively with a manic fervour. Her initial descent into deep depression had been transformed into an adventure, a wonderful flight into the unknown and she submitted herself to the experience becoming in fact, quite lost.

The memory of the existence of the chest under the oak tree, had opened the lid of Pandora's box as far as Jessica was concerned. It was as though she was being encouraged, in a most urgent way, to continue with a mission as yet unfinished. She was dreaming again, of beautiful forests of oaks, of Father Donovan, the past and the future? It was so beautiful to be in his company once more, even in a ruined world in an undefined time zone. Discovering the site at the foot of the tree had brought her back to life. Though feeling so very reclusive and hampered by an incredible torpor, she eventually phoned Julia to sound her out about her plans to investigate the site.

Organising the dig, an excavation of sizeable proportions that would leave a big hole in the ground at the foot of the oak in pursuit of 'God knows what', was not quite as complex as Jessica had imagined. She contacted Ray, the groundsman and put it to him. She explained that her interest was a professional one and connected with the recently cleared Lucius Grey. In the event, Ray was helpful in the extreme and offered to clear it with the housing association, the governing body made up of the residents of Mortlac and the owners of the freehold. When she herself raised some potential reasons for objection, he waived them aside, claiming stolidly that he could fix it all. He even offered to help with the digging. Among the helpers, Jessica also secured the assistance of a very contrite John Stringer, his deputy Lewis Armstrong and a crew of bobbies. The whole 'Grey' scenario, though considered resolved, still commanded attention. Despite John Stringer's profuse apologies for his behaviour some weeks previously, Jessica had been very cool with him on that occasion and ever since.

" What can I say love, made a right twat of myself again didn't I? I honestly thought it a complete waste of time. I thought you were quite barmy but I had no right to be so offensive or judgemental."

By way of a peace offering he had bought Jessica an antique stamped metal 'AA' badge for the Bentley, presumably, Jessica thought, a treasure gleaned from his virtual addiction to 'ebay'. That it was a treasure was not open to dispute; Jessica however, refused the offering very graciously but firmly, she felt that she had to make a point. When the proceedings for the dig gathered momentum and John had offered to help, she had finally relented and invited him along as she was simply too tired to maintain hostilities. He spoke to her as they gathered by the oak to begin the proceedings;

"Are we alright now love?" he looked pale and miserable. John Stringer was a tough and jaded old copper but Jessica had always admired the fact that he was a fair man, if a trifle moody and always held himself accountable for his actions, admitting when he was in the wrong. It made him a bigger man in her eyes and despite his sometimes abrasive manner, he was an ultimately supportive colleague and friend. She gave him a warm smile which melted his heart;

"Yes we're fine John but do you still have that lovely old badge?"

He smiled, looking relieved and handed her the badge which he retrieved from his overcoat pocket and which was still wrapped in scrunched tissue, anticipating her acceptance; "You did alright love, you know that don't you."

When Julia had spoken to Jessica late on the previous evening, she had told her that she was going to drive up early in the morning for the dig which was great news. The thought of Julia's presence lent the enterprise a much needed balance and Jessica was happy that she would be there. Julia subsequently turned up in a mud bespattered and very rusty Volvo estate wagon with questionable tyres and an out of date tax disc. John Stringer and his men stood open mouthed as an extremely petite but delightfully attractive young woman alighted, looking like a film star. She was, rather typically, not dressed for work, wearing beautiful ankle length high heeled boots, a long Indian skirt with a white lace petticoat underneath, accompanied by a frivolous white lace top of Victorian origin. In addition she was enshrouded in scarves, bangles, necklaces and a lovely short waisted fitted jacket. The overriding impression was of purples, russets, deep reds and golds and her long blonde hair was tied into a long braid and glinted majestically in the watery sunlight. She gave an expansive, refulgent transatlantic smile, her dazzling teeth contrasting gloriously with the scarlet of her lipstick and her healthy outdoor tan. As luck would have it, the invincible John Stringer was bowled over by her, his heart being lost entirely, forever a slave to her whims! Jessica noted with a degree of wry amusement that Julia may not have dressed for work but her work was over and done with in seconds.

John Stringer, to hide his evident awkwardness, involuntarily examined the grubby Volvo as a diversionary tactic to hide his embarrassment but hen wished he hadn't when observing that the car flouted the law in so many ways. It was an automatic response, a force of habit even though his humdrum bobby days were long over! Jessica was over the moon, she needed an ally and Julia was just the right person for the job.

"You don't look so good," Julia had remarked as they hugged and she looked at Jessica with some concern. Jessica was excited and optimistic but did feel decidedly under the weather; she was running on adrenalin.

"Oh thanks! I'm alright Julia, I've been off colour for a while but I am on the mend, I'll be okay honestly."

Jessica was reluctant to admit that she really did feel pretty rough as that would be tantamount to an admission of defeat in her book.

She had dreamed on the previous night, as she had done almost nightly since the decision to dig had been made. In her nocturnal quest she saw that a treasure chest and the key to other worlds was buried at the foot of the tree. She had been with him again, her 'love', in the realm of her subconscious that was so uncannily more real to her than life. In that world she was with the man she loved. Life was idyllic, she wanted so badly for it to go on forever but on this occasion the elements had changed for the worse, the dream had turned nasty. The twist in events really bothered her as she bridged the threshold to wakefulness in the morning and the sense of anguish and loss did not really go away but lurked deeper in her mind despite the impending excitement of the day. In addition to the haunting atmosphere that prevailed, she had awoken feeling feverish, chilly and nauseous. In her typically scientific way, she had put two and two together and concluded that her encroaching sickness had been the factor that had turned the nature of the dream sour. She refused to allow the malevolent aftertaste to ruin the joy of the memory of being re-united with her love. She took some influenza medication, started to feel a little better and commenced with the dig.

The crew worked for some hours, excavating a nice rectangular hole almost dictated by the nature of the packed soil, even though in the intervening centuries, the level of the ground had risen considerably, there was the same effect as you find so typically on a paint chip that has been touched up. Despite the number of layers of paint, the outline of the chip would always be mirrored in the surface of progressive layers. The chest was buried very deep as it transpired and there was a point when it seemed that nothing was there to be found and that the marking above ground must be an aberration. Jessica, despite her mounting feverishness was determined;

"Are you all right love, you really don't look too good, maybe you should go and have a lie down?" John had suggested. She shook her head vehemently, not wanting to hold up proceedings. As the digging progressed, Ray was becoming increasingly agitated and because of his urging, a decision was made to shore up the sides of the hole with a wooden frame such as the type used to support the sides of a burial pit. Jessica, studying the disturbed and muddied ground and the deepening hole, thought of the summer bluebells.

'It's a good job that the bluebell season is well and truly over otherwise I don't think I could bear the carnage.'

In truth Jessica was starting to feel too ill to carry on, the grumbling of the diggers was additionally tiresome. After many hours of exhaustive work, the sun was setting and it was getting quite dark. They had dug to a depth of almost twelve feet and the task seemed never ending. John Stringer who was patently unfit, was sweating profusely and evidently very tired, suggested helpfully that if they were to continue, he could requisition a mechanical digger. Julia at that moment appeared with tea and cake and urged the team to keep going, promising more to follow. Just as tendrils of doubt were firmly taking root in everyones minds, there was a dull metallic crunch as corroded metal was breached by a sharp instrument.

Suddenly everyone was jubilant, excited again and a general patter of happy conversation and light hearted banter replaced a deepening ambience of gloom. Lewis Armstrong, an older man than John Stringer who was within weeks of his retirement, chipped in with his opinion that it might be an unexploded World War II bomb. His suggestion yielded a wry expletive from John and chuckles from one or two of the helpers but they were careful nonetheless. They dug down and around the object and finally were able to lift it out. It was an ornate chest which appeared to be constructed from bronze plates, very thick and beautifully engraved and with a lid that was heavy and well fitted. Though encrusted, impossibly ancient and latterly fragile from being buried underground, it was not in bad shape. In places, there was much corrosion, especially as the lid most unfortunately, bore also the fresh scar of an impacted pick-axe head.

The buzz of excitement as everyone leaned over to have a look at the treasure, filled the air with expectation. Julia wanted the lid taken off straight away. The chest, an object of fascination was considered an artifact in its own right; the prize within was a gift that should be savoured later when an expert could be consulted.

"Looks to me like it was put in the ground long before Lucius Grey's time love, shouldn't we call some archaeological or historical boffin who understands these things and how they should be treated?" John Stringer had suggested, strangely perturbed, cautious, uncharacteristically out of his depth. "Might turn out to be a national treasure and extremely valuable." There was a subliminal fear of what might be discovered, though no one could acknowledge this consciously. They experienced the same thrilling apprehension that children experience when daring each other to dash into the gloom of the woods on the night of a full moon, with an eerily refreshing wind and scudding moonlit clouds; they all want to brave the elements deep within the cimmerian shadow of the trees but they postpone the event, overpowered for the moment by their fears, giggling nervously. Then Jessica spoke up unhesitatingly;

"I know what you are saying John but this is private property. I understand this could be a National treasure but I feel that, as the discoverers, we need to look inside before handing it over to any other authority." Julia concurred enthusiastically, supporting Jessica.

" We have a duty to look inside first, that is what we are all here to do and really, this is a part of Jessica's destiny, her Karma."

There were skeptical remarks and not a little sniggering at Julia's suggestion but no one voiced any real objection.

By consensus of opinion, the heavy box was to be carried into Jessica's apartment in order to be carefully examined. John Stringer was frankly too exhausted to argue by this stage and secretly didn't really care. He badly needed a pee and wanted to slope off home to his comfortable arm chair, a couple of tins of beer and some wrestling on the telly.

" Looks like that might be worth a bob or two cleaned up love. How old do you think it is?"

Jessica intimated that it was probably just another relic from the civil war; many a chest containing treasures or documents were buried at that time. Secretly, she suspected that if her dreams were anything to go by, the chest was almost certainly as old as the tree, if not older and even quite possibly priceless. John Stringer's suggestion that before opening the chest, they should go to the pub for a well earned drink was accepted with considerable alacrity and not so surprising really, they were all tired and hungry . The last thing Jessica felt like however, was a boozy pub visit, all she wanted to do was curl up in bed and go into a blissful and exhausted sleep. She bit her lip and readily agreed, feigning some enthusiasm. She acknowledged reluctantly to herself that it was the least that she could do and suggested that the meal and the drinks were on her.

In the event and just as they were getting cleaned up and making ready, Jessica realised that she was simply not up to the occasion and forcing money into John's hands, excused herself saying that she felt too rough and very tired and felt that she really had to call it a day. John Stringer, accepting the money, looked at Jessica with some concern;

" Get yourself to bed young lady. Take my advice, stay in bed tomorrow and deal with this 'box' when you feel better, there's no rush. I'm not long for my own bed if I'm honest, love; I'm knackered!"

John Stringer was feeling indulgent where Jessica was concerned especially after recent events. In any case, the chest was in safe hands. He was curious of course but once he was ensconced in the warm pub and feeling deliciously mellow after a couple of heady brews, he just wanted to relax. The compelling need to enjoy a few convivial pints followed by a replenishing steak and chips overrode any other considerations; other considerations started to fade into an alcohol induced oblivion, nothing much mattered any more.

Julia accompanied Jessica home realising that she was not at all well but she was determined to be to be an accomplice in secretly opening the chest. Julia really had to get back to the farm that night and was therefore desperate to discover what was inside before leaving. In the event, it took some effort to lever the lid off with a pry-bar, sacrilege maybe but they were too tired and desperate to care. Finally the corrosion gave way as the lid broke free, snapping the corroded hinges in the process. Inside was a virtually rotten waxed container which, like a set of Russian dolls, contained another container and yet another. Despite Jessica's deteriorating state of health they were both frantic with excitement; the secret, held and enclosed for many centuries, was about to be exposed and neither of them had any concept at that moment, of the importance of what they were about to discover. Finally, as the last container was opened, a large sheet of curled vellum lay within. Though faded and in the final stages of disintegration, it was still legible, the spelling 'quaint' and interpretation elusive. The border of the document was delightfully ornate, a skillful monastic scribe had obviously worked exhaustively to embellish it in every way possible. They perceived this document as if it were some divine incantation, a holy relic of the most fantastic importance.

It took a lot of deciphering and Julia read out short sections, playing with interpretations of words and phrases while Jessica made notes. In a state of feverish doubt and mounting excitement, they managed to put together a copy of the document as coherent English text, based on their painstaking reconstruction. They read and re-read their notes, making changes where they saw incongruities. The entire corrected text was entered into Jessica's computer and stored. Everything was saved on the hard drive in multiple formats, also on a u.s.b stick and two cd's. Ten copies of the text were printed in sixteen point 'Times New Roman' which were to be distributed to various named people, including Benjamin Wallace. Finally, the original was scanned and copied, which required a series of adjustments to be made in order to preserve it in it's original state. Then Jessica put the original document, which was drying out and in danger of disintegrating completely, into a large zip-lock bag. One of the copies was also put in alongside the original, though it was separated by a sheet of waxed paper. A printed transcription was also added and all three were placed back in the chest. Jessica continued doggedly for the next hour and then finally, feverish and exhausted, she slumped back in her chair, the task complete.

By that time, Jessica had become visibly quite ill but she remained 'driven'. Her face was dusky and her eyes glassy but they were glinting with a fire of manic determination. Julia noticed that Jessica was visibly perspiring and was evidently in the grip of some hectic fever. She was also aware of a strange astringent odour emanating from Jessica and in the enclosed space, the smell was becoming more intense and really quite irksome. She concluded that it must some kind of decongestant rub. Julia tried to pack her off to bed to get some rest but Jessica would not be sidetracked. It was almost as if her life depended upon the completion of this task. Sitting by the fire, she closed her eyes and asked Julia to read to her, the contents of the text and then having done so she asked that she re-read it. Jessica sat for a while, her eyes still closed as she tried to banish a pounding headache in order that she could more fully absorb the implications of what Julia had read to her.

Afterwards, they sat in numbed silence and for the first time in their lives were both simply too stunned to speak. The clock in the hall cracked the silence with a sonorous chime. Becoming convinced that her fever was causing her to hallucinate, Jessica spoke, a plea of sorts, for some confirmation of the reality of what she had just heard.
" This is not possible Jools, how did it get there? I am dreaming aren't I, you are not really here at all are you? This must all be a fantastical product of my illness."
Julia started to speak, then pausing, deep in thought;
"Maybe we are both dreaming. Listen Jess sweetheart, I'm getting really worried about you, you need to go to bed. I'll make you a warm drink and heat you up some soup. I have my homeopathic remedies with me, Gelsemium should do the trick. I'll just phone John and tell him I'm staying for a day or two to look after you."
Jessica became agitated, insisting that Julia must go home.
"You can't stay here just because I have the flu Jools, your husband and your children need you. Anyway, I prefer being on my own and I'm not just saying that. You know me!
I have to creep away like a sick cat and tend my wounds on my own; I really can't cope with anyone being around. I'll phone you, I promise!"
Julia finally waivered;

"Who can I call to keep an eye on you?
Jessica felt her residual strength ebbing away, frustration made her impatient, peevish.
"Oh don't make such a fuss for goodness sake Julia, I'm not one of your children. I've been sick before and I'm sure I'll be sick again. I just need to go to bed for a couple of days with some aspirin and a few really good movies, I'll be fine and in any case, I'd hate myself if you cought this."
Julia reluctantly agreed and reached for her coat looking very concerned."

Jessica sensed that she might have offended her dear friend and tried to make attempts to appear more upbeat than she actually felt.
"I'm still not sure about that parchment though, do you think it's a sick joke, it must be mustn't it!"
"I don't know Jess, I honestly don't know but do you mind if I take a copy?"
" Of course not but I've already e.mailed it to you."
Julia hugged Jessica and then gave her the homeopathic remedies that she knew she would not touch and then, retreating through the front door, gave Jessica a radiant smile by way of an 'Au-revoir'.

Feeling far too depleted to bother with anything for the time being, Jessica took the hot water bottle that Julia had filled and went to bed. She lay shivering, though comfortably enveloped in crisp sheets and an electric blanket all of which were warming deliciously from her added and feverish body heat. She relaxed a little thanks to Julia's drink, a very little soup and more flu medication. She slept fitfully for a couple of hours and then awoke bathed in sweat. She felt too ill to go back to sleep but was not capable of movement or thought, her head was spinning intolerably and she ached everywhere. It was pure malaise that kept her in the bed and feeling as if she was in limbo between two worlds, a semi-comfortable drugged stupor. It started to rain heavily, she could hear it rattling against the windows, an unusual torrent that came in a deluge that drenched her part of the world that night. She could even hear the rain hammering on the roof of the building and as she listened so too did she finally slip into another realm that was not really sleep but nor was it wakefulness. There was an odd sense that water was spraying from the ceiling and upon her face and she was aware of making the effort to pull the sheets over herself to avoid getting wet and yet the sense of the spray remained. After several hours of restless sleep Jessica awoke still feeling very ill but slightly better though that might have been the drugs. A strong compulsion overcame her, an imperative to open the chest and read the contents of the text for herself once more.

After re-examining the transcription, Jessica was just as mystified and astonished as she had been upon hearing Julia read it out. Exhausted, slumping back into the armchair, she gazed listlessly at the parchment that quickly fell out of focus and became just a distant blur. Finally, she summoned the energy to stagger back to bed but the expected sense of relief was quite simply unattainable. Jessica was tortured by personal discomfort, something that she had never experienced before; a splitting headache, a body of ice but also sweaty and she ached to her very core. Falling asleep, she nonetheless tossed and turned restlessly in the bed. Lurking in some deeply remote but sentient part of her being was a prayer for some respite from the nightmare illness in whatever form that might take. Then she awoke again feeling even worse; in desperation, she flipped on the bed side lamp and reached for the flu medication, knowing as she did so that it was far too soon to take another dose. Finally there came a detectable change and within half an hour, a period of hiatus. At last, there was blissful relief; her toes warmed, she stopped shivering, a delicious languor swept over her and she finally fell into a deep sleep and yet it was not sleep however, for she had actually lapsed into unconsciousness.

CHAPTER 25

Jessica sauntered up to him on the fore deck, re-united with the man who was a stranger to her and yet known to her in every way possible. The air was even more than usually sultry, a heavy humidity hung like lead over them and stifled the world in a blanket of sweaty heat. Rain was falling in a deluge, the downfall was warm almost hot and as it fell onto the ocean in a precipitate broiling torrent, there was an impression that clouds of steam were rising. Jessica was so hot that she decided to go for a swim and stripped off her clothes while standing at the bow of the boat, uncharacteristically bereft of self consciousness. She heard a shrill whistle and observed Father Donovan waving his arms, intent on trying to attract her attention; she briefly held a pose for him and smiled back cheekily. He seemed to be shouting something but the noise of the rain drowned out his voice; he looked serious but then of course, he always looked serious. Ignorant of his warning, she performed an elegant swallow dive into the deep azure of the ocean. As she entered the water there was a shift, as the shadow of a spectral cloud descended upon her. There was no mistaking the chill wind of malevolence that was starting to blow as Jessica felt herself gripped by the merciless tug of wakefulness.

She finally awoke at sunrise, her breathing shallow, her heart beating arrhythmically and her body bathed in a vile smelling and strangely astringent perspiration, the world seeming a strange shadowy place and beyond the grasp of reality. In her semi-conscious state, beams of watery sunlight from a bleak midwinter sun sneaked through the clouds and through a gap in the curtains; the room became illuminated with ethereal shafts of light. The wind was still blowing tempestuously, though the rain had finally stopped. Jessica was vaguely aware of things crashing about outside and was able to study the form of the frantically agitated but denuded limbs of the oak tree from her bed. So angry was the wind that Jessica feared for the tree's survival but then the tree had probably endured a thousand storms of a similar intensity. There was a malignity in this storm that seemed out of the ordinary and her disordered mind contemplated the elemental weather with a combination of bemusement and depression. The tree, so bereft of leaves, resembled the tree in her dream; dead, petrified and with no outward sign of the once vibrant animus that had radiated from within. Amazingly, her tree was unscathed, still standing and ever defiant to the talons of natures sometimes cruel capriciousness.

The night had seemed never ending and now the perpetually hungry and demanding William was wailing for his breakfast. Jessica's head was starting to clear a little, the funk from the excessive flu medication was retreating. She wanted to get up, make a cup of tea, to feed William to stop him from being such a nuisance but upon trying to rise, Jessica knew with a dreadful sinking sensation that she did not feel capable of getting out of bed. Her illness had advanced to that point where she had become increasingly numb to her symptoms and was no longer bothered particularly by aches and pains. Normally she was so well and healthy, so vital that it came as a dreadful shock to her, she was rendered almost inert. She had obviously continued perspiring heavily in the night while asleep as her bed smelt offensive, horrid. As someone who was typically very circumspect with regard to her personal hygiene, Jessica's sensibilities were affronted. After a time and with and extreme effort of will, Jessica tried to sit up in bed, becoming overtaken by new and alarming symptoms, indescribable giddiness and nausea. Her deep sense of duty compelled her to reach for the phone in order to explain her absence.

"Good God Jessica how ghastly for you," Benjamin Wallace sympathised somewhat patronisingly.

"As for work, please don't give it a thought my dear, you just get yourself well. We shall miss you terribly of course, that goes without saying but we will see you soon. Far better that you stay at home in any event, a very sensible precaution in my book. My advice to you m'dear is to repair to your bed with a hot toddy and a hot water bottle and forget about everything. I highly recommend Brahms piano concerto no 1 in C minor, elevates the spirit marvelously. Take all the time you need m'dear."

Jessica feebly tried to interject so that she could outline details of the cases that she had been working on but he would have none of it. After the conversation, she suddenly felt unutterably tired and cold, even when huddled up in bed with two hot water bottles, one for her feet and one for her back. Then, she drifted helplessly into an exhausted sleep and instead of continuing with her previous nightmare, she revisited that special place where the dream had originated.

That strange scarred and hostile land, the place to which her nocturnal adventures had taken her over the past months, ironically seemed so much more familiar than her current reality. The whole adventure had commenced when she had found herself walking along a beach on what appeared to be a small remote island. There was no sand, just grass to within a few feet of the waters edge and then muddy soil disappearing into the water. The shoreline was strewn with hundreds of stranded and obnoxious looking purple jellyfish in various stages of dessication; they were large, slimy and venomous looking and Jessica avoided them instinctively. It was sweltering and intolerably humid; never had she experienced such oppressiveness, not even when she had lived in Hong Kong as a child, a place to which her father had been assigned. Jessica had no idea how she came to be here, no memory of having been brought here but that seemed strangely unimportant. She studied the coastline, baffled; the area seemed so familiar and yet so alien. There were many buildings, some of which lay submerged and countless roof tops discernible below the surface of the water. There was a steep road that descended into the murky depths.

A great tree stood well above the water line, most of the limbs dead as the roots had been inundated by the encroaching waters. Yet still there was a tenacity for life that was evident in the few branches that were still heavy with leaves and acorns, as if the task of staying alive was not yet permitted to be over. There was a hole at the base of the trunk which had become a small pool as it had filled with water and for some reason this triggered something deep in her subconscious. The discord within Jessica quickly turned to terror.
'Where the hell am I, how did I get here? I must be dreaming! I must try to stay conscious, keep a level head.
It all sounded so sensible but the thoughts rang hollow, she was inextricably trapped in the material reality of this alternate world. Like a bird whose wings had been clipped, she was incapable of flight.

Then coming towards her across the turbid water, Jessica espied a boat, a large cruiser that in its day was one of a type that only the wealthy could afford. It looked so like Uncle Alistair's own immaculate example but the superstructure was green with moss and algae and evidence of advanced barnacle encrustation could be seen just below the waterline; apparently the boat had not been out of water for a very long time. Anachronistic masts and sails had been erected on the fore-deck and those sails had somehow collected and gathered the scant, almost imperceptible though sultry breeze and billowed sufficiently to propel the boat forward. Large three bladed wind turbines were situated at points along the deck. From the flying bridge, a tall man with a kindly face waved at her. He was muscular but also skinny, verging on but not quite undernourished. His Robinson Crusoe-esque trousers hung off his legs in tatters, his upper body was naked and habitually so judging by the deep weathering of his skin. His long beard, hair and his eyebrows were sun bleached and his face and the corners of his supernaturally blue eyes were lined from constant exposure to the elements. Jessica recognised him instantly, there was something so familiar in his face, in his look. He was a handsome man with features, Jessica felt, belied intelligence.

He pulled up to a nearby moorage, a jetty of sorts, in fact it was the tin roof of an old building, decaying and canted over at an impossible angle but evidently stable enough to walk on. He beckoned to Jessica and she jumped aboard without preamble, guided by the hand that was held out to her. There was something reassuring about him, strong, wise and she trusted him. He had a lovely voice, rich and vibrant, his words were exquisitely enunciated like that of a practiced baritone, though he was also possessed of a speech affectation. He spoke slowly, deliberately and with a periodic pause which he punctuated with an 'um' as if he were thinking, considering what he was going to say. There was an oddly clerical air about him which was confirmed when he introduced himself as Father Donovan,"Though sadly lapsed in my um, divinity my dear."

From the outset, Jessica knew that she was completely captivated by him and for the first time in her life was consumed by her need. Up close he smelled amazing, fresh, outdoorsy, a little of salt air and with a faint hint of fresh perspiration. It was a vital and feral human scent that was intoxicating, no doubt enhanced by some subliminal pheromone that reached out and aroused her sensibilities. She felt as though she had always been in love with him.
" My name really is Father Donovan," he had told her laughing just a little, the corners of his eyes crinkling as he smiled at her. Jessica inexplicably yielded to him, allowed herself to display total vulnerability which she would never have done under normal circumstances. He could tell almost immediately however, that she wasn't terribly comfortable with his name and he smiled at her again, amused.
"Just call me um, FD, everyone else does or at least the very few that I still talk to do!" Then he realised in that instant of making the suggestion that of course, she was never going to call him FD. They gazed into one anothers eyes for a moment, glimpsing into the portals of their souls until Jessica, suddenly becoming embarrassed, realised that despite their obvious and very real connection, she had not formerly introduced herself;
"Oh gosh, sorry, I was in a world of my own! I'm Jessica Stearne, well just Jessica actually. Do you mind if I ask why

'Father' Donovan? Are you really a priest?" she had asked half hoping that this would not be the case.

"Yes, actually, I am a priest or at least I was once but as I said, inherently lapsed now I'm afraid. The world has changed and ….um I with it, or so it would seem."

" What on earth happened here? I feel as if I know you. Am I dreaming, I am aren't I?"

" Well, all life is merely a dream some might say...um, yes you do know me as it happens, very well and I you of course."

He made the statement so pragmatically that Jessica was stunned into silence for a moment. Jessica studied him skeptically, her forensics skills coming to the fore, the scientific aspect of her very 'being' needing answers.

The sun was setting and what little breeze there had been dropped completely. Jessica, already very warm, became almost superheated and was sweating uncomfortably in the sultry heat, her top quite saturated and sticking most uncomfortably to her skin. Jessica was desperate to remove some layers of clothing and decided that the best course was to simply take off her blouse without fuss, though she felt very self-conscious and looked away as she did so. Now she was wearing only a long cotton skirt and a frivolous lacy white bra.

Why the hell am I not wearing one of those boring sports bras that I nearly always wear!' The strangely practical thought intruded upon this other realm. Father Donovan was a true gentleman, he pretended impartiality, subtly averting his eyes and appearing to study the distant horizon against the glare of the sun.

"We are going to have to leave here to gain a safe mooring for the night. This place can be tricky when a storm blows up."

He flicked a couple of switches and there was a slight surge as the boat moved under a different type of power, the wind having dropped. Once underway, he became quiet, slightly awkward, not knowing what to say but then it occurred to him that Jessica might be hungry.

"Would you like something to eat?" He asked;

"It's ...um, mostly fish and simple vegetables I'm afraid as there isn't much else available these days; basically only what we can catch in these depleted waters or grow for ourselves.

"I am quite hungry actually," she replied, suddenly realising that she was very depleted but unsure as to the nature of the reality in which she found herself. She caught him surreptitiously looking at her and for the first time, she actually experienced a thrill of delight at being surveyed. He of course looked away instantly but was brave enough and dignified enough to apologise.

"I am sorry if I was staring, its not often that I have company, especially that of an attractive young woman. I suppose I am deeply incredulous if the truth be told!"

He barbecued some fish and roasted vegetables and they talked about anything and everything while gazing out at an ermine sunset over a limitless deep crimson ocean. Jessica surveyed her surroundings. The rear deck sported an open topped water tank and a galley built from driftwood and other odds and ends which included a firepit made from an oil drum with the top cut off. An area of the fore-deck was covered with raised beds containing vegetable plants of various types; tomatoes, carrots, potatoes, peas and corn. Incongruously situated in the middle of the deck was a small replica of the 'Venus de Milo' and an old deckchair. There was evident ingenuity in the set-up and Jessica noticed that there was even a small but laden apple tree in a very large tub. On the stern was a rusty old motorcycle, a Triumph she thought but it was in very poor shape.

"Where are we?" Jessica asked.

"Don't you recognise this place?"

"I really don't know! It reminds me of a place I know but it feels like somewhere quite alien."

" This is ...um your home in fact but in another time, in your future. Do you recognise the old tree? I planted that tree a long long time ago in a fresh unsullied world full of magic and promise."

" What happened here?"

"We live in a ruined world, ruined by man, ruined by us."

"Is this really our future?"

"Well yes, it is in this scenario."

Jessica raised her eyebrows, tendrils of doubt creeping into her mind. Reading her expression, Father Donovan changed the subject, the time was not yet ripe for this conversation. It had been many years since he had felt this happy, he desired company and he wanted Jessica all to himself.

" Please tell me truthfully, are you really an ordained priest?"

Father Donovan paused for a moment and then smiled shyly.

"Like I said, I was once, ….um several times actually, one of my many roles. I gave it all up though, religion I mean. Rather I had given it up but I am what I am, doomed to walk the earth as a creature who defies the adversity of mortality as some kind of priest. In my last incarnation I died of grief as a young man. I believe I had the pleasure of a brief acquaintance with you at school."

Jessica was astonished and quite unable to discern what he meant but was distracted by him, almost entirely mesmerised.

When he casually put his hand on her shoulder to guide her, she shuddered involuntarily, deliciously. She realised that she wanted him in a way that she had never wanted anyone in her life.

He took her to a cabin beneath the fore-deck that had apparently been left untouched since the boats original owners had abandoned the craft, having either perished during the cataclysmic events of recent times or just didn't care anymore. There was a semi-complete jigsaw on a small table next to the bunk where there was a well loved Rupert Bear propped against the pillow. The bed was made up though when the sheets were pulled back, they could both see that they were mouldy and partially rotten.
"As you can see, I haven't been in here much, I shan't be a moment," he said as he left hurriedly to find something suitable with which to replace them.

Jessica, on finding herself alone in the cabin, realised that the space did indeed look familiar. On the floor in the corner was what Jessica recognised as a personal cassette player and some tapes scattered about. In the cupboard there were clothes for a girl of about nine or ten years of age that were obviously fashionable for the time, with recognisable names. There were jeans and tee shirts, a couple of dresses and skirts and some underwear, still folded neatly on a shelf. Jessica briefly studied the clothes, obviously female yet strangely androgynous, not tailored for a developed female form. Then she experienced a momentary pang, a strange sense of familiarity and felt a strong connection. Her reverie was broken as Father Donovan returned with a sleeping bag still wrapped in the original plastic and laid it down.

"It's all I have I'm afraid, I'm not really used to having guests."

"You live alone?" Jessica prayed for him to say yes.

" Um....quite alone, I always have, although I don't really have much choice these days."

"Are there many others?"

He paused for a moment, trying to decide how to answer, looking uncomfortable and a little vague, obviously hoping to evade the subject. In the end he settled for the dismissive, "Not many, especially with any degree of sanity!"

Jessica, confused by his response, was tempted to pursue the subject to get more out of him.

" There is a lot to tell you and this is not the time, just wait a couple of days, settle in and then I'll tell you everything. I ....um, assume you will be staying?"

He was amused at his joke but Jessica became instantly aware of his sadness, his loneliness and his obvious sense of desolation. She wanted to reach out to him, to sooth him in some way but she was an awkward and thoroughly non-tactile person and just didn't know how. Besides there was electricity between them, they were both aware of it and this ironically made them less inclined to touch. The space between them fizzed with potential and made them forget what they were saying mid-sentence. He bid her good night; she turned from him to open her sleeping bag and he gently leaned over and kissed her on her neck. She froze for a moment, a little fearful, uncomprehending but unbearably aroused. Then he reached for her waist, turned her and drew her face to his, kissing her on the mouth. Within moments Jessica was on fire, she had never been so intoxicated by carnal desire. Normally embarrassed and annoyed by her body, she was for the first time in her life suddenly proud as he removed her remaining clothing, revealing her beautiful full breasts. Here was a man under nourished in these respects, but also, there was a starving woman too.

Days turned into weeks though having lost all sense of time, a blissful life unfolded for Jessica; for the first time she was truly happy. The level of intimacy that she had found with this man was a revelation to her. Often, while lying in a state of post coital lassitude, Donovan would share his thoughts with Jessica, telling her of the harsh realities of the time and of the plight of mankind. She wasn't filled with a sense of doom and gloom in the remotest way, she had him all to herself and she had never been so happy. She loved to hear him speak, and listened to him for hours as he told her of his life in this strange doomed world.

"The polar ice caps have been melting at an exponential rate and Britain's tilt is increasing as land to the west rises and the east drops. Our tree will be almost totally submerged in ten years time, the climate has changed so much. The world economy has totally collapsed and the banks have failed. The governments are non-existent as far as I know and we are all but destroyed through constant war, disease and deprivation. There aren't many of us left, only the fittest survive and I am doomed to immortality it would seem. The most …..um tragic aspect of this is that the ocean has changed and it is actually dying; the world cannot survive without the ocean. Decades of pollution by man and carbon dioxide emissions have made the ocean very acidic and therefore poisonous. Recently increasing geo-thermal activities and an unstable climate have made this situation worse. The very basis of all marine life, the plankton are disappearing fast, consumed to a great extent by the purple jellyfish. They are also unable to survive the growing toxicity and are of course the vital link in the whole oceanic food chain. It's very rare that I am able to catch shell fish now and marine mammals have all but disappeared as far as I know."

"My God, is there no hope?"

"Oh there's always hope, this is what drives us. Without hope there is nothing."

During the days, he fished and she prepared the catch, gutting and salting, throwing the fish guts to an expectant large furry tabby cat that looked extraordinarily like William. He had appeared one day and became their constant companion. Jessica also tended the precious vegetables and plants which were such a vital part of their diet. Each evening she tried to produce a special meal using the limited resources available, creating a romantic ambience with stubs of candles in tin cans and music from the seventies played on the compact disc player when energy supplies permitted. After supper he would lead her to their cabin and they would make love.

Jessica awoke one morning feeling faint and nauseous and after further days had passed in a similar vein, she finally 'twigged.' It had been almost two months since her last period and her breasts felt heavy and sore, boasting a recently added filigree of tiny veins on the surface of the skin which added conviction to her suspicions. Jessica had never really known what to think about having children since her own childhood had not been a particularly happy one. Not only that but the prospect of bringing a child into a burnt out and dying world where it was doubtful that life could be supported for many more years was terrifying to say the least. Yet she felt jubilant, joyously proud of her conception. Once she was certain, she sought out her lover in order to tell him their news. Silent tears ran down his face as he placed his hand on her belly, trying to detect evidence of the little being who resided and grew within.

CHAPTER 26

One of the conundrums in the realm of dream is that 'time' has no relevance. The scenarios enacted during those diurnal adventures into dream state may be as real as life; come to that, the day to day routine of life in the material world may well be the illusion and the dreams in fact, reality. Who really knows? It could be argued that Jessica's grasp of reality from her place in a twilight world was entirely compromised but so far as Jessica was concerned, all that she perceived was real.

Steven Savage had pretty much bowed out of Jessica's life. The last time they met they had quarreled horribly and he had stormed off, determined never to have anything to do with her again and yet he still had a soft spot for her. He supposed that was the reason why he always dropped everything to help her when she needed it and why he was a surrogate guardian for William, he loved cats and particularly adored this one. In truth he was very fond of Jessica but his appreciation, noble though it was, was quite unrequited. There were times when he could have kept William for himself had he been at liberty. Steven was a died in the wool bachelor and was used to having his own way but where Jessica was concerned that rarely happened. He was not a bad person though he held little regard for humanity; as far as he was concerned, people were there to be exploited.

He had just successfully invested the fortunes of a recently deceased widow into a vineyard in the Dordoigne. Her beneficiaries were distantly related to her and were widely scattered, having no more connection to the widow than did Steven Savage. She had come to see him years previously upon the recommendation of a nurse friend of his who worked at an upmarket old peoples home and who was naturally good at enticing even the sharpest and most acerbic of elderly people into her confidence and thence into Steven's, a combined operation that was as scurrilous as it was 'compassionate'. Steven knew that it was only a matter of time before he would be asked to represent the estates of this lady as 'executor'.

In clear cut cases where there were obviously close relatives and expectant if acquisitive beneficiaries, he was diligent and saw to it that things were done as they should be. Ironically, his reputation did not suffer and in fact he was held to be a paragon by the very people he had set out to exploit. Where bequests were more vague he set to work to 'legally' defraud his clients. Often this would consist of a clause in a signed 'will' where the client had consented to let Savage take full control and invest their estate 'prudently' or as he deemed fit. This virtual power of attorney and the following verbal understandings during confidential meetings would enable Steven to act on the behalf of the beneficiaries at an interest rate that he deemed appropriate. Often much of the value of the estate was invested in stock bonds or other property and so Steven Savage issued payments to beneficiaries but also held onto the main bulk of the estate in the process. He was rich, clever and relentless and very able to throw up a smoke screen of legal flim-flam which effectively covered his tracks.

Even though Jessica held deep suspicions about his exploits, often accusing him off duplicitous behaviour, he would hold up his hands and giving a disarming smile would claim that he always acted meticulously within the constructs of the law. Julia, on the other hand, knew exactly what he was about and challenged him at every opportunity. On very rare occasions however, Steven would find himself floating on thin ice when pursued by sharper and more legally aware and astute relatives. He managed invariably to wriggle out of any such predicaments using various tactics at his disposal; unfortunate delays in probate, legal complications, contested wills, anything he could think of before finally having to hand over the estate, less the amounts he had legally pillaged.

Just recently, Steven had discovered that a man who was a distant legatee whom he had mildly defrauded, was a successful member of the underworld. A family row had caused him to detach himself from any further dealings with his minuscule share of the estate, an expedient measure he thought but this man had come across enough inconsistencies to catch Steven on the hop and did not appreciate being made a fool of. Steven found out fairly quickly and with a sinking sensation of impending doom that he was in very hot water and no amount of ducking and diving could help this time. On the brink of despair, he was saved very bizarrely when the man was murdered in a shoot and run incident. In his inimitable fashion, Steven had sighed, poured himself a large vintage malt, climbed into a hot bath and then allowed himself to luxuriate and bask in an enormous sense of relief; the ordeal was over, or so he thought. Just as the matter had passed from his mind, the police started to investigate him for reasons of which, on this one occasion, he was entirely ignorant. He had undergone gruelling questioning for hours, then reluctantly, the police had released him though muttering ominous imprecations that they were 'onto him'. In a curious turn of events, it seemed that Steven was to receive some rough justice for a crime that he had genuinely not committed, to whit, the murder of a crime boss! Witnesses reported having seen him, it was alleged, at the scene of the crime. The initial suspect who had apprehended for the murder had been released following Jessica's apparently 'whimsical' forensics report. The victim was a man of influence and the police were under pressure to produce a culprit and so Steven found himself well and truly in the cross hairs. He was both outraged and frightened and decided to petition Jessica for help. Whether she would give it or not was quite another matter but he was desperate and he was well aware of her high legal office connections following the Lucius Grey case. What he didn't know was that Jessica was also involved in the case of the murdered crime lord or indeed, that she was off sick.

After days of phoning, sending text messages, writing emails and even mailing pleading letters to her to no avail, he decided to throw caution to the wind and contact her at work. He knew that he would have to tackle that fool Benjamin Wallace but Steven was desperate. Despite his exceptional and refined good looks, diminutive and dapper though he was, his good though slightly clinical taste and his love of the good things in life, he was at heart an east London boy from Skinners Lane. His slight lingering trace of a cockney accent was detectable though charming. Steven however, felt haunted by it; it was his own personal sword of Damocles. Sometimes he took a dislike to people who spoke like 'friggin' toffs' and who put on 'airs and graces'; Ben Wallace was a case in point. For some reason that Steven Savage could not point a finger at, Wallace made him aware of his own shortcomings and it irked him considerably. The irony was that while Steven aspired to 'high society' and sought the finer things of life, he bitterly hated people from the upper classes in general, though there were exceptions. Benjamin Wallace was the last person on earth who Steven wanted to speak to under any circumstances. Not only was he undeniably a snob but unfortunately, Steven perceived that Wallace put him down as an act of sheer spite. He had seen right through Steven's schemes, and had accused him, to his face, of being an embezzling gutter-snipe when at a party and in front of several of his friends. Ben Wallace continued to display his disapproval of Steven when their paths crossed by being irritatingly obsequious and polite though almost imperceptibly mischevious at the same time.

It was Wallace, of course, who answered the bloody phone which Steven knew, deep down, that he would.
"My Dear Steven, how the devil are you old chap, still taking great care of our senior and more well heeled citizens no doubt, good for you! Where would we be were it not for such exemplary selflessness?"
Steven gritted his teeth and ignored him.
"I wondered if Jessica was there by any chance?"
"Is who here?"
"Jessica?"
" I'm awfully sorry to have to tell you that she is not. We've been denied the pleasure of her charming company for nearly two weeks, poor thing! I am getting rather worried about her to be frank with you Savage. I have tried repeatedly to telephone her but to no avail. I was just thinking I should pop round to see if she has made a recovery yet but I hate to

trouble her. Y'know if I did not know Jessica so well, I would begin to suspect a severe bout of intemperance during her time off- ha ha!"

Steven ignored Wallace's inference.

"Is she on her holidays or is she sick then?"

"Holidays ermm? Oh you mean 'leave'. Good God no, she was a bit below par, influenza I believe or so she said, frightful drag for the poor girl. To be honest, we could really do with her now as it really has become the most ghastly shambles here and quite apart from anything else I do miss the gal. I shouldn't be telling you this but between you and me, we have a murdered crook in here who will have to be released and planted soon before the smell gets too much to deal with."

Steven went cold at the mention of the crook, knowing instinctively who it must be and he let down his guard just a little.

'So Jessica's involved, what a turn up for the book!'

"Maybe I'll try and reach her at home Mr Wallace?"

Steven then mentally kicked himself for calling him, Mr Wallace, who on the other hand, Steven noted, was actually being a lot more pleasant than normal.

"If you do get in touch with her, would you send her my fondest love and ask her to let me know if she has any idea when she will be able to come to work?"

"I shall do my best sir."

Benjamin Wallace smirked and Steven squirmed,

"I'm most grateful but really there is no need to call me sir dear boy."

Steven was taken right back, in brutal fashion to similarly harrowing experiences while at school. In that moment he felt as though he was right there in the classroom being shouted at by a vinegary and sarcastic teacher.

" Well let me know how it all goes with Jessica eh Savage?"
"I'd sooner eat glass you fuckin' pompous, pedantic old queen!" Steven muttered under his breath.
"What was that Savage young feller?"
"Nothing Mr Wallace! Speak to you later; thank you and well, Bye!"
"Well Goodbye; until I hear from you. Oh and don't be too hard on those poor unsuspecting old ladies eh old chap?"
In hindsight, Steven would come to realise that the comment was almost certainly innocent, meant as a light hearted jest, something to break the ice, an olive branch even but at that moment, Steven was rancid with indignation. He toyed with the idea, over the next few minutes, of somehow being able to drop poison into Ben Wallace's gin; moments later, he felt slightly better.

The drive across London from his plush pad on the Thames in east London to Mortlac was quite a distance and even when relaxed and in good humour he drove like a demon. He really was an excellent and skillful driver but his talents were better suited to a race track than a busy European capital city. In his stressed and irritable frame of mind, he carved up other motorists and even deliberately drove into the path of an oncoming dispatch rider sitting astride a well used and heavily laden BMW motorcycle. The dispatch rider kicked at his Jaguar's rear lights smashing a lens and yelled at Steven while riding alongside. A course, uncouth and habitually angry voice.
" Fucking stupid cunt, can't you drive that fucking wheelbarrow properly? You fucking nobs are all the fucking same. Fucking Wanker!"
Steven smiled pleasantly, mouthing silent apologies, he waved apologetically but also imperiously. He had no time or

stomach for a confrontation with a large hairy motorcyclist and in any case he was rather flattered that he had been called a 'nob' because, in truth he really was.

Steven still had keys to Jessica's flat even though she had insisted many times that he give them back. For some reason he wanted to keep them and invented many and varied excuses such as;
"Oh Bugger! I don't believe it, sorry Jess, I left them in my other trousers, really sorry love, I'll bring them next time, promise!"
With that he would give her a pleading puppyish look and she would cast her eyes to heaven.
"Next time Savage, I'm counting on it, please do remember! I mean no offense but I don't want keys to my flat out in the world at large. Believe it or not there are people out there who hate me and might want to do nasty things to me as a result of what I have to do in my job; I've had death threats you know?"
"I promise love, no really I do, don't give me that stroppy look. Who would want to harm such a gorgeous bird as you anyway?"

As he drove up to the front of the house, the wheels of his Jaguar making evocatively expensive noises on the gravel drive, Steven espied William running up to him from beyond the old tree. Steven scooped him up and cradled him like a baby; he was the only person that William tolerated such liberties from and in fact he was entirely happy with it. He lay with his eyes half closed and his paws kneading the air as he purred like a kitten. Alarm bells began to ring in Steven's head and he was puzzled, William's reaction was almost over the top.

"Your mistress been starving you, you've lost some weight your highness?"

William kneaded the air a little more, the tips of his canines visible as he stretched his head back blissfully.

" I have to go and find missus if that's okay with you, are you coming old chap?"

Holding him indecorously by his midriff, Steven deposited William back onto the floor and prepared to walk to the main entrance. Just as he took his first step, William ran in front of his legs repeatedly, almost causing Steven to trip.

"Whoa, what's going on matey?"

Steven picked him up again and held William against him with his left hand under his chest, two fingers poking through between his front legs. Steven had discovered that for some strange incomprehensible feline reason, William always preferred being carried this way and so it was that they went together to the main entrance. They encountered Mrs Wainwright just as she was about to leave her flat.

Steven and Mrs Wainwright knew each other through Jessica and their connection was usually friendly. Steven treated her like he treated all his older ladies, with a sort of condescending cheeky charm.

" Hello Mrs W. How are you on this this wintry day, looking very gracious and extremely elegant if you'll forgive the impertinence."

Mrs Wainwright was as sharp as a tack and was actually well aware of his machinations, being wise enough in her advanced years to ignore his behaviour. Indeed she even found Steven roguishly charming to a degree, despite his faults and that was precisely the response that Steven always illicited, that was his great trick.

"Why, hello, it's Mr Savage isn't it dear...?"

"Indeed it is Mrs wainwright, larger than life and twice as ugly."

Given Stevens diminutive stature she smiled, despite herself which of course was his intention.

"Such a shame that we don't see so much of you these days Mr Savage?"

"Oh well, you know, work, commitments, life and all that nonsense."

Steven was in a hurry and Mrs Wainwright detected the subliminal squeak of irritation, more than that, there was a determination to be civil, he was being just a little too chummy.

"I haven't seen the young lady for a couple of weeks, is she away perhaps?"

"I really don't know to be honest. She never tells me what she's doing. Come to think of it I don't tell her much either."

Steven was determined not to offer any extra information for fear of being trapped in further conversation.

"Must dash though, excuse me love, errands to run, people to see, I have to get something from Jess's flat before I leave."

He brandished Jessica's keys and shook them in front of Mrs Wainwright as if to convey that he held unequivocal rights to her abode at any time the whim took him.

"Do you think I might come with you Mr Savage, only it's been so long since I have seen Miss Stearne and her cat has been hanging outside my door for the last week making all sorts of fuss?"

The last thing Steven wanted was to be accompanied by the old lady and he tried to put her off but he was, he had to admit, alarmed by Williams strange defection.

"I'm really not sure if she is there Mrs Wainwright, I only came over to pick up my dinner suit for a 'do' I'm going to tonight."

"That sounds like fun, somewhere nice I hope?"

There was a brief tangible and terrible moment of reality, his intolerance bleeding noticeably through his veneer of charm and bonhomie.

"Please don't think I'm being rude Mrs Wainright but I really am in a hurry."

With that he made off at speed through the entrance, turned right through a fire door which was a tasteless 'sixties' addition, fitted with a large window pane which was rendered almost opaque by the matrix of criss cross reinforcing wires incorporated into the glass. Then he raced up the stairs, his foot steps ringing off the walls and with a very tolerant William cradled in his left arm, who was being shaken at every step.

He repeatedly knocked on Jessica's front door without response, then he tried calling her on his cellphone and could hear the phone ringing in the flat. He waited for some moments and then, having failed to illicit any answer from within, decided to use the spare key. It was then that he noticed a noxious highly astringent odour in the hallway, simultaneously he realised with irritation, that Mrs Wainwright had followed him. The look on her face was of steadfast but affable determination as she climbed the stairs and made towards him but to his amazement, Steven found that he was suddenly and immeasurably relieved that she had been so intent on joining him.

"Such a curious smell don't you think Mr Savage?"

"Yeah, it's really quite extraordinary."

"I've noticed it for some days and it does seem to be coming from Miss Stearne's abode."

Grappling for a moment with a key that had always been annoyingly tricky, he opened the door to the flat and was assailed by the smell, suddenly intensified a hundredfold. He felt dizzy, nauseas, the sort of reaction you have to acetone or to gasoline when exposed to large quantities. William, in a flurry of panic, broke free from his embrace and jumping down, made a beeline for the bedroom. Steven followed and so did Mrs Wainwright hot on his heels. Jessica was lying in bed on her usual side; he noticed with mounting horror that her face was pallid, an expression of agony frozen onto her features. Steven was about to rush to her when he was deterred by a gentle but powerfully restraining touch on his arm. He looked at Mrs Wainwright with a look of anger and bewilderment.

"She's dead Mr Savage, quite dead I'm afraid."

"Why, how, are you sure?"

"Yes, I'm completely sure. She looks like she has been very sick, poor love, whatever was it that caused this I wonder?" Steven was quite out of his depth and powerless in the moment to do anything but mutter inanely."

"She can't be dead, she's too beautiful."

"Oh she's dead alright my dear, we must call for assistance." William had jumped onto the bed, curling up resolutely against the mortal remains of Jessica, his mistress, as if trying to infuse life back into her. Steven, after a moments indecision, dialed 999 on his I.phone relaying to the operator their horrific discovery. The intervening moments before the ambulance arrived seemed interminable. Only then was Steven able to survey the interior of the flat.

There eyes were drawn to a very ancient looking metal chest on the floor. Steven's sharp eyes were immediately drawn to a zip-lock bag which contained what appeared to be a parchment, curled with age, as well as some sheets of A4 paper which appeared to be copies of a translation. What made this all the more compelling was that Jessica had a piece of paper in her hand which looked to be of the same text. Steven overcame his horror and his squeamishness and went over to Jessica, looking at her for a moment and reached out to touch her but then, at the last second he withdrew his hand. Then he reverentially withdrew the scrunched sheet of paper from a partially clenched, dessicated and skeletal hand frozen with rigor-mortis and spread the paper out on the bedside table.

At first, Steven scanned the sheet, snippets of information arousing intense curiousity and then, deciding that the information contained therein required another rational mind to be involved, he read the text out loud;

" *My name is Laurna but I speak in the name of Jessica Stearne. I speak for myself and I speak of my home, this sacred land of Albion and I speak also for this world. This land is already blighted by invaders and the influence of invasion. The island will be destroyed by pestilence and mankind's lack of respect for the world. This beautiful place will fall into the hands of people who do not understand her and will not have the best interest of the land at heart. Until such time as the original inheritors and respecters of this beautiful place shall once again rightfully take control, the conquerors will have dominion. If and when this message is found then the process has already started. You will one day have a queen, a mortal being but an emissary from other worlds and dimensions. She will reach back from the future and purge this land, restoring it once more to the magical place that it should have been. The entire world will enter a period of crisis by the 21st century. Bureaucracy and government supported greed will have the upper hand. The evil that thrives in the society of man which hides behind a mask of good shall finally be driven from here and those disciples of the devils, the slaves to ego, wealth and power will be removed permanently. On the 21st December 2012 this land of ours and the entire world will experience a great cataclysm! This might seem to be a terrible prophecy but a great tidal wave of spirit light will cleanse the land and render it once more the magical place, the Garden of Eden that it should always have been. The spirit of Mother earth which thrives in the hearts of people such as the great queen Boadicea will prevail and defend Albion from its countless invaders. I am Jessica Stearne and I am from the future but until such time as I discover this message, I too shall be as ignorant as the rest of mankind.'*

As if mesmerised, not sure what he had just read he glanced over at the parchment in the zip-lock bag like an automoton, his quick mind gleaning enough information to know that the sheet of paper that Jessica had been clutching to the bitter end was some kind of transcription.
"Is this all some strange joke Jessica love?" he muttered aloud.
"I beg your pardon Pardon Mr Savage?"
Without preamble, he passed the sheet of paper to Mrs Wainwright who reached into her handbag for her reading glasses. Like Steven she scrutinised the text with a mixture of disbelief and intrigue and then reread the text twice more. Removing her spectacles, she turned and looked Steven full

in the eyes, a look of bafflement written on her face. In that
rather inappropriate moment, Steven was suddenly compelled
to admit to himself in a rare moment of honest insight, that
Mrs Wainwright really did have the most beautiful eyes.
"What can it all mean Mr Savage, do you think?"
" Beats me love, its obviously a transcription of that
parchment thing in the bag, do you think she was raving
when she wrote this?"
"I honestly don't know my dear, I couldn't possibly say."

Steven knew with a sinking heart that he was going to
have to phone Ben Wallace again and then become involved
in one of his macabre and theatrical investigations. At this
point an ambulance and a police car arrived and the drama
continued.

CHAPTER 27

In those last excruciating hours before she died, Jessica was barely lucid, the agony of her condition being her only link with reality. She had lain in a state of purgatory, somewhere between her own world and some shadowy twilit realm of phantasm. She wanted release, craved escape but was anchored by a prevailing and haunting sense of responsibility. There was such a conflict between the forces of life and death within her but she was desperate for the hurting and the aching to be gone. Ironically, even in those moments, the dichotomy of her sense of duty added to her unbearable predicament. She was on the brink of entering a barely acknowledged ephemeral world of spirit and so desperately wanted to break those last few bonds. She was held, as if by elastic that was yielding at first but the tenacity of which became rigid once the maximum stretch point had been reached. Jessica finally, was beyond caring and she simply let go, the ties that had held her so fast dissolved as if they had never existed.

That mysterious moment of death was not an episode that she could pinpoint or remember in the remotest sense but it was a dreamlike transition from a world of pain to a blissful state of dream sleep, a condition of semi-awareness without any definition. The only way to describe Jessica's consciousness at that moment was that of a 'sleeper'. After a long, strenuous walk in the rain and then upon returning to a warm dry room and a comfortable fireside chair, it is possible to enter into a sublime state after one closes ones eyes for a few moments. During those precious moments one might be vaguely aware of entering a domain of unspecified limbo and this is what happened to Jessica. She floated for a time in a nirvana of blurred awareness, contented timeless bliss with no borders. She could have been in that state for one second or a billion years, there was simply no measurement and no markers for consciousness and really no need. All that was necessary was simply to rest and to 'BE'.

What followed then was a moment of seeming awakening, of increased and painful cognisance as she looked upon herself upon her bed, a pathetically ill, wizened and almost unrecognisable pale ghost of a female human being, whose vitality had been devoured by the poison of the purple jellyfish. Indeed the toxin was so virulent that it not only affected her future self, a revenant being of a dream world devoid of corporeal substance but it also leached back into the past and took her mortal life. The toxin of the jellyfish was not just any crude poison but a multi-dimensional singularity of immense venom. It was a quantum substance that was both chemical and energetic simultaneously, an agent that was a manifestation of all the combined toxic pollution, both of Earth's environment and of the temporal realm where it existed on all levels. The end result was a vile by-product from the cesspool of human consciousness and of the ill-considered manufacturing and extraction processes. All the evils of the world, both psychic and material, had resulted in a substance so malevolent that it had breached the defenses of the temporal realm and beyond the thresholds of time. The toxin seeped like a sulfurous yellow gas into the future and into the past and further even into a domain where time did not exist. The spirit of Jessica

338

contemplated this once beautiful human being who had been destroyed by the poison and was lying in squalid and soiled bedsheets. At first she felt sad, bereft and then suddenly she felt not the slightest hint of remorse or sorrow, merely sublime relief and empowerment of the most beautiful and wonderful kind. A concept came to her being that was, impossible to put into words or even thoughts but an 'energy'. *'Glorious liberty, now I can do all those things that as a human being I could only imagine.'*

At the moment of her death, the entrance to a tunnel materialised in some indiscernible form, the almost cliché beacon of light from deep within that beckoned to her and Jessica seemed to have a choice, she could linger for as long as she wanted, an earthbound wraith destined to haunt a monochrome world of illusion mixed with a mosaic of places and daily events but there was no need. She allowed herself to be drawn into the tunnel, a little like the tractor beam that draws stricken spacecraft in Star Trek. Jessica was both compelled and pulled simultaneously and entered into the light. Gradually the conception of 'what is' and 'what is not' and of boundaries became eroded, no more perception of time or of limits, no more imperatives, no more guiding emotions or ego and no more thought. Jessica was neither conscious or unconscious and the prevailing sensation was that of floating, of awareness, of nothing and of everything. There was no space or shape or form, there were no outlines or worlds or delineations of any type but there were beacons in the void, focal areas of light energy.

'Light' is the wrong expression really in a realm where physical light and photon emissions do not exist and are abstractions. These energy centres were simply focal points

339

of sublimation, of energy but 'light' is the only word that infers a relative meaning. In some places there were clusters of these lights and in others just solitary ones but the one common factor was that they were all linked to a greater or lesser extent, depending upon the will of the essence represented by a light. Indeed Jessica herself was a creature of light, a being of pure energy, of concepts and ideas, a unique individual but also linked to all of the others. There was no sexual orientation in a physical sense but she represented that female energy, she was the yin.

Each essence of light represented a thought form, the consciousness of an individual being but was linked in some divine way with other conscious energy centres. The connection to the matrix of other clusters of light represented others who were connected in ones life who shared beliefs, experiences, ideas, loves and dislikes. These energy sources became a part of the destiny and lives of each with whom they shared a close connection and interaction. Every willful construct of an individual light form had a repercussive effect on the entire matrix with differing consequences. The perceptions, realities and destinies of all were involved in a dynamic confluence of change affected by the concepts of the individuals; a temporal dance moving to the rhythm of the collective consciousness. Jessica was aware that in this realm, she was privy to information that was denied to all but the wisest and most aware of mortals, the old souls. She realised also that as a being, whether they were mortal or spirit, they were all of one and the same reality in this realm; the lights were the representation of the energy and vitality of conscious entities. Jessica could see that the world of people that she had shared a life with were just as present in this domain as the dead; the centres of light with whom she shared this connection had a vivid commonality.

She could not help but be aware of lights that were of a different hue and shape, constantly on the move and completely dis-connected to any of the others, at the same time seeking desperately to become joined, looking also for rejuvenation, as if they were destined to become simply nothing and to disappear entirely. These were the restless spirits, beings or souls who were tormented with a belief that they were 'unconnected'. They unrelentingly sought connection with anything living or dead and needed to be a part of the matrix to survive in any form. They were parasites in this realm but ghosts or dark spirits in the corporeal realm. There were also flashes of light like sprays of sparks, incandescent at first but quickly dwindling to nothing. The sensation that Jessica felt from these was a powerful wave of intense sadness and suffering, almost unbearable and highly contagious; they were beings whose lives had evidently been brutally cut short. She wrapped a protective aura of energy around herself and willed herself to transmit waves of uncompromising love to these hapless semi-aware beings, victims of mass murder, humans slain or factory farmed animals slaughtered without love or care. Similarly she protected herself against the protozoan-like ribbons of dark green; blastema's of malevolent thought-forms that were the manifestation of darkness, of pure ugliness and purulence.

The toxic influences of the purple jellyfish were very much in evidence, as they were a culmination of all that was pernicious in the creativity of the mind, the disaffected imagination and from the cauldron of the chemist. There had to be a repository for the waste and garbage of negative energy influence and, unfortunately for the future Earth, this had manifest as giant purple jellyfish. All of the excesses and dissipation of latter day Rome leading to the so called civilisation of a sick 21st century world had to end up somewhere and to become something.

There was a timelessness to this episode for Jessica and she was happy, contented in a way that she never had been before and well protected in a divinely comfortable but subliminal fashion. Jessica however, developed a sense that things could not stay this way for an eternity, at least not for her. There was no one realm in which she could exist everlastingly and blissfully, as her fate and the fates of others were as yet to be completed. Like a fine knit sweater, her world was far from complete and she felt a pull and an increasing urgency. There was one to whom she was promised, to whom she must become attached, with whom the connection had not yet been established and by whom the rift that was pulling the world apart, could finally be healed.

At the end of what had seemed an eternity came a change, an upheaval. There was a sense of being funneled and contracted and finally compacted into a finite space and once again, becoming aware of boundaries and limits. Yet again a transition was taking place but she had no means of gathering information or understanding what was happening to her. Jessica's next incarnation in the Earthly realm was to be a tree, an oak which was a fitting and appropriate manifestation and so she arrived, having been deposited from a tree as an acorn. From a human perspective, trees have few senses; they cannot see, hear, taste or become excited at the tender touch of a life partner. Jessica in this incarnation was no different but she could however 'think', cogitate, meditate, ruminate.

There is no way of knowing if there is a natural interface between the human mind and tree physiognomy and any such process must therefore be developmental. What Jessica could do she did, she explored with her mind and this she did constantly in this state of vaguely comfortable but robust imprisonment. Though she was to have no vision in the human sense, she would experience sensations that could be worked upon and interpreted. As she grew from an acorn into a young sapling, so too did her awareness, newly re-awoken as an armoury of senses. Jessica became aware that she was not one but two beings, essentially male and female. They combined to become the tree in keeping with the hermaphrodite consistencies of most plants and especially of the oak tree. Her other half, almost literally, was a being whom she had known and with whom she resonated but beyond that, she was unaware and incapable at that stage of knowing more. There was also a presence, a blurred awareness of a third being, external to themselves but one of the 'trinity' nonetheless. She could sense his energy, his vitality, his kindliness, wisdom and his caring. There was a feeling, an understanding of a complex electro-dynamic pattern of energy that represented the vital body of a 'being' physically separate though eternally connected. The old druid was aware of his role and spoke to the sapling oak tree, humming prayers, litanies, mantras, communing, their collective entities becoming one in these moments.

The seasons changed, spring to summer and then Autumn. The joy of feeling the sun and the exquisite expedience of drawing life, sustenance from newly grown leaves was replaced by a sense of creeping tactical withdrawal, the few leaves were shed and the mistletoe took hold. Jessica experienced a sense of many lifetimes; images flashed before her. Hers was not to be a life of cogitation or contemplation but a life of sensations, or knowledge of a strongly compelling need to reach out and connect with her Mother earth and to the beings with whom she shared her existence. More and more as time passed, she felt herself tuning in to a male presence, a yang energy, could feel him in her mind, was sharing a life with him and was content to live with this wholly absorbing and comfortable notion where there was balance and equilibrium. There was also the exquisite understanding that they were not only connected to each other but to every part of the entire planet; every microbe, every plant became a part of who they were. Where there had been resentment once, a lingering trace of consciousness, of imprisonment, of lack of liberty, Jessica realised that she was perhaps for the first time ever, entirely free. She/they could be anywhere and the fascinating electro-dynamic diversity and character of all who dwell on the planet became known. Birds nested in the great branches in the spring, both he and she sensed their urgency and their excitement and most of all worshipped their ability to fly, to dance with a joy of life in the mating game, to pirouette and to soar in the skies beyond the clouds, birds were their very emissaries to and from the heavens.

In fact it was the birds that helped Jessica and Lucius to endure the pain and anguish as their brethren were cut and harvested to provide food for others, or were trimmed to keep nature in check. Nothing compared however with the agony when mighty oaks, chestnuts, maples and beech were brutally hacked down by machinery, their collective souls

344

alive but in living torment for days, weeks and even months. The great trees continued, rather tragically, to shoot and bud despite their loss of connection with the life giving Mother earth, their displaced roots withering in the sun. Father Donovan's tree, the trinity, Jessica, Lucius and his counterpart, became well versed in enduring the devastating loss of close brethren on forested plateaus and on each occasion, the trinity felt themselves die just a little. Fortunately for them, their position on the lake shore seemed unassailable, as though they were guarded and kept safe in some way. There were times, however, when there was a brush with mortality. The old druid, Father Donovan, had planted the tree in that spot for a reason and for apurpose, being driven to do so, knowing on some level that his own fate was intermingled with that of the spindly little plant.

As time passed, Jessica became aware of a fourth spirit who had been drawn into connection with the 'trinity', a novice priestess, an innocent; Laurna was her name. Jessica had been reluctant at first to acknowledge this divine aspect of her 'self'. Some residue of her pragmatism was like the hardness of a diamond seam in an an open pit mine; this aspect of her character resisted erasure. At the planting of the tree, they had all been there of course and were well aware of the powerful conjuration of magic or divine forces through the mists of time. A swirl of colours, the beauty of a star nebula and the sensational aspects of the aurora borealis had accompanied them all as the Druid had invoked the forces of the universe.

One day, they became aware of anothers presence, specifically Derryth's son no less, a true elemental and nature spirit in essence; Dewin had entrusted a treasure, a metal chest to be buried within the sanctity of the oak. To be encumbered by an inanimate object devoid of life, had at first filled the tree with uncertainty, especially as bluebells at the foot of the tree were dug up and trampled in the process. There was, however, a sense of magic emanating from the chest which inspired 'they' who were the tree to protect their charge. At the behest of the young druid, the bluebells were encouraged to regrow and to hide the chest from the forces of evil. Fox and deer sought shelter under the canopy when hunted or when the rain fell. Stags rubbed the itchy dead skin from their antlers on the rough bark. Rabbits and badgers built warrens nearby and mated profligately, making the most of and contributing to the great bounty of Mother nature. Over the ensuing decades, lovers in human form were enticed by the shade under the tree, by the great protective canopy of the oak's mighty leaf adorned limbs. Once, a rope was thrown over a lower branch by a renegade militia group during the Civil wars and a man on Horseback with his arms tied behind his back had a noose put over his neck. Jessica and Lucius, aware of the impropriety and injustice of the intended execution, conspired to cause a limb to suddenly wither and break away as the horse was slapped on its rear end, the man fell to safety with a bump, on the earth. The mighty limb fell too, right on top of the ugly men of the militia who had death and pillage in their battle rotted hearts. Those that escaped the impact fled, running for their lives while fearing that the wrath of God was upon them.

The centuries passed and the tree grew ever bigger and more magnificent as the druid's spells prevailed. Any attempt by the forces of nature to uproot the tree, or by man to chop it down, were inevitably frustrated for such was the role of the tree; there was a destiny to follow and this could not be curtailed. There had been an attempt once, to fell the tree and in a mighty effort to secure the allegiance of the forces of nature, a protector was conjured into existence. A marching man who was indeed a giant in appearance bore down on the tree's attackers but the apparition was in fact a lifeless form created from leaves previously shed and which had been gathered up and shaped by a sirocco that was summoned by arcane forces. The band of would-be tree fellers had run from the place screaming, their tales shouted far and wide, which of course ensured the tree's protection. On another occasion, a fire was lit and once again the elements were summoned by the spirits of the oak and a deluge put out the fire before serious damage was done. Once, a man, not just any man but an immortal being unwittingly but irrevocably linked to the oak, climbed the branches and cut into the bark with a knife. Though it was painful, 'they' understood his purpose. Once again they felt that somehow, the skin was being branded with intelligence that was a message that was to bridge the time lines until synchronous events led to the message being received and understood by the person for whom it was intended.

The universal blueprint had already been created and there would inevitably be a time when Jessica would be made aware, as if in some long forgotten dream, that she had dug up the chest and read her own prophecy, a foretelling that had been laid down in print almost a thousand years earlier. In her dreams and visions, Jessica observed a young priestess, Laurna, knowing in some deep part of her psyche that the priestess was herself. She had been a maiden and knew little of the ways of the world or of men and had been in a state of mortal terror in the face of what constituted her role in the ceremony which involved her being handed over to an old man like a sack of meat for the purpose of ritual procreation. He was a handsome elderly man and kindly but obligated by the demands of the ceremony to take her, a very reluctant partner, by force. At the moment of consummation, his presence and his otherworldliness had paradoxically banished her fear and aroused a wantoness that she had not known existed. Laurna had conceived in two ways that fateful night. Mindful of the laws of the ritual however, she knew that she was destined to live the rest of her life loving a man she would never see again. Nine months later she delivered a child into the world who would never meet his father. The sacred circle of Oroboros was almost complete.

CHAPTER 28

The spark of creation is a jewel of intent that is infinitely small or boundlessly large, it is a quantum idyll but nonetheless, it is immeasurable. A painting in oils, a novel, the germination of a seedling and the whim that brought a universe into being are all drawn from within primordial chaos as metaphysical constructs. In the last years of the life of Father Donovan's ancient and dying tree, the rising oceans caused floodwaters to lay siege to the worlds lowlands, among them Tower hill. This area was not some lofty plateau but a marginally elevated section of land in London's flatlands adjacent to what was once the River Thames, an estuary now absorbed into the worlds burgeoning oceans. The surroundings became inundated and the ground in which the tree was rooted gradually became submerged. Though the oak was ancient and approaching the end of an extremely long life, the salinity of the encroaching water was, by degrees, saturating the roots and the process of death was therefore accelerated. In places the sap withdrew and more and more limbs, bereft of foliage and bark, became weathered and sun bleached. Like a malnourished and weathered crone with a skin of parchment, the skeleton of the tree was becoming more and more evident as the seasons passed.

The spirit guardians of the tree were aware that this phase of their incarnation was coming to an end and anticipated their release without fear. Not so much a memory but a 'sense' of other shorter lived incarnations came to them. There was a feeling of urgency and anticipation which grew as time approached. The concepts of time and dimensionality started to take a foetal form in their understanding. Greater awareness typically takes root in people as they age and gather wisdom and so it was with the grand old oak tree. The lives of the ones who represented the spirit of the tree, bound together as they were as its soul, had also led very different lives on the earth and they hungered now for an alternative existence. Life as the spirit essence of a tree had been good, though sometimes full of turmoil but it was a process of gaining wisdom. Their connection had anchored them to each other for eternity; they had been united, of one mind and in that incarnation they had wished for nothing other than for harmony in the world.

As if in some diurnal and interdimensional phantasm, the great oak's skeletal image was reflected eerily across the lagoon one moonlit night when it was approached by a visitor. An elderly, still beautiful but painfully thin woman with long silver hair and wearing the colours of nature; russets, deep reds and golds could be seen wading across the watery stillness. The moon was full and bright and the visitor's shadowy image, blending with that of the tree, lay long across the millpond calm of the water. She held her skirts up clear of the water that reached beyond her knees almost up to mid-thigh. She was coming to the tree with a mission and had started to speak. Of course the oak could not hear, was deaf to her eulogies, her entreaties and her sentiments but the tree sensed a presence, recognised her energy, her love and her wisdom and for the first time in this incarnation yearned desperately to communicate. Julia stopped at the foot of the oak and looking up, tears streaming down her face was pleading;

" I know you can hear me, I know who you are and you can listen if you only believe it. Please tell me, what will become of us, of my children who are grown and with families of their own and who have no hope. We have almost lost our farm and our livelihood, our sacred space; the waters are continuing to rise, we are starving to death and I'm desperate. Yu know what will become of us because you have told me in my dreams but I can't remember what you said. Please Jess, if you can hear me, then help me!"

It was then that after centuries of utter quiescance that Jessica in this incarnation as a magnoliophyta could inexplicably 'hear' sounds, an astonishing sensation that at first ravaged her centuries old state of utter silence and tranquility. The sounds were very distant at first, extremely muffled, almost inaudible, a disembodied vibration somewhere in time and space. Then, oddly, there were moments when the sound became almost painful, had a shrill clarity as though Julia were talking loudly right into her ear, just as people tend to do at parties when very loud music is being played. Frustratingly, these moments were fleeting and randomly spaced, a colourful mosaic of noise and dissonance but gradually a change took place. These brief moments gathered momentum, coalesced, the sounds started to gather force and intelligence. Then Jessica recognised that the sounds were a human voice trying to communicate information. She could not ever remember 'hearing' such sounds in all her centuries as a tree. The concept came to her all of a sudden, that although vocalisation was a normal everyday event in some other incarnation, the sounds that she was hearing were not after all, borne on the airwaves and were not sounds at all. Jessica felt an imperative need to become conscious, lucid, sentient; she wanted to communicate, to speak. A strangely alien impulse to verbalise overwhelmed her but she was, she realised, quite impotent; nature had not equipped her with the power of speech. Then Jessica tried, with all her might, to reply with her mind but trees are not equipped with consciousness in the same way as human beings and despite Jessica's heroic effort, there was nothing that could be done. Why had Julia come to a tree to ask for help? There was something so singular in this course of action that Jessica recognised in this person, her desperate need. Without really knowing what to do but with a vague memory of having saved a man about to be hanged many centuries earlier, she and the others made a valiant attempt to create a similarly extraordinary event. Somehow, she had to acknowledged the presence of her soul sister, to give her a sign, some hope. Jessica urged their collective consciousness, the entity of the tree, to respond. There was little left that was alive on this petrified giant in the shallow watery stillness. One small limb, withered and dying; the only one adorned with mistletoe, a handful of leaves and one solitary acorn, represented the last dying gasp of this beautiful old giant.

As Julia gazed up beseechingly, driven almost mad with frustration and despair, she thought she heard a small crack and looked up just in time to see a branch falling towards the water where it finally landed with a big splash. The branch was too big to lift or carry but as she inspected it, driven by intense curiousity, she noticed two things about it. Incredibly, there was an inscription on the branch, a plea to the world for justice though it was hard to read. This was the very message that had prompted her dear friend Jessica to reopen the controversial forensics investigation. Something else that caught her eye was an acorn, just one solitary little seed clinging amidst a clump of leaves to some vestigial part of the limb. Julia contemplated the enormity of the number of acorns that the tree must have produced in its long life; this specimen was the result of a last gasp by the great oak to perpetuate life and was in itself a miracle. The beginnings of an understanding dawned on Julia's face as she took the acorn, carefully removing it along with the shroud of leaves. Wrapping it gently in her scarf she tucked it deep into the front of her blouse between her breasts and close to her heart, some maternal directive guiding her and assuring her that this really was the safest place. Satisfied that her mission had been accomplished, she started for home feeling suddenly optimistic, lighter; the curse of mystery and lack of comprehension removed and the gift of understanding making life suddenly bearable again.

She prepared to return as she had arrived, walking back to her home in Glastonbury, which was a good seven or eight days walk. The highways and motorways were strewn with rusting and damaged vehicles, abandoned when the fuel had run out; great sections of the highways were lost to the ocean, having disappeared into water inundated valleys and lowlands. There was little point in walking on the roads as they had become reclaimed by the relentless advance of nature but they were nevertheless, a means of navigation. Julia knew that if she followed the M4 west then she was ever on the right track. It felt so odd to her to be navigating what had once been a seething motorway, now transformed into forests of bushes and small trees, small areas of broken blacktop still visible in places and broken cars strewn haphazardly wherever they had come to a halt. In every case, there was evidence that the driver and occupants had been making a run for it to some important but unknown destination. Many vehicles were badly damaged, patent evidence of sheer panic by the occupants but in many cases they had evidently run out of fuel and could go no further. There had obviously been a serious collision between a car and a van that were impossibly mangled, a 'train wreck' as Julia would typically have described it. A lone skeleton, partially clad in tattered clothes but with a gaping and splintered impact injury in the left parietal bone, sat in what was left of the drivers seat; it seemed oddly unlikely that the injury was sustained as a result of the accident and Julia sensed foul play. Humanity had been driven to the brink of madness by panic and a desperate need for food and there had indeed been a period, she remembered with a shudder, when sensibility had been forgotten and mayhem had reigned supreme.

The walk to the tree had taken her eight days and she expected that the return trip would take a similar amount of time as she was deeply fatigued. It had become tradition in these times for travellers to be offered shelter and any little food that could be spared. People on the road were viewed in a similar light to the pilgrims of ancient times, as they represented hope in some strange way. Julia paid her way with her visionary observations and psychic intuition and she could only improve the respect and expectations toward travellers like herself. She found that people were pleased to be of service to her and were usually happy with the trade. Not everyone was of the same mind however and life on the road for the travelling wayfarer could be risky. There were many homeless people brought low by hunger and adversity; among those were too many predators who took by force, food, clothing, and carnal pleasures and who were decidedly dangerous but Julia's sixth sense had guided her well so far. She had expected to arrive back at the farm on the eighth day of her travels, then discovered that her sense, on this occasion, had betrayed her.

She was hungry, exhausted and her judgement was impaired, she was driven by her desperation to recall alternative and shorter routes across country and she entered territory that wasn't altogether familiar. Since visiting the tree, she had been sustained by a sense of greater vision and had lost much of her fear. She could see a place in the distance that beckoned to her, it was typical highland, verdant and green and well beyond the reach of the risen waters, being exquisitely unblemished which added greatly to its appeal. She rechecked her bearings and looked for familiar land marks. Where moments before, there had indeed been a few recognisable signs, suddenly these were no longer visible, as a low lying mist had appeared from nowhere and obscured any residual points of reference. Julia was puzzled. The hills could not simply have appeared from nowhere but maybe, just possibly, she never noticed them before? By her calculation she was within a days walk of the farm. She and John had walked over much of the surrounding country and she assumed that she knew it well. She was compelled to keep going, despite her depletion and extreme hunger. She climbed the hill to a point where there was a natural entrance to a glade, where the mist had cleared allowing a shaft of sunlight to illuminate her path.

As Julia entered the clearing, she found herself in a beautiful woodland valley and was enticed further by the sound of a rushing waterfall and shimmering patterns of

reflected light in the bright balmy sunshine. Suddenly feeling very weary, Julia lay down on the grass and closed her eyes, exposing her face to the sun. Within moments she was surrounded by strange bird-like animals, beautiful semi-naked beings, enjoying the paradise in which they lived. They crept toward her warily, acknowledging Julia's need for peace. Hearing a noise, she opened her eyes with a start; fearing that the effects of starvation had caused her to hallucinate, she gazed at all who surrounded her in disbelief. She could not allow herself to become enthralled or even to believe what she saw. This was altogether another world, a realm that was idyllic but strangely unlikely and she was just not strong enough to cope with the disappointment if the vision should fade. The thought crossed her mind, in a dispiriting moment of rationale, that while she felt warm and comfortable for the first time in months, she was in fact suffering from a sleep and food deprived rapture. Then feeling so terribly weary, she permitted herself to close her eyes for a moment and within seconds she was in the arms of Morphius once again. Just as she entered that pleasing and encompassing realm that sleepers inhabit, another residual tendril of rational thought crossed her mind;
'How can this place exist in southern England and remain so anonymous; certainly it's no where in the Somerset that I know of!

Opening her eyes after what must have been hours judging by the position of the sun, she looked around in a still sleep enveloped haze and expected to observe an empty and ruined housing development. She had anticipated that the reality of all she had experienced before she went to sleep was the manifestation of an exhausted mind. As far as Julia could remember there should have been a large housing estate in this locality; a million 'bijoux' shoe boxes of mock Georgian architecture, planted by greedy developers deaf to the entreaties of preservationists and cunning in their dealings with government legislation and corrupt council officials. Like anyone seeing great remuneration at the end of a deed, they had reasoned that all those rules and sensibilities were for other people. Surely they could get away with building a few houses and not upset the Earths balance!

Julia rubbed her eyes and looking up was astonished to note that nothing had changed, the 'vision' was still with her; all around her, the deep blue sky was clear and the air clean and fresh. For excruciating decades, Britain's weather had worsened progressively, most of the country being deluged in continual drenching rain or swamped in muggy heat. The colours in this vision were like the surreal clarity of a blue-ray image; the oxygen rich air was so pure, unsullied and refreshing that she felt drugged. It was the first time that she had drawn such a beautiful breath since a childhood camping trip to Jasper in Alberta one summer. Julia could not believe how bewilderingly beautiful this place was, a genuine Garden of Eden but she had absolutely no idea why or how she came to be there.

Hunger had been a constance companion for some years but suddenly she experienced not only the familiar pangs but was indeed, absolutely ravenous. After a brief forage she was surprised to find that she did not have to look very hard; berries, nuts and fruit were in abundance and she grazed contentedly. Sitting in a soft, sun drenched depression in the grass, Julia happily devoured fresh revitalising food for the first time in months and wholly unimpeded by a sense of lack; she began to feel her old vigour returning. Once replete, satiated in fact, she felt inexplicably drowsy again. Resting and dozing and becalmed by the sound of life; birds twittering, bees buzzing and the gentle rustle of grasses in the warm, healing breeze that caressed and soothed, Julia fell once more into a deep and dreamless slumber. She went to a place devoid of anxiety, stress or those horrific dreams as had become so normal in recent times.

When she awoke once again, some time later, her awareness heightened, she knew with an overriding sense of urgency, that this was where the acorn must be planted. Julia looked around for a suitable spot in the lee of the wind and found the perfect place. It was in an area of woodland adjacent to the shore of a placid and magical lake which reflected a perfect mirror image of all that was around her, an inverted but pristine world. She dug into the fertile earth with her hands, and planted the acorn, then constructed a low wall around the site with as many rocks as she could carry in order to protect the acorn during this time of extreme vulnerability. Julia knew on some deep level that the acorn would germinate and grow tall and straight, providing shelter for those in need of the encompassing shade of an enormous and gently rustling canopy.

The true paradox in 'reality' occurs when a person is under no illusion that what they perceive is real. The nature of enchantment is that the credibility barriers of the mind have been quite broken down; there is no doubt, no question and therefore the mind will grasp all that is presented and devour it hungrily. What is 'reality'? This is the eternal riddle that has baffled and confounded philosophers since the dawn of thought. The problem of course, is that criteria cannot be applied to the nature of reality to impart the nature of what 'is' and what 'is not' real because that criteria is in itself the eternal conundrum. Julia, exhausted, mal-nourished and pushed to the limits of her resources had cried out for help which had somehow opened a doorway that had taken her to another dimension. A realm where she had been set at ease and where the extraordinary ripples of syncronicity within the continuum brought her into contact with Jessica as had been ordained. Julia, having completed her work, stepped back, surveying the result and was filled with satisfaction and a sense of completion knowing that her quest was almost accomplished. As she bathed in the energy of her surroundings in this mysterious domain of undefined borders, she beheld a beautiful naked young woman who was approaching; she cried out her name in astonishment, "Jessica, can it really be you?"

The woman looked at Julia for a moment, uncomprehending and then the dawn of recognition flashed across her features and she spoke;

" It will be alright you know, everything will BE according to the Great plan. It is impossible for me to explain to you how I know this but I do."

A tall man approached and encircled Jessica's waist with a protective and proprietorial arm. He too was almost naked and his skin displayed the feral golden glow of one who lives perpetually outdoors. He was broad, muscular and powerful with long sandy hair and a fine sculpted nose. It was his eyes that Julia was drawn to however, a hypnotically pale green and she felt herself drawn into them as though she was being plucked from the edge of an abyss. She found that she was stirred by him, emotionally and sexually but there was more to the attraction than raw physical desire; it was as if she had always known him. He represented the masculine archetype and his union with Jessica was an indication that

the schism between the Divine masculine and the Divine feminine had finally been healed; a marriage made in heaven and consecrated on this earth. He studied Julia for a while and then he pointed to where she had placed the acorn in the ground. To Julia's amazement, a sapling oak stood there, proud and straight. Then he knelt before her;
" Mother Goddess, you have our undying gratitude for restoring the balance and we shall forever honour you."

In this timeless state of unreality, Julia was distracted by the incongruous sight of a dog nearby, snuffling playfully in the bushes. He was a large shaggy creature, quite wolf-like, ears erect and alert, one uncanny pale blue eye and one brown softened by overtures of friendship, his tail wagged in greeting. Julia had some vague recollection of Jessica once talking of a dog that matched the description of this fellow, one that she had met when she got lost on her walk near the farm. As the unbidden thought flashed through this idyllic world like a thunderbolt, the image before her started to waiver and shimmer, the colours losing their distinction and sounds becoming an echo. Julia held out her hands to grasp those of Jessica's in an attempt to hold on, to cling to this reality but to no avail. She let go and then collapsed onto the earth as her vision dissolved and she surrendered to the all pervading sultry gloom, by the side of a broken motorway strewn with abandoned vehicles.

John was gently holding her, stroking her hair and kissing her head in the early morning darkness.
"Its alright my love, it's okay, It's just a dream thats all, its a beautiful morning and there is nothing to be sad about."
Julia started to come to, sobbing, realising where she was.
"It was that same dream again."

"The one about Jessica."

"Oh yes, John it's so beautiful there! I feel as if our destiny is there but I don't know if we could ever find that place again. Do you think I will ever see Jessica again? What is all this about, what the hell really happened to her?"

" She was poisoned my love; you know that, though we will never really know that she ingested a lethal toxin, some kind of fungus, I'm not sure we will ever really know what happened to her."

"I keep telling you John, I knew she was ill when she came back from that walk."

John reached for a glass of water and then stopped to think for a moment.

"It does make sense; that was obviously why you became ill too, because of the spores on her clothing but why couldn't we find the mushrooms? Thank goodness your exposure was only a fraction compared to poor Jess. But listen to me my love, I'm here and I'm going to take care of you..... well at least until I have to milk the cows at any rate!"

John then smiled, a cheeky disarming grin barely visible in the half light of early morning.

"I suppose a bit of early morning frolicking is out of the question?"

Julia smiled at him despite herself, then she became serious again,

" One more thing and then I won't mention it again. I just have this feeling that Jess is trying to tell us something, I really do."

"Maybe she is warning us and assuring us at the same time," John suggested with an uncharacteristic expression of insight."

Julia gently took his hand and bit gently into the fleshy part below his thumb;

" You are absolutely right my love but we do have half an hour don't we, before you have to get up and the world won't change just yet will it? Just be gentle with me Farmer John okay?"

CHAPTER 29

In those quiescent moments of serenity that often occur in the early morning, one has time to ruminate and to contemplate on life; to philosophise on the complexities, the sorrows and the joys of existence. A young woman, recently awoken from a night of bizarre but fascinating dreams lay in bed and considered her adventures and her many lives that had taken place while in that other world. Her lives had spanned a period from the distant past into the not so distant future. The people that she had become were not so strange to her as one might have thought and in them all she observed a fundamental element of herself. She remembered the obtuse pragmatism and restricted credibility barriers of someone named 'Jessica Stearne', forensics scientist and professional woman; she recognised a closed and intransigent female who had unwittingly shut out so much in her life.

Through this curious window of perspective of her being, the dreamer gazed at her husband who lay beside her, a man whom she adored. In one of her dreams, she had been a young priestess who had been offered to this dynamic man. She had been compelled to endure a ceremony that had, at first, filled her with great fear but this was the course that had to be followed as set down by the elders, a procedure that would hopefully auger a less disastrous reality far into the future. As a result of her terror, the spell consequent of their union was not well woven but it was nonetheless powerful. What spell was it that the dreamer was recalling? Her subconscious seemed fully aware, though her mind was less able to grasp the facts. Something told her that there was hope and that the end result would be achieved, though precisely what that was remained a mystery to her. In examining her dreams, the very act of doing so brought the experiences into her waking world, making them real.

The ceremony had been planned as a matter of expediency, in order to change a world where, it had been foreseen that impending disaster awaited humanity; not only humanity but other harmonious life forms on this wonderful and unique planet, truly the veritable Garden of Eden. Timing was the issue in a realm where time does not exist but synchronicity is an event borne of precise timing just as the gears of a complex machine enmesh at critical moments. The ceremony created 'a seed' that would lie in wait, dormant for almost one thousand years. If the seed failed to germinate, due to the absence of the active ingredients or the catalysts, then the future for mankind would be relegated to oblivion. Jessica thought through all of this and yet was only dimly aware of the complexity of the mechanism at work. Within the labyrinthine conundrum of thought form and creation lay the secret of her new life and her old life; such were the intricacies that it could not bear investigation or analysis with thought alone. Hers, she relearned, were the old ways, the ways of nature, the way of universal and pagan law; they are, of course, one and the same thing.

As she awoke fully, rubbing her eyes, her memories were already blurring but she was still immersed in the atmosphere of her nocturnal vision and in this dream she had a strong connection to people whom she had never met; yet there was a subliminal link between them all. She knew, on some visceral level, that somehow and somewhere in a the path to the future, things had gone badly wrong. Some trick of fate, a distortion in the DNA had dictated a path for mankind that had become out of control and entirely dangerous to the planet, to Eden. She recalled the discomfort of stifling polluted air, over-fished and horribly tainted oceans, a world on the brink of disaster. Her island, bewitching Albion, was a land that was the heart of the earth but which lay shattered and wasted by greed and overpopulation. There was still magic and wonder to behold but the ugliness had progressively outweighed and overcome the spirit of the land with the malevolent stealth of dry-rot.

As she lay basking in the luxury of awakening to a new and enchanting day, her partner yawned and stretched then opened an eye that was hypnotically pale and ageless, which was animated, intelligent and compassionate and through it he gazed upon his woman. He reached over to her and she felt the sizzle of electricity in the air and a fire of want coursed through her once again. Was it possible that she could want him again, their constant hunger for one another had abated from sheer exhaustion but after sleeping, as they awoke, their need awoke also and was as vital and as thrilling as ever. This kindly man who had been forced to take her in a previous incarnation, was also the person that she loved more than anything in the world and she clung to him as if her existence depended upon it.

Later that morning they embarked upon a daily ritual, the significance of which was deeply ingrained in their souls. They went to the tree, a sapling that was fragile, newborn but straight and full of life. He looked into her eyes,

"We have been given a chance, my love, to make this a world that is good and benevolent, a world that can support us but we in turn must honour the Earth. We must never abuse this gift of life, this chance of living in the realm of nature. There is enough for us all, shelter, food and clothing. We live in a place that is potentially idyllic but evil, greed and avarice are the propensities that will create our downfall if unchecked. Man needs to embody the importance of circumspection, management, balance and self control. Future man will discover the folly of nurturing a gaping maw of material acquisition and power. The little oak tree is a symbol to mankind to remind us of our priorities. They gazed out over the enchanted valley of this land. All of those people that she had held dear were with her in one way or another, all of them with the exception of one, someone who had once been very important to her.

Later that evening, falling asleep by the fire as it crackled and sparked, emitting fireflies of light into the balmy darkness, she gazed at the stars, feeling as though she would fall into them. The sound of the fire was hypnotic and she gave in to her drowsiness, taking comfort from the arm of the man that held her, anchoring her, making her feel safe and she drifted into the bewitching realm of nirvana. Once again she floated in a sea of consciousness, a hazy sort of awareness, delicious, safe and healing. A tunnel beckoned to her and she allowed herself to be drawn like a moth to a flame, toward the entrance. Like a young animal venturing beyond the safety of the lair she was alert, slightly apprehensive but above all, curious. This was a journey that she was compelled to embark upon, though on some level, she sensed danger that was all around her, though somehow she was kept safe. Emerging for a moment into semi-wakefulness, she felt the reassuring grip around her waist and then permitted herself once more to drift towards the beckoning light that drew her to some distant horizon. There came a point when she feared that if she did not turn back, it would be too late but simultaneously, she realised that there was no turning back, she no longer had any choice.

As she surfaced, her consciousness gasping for air, fragmentary impressions came to her, then more, then a deluge; concepts, impressions and familiar voices. A light shone on her face, streaming sunlight from a window. A summer breeze brushed her cheek as it passed like a beneficent spirit, wanting to awaken her but gently,
" She really is very lucky to be alive."
Glimmers of sentences, some distant, nonsensical but some clear and beckoning. Then she heard Julia's voice;
"Thank you Creator, thank you spirits for bringing her back."
An unknown male voice, slightly officious, close to where she lay;
"We know that she must have ingested some of the toxin when she was in the woods, a very rare type of mushroom that normally you don't encounter in Britain, though we do seem to see more of it now thanks to global warming. It is normally specific to Indonesia and the tribes people use it as a nerve poison. The spoors from the mushrooms are released into the air and if you are in their proximity on a still day, they can really get a grip on ones system and hers was substantially compromised. It is both hallucinogenic and often fatal. She really must have an iron constitution but it is a good job you found her when you did."
Jessica yearned to sleep again, to be by the fireside, beside her man in her beautiful world but then a question arose;

was she awake? Was this her reality or was it the product of her mind, in its apparently poisoned and distorted state?
" It is said that in the days of pagan worship that priestesses collected this stuff when they could find it. During ceremony they would ingest very small amounts of this substance so that they might embark upon vision quests, it was known to be a very potent plant medicine."

Julia bent down to her;
" You are awake aren't you dearest, are you able to speak?"
"Where am I......? Julia is it really you?
"It really is me my love, you are in hospital, have been for almost nine months and have been in a deep coma; at first we feared that you might not make it. We are taking you home soon, back to the farm. I've made up the spare room especially for you and you can stay as long as you need to."
Jessica was overwhelmed, suddenly it seemed that she had lost everything, her beautiful world with its strange but beautiful creatures and of course, her man, the only man that she ever loved and truly wanted. An unbelievable sense of loss and sadness enveloped her as tears sprang from her eyes and rolled down the sides of her face but then, strangely, there grew in her heart a sense, a feeling, a tinge of relief. Though reluctant to see it at first, there was a definite comfort in seeing her dearest friend alive and well and some sense of normality after what had been the most fantastical adventure. She cried uncontrollably, letting everything out that had been cooped up inside her for so many years.
"Oh Julia, have I really just been dreaming? The places I have been, the people I have seen; the man I love! I really thought I was dying, Steven Savage found me in the apartment didn't he? It all seemed so real. I'm so bloody confused."

On that last note she endured more paroxysms of unassuaged grief, pouring her heart out. Julia, tormented by Jessica's misery, helped her into a sitting position.

" What the hell happened to me? I feel as if this has been some sort of extraordinary, nightmarish and sometimes heavenly dream; am I still in the midst of it, because I don't think I can take any more?"

Julia continued to hold her for a while, comforting her, giving her the warmth of human contact, the connection of a lifelong friend.

"No you are here with us my love. You poisoned yourself when you went for a walk to the lake, though lord knows how you did. Those odd looking mushrooms that you had apparently discovered must have proliferated there for a day or two but then disappeared as mysteriously as they had appeared once the weather changed. We looked and looked and could find no evidence of them."

"Is this real, are you real, could you pass me a mirror?"

"You bet this is real, just about as real as it gets but then none of us really know what is real."

Jessica looked in the mirror that was passed to her and was horrified at what she saw. Her face was much thinner, there was a grey streak in her hair and deep black rings circled her sunken eyes. An appalling sense of loss surrounded her, consumed her and yet, underneath it all, there was a fine filament of optimism was growing and threading through her consciousness.

Though weaker than she could ever have imagined, she managed to reach out and hug Julia, holding her as tight as she could, needing an anchor.

"They are going to keep you in for another couple of weeks or so just to make sure that your kidneys keep operating okay on their own but John and I will keep popping in to make sure that you don't get up to mischief."

" What about work?"

"Don't give it a thought! Oh my love, I knew you would come back to us."

"What about William, where is he?"

"Oh that munchkin, well he fared better than all of us. Your Mrs Wainwright has taken him in and is feeding him a non-stop diet of rich tea cookies from what I hear. I never liked Steven Savage particularly but you know it was him who suggested the idea and I was very surprised. Initially, when he heard you were sick, he said he was going to take William and seemed very determined but then he phoned Mrs Wainwright and suggested that she take him in. It was all very odd really because he doesn't know Mrs Wainwright, she had no idea that you were ill and she doesn't even like cats very much. Anyway she has William and utterly adores him but she also lives for the day when you can reclaim him; isn't that a strange tale?"

Jessica relaxed a little, smiled and touched Julia's cheek softly with the backs of her fingers. Then just as calm had prevailed, her eyes flew open and she appeared suddenly alert, anxious, her eyes wide with panic.

"What about the chest?"

"What chest?"

" The one buried under the tree!"

Julia looked thoughtful for a moment as if trying to decide what to say and in fact trying desperately to find something to say.

"You know at first, before you went into a coma, you raved about some box being buried under that big old tree and you would not stop. Finally and just to calm you and to prevent you from being so agitated, we searched for it, digging big holes, destroying the bluebell bed and upsetting the gardener; amazingly though, we did find something! I think I was more surprised than anyone."

Jessica looked relieved, intransigently hopeful.

"But there wasn't much there, some rusty pieces of metal, with a few rotting splinters of wood and the faintest remains of parchment inside what was left of a waxed envelope. I have to tell you Jess, no one was more astonished than me."

Jessica looked at Julia intently, desperately curious.

" Did you read the parchment, did you see what it said?"

"Nope honey, we really couldn't. What was left of it fell to pieces as soon as it was touched, despite the best efforts of the experts. But you know what was left of it is a national relic of great historical interest, buried by a priest so it is believed."

" I know it all, I read it! I can repeat it all verbatim."

Julia looked shrewdly, knowingly into Jessica's eyes;

" The parchment no longer matters you know. You are the new parchment and you have that information as you so rightly say."

"Is that my friend talking as my psychic or are you just comforting me?"

Julia paused for a while, obviously some caldera of emotion bubbling within.

"I have been very linked in with throughout your illness Jessica. You showed me some of what you saw and I dreamed some of what you experienced. I was in that place you know, the moonlit lake where the acorn dropped from the dead tree."

Jessica was silent for a moment, unable to speak, unable to really comprehend what was unfolding. Julia could see that Jessica was consumed by emotional turmoil and decided to bring things back to earth.

"Ooh, hey Jess, before I forget, I need to tell you that there is a solicitor by the name of Whitton, Baron Whitton I think his full name is, who has been trying to contact you. God, you Brits really do have some weird names! He's been phoning just about every week or so for the past few months, has made a regular nuisance of himself. I promised that you would get in touch as soon as you were better."

" How curious!"

Jessica's professional etiquette, having lain dormant for so long was re-awakened, she became very curious.

"Did he say what it was about?"

" He really wouldn't Jess and I tried my best to get him to, you know me? He kept repeating that it was very important but between you and him. He was very insistent that I pass on the message and to let him know the moment you regained consciousness."

Jessica growing very weary, suddenly lapsed into tears again, shuddering with grief,

" I've lost him Julia, I've lost the only man I ever loved and I don't know how to get him back. What will I do without him? I don't want this life, it's not really mine, I don't belong here."

Julia feeling the full impact of Jessica's torment, was unable to say anything for a moment and just hugged Jessica tightly, gently rocking her to and fro like one of her children and stroked her head soothingly. Finally Jessica lay back exhausted and drifted off to sleep. It broke Julia's heart to see her friend so stricken both physically and mentally. There was indeed going to be a long road to recovery for Jessica but then a thought occurred to Julia.

"Oh before you go to sleep, I'm so sorry, there's something else I must tell you."

Weary eyes opened for a moment, fleetingly.

"Jess, can you hear me?"

" Umm..... what is it Julia?

"Jess this is important!"

Jessica had lapsed back into a state of semi-consciousness, not life threatening any more but just the sleep of the deeply exhausted. A young nurse came over and pulling the curtains around Jessica's bed, indicated in her professional bustle that perhaps the time had come when the patient should be permitted vital rest once more.

Jessica slept for another fourteen hours and then awoke feeling a little stronger, rather more positive. Her experiences, though still painful, were by that stage, partially banished. Throughout the remaining day, her trepidation and sense of loss gave way gradually to a new optimism and a hunger for life. Her innate vitality was restoring her to health by unwavering degrees and her mind was spending less time trying to make sense of all that had happened to her, focusing instead on getting well and looking to the future. She had speedily come to the conclusion that the answer was not to run away but simply, to tackle life head on.

'The world is a beautiful one and there is time to make people aware and to make changes necessary to avoid disaster and I know also that there are many people of like mind. Not everything man has done has been destructive; there is so much good in the world, so much richness and so much life. Rather than concentrate on all the negative aspects and dissolve into a state of impotent misery, we need to be positive and make this our focus. The face of evil so often wears the mask of good, time to root out those hypocrites, this is the way to start. There are plenty of willing, selfless, constructive people who have a real desire

to become organised and to do something that will be beneficial for the world. It's not too late, it really isn't. I know we can do this, especially once kindred spirits find each other. The world doesn't have to be doomed if we all make sure that we perceive that it's going to be alright; just a matter of our perspective on reality.'

Inevitably Jessica's thoughts then turned to the man she missed so desperately. With that last thought and a lingering sense of loss, Jessica turned over and slept again, though she was comforted by the knowledge that her life was becoming more meaningful.

CHAPTER 30

Jessica's recovery was slower than she had expected at first and fraught with setbacks and frustration. For some reason she fell prey to a persistent tinnitus, a loud ringing in her ears which haunted her waking hours. She was given food little and often, a kind of watery and rather tasteless soup which did little to satisfy her palette despite the fact that she had been given appetite stimulants. Then came the day for her first desperately needed bath; holding onto her mobile intravenous apparatus rack, her first shaky steps to the bathroom were incredibly arduous, as if she were climbing Everest. Jessica had never felt so winded and short of breath in her life. Nausea and weakness came next, along with another plummet into the abyss of depression. She burst into tears of helplessness when a nurse had assisted her in taking off her night clothes. The jaundiced, pitifully thin and shrunken waif reflected in the mirror was a complete stranger to her; Jessica studied the reflection for a moment in mute astonishment. The hot bath, though exquisitely cleansing and relaxing, sapped what remaining strength she had and once back in a freshly made bed, she sank yet again into a peaceful sleep. She slept for the next twelve hours but in a sleep so shallow that she experienced the world through an ambience of twilight impressions, odd sounds and smells mixed with the miasma of fantastic dream imagery, a mosaic of impressions but bereft of continuity.

When she awoke, feeling that she had slept for an eternity, she felt rested mentally but still physically exhausted. The tinnitus was so loud that conversation was difficult without the other person shouting. Jessica noted that while her hearing during the day was afflicted with the terrible ringing, as if her ears had been damaged by an explosion, by night her hearing was sharp and bereft of interference, an odd and apparently unaccountable reality. Jessica nevertheless, encouraged by the views of others, held steadfastly to the notion that once she was discharged, she would trip lightly down the stairs and exit the hospital, full of fizz and vitality. She had anticipated improvements in the same way that one recovers from influenza, initially slow but then hastening exponentially to a full and energetic recovery. In fact, the very reverse appeared to be the case with Jessica. Her recovery and awareness ironically making her more and more conscious of her poor state of health and therefore more debilitated.

To a great extent she was still highly disorientated, unable to be sure of where she was or come to that, 'when' she was. Almost unhinged by her recurrent and free access to places where mortals are normally forbidden, Jessica was quite at sea. She concluded, during those tortuous hours when all she could do was think, that there was no standard with which to compare her sense of reality. 'Actuality', she had decided, was simply a point of reference to which one became steadfastly attached. All one needed in order to be in a different plane of consciousness, was to focus ones belief structure and psyche to a fixed and known scenario. Certainly Jessica had endured many 'realities' during the intervening months of her illness but the place that she felt the happiest and most complete was on the boat in the dying world of the future and with her true love but then her life had been curtailed. A beautiful recollection came to her of the realm that she had inhabited just before entering into the tunnel and waking up in a hospital bed. There were ironies she decided, in choosing such fates in uncompromising dimensional aberrations. The world was coming to an end, destroyed by man and yet man for all of his faults was not all destructive; there is so much man made beauty in the world, the arts, music that takes one on transcendental journeys, majestic and impossibly labour intensive architecture, and the fascination of literature. There seemed to be an imbalance at this time, the forces of darkness attempting to engulf the forces of good. The tragedy of modern times is that the forces of evil have become very adept at parody and the divisions between the two have long since become blurred. For no reason at all Jessica suddenly had a flashback of herself as an innocent young priestess, about to be thrown in sacrifice to a kindly and handsome though terrifying druid. This was an offering, an act of sacrifice that was intended to put the world to rights that by its very nature, reeked of fear and revulsion, another divine paradox.

After six more weeks in care, Jessica was starting to feel a lot better and had gained much needed weight and energy. Hospital food administered latterly was, if nothing else, exquisitely calorific but she knew that her days of appreciating treacle pudding and custard were over. She was told that all being well, she would be discharged within the week; that indeed was grounds for celebration. Mr Whitton of Baron Whitton, the solicitors came to see her one evening very late and well beyond visiting hours, somehow aware of her miraculous recovery. He was, however, denied access to her curtain encircled bed while she was receiving medical attention, though Jessica could see him through a small gap in the sterile enclosure; a tanned and expensively dressed older man with a pleasant if official manner who, she observed, smelt exotically of expensive aftershave. He had spoken to a ward nurse, expressing that his visit was a matter of great importance. The nurse thanked him in a perfunctory fashion but promised to relay the message to Jessica who had, in fact, overheard him and was curious about her strange visitor although not so curious that she wanted him to see her in her dishevelled state.

Finally, the long awaited day of her discharge arrived. Julia swept in leaving in her wake a glorious scent of fresh honeysuckle tinged with summer air and looking more beautiful than ever. Jessica saw that it was not merely how she looked but what she radiated that people became spellbound by, they were drawn to her like moths to a flame. Jessica realised in her newly awakened sense of consciousness, if indeed that is what it was, that for the first time she was able to sense this, could almost see the radiant aura surrounding Julia. It was a day of elation though Jessica did not dance down the steps cured but was escorted to Julia's car in a wheelchair as hospital policy dictated. She was still feeling weak and unequal to the task of simply walking or even of living. Jessica nevertheless, had convinced Julia that she needed to be back in her apartment and that while the thought of going to the farm with Julia was appealing, she really did desperately desire to be back in her own surroundings, at least for a few days. Julia agreed, insisting on staying with her for those few days to keep her company.

Jessica remained quiet while being driven back to Mortlac in Julia's ramshackle Volvo. She so yearned to be home but there was a part of her that was apprehensive; the same feeling that one has when at an interview for a job. Predictably enough, once the tyres of the Volvo had scrunched up the gravel driveway, Jessica was overjoyed at the sight of her home. Once she had turned the key and was assailed by that familiar ambience of her home and overwhelmed by the spectacle of William lying on the kitchen table, kneading the air with big soft paws, she was in heaven. Mrs Wainwright, knowing of Jessica's return had tactfully withdrawn, leaving a note and a saucepan of stew, gently simmering on the stove.

'Welcome back my dear, you have been so missed by us all. I knew you would be weary so please forgive me for not dallying but I look forward very much to having a chat soon. I shall miss William, what a lovely fellow he is. Fondest regards, your neighbour. Patricia Wainwright.'

Jessica realised that in all this time she had never known Mrs Wainwright's first name. Julia and Jessica made inroads into the delicious stew and chit chatted mindlessly about nothing in particular until Jessica, desperate to sleep, excused herself;

"Sorry to abandon you on your first night but I really am pooped. Do make yourself at home, there's probably something to drink in the fridge."

"Oh it's so nice to have some space away from the farm for a change, so lovely to see you up and about. I'll find myself a movie to watch and pillage some booze, I'll be fine."

" No snakebite I'm afraid, will you manage with a crisp chardonnay?"

Julia gave Jessica a wry smile and hugged her good night.

That night and once safely in her own bed, Jessica dreamed again. This time she was walking along a forest path on a wet wintry evening at dusk, in a place that she recognised. She was walking to a circle of standing stones not far from a lake by which a sacred oak tree was yet to be planted. When making her way along a path, she encountered a most enormous and utterly beautiful stag with an incredible but intimidating set of antlers. At first she was startled, as was the stag; the thought crossed her mind in that instant that he was going to bolt. She spoke to him very softly,
"It's okay beautiful, I mean you no harm, I promise. You really are magnificent, there's no need to be afraid......"
The stag moved away from the path but not quickly and not too far. He stood nearby eating the lower leaves of a tree and while doing so exposed a strip of white fur that ran from his throat to his underbelly, a colour that was in stark contrast to the deep red/brown of his winter coat. Jessica carefully made her way into the circle of stones and sat in the middle on mossy ground that seeped cold water through her robes and chilled her behind. After a short while the stag came closer and he lay down in a hollow right next to a fire pit beside the circle. He neatly folded his legs beneath him and held his head proud and erect. He observed Jessica from a perspective of inquisitive caution; for her part, Jessica was enchanted as she beheld this beautiful creature of the forest, spellbound by his potent proximity. They observed one another for a time, exchanging thoughts and views, communing on all but an audible level. Finally, the moment came when she had to leave and besides which, her bottom was getting very cold and damp. As she walked away, he just watched her with no hint of alarm, merely a look of serene majesty and wisdom.

Jessica awoke just at that moment, then she lay in bed in the darkness thinking about the dream, the memory of which had remained etched in full detail upon her conscious mind. It was almost as if the dream were some kind of farewell but she was ill equipped to make much sense of it. In the midst of her whimsy, a more pertinent thought crossed her mind. *'How is it possible to have a memory of a time when I did not exist? The lake was there but the tree was yet to be planted. I sensed something, knew where and when I was and yet, how was that possible?'*

Julia helped Jessica go through a ton of correspondence that had been building up in her absence. Thanks to Benjamin Wallace, Jessica's essential bills had been paid but there was still a great deal to plough through and an enormous pile of flyer's to be dumped in the recycling bin. Among the piles of envelopes was a letter from Baron Whitton, Solicitors at Law. Jessica had quite forgotten about him and promptly phoned to make an appointment. The receptionist who answered the phone was a typically rancorous and defensively hostile forward guard who gave little away. She declined to answer any of Jessica's questions, indicating that all would be resolved at the meeting but she did allow, in her rather austere and vinegary fashion, that the matter concerned Jessica's late Uncle Alistair. Jessica was quite puzzled, knowing that the matters of his estate had been dealt with months previously and that there was nothing to resolve.

Julia placed a cup of tea in front of Jessica and looked at her searchingly, sensing her confusion.
"Just had a very odd conversation with the solicitors office; the want to see me in connection with my 'late' Uncle Alistair and his estate?"

"I'm so sorry, I know how fond you were of him. Actually when that lawyer guy kept coming to the hospital wanting to see you, I guessed what it was about and I did try really hard to tell you but you were too out of it."

Jessica was baffled, she knew Alistair had died but then of course, that was in her dream. What was this really all about?

"Julia my sweet, I can manage now; I really think that you need to go back to John and the kids. I feel so much stronger. Why don't we go out tomorrow and have a really fun day and then you must go home. Let's get drunk just like we used to, have a day of unbridled lunacy, I so need that right now!"

" Are you sure Jess?" Julia looked at her intently, tuning into her in her inimitable psychic way.

"I must admit that it would be great to get out for a while. I've been in London a week already and haven't even seen the Eiffel Tower yet? I've heard so much about these European monuments!"

The devilish smile on Julia's face as she spoke made Jessica laugh.

Jessica was improving by leaps and bounds but odd lapses in her memory were disturbing to her. As it transpired, Jessica was not really up to a day of drunken gay abandon but they did go to Regents Park and rented a rowing boat. Julia rowed while Jessica handed her glasses of sparkling wine and crackers with smoked salmon and cream cheese. The sun was shining; a cloudless blue sky inferred a promise of joy and happiness and Jessica started to feel quite upbeat, interested in life once more. They shouted nautical epithets as they navigated the waters of a lake made choppy by other exuberant boaters. Later they went to the Tate Gallery and spent a happy couple of hours battling with tourists. Finally, they went to a bistro, had a decidedly miserly meal of 'nouvelle cuisine' aspirations with more wine, most of which Julia drank and then they eyed up the waiters to see who could get the most encouraging response. Julia was gladdened to see Jessica looking so much better if still a little thin. The streak of white that had appeared in her hair was there to stay but in some odd way, the contrast suited Jessica even if it did make her look a little older. A tendril of raw compassion reached out to Jessica from Julia's heart while Jessica was engaged in a bit of uncharacteristic light flirtation with the wine waiter and Julia smiled whimsically at her, so glad to see her alive.

Julia departed the following day. She opened a creaking drivers door and climbed onto the ripped seat that exposed some of the underlying foam cushion, in the muddy and battered but ever willing Volvo wagon. It was a decidedly incongruous sight in that part of town.
"I knew you wouldn't come with me today but promise me you will visit soon?"
"I promise, I really do! I would love to be with you all, I just need a few weeks here to get my head completely straight."
Julia waved as she left, shouting her intention to pop back very soon for a girls weekend of window shopping and riotous self indulgence. As she waved her off, Jessica pondered upon the appointment with the solicitor which was to be the following morning and decided to check the Bentley to make sure that it was functional. When she opened the garage door with its characteristic squeal of tortured metal she was horrified to find the car covered in dust and that one tyre had gone flat. The portable compressor that John Stringer had given her at a 'works' Secret Santa one christmas, soon restored the tyre to full inflation and after some hours of sweat and toil the car was once again shiny

and fit to use, though the scar of vandalism looked worse than ever. She had already re-insured and 'taxed' it and now the old car just needed a good run. Though Jessica adored the Bentley, she decided while cleaning and polishing it that, finally, the time had come when it should be retired and possibly sent on loan to a museum. There was no place on the road now for such environmental dinosaurs, beautiful though they were. The person who had keyed the side, written that offensive note all those months ago was actually quite right in his excessively and annoyingly moralistic way, though she felt that his actions ran counter to his ideals and were based principally upon the hypocrisy of raw envy.

The following morning, Jessica was welcomed into a swish and expensively appointed solicitors office by Mr Whitton.
"Please don't mind Mrs Pratt." he said genially;
"She's our guard dog but she truly has a heart of pure butter once you get to know her. She really is invaluable and I honestly don't know how I would cope without her."
Jessica accepted the explanation with good grace, though her hackles had risen upon first encountering the redoubtable Mrs Pratt, sitting at her desk in the reception area and who had given Jessica an unnecessarily hard time. Mr Whitton continued;
"I must say you look so much better now than you did when I saw you briefly in hospital Ms. Stearne. To business though, I expect that you know why I have asked you to come and see me?"
"My friend did say that you had inquired after me on several occasions but no, I don't have the least idea why you want to talk to me."

"Ah, yes, the somewhat eccentric but very attractive American lady, Julie I think she said her name was. But to come to the point, I was terribly sorry to hear of your uncles death, of which you have been made aware as I understand; he was a good friend of mine. I apologise also if I seem tactless but one must be devoid of ambiguity in these matters, as I am sure you will understand."

" Actually it's Julia with an 'a' and she's Canadian and my closest friend but yes, to answer your question, thank you, I am aware that Uncle Alistair died some time ago."

The solicitor looked momentarily puzzled but resumed his speech."

" Mr Gray passed away some months ago while you were still mortally ill and effectively out of touch with the world. He did of course, leave a 'will' and with the exception of a few minor dispensations here and there, you are to be the sole beneficiary of his entire estate including, as I understand it, his house, Abbotsfield and- oh dear ....please bear with me a second, I do apologise...!"

A file was consulted and the solicitor put on some glasses for a moment as he scanned through the text.

"His motor cruiser moored at Hayling Island....... quite why he made such a point of that is unclear to me but he had this outlined in an Addendum which indicated that you would understand."

Jessica froze, quite at a loss as to how to react. She didn't understand at all, was really confused, none of this made sense and she sat in stunned silence for a number of minutes, feeling nauseous and attempting with all her might not to faint, while goose bumps ran riot along her arms.

"Are you quite alright Ms. Stearne; would you like a drink, tea, coffee?"

"I don't suppose I could have a whisky or brandy or something, I know that this is a most odd request but........."
Mr Whitton smiled graciously, reached into his desk, retrieved a bottle and two glasses and poured them both a drink.
"Think I'll join you if I may, I do understand that this has all been rather a shock, especially as you have been so ill."
Jessica took a sip of her cognac;
"I'm sorry, I really had forgotten about his boat. Also I could swear that I was told he died intestate, no will and large debts and so forth."
" Well I'm not sure where you heard that my dear Ms. Stearne but I assure you that he was more than comfortably off and as a member of the bar was only too well aware of the importance of leaving a signed and witnessed 'will' in my care. Look, here it is, a legal document in every sense. I have already applied for probate and have fully resolved any of the few outstanding issues regarding your uncle's finances. His entire estate and house is yours once probate is granted and that should be within the twelve month, as the case is clear cut and his affairs well managed. I believe I am correct in stating that you can move into Abbotsfield now if you like, though you understand that it won't legally be yours just yet; you would technically be a custodian so to speak. It is a wonderful old place and I have many happy memories of visiting your uncle and aunt there and you of course, though I see that you don't remember me. There are no contestants and nor, I feel it safe to say, are there likely to be any. I have handled your uncles affairs for many years and they are meticulously well organised."

Jessica left Baron Whitton in a state of astonishment, her disbelief mixed with raw excitement.

" I don't know what's happening, how can this be? I was there when the unsigned will was discovered and read. There was little money and no chance of a simple legal solution. What about Mrs Wainwright, she could be a contestant, couldn't she?"

Jessica ran back into the office brushing aside Mrs Pratt's Objections and without pausing to apologise, asked about Mrs Wainwright.

"I've never heard of her my dear, she's not a relation that I know of and I have checked most carefully for any family members no matter how distant. As I mentioned to you, there are no other named beneficiaries."

Jessica left once again and gave profuse apologies for the interruption, she felt as if she had behaved like an idiot. She was still very confused about the house, that beautiful Georgian residence with its many rooms and the fountain and the exquisite memories. It was all hers!

Jessica phoned Ben Wallace who was surprised when said she would be back at work the following day.

"Are you sure you are quite up to it my dear?"

Jessica felt that she was being patronised.

"Yes of course, I wouldn't have phoned in otherwise, I want to come back to work."

"Good Heavens! well well, we shall look forward most earnestly to seeing you my dear."

"Ben?"

"Yes my dear"

" I did help you exhume Lucius Grey's grave didn't I?"

"I'm not with you dear lady?"

" Lucius Grey! You know the man who was hung for a murder he did not commit."

" Oh, you mean the Victorian gentleman. As for exhumation, good gracious me no, what an idea, we don't have time or

387

resources for all that nonsense; we are not archaeologists. Of course we did investigate the site where the chest was discovered but you know that. When you were ill and delirious, the only way we could shut you up was to do as you asked but it was a very cloak and dagger affair, let me tell you."

Jessica was deep in thought.

"Jessica?"

"Oh sorry I was miles away. See you tomorrow, we'll talk then. I think I was hallucinating about all that."

"Quite so my dear, well jolly good, until tomorrow then."

Despite her logic and Julia's constructive input, Jessica really was starting to question her reason and even her sanity.

'Oh this is all so strange, like a nightmare, is this real, or isn't it? No! I am imagining this too, I must be.'

Being back at work and once more into a routine was comforting in a humdrum kind of way. Jessica resumed her role though trying too hard and earning the disapproval of Ben Wallace who thought she was overdoing things.

" Good Heavens my dear, you do have a home to go back to don't you? For the sake of my nerves, take a break my dear. That poor cat of yours will move out again, you mark my words."

John Stringer hardly acknowledged that she had been absent for months and simply gave her instructions as if she had left for home just the previous day. Finally, at the end of the first week, he cracked, winking and then smiling as he left some paperwork for her to look at.

"Welcome back Love."

CHAPTER 31

Now that Jessica was almost completely recovered and back to her old self, she realised that she was on the brink of attaining something akin to contentment if not actual happiness. Nevertheless, there remained for Jessica a subtle but haunting element of sadness, a sense of emptiness where there had been none before. Her overriding awareness however, was one of gratitude and of the joy of being alive.

She was was still plagued by her aberrant memory; scenarios and settings brought on during the course of dreaming became a part of her entire memory and somehow mixed up with her day to day routine. Jessica tried to analyse the situation and came to the conclusion that there was little difference between these apparently groundless memories from her recent nocturnal adventures and the memories say, of her childhood, of her teens and of earlier adulthood. If these memories could be sorted through, they would be numerously complex scenarios stored in mounting abstractions and not practicably divisible. She felt truly, that she really had somehow glimpsed the future, peeked into alternate universes and been a spectator observing the past.

Awakening very early one morning, Jessica fidgeted restlessly, unable to go back to sleep; the phantom scenarios flitted through her mind over and over again. Realising that she was probably still very traumatised and would probably remain so for a long time, she decided that she needed to talk to someone. Of course she immediately thought of Julia and reached for the phone, 'sensing' that this was a good time. Julia would have finished her chores and was probably having a cup of tea before getting the children ready for school. In the event, she answered the phone sounding very bright, cheery and delighted to hear from Jessica.

They exchanged the usual preliminaries, enquiries, a little banter, initially skirting the issues that they both knew were on Jessica's mind.

"Is this a good time to talk Julia?"

"Absolutely Jess, tell me, what's going on?"

"There is so much going around in my head, I just need to at least try and understand what happened to me. This is all so much beyond my experience or understanding that it frightens me"

Julia listened, tuning in to her friends disquiet, sensing her fundamental unease with what she had so far in her life, up until the mind expanding 'poisoning', adhered to as her reality. Julia hadn't intended to be preachy but then she found herself talking of something she referred to as the Tree of life which, she explained, was a metaphor for the livelihood of the spirit. Her description, it seemed to Jessica, was engagingly 'new age' but then Jessica felt there was a kernel of truth within, there was a resonance of thought. Julia continued,

"The tree of life theory suggests that such memory storage as we have, as creatures of the universe, comes about as a result of an intrinsic link with ones eternal soul. This is represented by the out-of-body brain circuit, referred to as 'circuit eight', where not only this life but all past lives, future life and all inter-dimensional memories are stored and are readily accessed, if only we could take the time to learn how. You took a shortcut Jess my love and it has taken it's toll but, Oh my God, what a gift! You have no idea."

"But even if I believe all this Julia, this mumbo jumbo, this tosh, sorry I really don't mean to be rude Jools but I'm drowning, how can we possibly remember something that hasn't happened yet?"

" We had a conversation once Jess, do you remember my never ending eulogy when I explained that 'time' doesn't exist, time is a man made concept borne of our desperate need to comprehend a process of events."

"Oh gosh yes, how could I ever forget that evening?"

"This out of brain 'circuit eight' is the dimension we access for all of our extraordinary powers, explains ESP, it's a scientific conundrum but one that is accepted as such by scientists. In fact, we are told that extra-sensory perception is simply an ability that some people have for an an unusually high degree of perception; well it's both true and nonsense at the same time. We all have this innate sensitivity though few are aware of it."

" I know Jools, you see things all the time, not just when you are asleep, you even tuned into some of my dreams, didn't you?"

" None of this really matters Jess because this perspective that we accumulate memories, real, imaginary, dream and illusion doesn't alter the fact that the memories are there and as such form the person that we become."

In her typically scientific fashion, Jessica had set up some kind of cognitive management system in her head and then she found that, like Julia, she could at times be free to be guided by her memories and her intuition. Jessica knew with every fibre of her being that she did not want to contribute to creating a burnt out world and there was absolutely no reason why it should be so. What occurred to her was the memory of an event that had not yet happened; that according to Julia's criteria, became simply relegated to the realm of fiction because of fore knowledge. Indeed, this was the ESP conundrum! Then Jessica remembered something she had once read by Dr Lyall Watson,

'The future may be preconceived without being preordained.'
She understood this to mean that knowledge of what 'might be' is precisely what causes that future to simply fade away, a divine paradox indeed. As usual, Jessica felt uplifted and hopeful after her long conversation with Julia; the level of understanding and awareness growing within her and causing her to view her life differently.

A few days later, Britain became enveloped in the grip of an almost Grecian summer. Eternal blue skies and soaring temperatures brought people out of their caves and like refugees released from an internment camp, they emerged happily into the bright sunlight, squinting light deprived eyes and bearing ultra-violet light deprived skin. Within days and under the onslaught of mounting levels of vitamin 'd' they shed their ill humour and their grim, grey pallor and blossomed like Norfolk tulips, entranced and embalmed by the nurturing effects of the sun. Jessica was certainly no exception and in deference to the idyllic conditions and her soon to be acquired inheritance, she strove to shed her mantle of gloom and to fulfill a life long dream. She located a motorcycle dealership, caught a bus and came home hours later, giddy with excitement and a brand new Triumph Bonneville T100 painted 'Intense Orange and Phantom Black'. She parked the glittering new motorcycle in the garage next to the Bentley where it gentley creaked as it cooled and emitted strangely heady odours of freshly heated new metal. Jessica, wearing a new jacket and carrying a crash helmet and goggles tripped up to the entrance to the flat full of the joys of spring and planning an adventure.

After three weeks of intense work, Jessica was finally able to get away for a long weekend and a much anticipated ride on the the new Triumph. Quite apart from anything else, she so badly needed to go to the house, to lay Uncle Alistair's ghost and decided to take the Triumph for a 'shakedown' run as she had been advised so to do. When she had taken posession, she had been given the keys for the house by Mrs Pratt at the solicitors office on the morning of her visit but Jessica had put them 'somewhere safe' and with a memory still abberrant and mischevous, had of course completely forgotten where! Maddeningly the keys had vanished into thin air and the house, she knew, was well defended against illegal entry.

The idea occurred to her to go to Hayling Island where the boat was moored, as the solicitor had indicated to Jessica that there was a set of spare keys hidden on board. The keys to the boat, she was told, were kept in a little magnetic box that was attached to the underside of a metal bracket secreted in a small cupboard on the flying bridge. There was a part of her that didn't want to see the boat because it was a painful a reminder of her Aunt Maria's absence and Jessica still felt a little too delicate for those memories to be rekindled but there was little choice. It was either that or go through the embarrassing process of calling and explaining her predicament to the alarm company and procuring the services of a locksmith; the ride would be fun. She set off on a morning full of summer promise with adventure in her heart.

Riding carefully at first, to Portsmouth along the A3, getting used to riding a motorcycle once again and enjoying the undiluted thrill of being on two wheels, she adapted quickly and naturally, leaning into the corners and smoothly up-shifting on beckoning straights. She actually giggled while riding, feeling truly alive for the first time in years. She even smiled while riding through Petersfield when some construction workers, observing a curvaceous young woman in well fitted leathers, wolf-whistled at her. On previous occasions, Jessica had become prickly, full of disdain and annoyance toward wolf-whistling men. Since her experiences over the past months, she discovered that they too were a part of the joy of living. In their questionably inappropriate way they were simply celebrating the rich tapestry of life, the heartbeat of nature.

Locating the boat was problematic as she really had little memory of Hayling Island, what the boat looked like or, more importantly, the name. Her only vague memory was of a large white cruiser. Initially, Jessica was denied access to the marina by an officious man who was unfriendly and had appeared to have judged Jessica based on her 'biker' look. The fact that she didn't really know what she was looking for did not help her case. Determined to win him over, Jessica smiled and cooed, discovering for the first time in her life that there were indeed great powers in a womans charms and in the subtle but powerful influence of true femininity. A reference to the register of owners yielded results.
"Gray, Alistair? I knew him well love, so sorry to hear of his death, he was a real gent. She's moored at berth number D402, fourth gangway on the left."
Jessica walked along the main dock and took the gangway as directed.

Upon successfully locating the berth, Jessica experienced first hand the effects of time slowing down; she became faint, her vision blurred and then her knees buckled. Then she became vaguely aware of someone running to her rescue, a distant voice echoing within the labyrinthine confines of her temporarily disordered mind, asking if she were okay, which of course, she wasn't. Then there were some sympathetic mutterings of concern, a strong male voice, clearer.

" Bring some of that lemon barley water over Yvonne love, maybe she's dehydrated, do you think we should call an ambulance?"

Jessica was helped to a nearby patio chair and quickly gathered her wits.

"I'm alright, honestly, I just had a bit of a shock, truly I'm alright, I'll just sit for a moment, I need to catch my breath. I've just come out of hospital and I suppose I'm not quite right yet but I'm getting there. It's okay, I'm fine now, truly I am."

'Yvonne' joined them and handed Jessica a glass covered in condensation, leached from the crisp refrigerated cool of the lemon barley water.

"Well if you're sure love, you look really pale; here sip this. Do you want a cup of tea, Bill, put the kettle on?"

Jessica sat for a while gathering her wits, feeling foolish, sipping lemon barley water and tea alternately; by degrees her strength returning.

"You had us worried there for a moment."

Jessica explained as briefly and simplistically as she could that she had been unwell although she was in fact, so much better now though she was periodically prone to spells of feeling faint.

"Just a passing moment that's all, I'll be fine."

Relieved by her returning colour and energy, Bill and Yvonne relaxed and started to chat.

"Is that your boat then," Bill asked a little interrogatively.

"No! Well actually, yes I suppose it is now. It belonged to my late uncle, I actually came to fetch something but I never imagined.............."

Everything was swimming again.

"Here, steady love....." Yvonne observed Jessica blanching again and swaying on the chair; she held her fast. It took a while for Jessica to convince them that she really would be alright and as she took control of herself, overcame her tempestuous emotional state, she forced herself to look at the boat.

The cruiser, named 'White Heron' was about 55 feet long, sleek and was entirely alien when she came to think about it. This craft had been her Aunt Maria's and Uncle Alistair's second home. Alistair true to form and a wag to the end had undertaken to write a subtext beneath the craft's name, a secondary name with a humorous twist, a play on words, *'Overdraught'* written in italics.

"It's been a few years since I've seen her out and about," said Bill.

"I almost thought she had been abandoned, except that as regular as clockwork a man comes to run the engines, clean her up and check that she's in fine fettle. Such a great boat, I'd love to have her, always hoped she might come on the market one day?"

Jessica's hackles were raised slightly as she felt the enquiry to be a little invasive, the wounds of bereavement were still raw. Bill and Yvonne had been kind to her and at that very moment, were suggesting that she come aboard their own craft for some lunch. She accepted the invitation graciously and then while eating, briefly explained the story of how she came to be the new owner of White Heron.

After lunch she climbed aboard and with Bill's help, looked for the keys; finally and after much searching. the magnetic box was found on the underside of a bracket inside a small cubby hole. Jessica did not want to waste time and armed with the keys, needed to be on her way to the house without delay. She thanked the helpful couple profusely but before departing, Bill stopped her, evidently wanting to speak and then he came straight to the point in his blundering businesslike way.

"If ever you want to sell her, let me know, business is good and I can easily afford her. She would be looked after impeccably, I can promise that."

Jessica could see the desire in his eyes and she really had no idea what to do with the boat; she was not a sailor. There was some instinct in her though, that was reluctant to acquiesce, preferring instead to delay the moment until she could make a decision in her own time.

" I don't actually own it yet Bill, as I am waiting for the deed of probate, all that legal nonsense but if I do decide to sell, I'll keep you in mind, I can promise you that."

A look of disappointment flashed briefly in his eyes.

"Thanks love, you do that."

Despite herself and the march of time, curiousity compelled Jessica to look around inside the boat. She found the whole experience to be utterly surreal. The boat was exactly as it was in her dream but in much better condition. She could almost 'see' the vegetable garden mapped out on the deck and the placement of the wind turbines. The funny thing was that while she did remember some lovely boating trips with her aunt and uncle, enchanting days of never ending sunshine and idyllic meals of ocean crayfish and giddying pink fizzy wine, she simply could not remember the boat in any detail. Some unseen force drove her to a cabin under the fore deck, a cozy and sumptuous abode. There was a semi-complete jigsaw on a little table and a stuffed Rupert Bear propped up against the pillow of the bunk, her bear. Even though he was Rupert, Jessica had insisted he be called William, just like her cat,

'Of course!'

How ever could she have parted with him? On the floor in the corner was what Jessica recognised as a personal stereo cassette player along with various tapes with names of bands like 'Wham' and 'Wet Wet Wet'. In the cupboard there were clothes for a girl of about 8 or 9 years of age; typically expensive fashion clothes with recognisable names. There were some jeans, a few tee shirts, underwear and a couple of dresses and skirts. Jessica briefly studied the clothes, obviously female and yet strangely androgynous, not tailored for a developed female form- still a child's clothing. She knew with a chilling sense of certainty that the clothes were hers. Overwhelmed, Jessica rushed out of the boat bade a hasty farewell to Yvonne and Bill, ran toward the office and then jumped onto the Triumph and sped away with a perfunctory wave. It was later and as she approached the drive to the house that she realised with horror that she had forgotten to lock up the boat.

"Bugger, damn, shit! I'll just have to go back to the boat on my way home; oh how bloody tedious!"

It wasn't just the prospect of another lengthy journey that bothered Jessica; it was having to see the boat again, to acknowledge its very existence and that was something which she found very unsettling if not actually frightening.

There was compensation however and Jessica felt a mounting flutter of excitement as she rode along the driveway and then having stopped the Triumph at the coach house, she put the kickstand down, took her helmet off and looked up at the great house. She followed the footpath that led across the lawn and then she stepped up to the entrance of an entirely familiar, exquisitely beautiful baroque style Georgian conservatory. The design was by an architect of exceptionally flamboyant renown named Thomas Archer. Jessica unlocked the doors and then grappled with the alarm system in a state of trepidation. It almost seemed as if Alistair and Maria were still there; there was the same atmosphere, a thoroughly familiar esthesis. For the first time in living memory however, Jessica ears were not assailed by music cascading through the floor to ceiling high sash windows that opened into the conservatory from the library. There was still a bewildering array of flowers in the conservatory and Jessica basked for a moment in their colour and the exquisite, almost overwhelming scent; Gerbera, snapdragons, lilies, geraniums and lisianthus but sadly, there were no familiar figures, one of whom was was usually busy writing in the library and the other, habitually seated in the now empty chair reading his newspaper; Jessica wept freely, wiping away her tears with the sleeve of her jacket that left black streaks on her cheeks.

The surreal period that had encapsulated her for most of the day gradually receded as she bathed in the capacious antique enamelled iron bath that, within minutes, had leached any trace of heat from the originally scalding hot water. The exotic bathroom still contained shelves of exotic unguents and perfumes that had belonged to her aunt. Later Jessica floated around the numerous rooms with repeatedly refilled glasses of single malt, obtained after ransacking Uncle Alistair's drinks cabinet. She was aware that she was getting quite drunk but in fact Jessica had never felt so happy, so complete and so intoxicated in every way. She had always adored the house, an historic, beautiful, solid, grounding mass of stone, moulded into an abode of exceptional perfection. It was a truly substantial place that had carved its very image not only in the world but also in the temporal domain, as far as Jessica was concerned, it was her only real home, always had been, her anchor and her retreat. She stayed at the house for three blissful days, playing music, tidying, opening curtains and windows, having endless conversations with Maria and also with Alistair. She felt exquisite, expansive, benevolent, wanting to share her good fortune with her lifelong friends and she phoned Julia. John was to have the Alvis, and Julia was to have her apartment at Mortlac if she wanted it, though Jessica would stay there while she was still working. John Stringer would have the Bentley as he adored the car and wanted nothing more than to have something to tinker with on Sunday mornings, he was the ideal person. Benjamin Wallace would have some exceptional vintages from her uncles wine collection. Steven Savage,

'Hmm? Well Steven is a crook and should not be encouraged but he has to have something but I'm just not sure what? So strange that I should have dreamed of his being in trouble and coming to my flat.'

After an idyllic weekend, Jessica awoke on Monday with a heavy heart. The balmy weather had given way to cloud and rain threatened. She knew that she would have to make a run for it to avoid getting wet on the Triumph. Then she remembered that she would have to make a detour to lock up the boat. The thought crossed her mind to contact the marina office and ask the kind couple, Bill and Yvonne to keep an eye on things. Then Jessica felt that to do so would give them access to the boat and instill some sort of proprietorial hope with regard to her selling, which she now knew she did not want to do. There was nothing for it, she would just have to go and lock up in person. Donning some 'country style' rudimentary waxed cotton waterproofs that must have belonged to Aunt Maria, she set out in the rain accompanied by a measure of trepidation.

Jessica locked the house and set the alarm or at least she hoped that her inexpert fumblings had armed the device. She strode along by the lawn and passed by her favourite place, almost a monument, which was a series of stone seats arranged in a circle and hidden charmingly by a lilac covered wall that was crumbing with age. She walked through the arched gateway and then stopped for a moment, remembering all too fondly those delightful and eternal episodes as a child when she had played for hours in an around this extraordinarily pretty corner of the garden and she had never tired of it. For the first time ever, Jessica experienced something akin to being broody; to see her own children playing in this magical spot, as she herself had so often done, would be such a joy to her.

Just as Jessica was walking toward the coach house where the Triumph was parked next to Alistair's poor dusty old Alvis that sat on flattened tyres, she turned to have a parting look at the house, her house, her very own place of sanctuary, when she noticed, just in front of her, perched low in a nearby apple tree, a beautiful raven, his plumage displaying a rich sheen of black with glinting lapis lazuli. Jessica gaped with amazement at first, some association emerging but not quite coming to the surface, something that bothered her on a subconscious level. She stood and gazed at the raven who lifted his wings and cawed at her, made some noises in imitation of other birds and then cleaned his beak on the branch; the raven was trying to communicate something to her, she was sure of it.

A torrential downpour, lightning and thunder enveloped her and the rich smell of hot but recently drenched pavement assailed her senses; there could be no more proof of the reality of the world in which she was an inhabitant. Riding the Triumph into a headwind and with hailstones hammering into the front of her full face helmet was disconcerting and Jessica was on the brink of forswearing motorcycles forever. Then as the sky lightened, a patch of deep blue gave access to the heavens, the sun came out and Jessica started to feel at peace with the world again. She understood that when one rides a motorcycle, one is not watching a movie but has become a part of the drama; the subtleties of temperature change, of odours, of changing light achieving far more significance then when one is in a car. Riding a motorcycle is all about contrasts, she realised and that this is a part of the magic of the experience, she had almost forgotten what it was like.

As she dismounted at the marina, she was about to pull off her helmet but feeling very cold, wishing to be anonymous and in any event planning only to be a few minutes, she rushed to the boat, keys in her hands. Then she noticed once again a raven, perched on the radar mast of the boat, tipping precariously back and forward, wings outstretched as it strove to maintain balance. Jessica stopped in her tracks and looked at the bird, some memory once again bubbling sluggishly to the surface. Then she saw a silhouette of a man standing high up on the flying bridge. She was about to be outraged but was arrested by his evidently responsible air, he seemed to be at work. Jessica assumed that the figure must be Bill but no, he was too lean, too tall. That left one other possibility, he must be the maintenance man originally engaged by her Uncle Alistair to look after White Heron.

He was indeed a tall man with a kindly face and he waved at her in unselfconscious greeting, seeming to know her. As far as she could tell, he looked ostensibly nautical, an habitual seafarer. Evidently, he must have been hard at work as his muscular upper body appeared to be unclothed. As she drew closer she could make out more detail, his long beard, hair and eyebrows were sun bleached and his face and corners of his supernaturally blue eyes were lined attractively from constant exposure to the elements. Jessica dared not recognise him, someone so utterly familiar. She removed her helmet while squinting into the sunlight in preparation to wave back at him, her bunched hair nearly as black as the ravens feathers, with the exception of a distinguishing streak of white.

In an instant she recognised him, the man was Andrew Morley and her one and only 'crush'!
She walked towards him smiling, he spoke.
"Hello."
"Can I help you?"
"I've ……um been expecting you Jessica."

This was a voice that Jessica knew so well, every intonation, every nuance.

" Andrew Morley! I never expected to meet you here of all places, I thought you had become a man of the cloth?"

"Oh I am...?" His voice was rich and vibrant, a little like Uncle Alistair's but deeper, like that of a practiced baritone but he was also possessed of a speech affectation. He spoke slowly, deliberately, words well enunciated but with a pause which he punctuated with an 'um' as if he were thinking, considering what he was going to say while talking.

" Actually I became Father Donovan for a time but I'm sadly lapsed in my .....um divinity dear Jessica."

"Do you know that I am the new owner of White Heron?"

He continued, ignoring her question.

"I suppose you could say that I am spiritual but not religious though I was once....um, deeply so in fact, you may remember."

" And now you clean peoples boats?"

Jessica did not mean to be petulant, impudent but her mouth betrayed her.

" As I've said, I've um, been waiting for you."

Jessica was stunned to complete silence, at a loss for words for moments. Too many slick tongued men of all ages had said words that were similarly facile,

"Where have you been all my life my lovely? Or, don't I know you from somewhere? " That kind of thing and yet there was a note of genuine honesty in his gaze and his words.

"Well I'm flattered, but do you think that you should be flirting with your new boss?"

He paused for a second as if trying to decide whether to say something.

"The last time I saw you, you were …...um dying on the deck of my boat, sorry, your boat, after an encounter with a poisonous Jellyfish."
He continued;
"The first time I saw you was at a ceremony a long time ago, you were a beautiful but terrified young priestess named Laurna. I tried to marry you once, much, much later, but I was imprisoned and then executed for a crime I did not commit. Our fates have dictated that we should be together but circumstances, incongruities have cheated us of that opportunity. The temporal storm is over, we are together now Jessica, you belong to me and I to you."
Jessica's head was spinning, her mind grappling to make sense of everything.
"We have shared the same dreams, in fact the same experiences. We can finally be together forever."
In direct contradiction to a habit of a lifetime, Jessica abandoned her reason, her fear of being hurt, her pragmatism and she reached up and tentatively put her hands to his face, beseeching him with her eyes to be sincere, to be truthful to her and to love her for all eternity; she was simply not strong enough to cope with any thing else after all that she had been through.

CHAPTER 32

Predictably enough, Andrew Morley and Jessica saw a great deal of each other in the coming weeks, finding the alternative of separation to be intolerable though the rigours of life conspired to keep them apart during the working weeks. Jessica lost interest in her work, she had become quite a different person as a result of her ordeal but she still went through the daily ritual that her job demanded. Andrew continued with his work on the boats on Hayling Island as he enjoyed it and it gave him time to think and to contemplate but he sensed that the time was coming when that too would come to a natural end.

His life had been simple but pleasurable in recent years, his sparsely furnished mobile home sufficient for his needs. It was a modest abode that he shared with his dog, Rufus, a great beast with pointed ears and hetero-chromic eyes. Andrew's only vehicle was an ancient and tatty, though dependable, short wheel base Landrover that he used for his work. Once a week he went to his local pub for a meal and enjoyed his self imposed three pint 'quota' of beer while Rufus sat on the front seat of the Landrover, looking out for his master. Sometimes, if he wasn't too wet and muddy and the pub not too busy, Andrew would take Rufus inside where he would lie beside his feet. The pub was one of those idyllic cottage Inns that exuded heady odours of good food and the combined aromas of pipe tobacco, shoe polish and the distinctive smell of hops. The ceilings were so low that the beams grazed ones head, creating a sense of extreme coziness. In the middle partition wall was a giant Inglenook fireplace which in the winter, gave great blasts of heat that banished the pervasive chill of the seasonal elements, a separate and very cozy 'snug' was however, offered to couples seeking a more intimate environment.

Andrew, despite his knowledge and awareness, was afflicted by the usual human frailties of self doubt and lack of confidence but his all consuming wish at that time was for him and Jessica to be together, forever. He decided that this Inn with it's uterine comfort and ageless charm would be the perfect place to ask Jessica to marry him and so he arranged a special evening for them both at the pub. He was compelled to admit to himself that he had nothing to offer her apart from his undying love. He had no money to speak of, no real home, a big hairy dog and a tatty Landrover and this knowledge acted like a vitriol upon his resolve, corroding and gnawing at his sense of self worth. Nervous and quite out of sorts, Andrew kept going to the bar and buying drinks for them both though. Full glasses accumulated in front of Jessica as she laboured for an age over a pint of beer, a beverage to which she was not usually susceptible. Almost autonomically, Andrew ordered food, steak-in-guiness pie with chips for them both. It was his favourite but he barely touched his though Jessica on the other hand, ate hers with gusto. She had observed with wry but amused candour as she snuggled up to him on the couch, that he was more than usually distracted and obviously very ill at ease but she knew exactly what was on his mind; she had after all, shared lives with him and in very differing scenario's. Throwing caution to the wind and to put him out of his misery, she grabbed his hand and looked up at him while he was aimlessly talking about some inconsequential facet of maritime law, interrupting him.

"Andrew?" He stopped mid-sentence and looked at her, slightly alarmed.

"Would you sit still and stop talking for a moment!"

"Well, um, I'm so sorry!"

"Shut up and listen to me. Why don't we get married? Lets get married very soon?"

Andrew was dumbstruck! Rendered speechless in the moment, he wrapped his arms around her, kissing her, relieved and all of a sudden, immeasurably happy.

They were married the following month in a registry office followed by a simple ceremony in the grounds of Abbotsfield. Julia attended the registry office marriage and then presided over the ceremony and though very earnest and serious at the time, she later collapsed into ecstatic giggles, repeatedly hugging both Jessica and Andrew. Then she took each of their hands in hers and looking at them said with tears in her eyes;

"Finally, you two are together; well of course you are together!."

Among the guests at the ceremony were Benjamin Wallace, John Stringer, Patsy Wainright and Steven Savage with his latest 'dalliance'. He had given Jessica a beautiful bunch of flowers and had hugged her warmly at the reception.

"You did well Jess, he's a good bloke. My loss is his gain eh, but I hope you will be happy, you deserve it."

Jessica was amused to notice latterly that Wallace and Stringer were having a good humoured if slightly drunken discussion about the state of the economy and actually seemed to be getting along. Julia, John and the children stayed on at the house after the wedding at Jessica's insistence and they had made arrangements for cows to be fed and chickens to be looked after. The children were beside themselves with happiness as they gambolled around the woods, the rarely visited vaults, the cellars and the dusty recesses of the rambling attic; discovering all sorts of treasures and playing hide and seek, drawing upon seemingly endless energy reserves.

On a tranquil summer evening, a few days after the festivities were over, Jessica, Andrew, Julia and John sat in the magical garden on the crumbling, though charming stone benches, within the shelter of a hedgerow shaped into a semi-circle where they drank wine and talked. Caught up in the magic of the evening and becoming a little drunk, they shared tales and intrigues, laughing easily and then finally, in the light of a glowing and plangent moon they became serious. Between them, they reached an agreement. In order for their world to continue to exist, they would have to create a schism in the fabric of their reality which would separate the whole into two parts which, as in he process of mitosis in a dividing cell, each half would become whole once again but with opposing polarities almost like matter and anti-matter. Each of these concepts of reality would represent opposite ends of the spectrum and would therefore represent a very different perspective of the future, one light and one dark, a 'Heaven' or a 'Hell' on Earth. The world they now lived in was a great deal more complicated and less material than they had grown accustomed to; recent events had made that as plain as day. Julia studied herself as though from afar, watching her thoughts and her ideas like a stranger eavesdropping on a forbidden conversation. Andrew Morley had so many memories that seemed not belong to him, were they all the product of some strange dream?

They made a pact, an unusual accord; this was not to be some flighty new age fad but instead, it was to be an affirmation. This was not to be the work of witchcraft, they were not going to be messing with the laws of the universe or interfering with the rules of nature. They were not going to draw rabbits out of hats or attempt to alter the course of past events, even if they could. Their intention was to rearrange their parameters of perception through their experiences and heightened awareness and to negate the wasted energy of conflict by separating what was perceived as the bad from the good. This was to be the evisceration in effect, that would create two quite different worlds, an untarnished refuge for the enlightened seekers looking for a better way and a place for those blinded by avarice and immorality; indeed the 'Heaven' and 'Hell' that they had talked of earlier. Andrew Morley, who was the most silent of them all but who had been listening intently to the conversation suddenly spoke up; "In this hologram that we refer to as 'reality', the experiences of the collective mind are but flotsam in an ocean of stimulus, nothing more than an infinitely vast sea of concepts and ideas that grow and change according to the whims and wishes of the collective. By 'tuning in' to the stimulus that seems relevant to us, to you my dear Jessica and to John and also Julia, we construct our perception of life and of universal limits from birth, based on the perceptions of our parents, teachers and society in general. Our reality, which in truth is every bit as nebulous as the phantom thought forms of the numinous dream world, is founded on a morass of possible misconception. In short, every person perceives a reality that they have themselves created. Those drawn to the realm of avarice, aggression and control and bent on flight into conflict and toxic oblivion have been taken there by their

410

own perspective on reality. Those able to enjoy the simple pleasures of wholesome living, the enchanting sound of birdsong and the joy of nature have likewise been able to do so."

There was a moment of quiet and introspection as each person considered what Andrew had said and then John spoke up, feeling a desperate need to make a contribution. "I feel that what you say is especially relevant in the world at this moment, with all that is happening globally and the fundamental sense of 'quickening' that many people are feeling now. So much strife and so many changes are happening and will continue to happen. We are, all of us, able to sense this; in fact we cannot avoid feeling it." Forces, as John had observed, were already at work that would somehow alter the mindset of the worlds people by more succinctly polarising their concept of reality. This was, they agreed, a difficult task for a demi-god and an impossible one for a quartet of idealists sitting around a fire in the garden but then the process had already been started and was well beyond their control. What they all agreed upon unanimously was that there was a great deal more to the Mayan prophecy than an intention to convey to the worlds population the sense that the end of the world was coming. Jessica had even more reason to hope that the world that they inhabited would be a benevolent one as she had recently discovered that she was pregnant, much to her and Andrew's mutual delight. She took this opportunity to tell the others of the forthcoming event. Both John and Julia were visibly moved by the news; John declaring this was indeed an auspicious start to their new lives and altered way of being.

The following morning after breakfast, Jessica, Andrew, John, Julia and the children walked deep into the woods by the lake shore as they had an important task to fulfill. A capricious wind harried leaves and rounded them up in spiraling vortexes. William, who was tagging along behind, tried to chase the leaves but then ran up a tree and surveyed the scene below with inscrutable feline eyes. The children played with Rufus who was endlessly patient and who constantly trotted after them, even though they tormented him. They threw sticks for him to retrieve which he didn't. They tried to ride him like a horse, Oliver attempted to probe his eyes experimentally with his fingers, and they all taunted him playfully. It was the sort of behaviour that ironically, often cements a relationship between children and dogs. During the walk, they all collected acorns from under the canopies of the great oaks. Then later, they reverently planted the acorns in pots full of damp loam. That night a storm swept in that rattled roof tiles and caused trees to sway manically, then the power went off. The children once more explored the dark and mysterious corners of the house shrieking with terror and excitement, having a wonderful time. Julia and Jessica read and then played scrabble by candlelight while John and Andrew escaped to the pub. Later, the girls walked arm in arm across the windblown park among the debris of tree branches and had a long and deeply satisfying conversation. They felt at peace within the eye of the storm.

By the time Spring came, Jessica was heavily pregnant. She had been looking after the acorns almost fanatically, observing those that had germinated and from which spidery roots and shoots grew, so fragile and precious. Looking at them, she wondered how could they ever aspire to the girth, height and colossal weight of a fully grown oak tree? She chose the plants that seemed to be the strongest and transplanted them to bigger pots. Finally out of those she selected one sapling which she intended to plant in the grounds of Abbotsfield but that task, she decided, was to be entrusted to her husband. As she pointed out to him with a look of amused irony, he did have some experience in this regard. Andrew chose the site for this sapling carefully and dug the soil in preparation.

Repacking the aged Volvo once again, Julia and John drove up from the west country for the ceremonial planting of the future 'Tree of Life'. The original Father Donovan's tree at Mortlac was reaching the end of its reign; tired now, its limbs withering with age and the sap receding or solidifying year by year. The time when finally this oak would falter, stagger and fall to the ground with a mighty crash in a cloud of dust, eventually to be reabsorbed by the Earth, was not so far distant. An heir to the kingdom was needed and indeed, was being nurtured as the ancient oak shed thousands of acorns.

The ceremonial planting of the sapling was to be another of the great paradoxes of time and of nature where the circle is completed. Andrew Morley placed the young tree reverently in the fresh soil, gently pressing the earth in order to stabilise the roots. The tree had been planted in the middle of the lawn, a central place with much space to spread and to become broad and strong. The intention in that moment was put out to the universal void, that people, whomever they might be, would have a chance to discover their new Eden while the old oak at Mortlac stood as a gateway. It would be a place that remained locked between the two dimensions, visible to seekers in both worlds, an access point to either world, open only to those who adhered to a wider vision. The brave new world, Heaven, the Garden of Eden would retreat gradually into the mists, populated by those beings seeking to live a simple life in accordance with natural law, in love and harmony. The eternal dream of mankind was to be made real at last and those who wanted a chance to start all over again were to be given that chance.

CHAPTER 33

Addendum

Britain in the 11th Century was a country that had been invaded repeatedly. Even then the curse of human kind's greed, avarice and depravity coursing throughout the world had left their marks upon the great Mother Goddess and it was going to get worse. By the early 21st century she was indeed growing haggard, the relentless toxicity of the modern world adding greatly to her deterioration. Her back was hunched, her body sagging and her wrinkles bearing a testament to her advanced years. The casual and relentless abuse administered unthinkingly to her 'physiology' by a burgeoning population of careless consumers had added to the burden and to her careworn condition. There was still hope however, that she could become dignified and healthy once again, for the regenerative and timeless powers of the universe to create magic to restore her to the vigorous, nurturing Mother whom we all rely on. In order for this miracle to occur, she had first to drink from the fountain of youth, to quench her thirst with the love and cooperation from humanity. All this had been foreseen by the great Druids, the priestesses of all ages and of course, the Mayans.

Long ago, during the time of King Canute, there was a man named Derryth who, with foresight, had made a decision to plant a tree, a sacred oak. It was his intention that a spell would be cast at that time which would take mankind on an altered path, though he had no idea what form this would take; the impulse to act was so strong that he was compelled to obey. An abbess of a nearby Christian order whose true vocation was that of a seer, she had received a vision of great portent in which she observed the planting of the oak. Then the vision had faded and was replaced by that of a young woman who appeared to be an incarnation of one of her order whom she recognised by her essence. She saw that this young woman would take part in events which would bring about great changes and begin to restore the Earth once more to her rightful path. The priestess, for that is who the abbess truly was, realising the importance of the vision summoned the other women of her order. They interpreted the visions and came to a conclusion; the spell, for that is what it was, would take many hundreds of years to mature, the timing was crucial and complex. A young initiate named Laurna who had not spoken since birth would one day be reborn. She would be a woman of her time and would have no knowledge of all that preceded her existence or of her role, until her cellular memory was triggered by an event of life changing proportions. All of this woman's life would pre-ordained.

At the ceremony when the oak had been planted, it was decided that the male and female universal components were to join in a great invocation. Derryth and Laurna were to join and to conceive a child. Once achieved, the couple would represent in their human forms the Yin and Yang of the universe and their issue would be a gift to the Mother Goddess. From the moment that Derryth and Laurna lay together, their association would be an eternal consecration but in order for the spell to work they would have to find one another once again across the gulf of time as was their destiny. The reluctance that Laurna showed initially in accepting her mate however, had set up a ripple of discord and this was to cause some repercussions. The Victorian era would have been the most effective time for this union, the world was on the brink of industrialisation which was already denuding and contaminating the Earth but events set in motion by Laurna's antipathy conspired to thwart the union between Lucius Grey and Georgina Brogan.

Almost a thousand years later and the oak, though ancient was still proud. From the moment that Jessica was born, the forces which had forged the spell had begun to work, unknown to her. Her early life was not auspicious, a semi-orphaned baby becoming a lanky and tragic little girl with scabby knees, a painfully awkward adolescent and a pragmatic young woman determined to prove herself in a male dominated professional domain, had suddenly found herself plummeting into an abyss of uncertainty. She had unintentionally embarked upon a roller coaster ride into the unknown and finding herself lost and abandoned within the labyrinthine conundrum of differing realities, Jessica had been forced to abandon her fierce grip upon the vital cornerstones of her security and 'normality' and had finally emerged from her cocoon, like a butterfly emerging from its Chrysalis.

When Jessica was a little girl, she had awoken suddenly from a nightmare and as all children do in such circumstances, had cried for her mother, a mother who never came. She was haunted by the nightmare into her adult life. The nightmare was devoid of complication and consisted of a series of images. She was in a dimly lit, stuffy and windowless room which had dark blue mouldering walls; the room was situated deep within the bowels of a house where

Jessica was sitting at a wooden table upon which were some folded clothes and a package of detergent. Alongside the table was an old fashioned twin tub washing machine that was steaming as it boiled the laundry within. In the background was a repetitive knocking sound, like a drum beat. The sound seemed to be coming from the other side of the back wall which, as far as she knew, was built into a hillside. Over a period of a few moments the sound, though not increasing in tempo, became louder and more insistent. With the noise came a wave of malevolence that seeped through the cracks in the walls like smoke and pervaded every corner of the room. Though not visible or detectable by any of the five senses, Jessica felt that she was being invaded and utterly violated by some unseen influence. She became rigid with terror and quite powerless to stop this influence that sought to possess her body and soul. As the beating became louder and her horror turned to petrified terror, she opened her mouth to scream but could utter no sound and then she awoke in some other world, a comforting domain in the darkness and silence of her room. She had cried for her mother, a mother that she had never known. Her father, she was aware, was either too sound asleep or too intolerant of her distress to care. He took a dim view of children who wanted lights to be left on or to be consoled at night. She had sobbed in the darkness, covering her head with the eiderdown and sucking her thumb, trying to banish the evil that had seeped inside her and which clung to her like dripping ectoplasm. Finally she had fallen asleep but that night had left an imprint, a scar on Jessica's mind that was to stay with her and to adversely colour her life and which lay like a curse in her psyche, echoing the terror of a mute young priestess forced to perform a ritual in another time.

This fear that had dogged her throughout her life and had thwarted her attempts to maintain successful relationships had finally been banished following her illness and the life changing revelations that had followed. The childhood dream that had instilled such numbing control over her sensibilities and that had so utterly posessed her was finally exorcised. It was then that a fire had been kindled in Jessica, a sublimation that bathed those who came into contact with her in a magical and invigorating light. Timing was the key. Forces harmonised at a synchronous intersection to create an event of great magnitude. Jessica had been reborn and had developed an incalculable hunger and a joy of life. As a result of this development, she had become susceptible to a union with another soul, indeed the person with whom she truly resonated just as Laurna had done so many hundreds of years previously. As a result of her 'subjugation' to her fate, she had experienced such an incandescent awakening of the senses that they had radiated out like the circular waves of a previously calm pool, which had been disturbed by the explosive impact of a rock hurled into its very centre. These waves had reached beyond the limitations of time and space, coinciding with those created by the union of Jessica Stearne and Andrew Morley, their combined energy providing the vital force necessary to manifest the original intention.

Others too were part of the equation like Julia and John, vital components in the tapestry of creation. Like a flake of snow gathering momentum and mass, so too did their ideas and intentions take on a life of their own. By degrees they eventually reached a conclusion and events unfolded before them like the release of a tightly wound spring. They would effectively become phantasms in their old world. A subtle shift in the nature and perception of reality would gradually cause those who were 'aware' to retreat into a realm which would become mythical to those who remained asleep.

If enough people 'believe' as one, then that belief becomes their reality, the change taking place on a truly quantum level. This change started from the moment that Jessica and Andrew found each other once again across the abyss of time Their union was the start of the great shift. Using the wisdom gained from future worlds, they were able to reach back and change the past so that a new future could be established. When Jessica had lived with Father Donovan on the boat in a burned out world of the future, she had known that she really was there but this was just another window of perspective in her being. The great paradox was that Jessica's presence in that world had already set events in motion that would change the past. She remembered a line she had once read that had been written by Doctor Lyall Watson, 'The future can be predicted without being pre-ordained'! Jessica and Andrew had been given a brief glimpse of their future; indeed, they had been inhabitants of that dying world and had seen, first hand, the cruel effects of the folly of mankind. Jessica's visions of the past and of the future had shown her that the planet was indeed a living being that was in much need of love and respect. There was a beautiful future awaiting those who sought a better world, a world in which they gave as well as received.

From her seat by the fireside in Uncle Alistair's favourite wing back chair in the library, with William sprawled across her lap purring for all he was worth, Jessica luxuriated in the moment, a sense of being warm and replete with life, enveloping her and making her feel drowsy. She had been reading a poem which spoke to her in a way that she had never expected, especially as it seemed so relevant; it was a short but uncompromisingly beautiful piece inspired, so she divined, by the sight of three trees emerging from the mists of a rain drenched day. She read the poem again and while doing so, absent-mindedly stroked the sides of William's face and he purred his absolution.

'Reality'

Three sentinels rise from the spreading mist,
Part of the monochrome world-
A backdrop, seemingly unreal
My eyes viewing all through a veil of ever-moving
water droplets.

Golden tree in vivid autumn solidity
Stands to the fore like a flame,
Clearly defined, truly in focus
Embracing warmly the dwelling beneath-
reassuring, familiar, eternal.

Two worlds portrayed, appear to mortal eyes-
Surveyed as whole,
A scene of contrasts, questioned not by mortal mind.
The collective thoughts of millions are the same.
And shape reality, as we know it for us all.

Becoming vaguely aware that she was being studied by Julia who was sitting in the opposite fireside chair, the one that had been Maria's, Jessica turned her head, looked at her and smiled. Julia dropped her eyes feeling momentarily embarrassed but not before observing in those previous fascinating moments of reflection that there was an unmistakable glow of happiness in Jessica that radiated from her like the embers of a fire. She would, Julia thought, be a wonderful mother; Jessica would understand what it was like to have grown up without maternal love and a warm protective bosom, just as Laurna had once done and she would love her child all the more. Julia knew then that Jessica was finally at peace. She was the person that Julia had fervently hoped she would be all those centuries before as she listened outside the bower as Laurna had growled, hissed and fought for all she was worth. This was the secret that Julia had carried in her heart from that time. Now she understood that the pattern was finally broken. Julia looked once again upon the face of a disciple, a maiden priestess fully released from her sentence of mute and chaste avowal. *'Yes Laurna looks well. Tonight will be a good night! The fires are already lit, the honey spirit is ready to be warmed and Derryth is on his way. Laurna awaits his arrival happily, even a little impatiently if I am not much mistaken.'*

THE END

www.ingramcontent.com/pod-product-compliance
Lightning Source LLC
Chambersburg PA
CBHW030239030726
47493CB00023B/193